KEPLER™

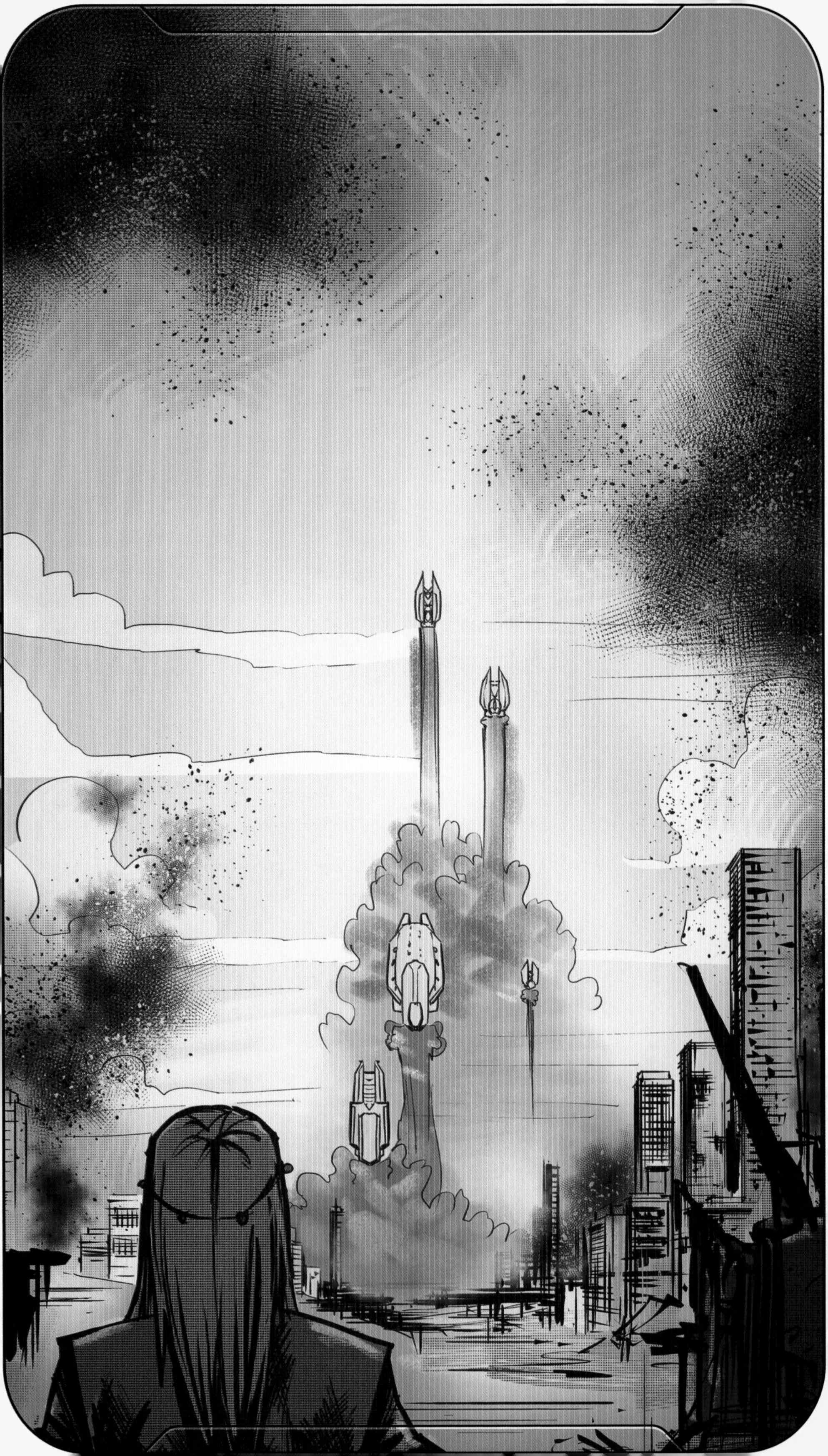

KEPLER

STORY
DAVID DUCHOVNY
& PHILLIP SEVY

ART, LETTERS & COVER
PHILLIP SEVY

DARK HORSE BOOKS

PRESIDENT & PUBLISHER MIKE RICHARDSON EDITOR MEGAN WALKER
COLLECTION DESIGNER ETHAN KIMBERLING DIGITAL ART TECHNICIAN CHRIS HORN

Published by Dark Horse Books
A division of Dark Horse Comics LLC
10956 SE Main Street, Milwaukie, OR 97222

DarkHorse.com

Facebook.com/DarkHorseComics
Twitter.com/DarkHorseComics

To find a comics shop in your area, visit comicshoplocator.com

First edition: November 2022
Ebook ISBN 978-1-50673-346-3
Hardcover ISBN 978-1-50673-345-6

10 9 8 7 6 5 4 3 2 1
Printed in China

MIX
Paper from responsible sources
FSC® C169962
FSC www.fsc.org

Library of Congress Cataloging-in-Publication Data

Names: Duchovny, David, author. | Sevy, Phillip, author, artist.
Title: Kepler / story, David Duchovny & Phillip Sevy ; art, letters & cover, Phillip Sevy.
Description: First edition. | Milwaukie, OR : Dark Horse Books, 2022. | Summary: "When the Benadem, benevolent space gods, return to KEPLER, a planet where homosapiens went extinct and all other hominid species thrived, their arrival threatens to plunge the world into chaos. West, a 16-year-old Neanderthal girl, is thrust into the conflict and is the only hope to prevent extinction. Her efforts, unique because of her mixed hominid heritage, not only change her life, but also reveal the merciless ambition and identity of the gods themselves"-- Provided by publisher.
Identifiers: LCCN 2022019629 (print) | LCCN 2022019630 (ebook) | ISBN 9781506733456 (hardcover) | ISBN 9781506733463 (ebook)
Subjects: LCGFT: Science fiction comics. | Graphic novels.
Classification: LCC PN6727.D834 K47 2022 (print) | LCC PN6727.D834 (ebook) | DDC 741.5/973--dc23/eng/20220608
LC record available at https://lccn.loc.gov/2022019629
LC ebook record available at https://lccn.loc.gov/2022019630

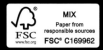

PREFACE

"Those who forget history are doomed to repeat it." That's a phrase that hits home for me these days. As well as the comedic corollary from *The Goon Show*—"Yes, I have learned from my mistakes and I can repeat them exactly." Those phrases, tragic and light, were rattling around my head when I was conceiving of the world of *Kepler*. What if we, humans, got another chance with a fresh new world we hadn't depleted and polluted? What if we entered into a new phase of colonialization, space colonialization—would we have learned from our genocidal colonial past? And what if, instead of indigenous peoples we were displacing and decimating, we came upon other types of hominids from our distant Earth past? Neanderthals, Denisovans, and other intelligent evolving primates native to Kepler. Would we treat them as the evolutionary brothers and sisters they are? Or would we play God and try to remake them and this planet in our own image? I guess this graphic novel is my working out the answer to those questions.

—DAVID DUCHOVNY

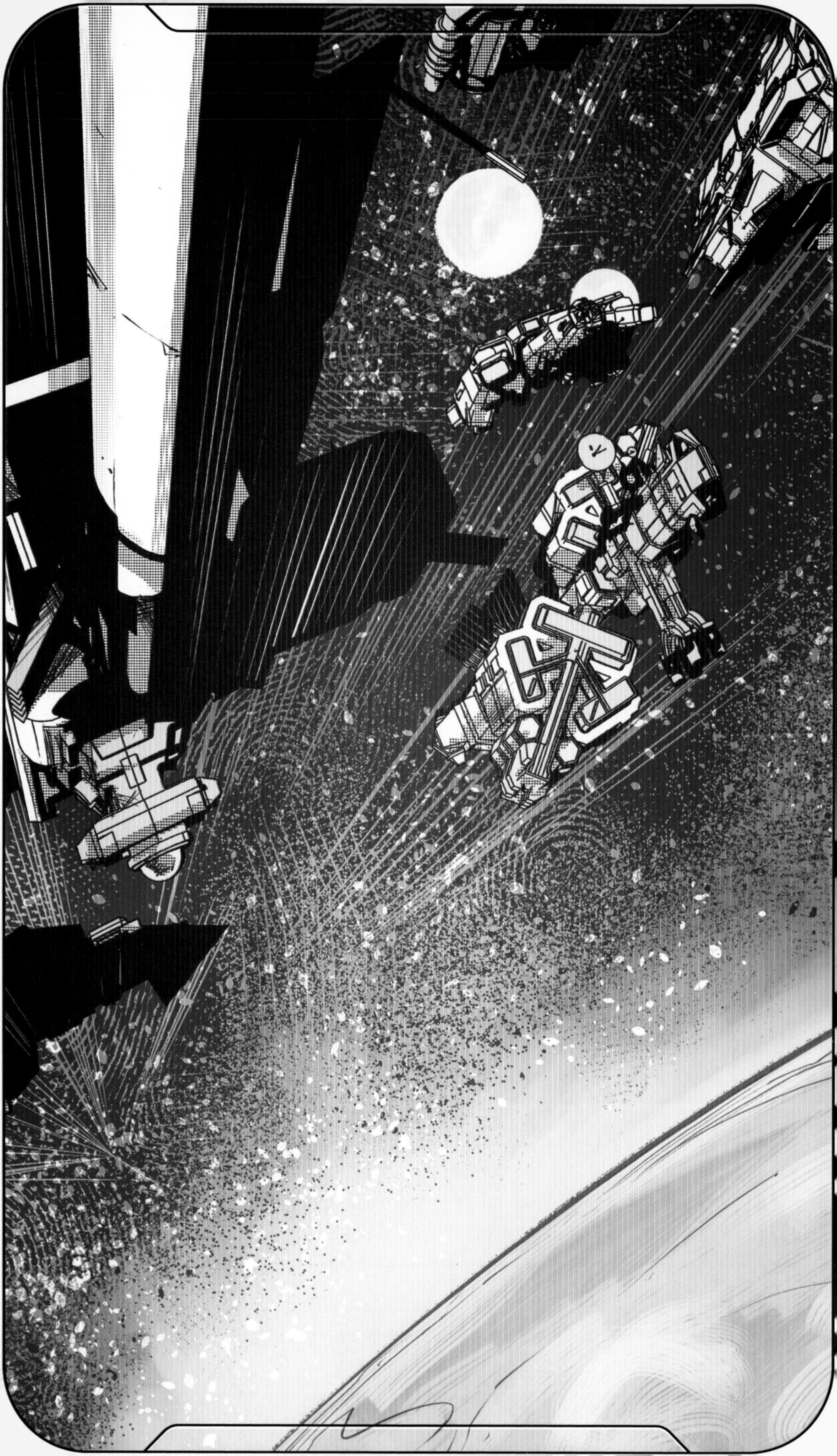

INTRODUCTION

'd get a call from Dave Duchovny. "This line in act four . . . do I have to say it? Or, at least, say it that way?" Way back in the twentieth century—certain I was the second coming of Richard Matheson, only in this century to accept I am not even a slug in Matheson's shrubbery—my immediate reaction was to reject anyone's suggestions, even those coming from the person who would have to make the line believable and true.

Here's why I'm telling you this. David would then explain, "I know you need the guy in that scene in act one, that Mulder isn't in, to say the same thing and Mulder is unknowingly echoing that guy's line, but could it be said this way and then the guy's line could be changed to say that and then it would be even more ominous." Take my word, the majority of actors focus only on their singular role throughout the story. David always understood the entire gestalt. Each character, not just his, the plot, how this plot connects with the plot two episodes ago, themes, humor, how it was all intended to work. He understood stuff in my own writing that I didn't know was there and always made it better. Always.

Where do we begin, hell, not even to resolve but, at the very least, untangle today's chaos, which we do understand involves an overwhelming interdependence of conflicting national economies in league with corporate partners that openly manipulate facts to achieve desired outcomes, while our individual lives are depersonalized and distracted through technologies . . . some nonexistent only a decade ago . . . all catalyzed by a sudden centurial pandemic, and, oh yeah, hey, how are we all affected, again, by that black hole fifty million light years away that we just snapped a picture of?

Kepler points the way. It understands the solution to "this" will aggravate the problem of "that." David and Phillip Sevy, with their comprehension not just of the complexities within entangled global issues—or in this case galactic—but also difficult personal struggles, present the case that we must each be willing to hear, consider, compromise, and sacrifice in the future if we wish to reach solutions that ultimately will be to the benefit of each part as well as the whole. *Kepler* shows that everything affects everything, and if your mind remains open, a solution is likely to arrive through anything other than you.

Don't just focus on your role. Take part in the entire thing.

Now, I gladly await the phone call improving what you just read.

—GLEN MORGAN, PRODUCER OF *THE X-FILES*

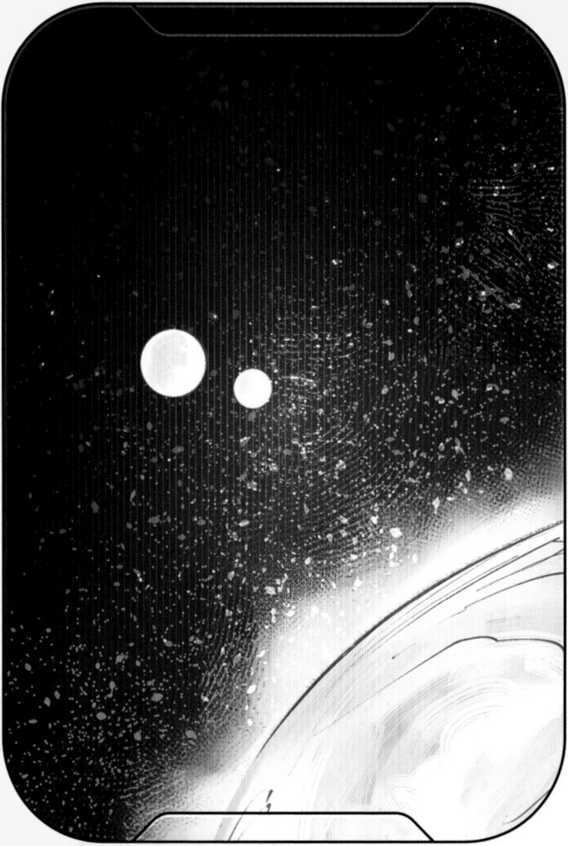

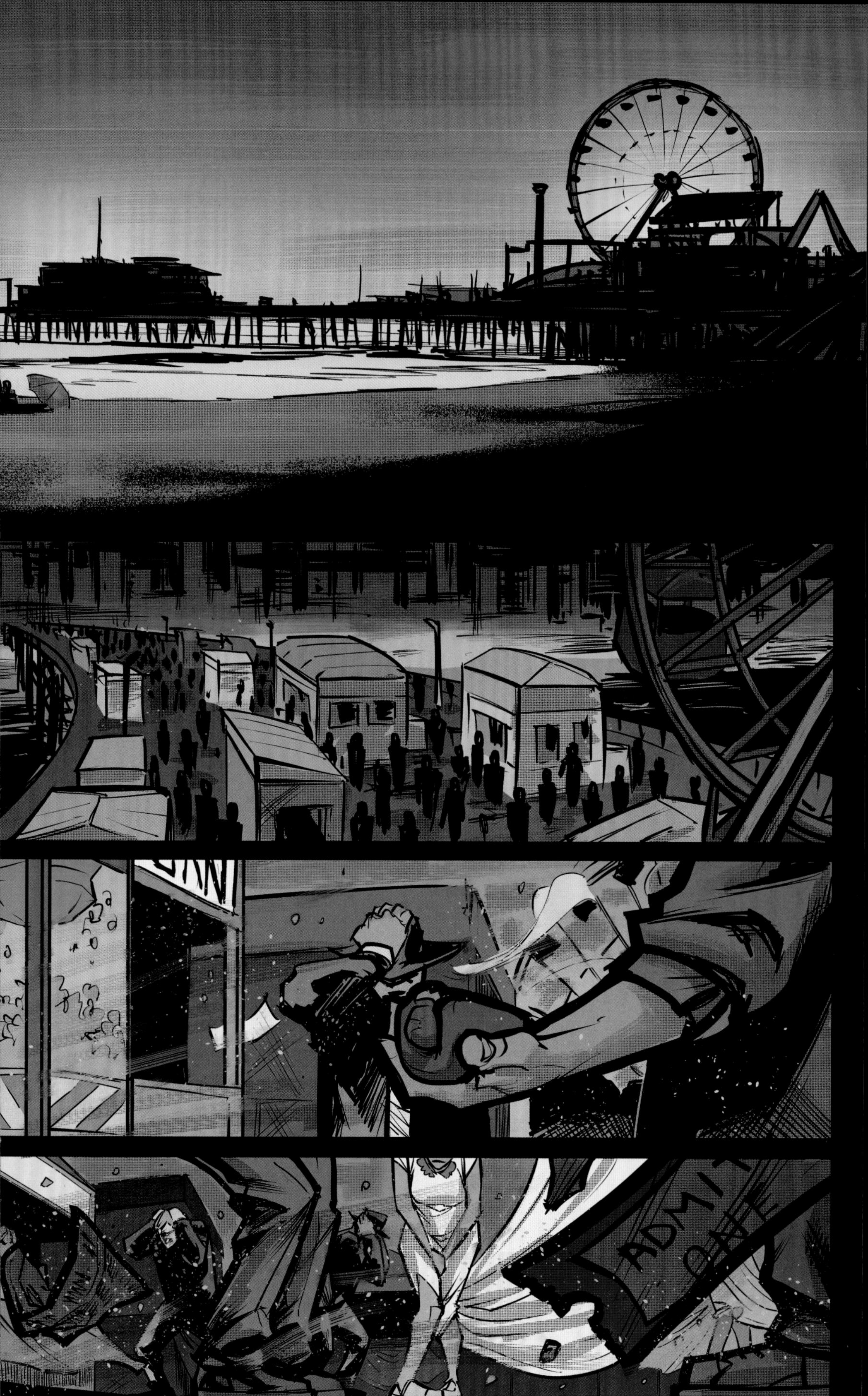

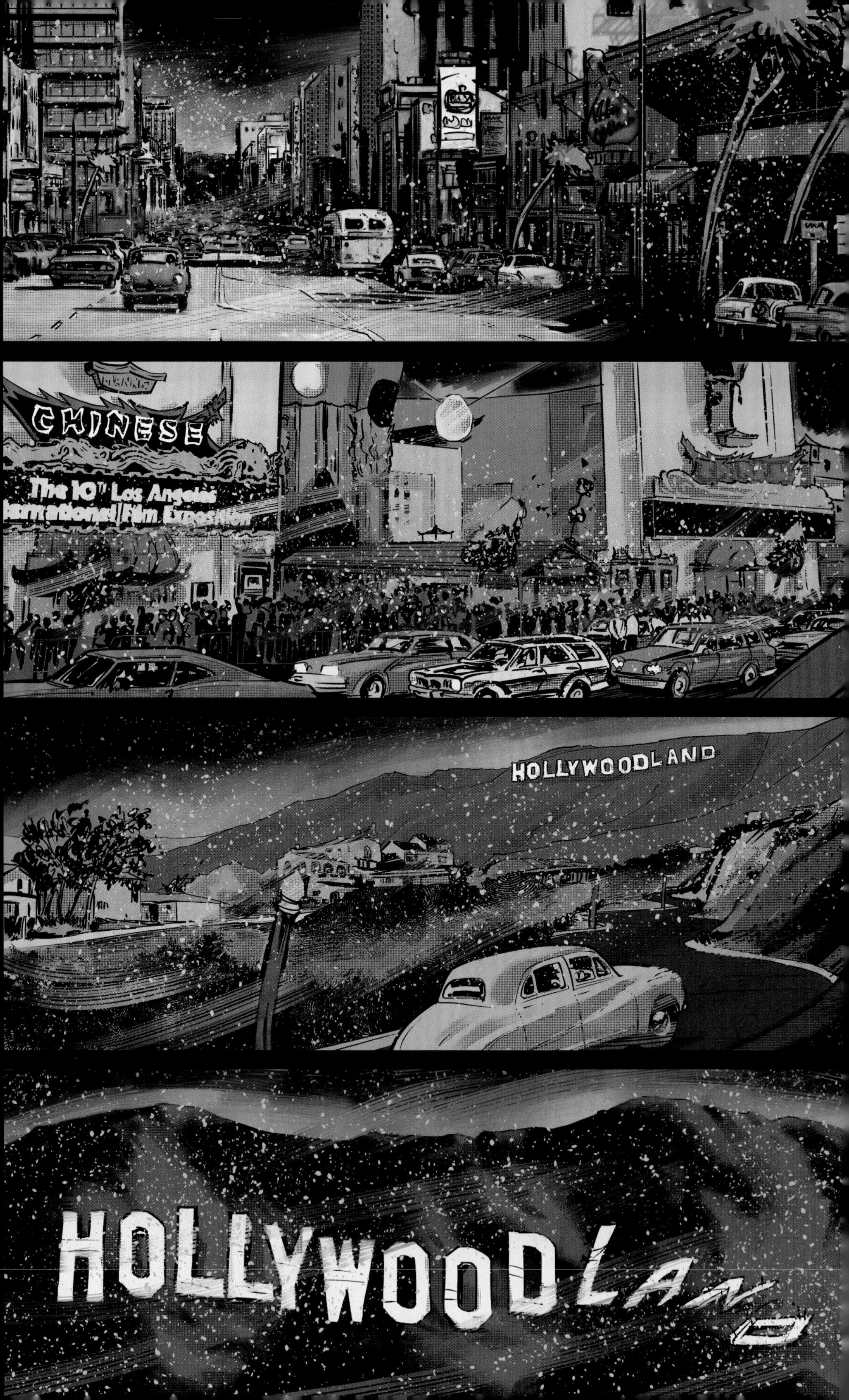
CHINESE
The 10th Los Angeles
nternational Film Exposition
HOLLYWOODLAND
HOLLYWOODLAN

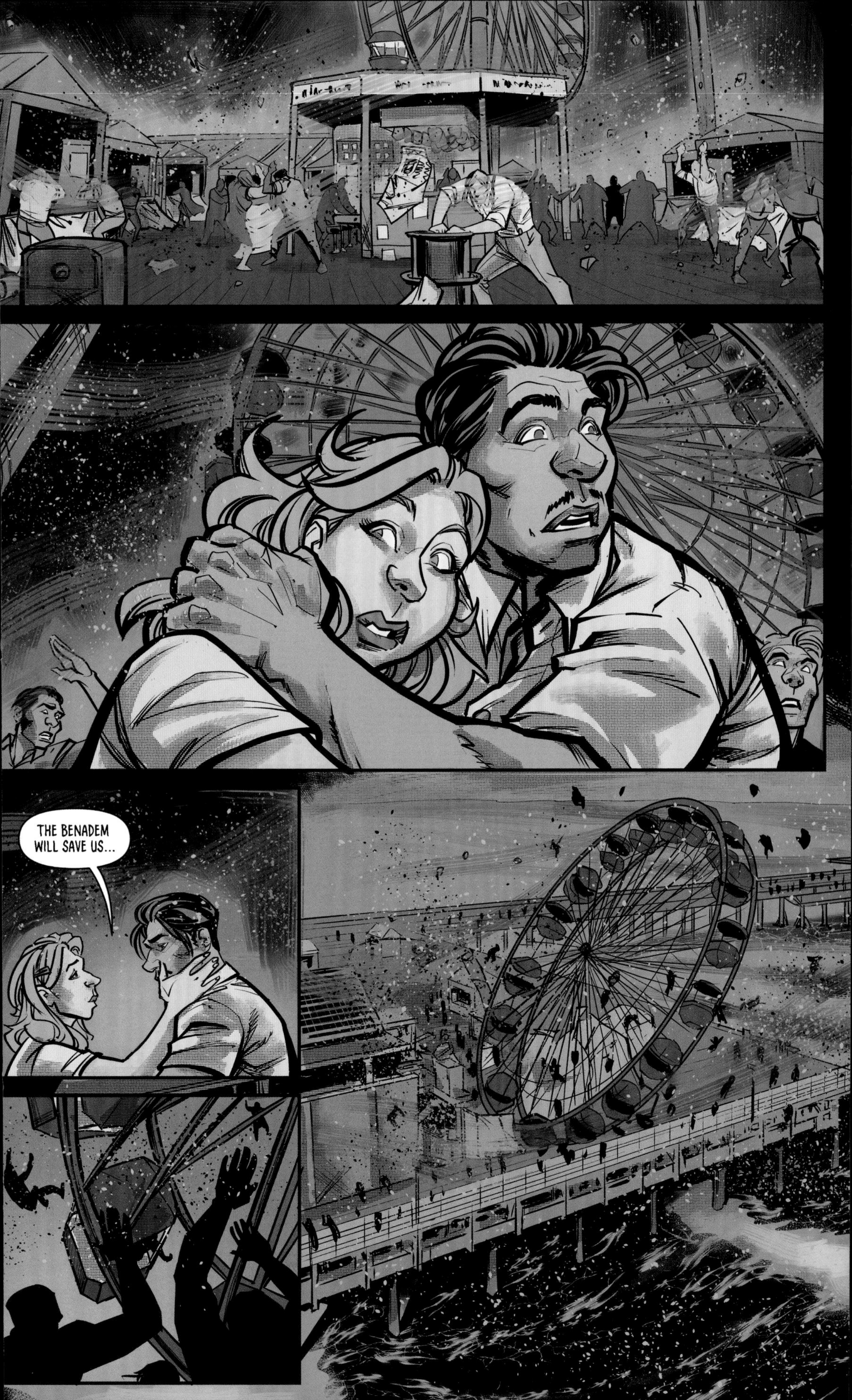
THE BENADEM WILL SAVE US...

Dark Horse Presents

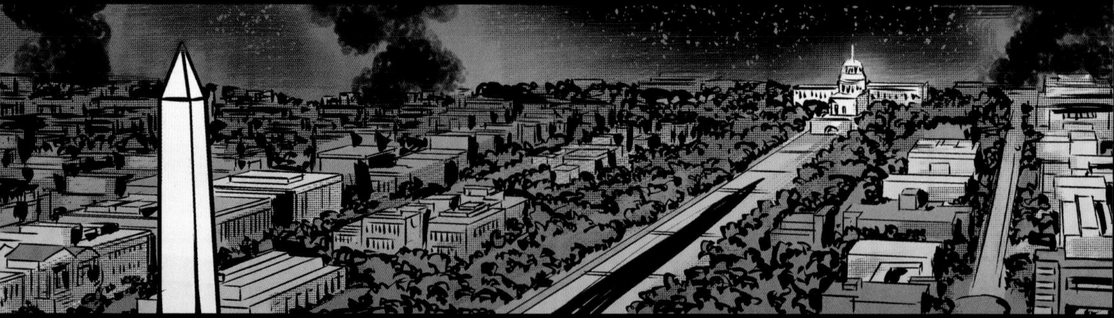

Kepler

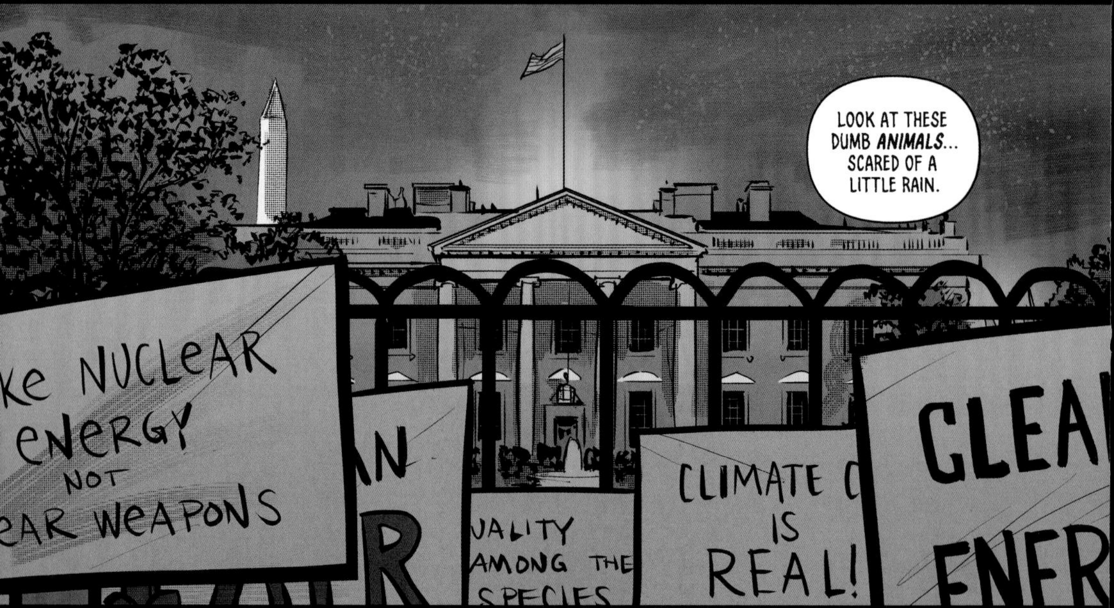
LOOK AT THESE DUMB *ANIMALS*... SCARED OF A LITTLE RAIN.
ke NUCLEAR ENERGY NOT EAR WEAPONS
UALITY AMONG THE
CLIMATE C IS REAL!
CLEA

by David Duchovny and Phillip Sevy

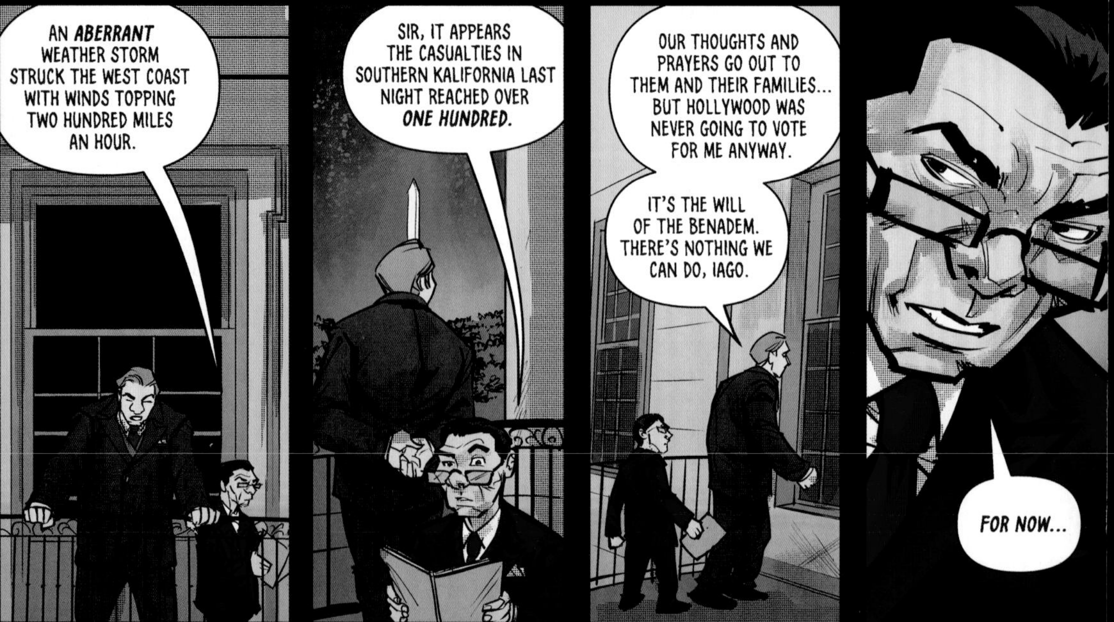
AN *ABERRANT* WEATHER STORM STRUCK THE WEST COAST WITH WINDS TOPPING TWO HUNDRED MILES AN HOUR.
SIR, IT APPEARS THE CASUALTIES IN SOUTHERN KALIFORNIA LAST NIGHT REACHED OVER *ONE HUNDRED.*
OUR THOUGHTS AND PRAYERS GO OUT TO THEM AND THEIR FAMILIES... BUT HOLLYWOOD WAS NEVER GOING TO VOTE FOR ME ANYWAY.
IT'S THE WILL OF THE BENADEM. THERE'S NOTHING WE CAN DO, IAGO.
FOR NOW...

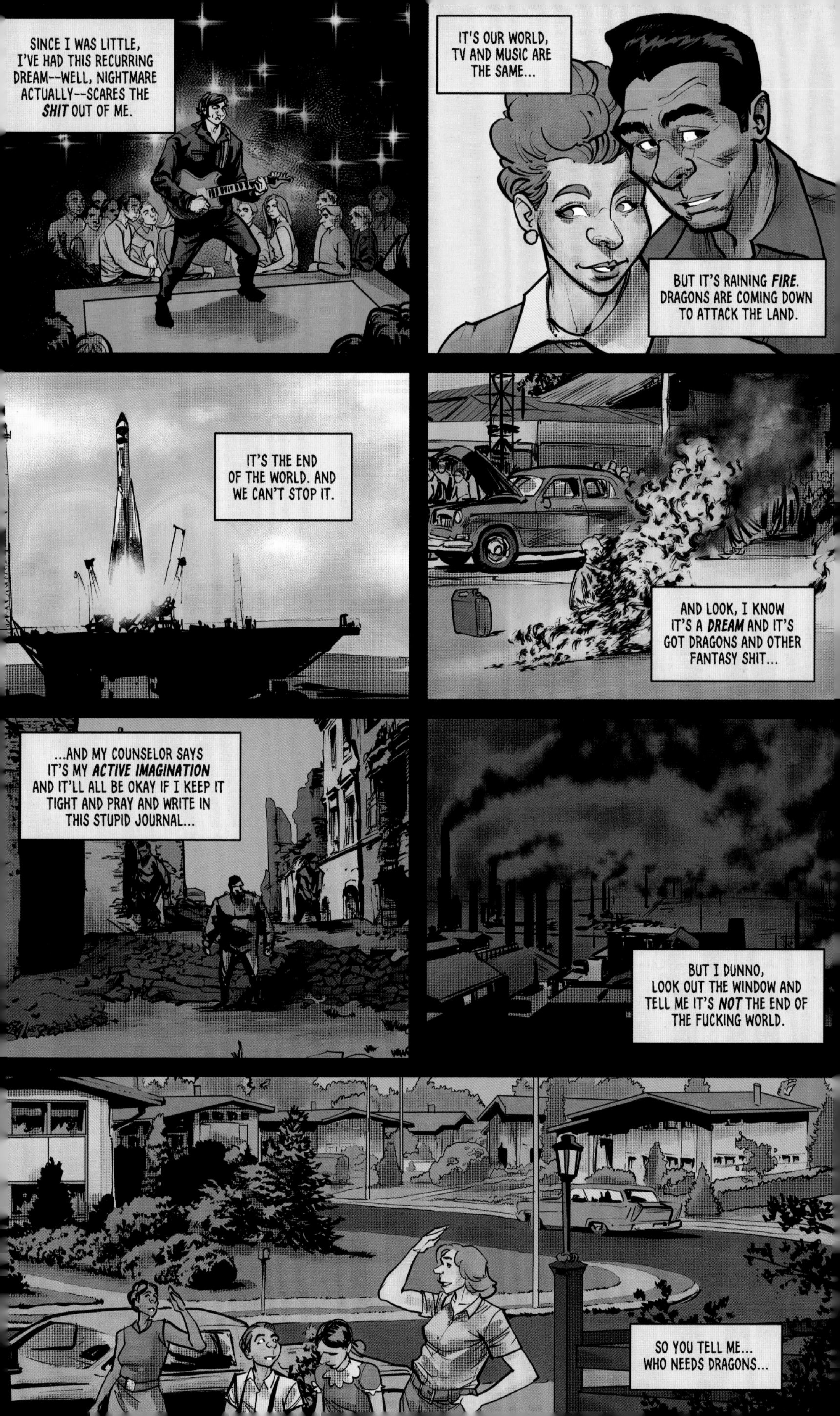
SINCE I WAS LITTLE, I'VE HAD THIS RECURRING DREAM--WELL, NIGHTMARE ACTUALLY--SCARES THE *SHIT* OUT OF ME.
IT'S OUR WORLD, TV AND MUSIC ARE THE SAME...
BUT IT'S RAINING *FIRE*. DRAGONS ARE COMING DOWN TO ATTACK THE LAND.
IT'S THE END OF THE WORLD. AND WE CAN'T STOP IT.
AND LOOK, I KNOW IT'S A *DREAM* AND IT'S GOT DRAGONS AND OTHER FANTASY SHIT...
...AND MY COUNSELOR SAYS IT'S MY *ACTIVE IMAGINATION* AND IT'LL ALL BE OKAY IF I KEEP IT TIGHT AND PRAY AND WRITE IN THIS STUPID JOURNAL...
BUT I DUNNO, LOOK OUT THE WINDOW AND TELL ME IT'S *NOT* THE END OF THE FUCKING WORLD.
SO YOU TELL ME... WHO NEEDS DRAGONS...

KEPLER:

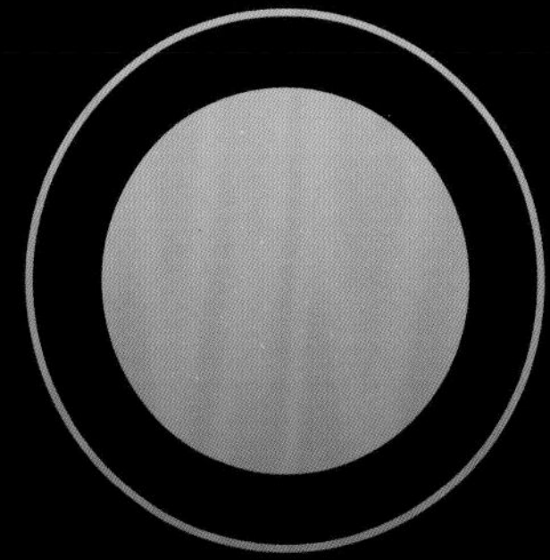

Kepler-452b is an exoplanet of the star Kepler-452 in the Milky Way Galaxy. Its existence was discovered in 2015. It is in the so-called "habitable" or "Goldilocks" zone, meaning that the planetary distance from its host star is such that liquid water can exist on the planet and sustain life.

It is estimated that there are over four thousand planets in the Goldilocks zone.

Designation: KOI-7016.01
Distance from Earth: 1,800 light years
Size: 1.5 times larger than Earth
Age: 6+ billion years
Host Star: Kepler-452, G-type star
Orbital Period: 384 days
Population: 165,000,000

SPECIES OF KEPLER:

THAAL:

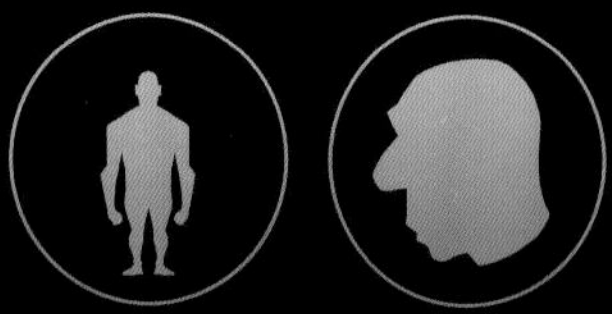

Most closely akin to the Neanderthal of Earth, this native Kepler hominid shares many characteristics of its Earth cousin—barrel chested with short, powerful legs, huge hands, and a facial aspect dominated by a protruding brow, short forehead, long nose, and large eyes. Thaals are the dominant hominids on Kepler, but unlike *Homo sapiens* on Earth, they have not outcompeted other Kepler hominids into extinction. Yet.

BONOBION:

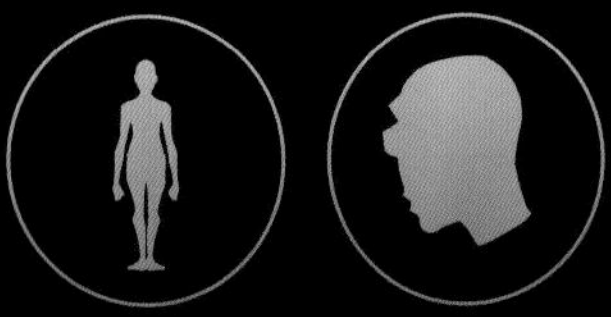

A gentle, peace-loving hominid descended from a type of Keplerian bonobo monkey. Bonobions are more slender and graceful than their Thaal cousins. With thinner torsos and finer facial features, Bonobions are a spiritual, empathic, and highly sensual species who prefer to resolve conflict with sex rather than violence. When a Bonobion child enters puberty, a third eye, their means of empathic communication, can become visible in the middle of the forehead.

FLOREN:

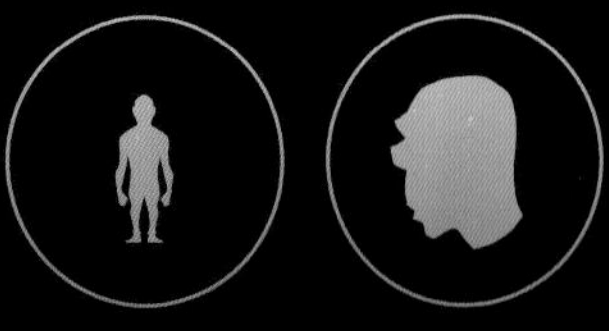

A small minority and a tiny hominid on the verge of extinction. Somewhat like *Australopithecus* on Earth or the famous Lucy. The Florens rarely break five feet tall. Because of their small physical stature, they have evolved to rely on guile and sociopolitical smarts. They are known as the Machiavellian hominid of Kepler, and they have the shortest lifespan—rarely breaking thirty years.

Note: There is no one skin tone associated with any one Kepler hominid. All Thaals, Bonobions, and Florens can display a range of skin pigmentation based on a variety of factors that are not connected to their species.

RELIGIONS OF KEPLER:

BENADEM:

The state religion of Kepler that centers around the centennial visits of heavenly beings bearing gifts of knowledge, wisdom, morality, and technology. Benadem would find its closest counterpart in twentieth-century American Christianity. The Bonobions, who practice a more natural, less technological way of life, grew tired of relying on these infrequent angelic visitations and preach a more humble Kepler version of self-reliance.

BONOBION BELIEFS:

As a counter to the external and consumption-focused beliefs of Benadem, Bonobion beliefs center around worship of and reverence for the planet Kepler. Only by embracing nature and life can the people grow and evolve. This, coupled with the mystical properties (such as various forms of telepathy and emotional manipulation) of the Bonobion third eye, causes Bonobions to be seen as both shamans and hippies.

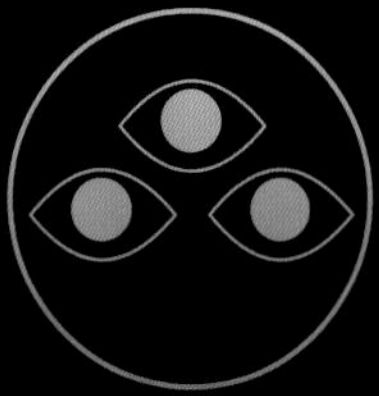

MAIN CONFLICTS OF KEPLER:

With the population's reliance on coal and other pollutant-heavy power sources, Kepler's atmosphere and climate are suffering accelerated instability and degradation. Nations of the planet are in an energy race to be the first to crack the key to nuclear power. No nation has yet managed the splitting of the atom successfully.

Kepler, home to a hybrid native culture with idiosyncratic Benadem accelerants, has evolved on its own into a sort of interplanetary equivalent of a mid-twentieth-century level. They have cars and planes and pollution and early rock 'n' roll. They do not have cell phones or nuclear weapons or punk. Yet.

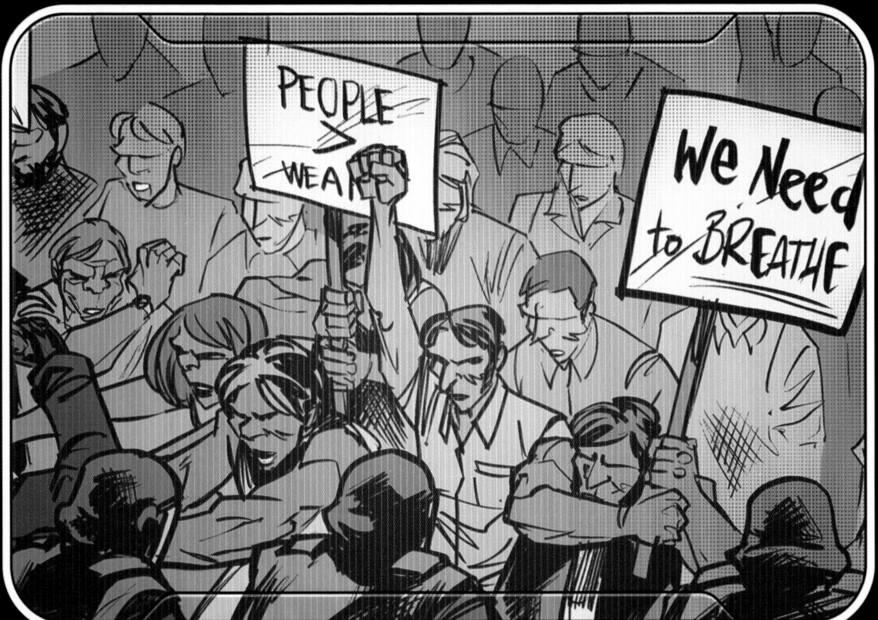
PEOPLE
We Need to BREATHE

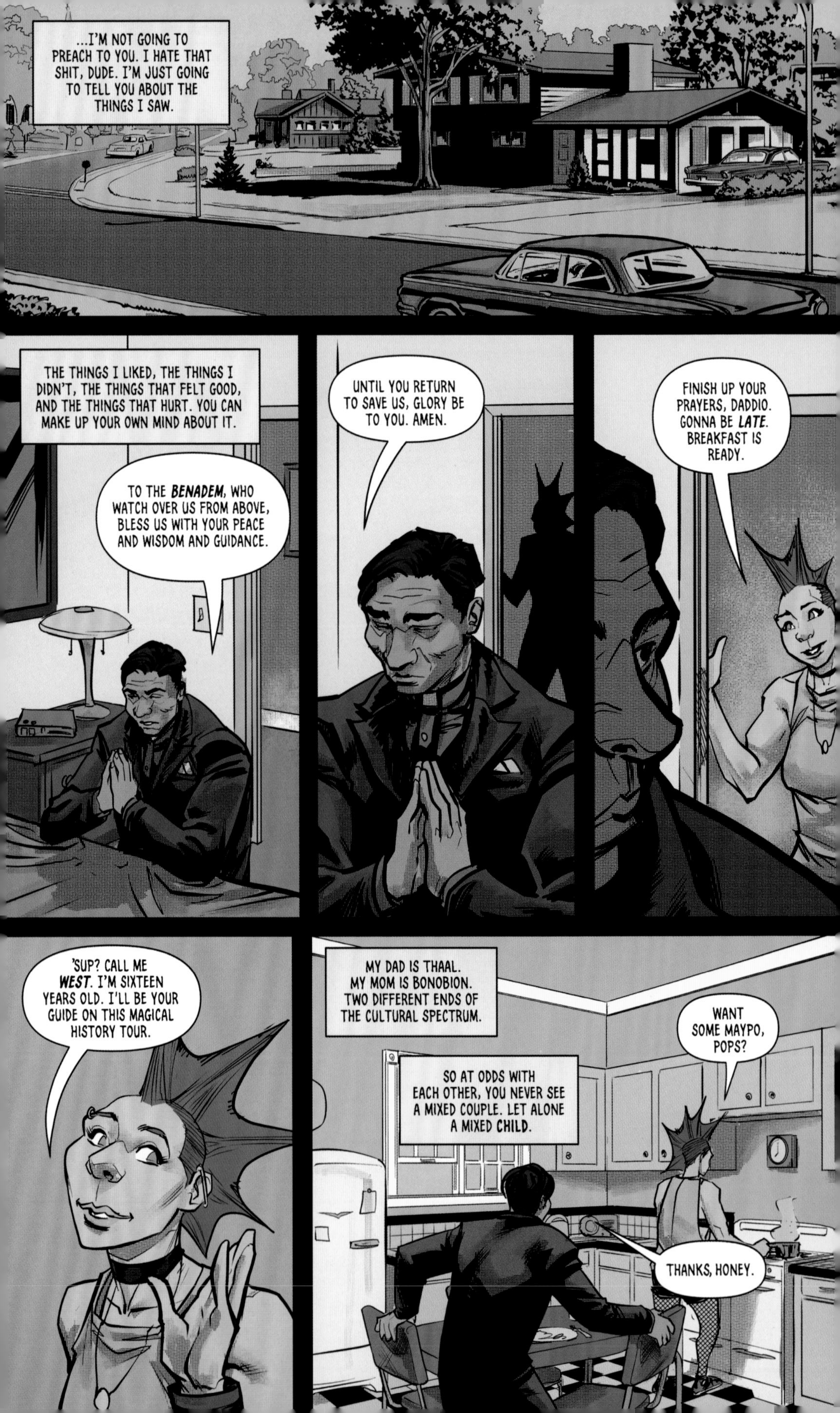
...I'M NOT GOING TO PREACH TO YOU. I HATE THAT SHIT, DUDE. I'M JUST GOING TO TELL YOU ABOUT THE THINGS I SAW.
THE THINGS I LIKED, THE THINGS I DIDN'T, THE THINGS THAT FELT GOOD, AND THE THINGS THAT HURT. YOU CAN MAKE UP YOUR OWN MIND ABOUT IT.
TO THE BENADEM, WHO WATCH OVER US FROM ABOVE, BLESS US WITH YOUR PEACE AND WISDOM AND GUIDANCE.
UNTIL YOU RETURN TO SAVE US, GLORY BE TO YOU. AMEN.
FINISH UP YOUR PRAYERS, DADDIO. GONNA BE LATE. BREAKFAST IS READY.
'SUP? CALL ME WEST. I'M SIXTEEN YEARS OLD. I'LL BE YOUR GUIDE ON THIS MAGICAL HISTORY TOUR.
MY DAD IS THAAL. MY MOM IS BONOBION. TWO DIFFERENT ENDS OF THE CULTURAL SPECTRUM.
SO AT ODDS WITH EACH OTHER, YOU NEVER SEE A MIXED COUPLE. LET ALONE A MIXED CHILD.
WANT SOME MAYPO, POPS?
THANKS, HONEY.

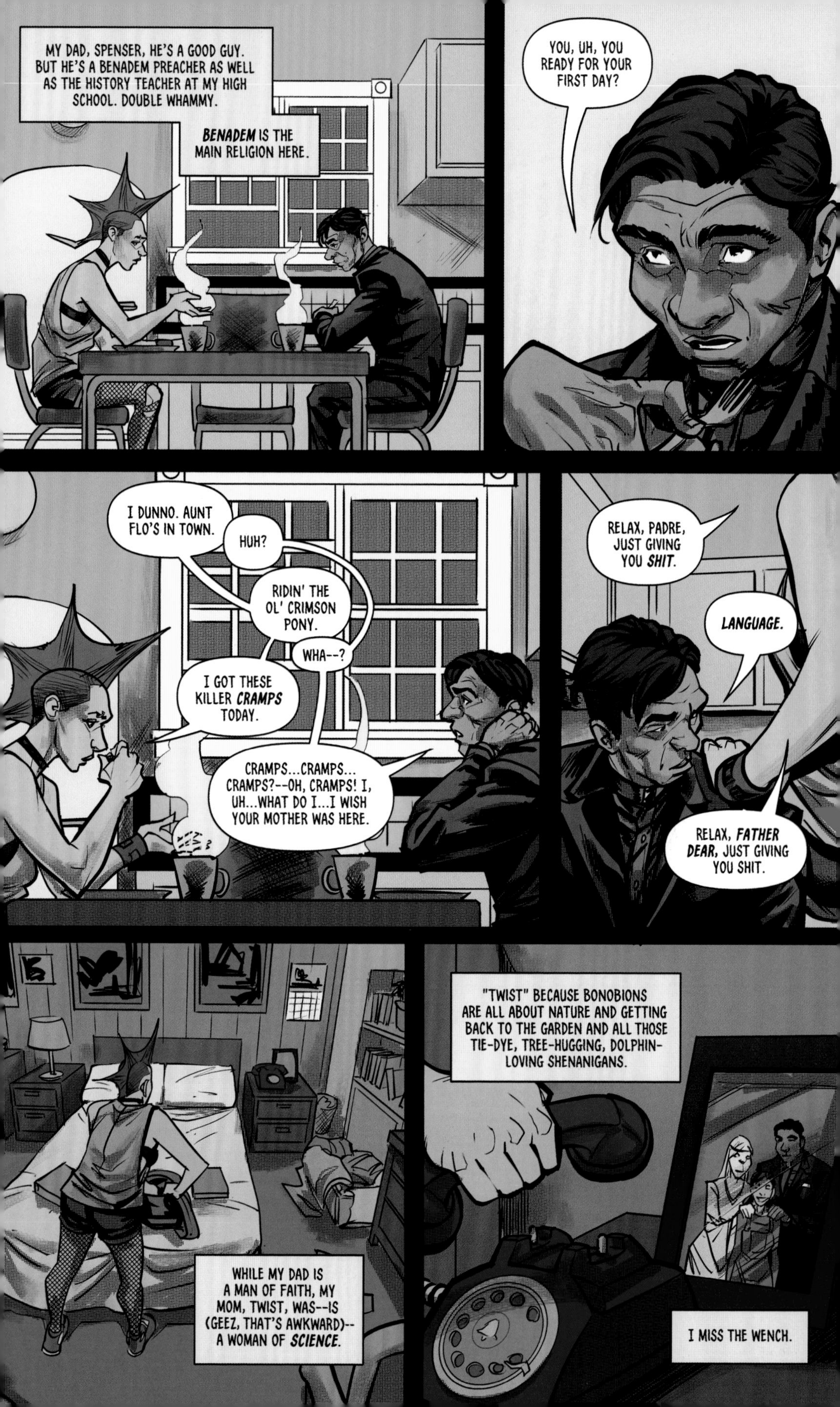
MY DAD, SPENSER, HE'S A GOOD GUY. BUT HE'S A BENADEM PREACHER AS WELL AS THE HISTORY TEACHER AT MY HIGH SCHOOL. DOUBLE WHAMMY.
BENADEM IS THE MAIN RELIGION HERE.
YOU, UH, YOU READY FOR YOUR FIRST DAY?
I DUNNO. AUNT FLO'S IN TOWN.
HUH?
RIDIN' THE OL' CRIMSON PONY.
WHA--?
I GOT THESE KILLER *CRAMPS* TODAY.
CRAMPS...CRAMPS... CRAMPS?--OH, CRAMPS! I, UH...WHAT DO I...I WISH YOUR MOTHER WAS HERE.
RELAX, PADRE, JUST GIVING YOU *SHIT*.
LANGUAGE.
RELAX, *FATHER DEAR,* JUST GIVING YOU SHIT.
WHILE MY DAD IS A MAN OF FAITH, MY MOM, TWIST, WAS--IS (GEEZ, THAT'S AWKWARD)-- A WOMAN OF *SCIENCE*.
"TWIST" BECAUSE BONOBIONS ARE ALL ABOUT NATURE AND GETTING BACK TO THE GARDEN AND ALL THOSE TIE-DYE, TREE-HUGGING, DOLPHIN-LOVING SHENANIGANS.
I MISS THE WENCH.

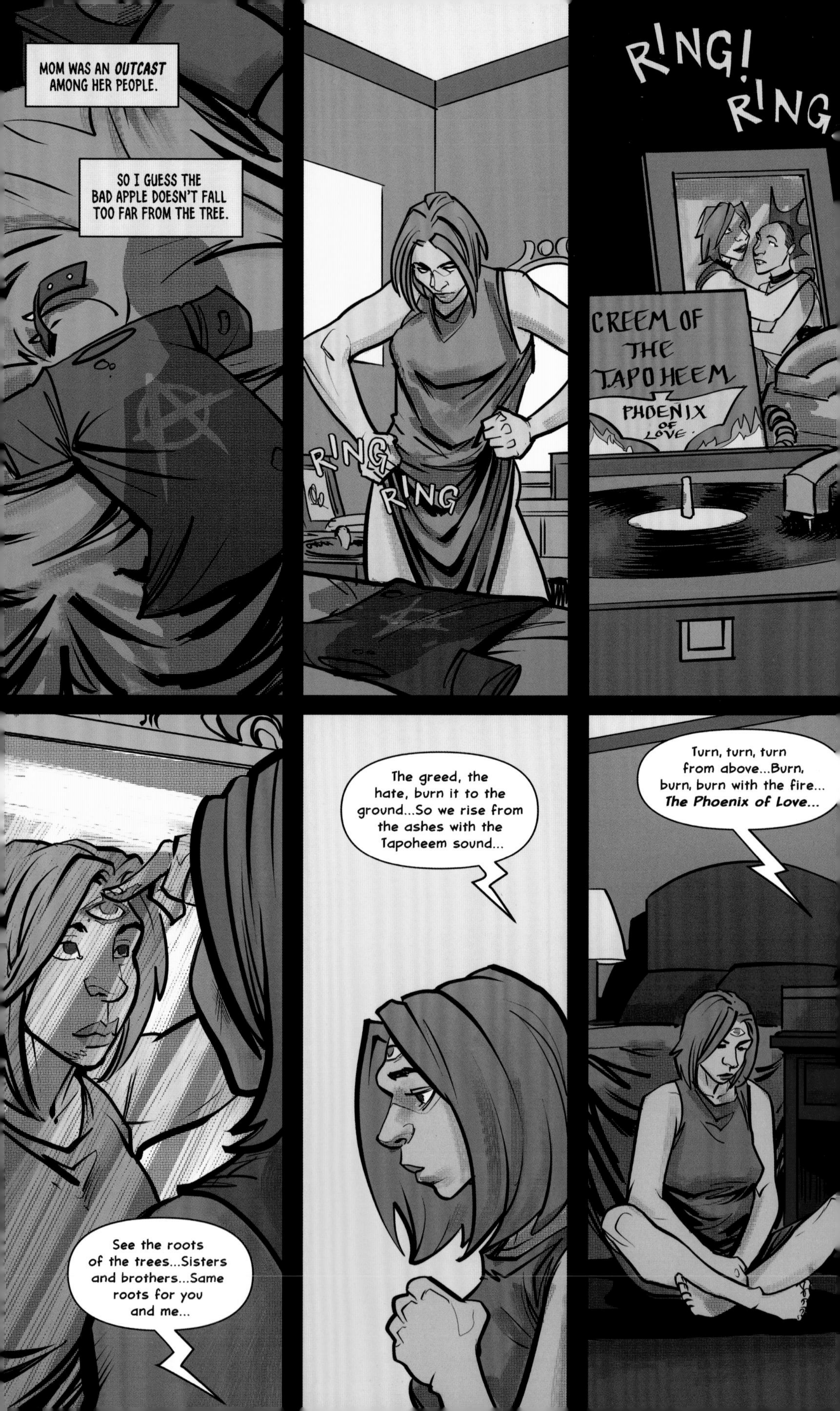
MOM WAS AN *OUTCAST* AMONG HER PEOPLE.
SO I GUESS THE BAD APPLE DOESN'T FALL TOO FAR FROM THE TREE.
RING RING
RING! RING.
CREEM OF THE TAPOHEEM
PHOENIX OF LOVE
See the roots of the trees...Sisters and brothers...Same roots for you and me...
The greed, the hate, burn it to the ground...So we rise from the ashes with the Tapoheem sound...
Turn, turn, turn from above...Burn, burn, burn with the fire... ***The Phoenix of Love...***

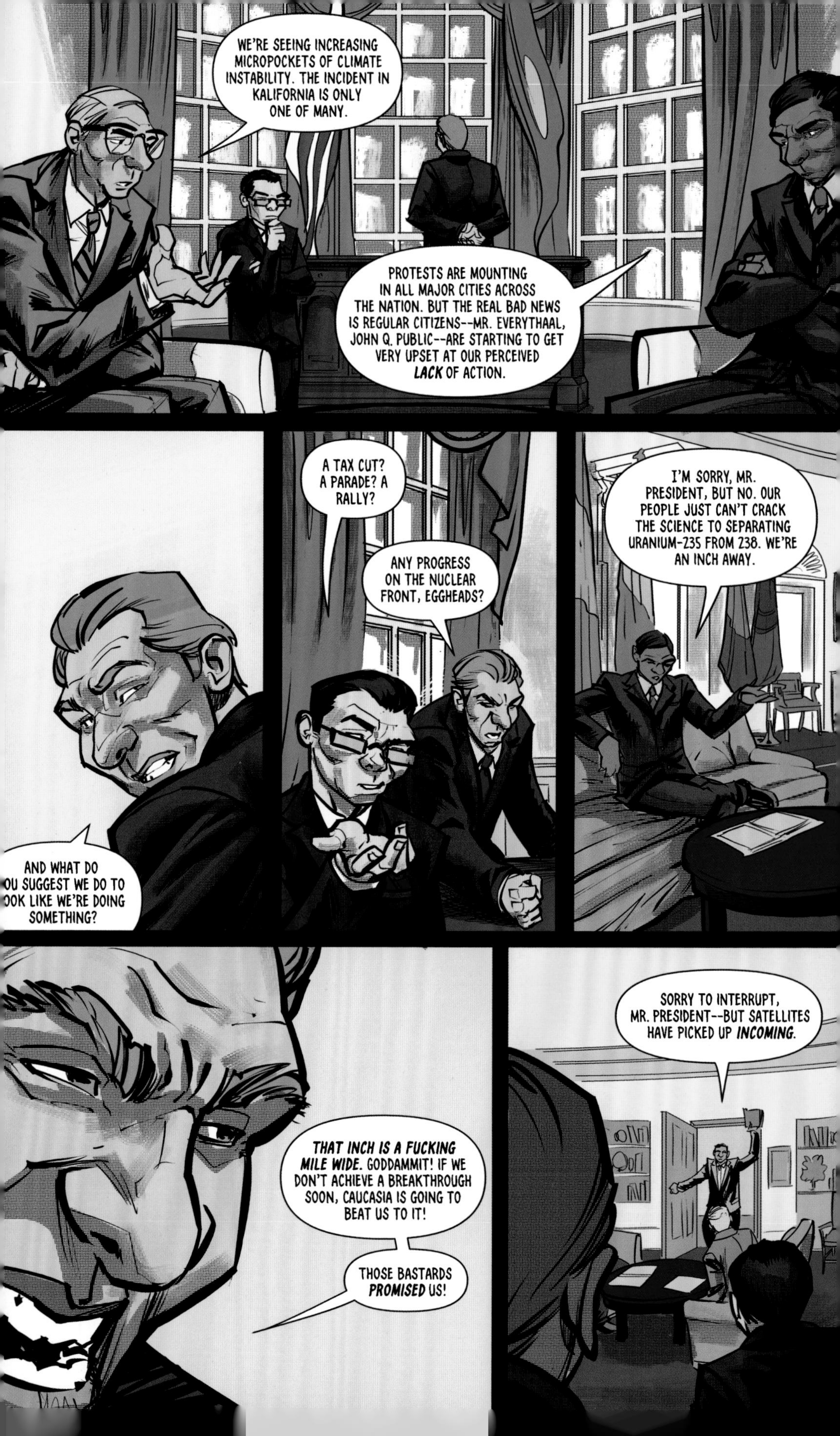
WE'RE SEEING INCREASING MICROPOCKETS OF CLIMATE INSTABILITY. THE INCIDENT IN KALIFORNIA IS ONLY ONE OF MANY.
PROTESTS ARE MOUNTING IN ALL MAJOR CITIES ACROSS THE NATION. BUT THE REAL BAD NEWS IS REGULAR CITIZENS--MR. EVERYTHAAL, JOHN Q. PUBLIC--ARE STARTING TO GET VERY UPSET AT OUR PERCEIVED LACK OF ACTION.
AND WHAT DO OU SUGGEST WE DO TO OOK LIKE WE'RE DOING SOMETHING?
A TAX CUT? A PARADE? A RALLY?
ANY PROGRESS ON THE NUCLEAR FRONT, EGGHEADS?
I'M SORRY, MR. PRESIDENT, BUT NO. OUR PEOPLE JUST CAN'T CRACK THE SCIENCE TO SEPARATING URANIUM-235 FROM 238. WE'RE AN INCH AWAY.
THAT INCH IS A FUCKING MILE WIDE. GODDAMMIT! IF WE DON'T ACHIEVE A BREAKTHROUGH SOON, CAUCASIA IS GOING TO BEAT US TO IT!
THOSE BASTARDS PROMISED US!
SORRY TO INTERRUPT, MR. PRESIDENT--BUT SATELLITES HAVE PICKED UP INCOMING.

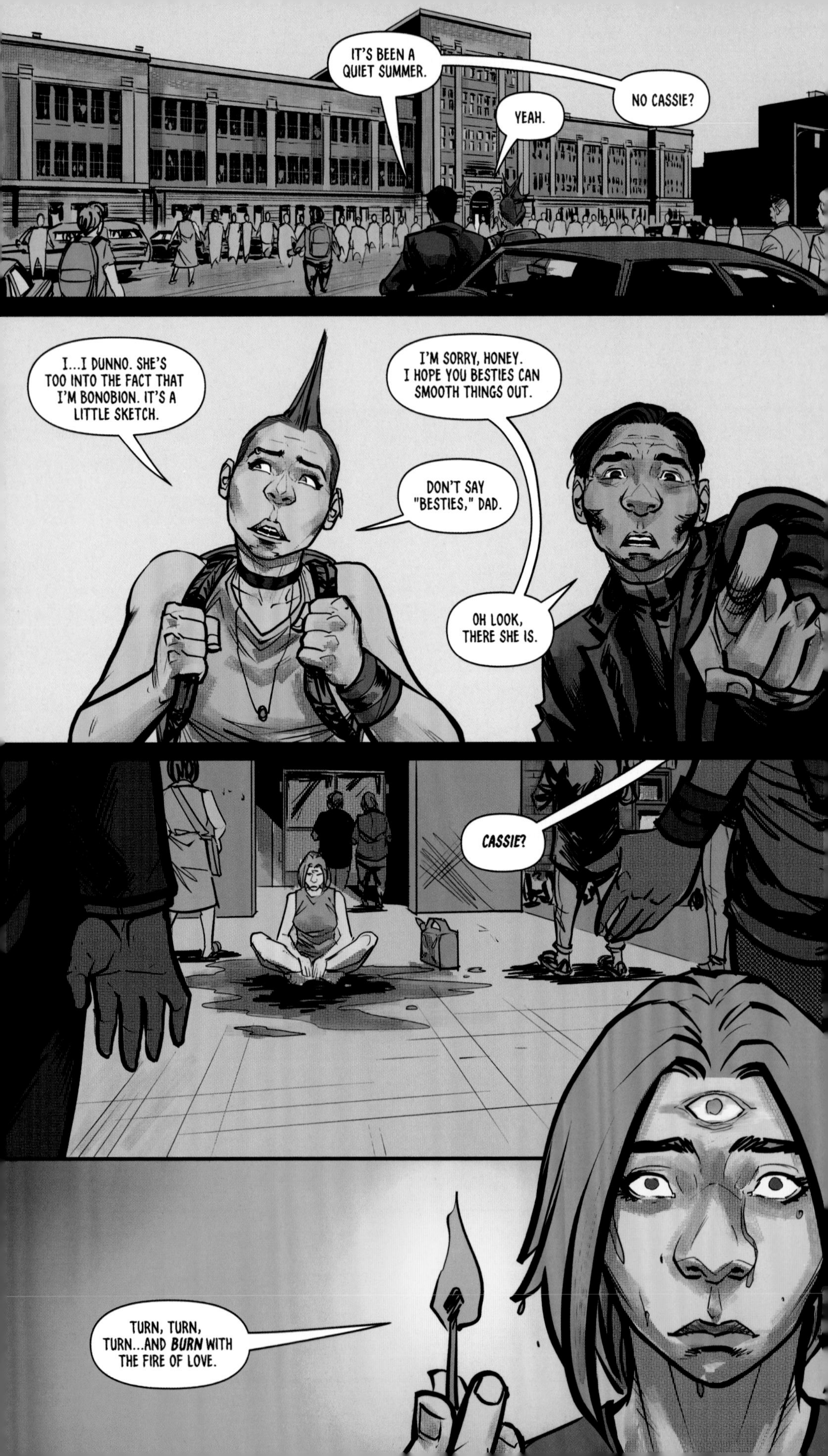
IT'S BEEN A QUIET SUMMER.
NO CASSIE?
YEAH.
I...I DUNNO. SHE'S TOO INTO THE FACT THAT I'M BONOBION. IT'S A LITTLE SKETCH.
I'M SORRY, HONEY. I HOPE YOU BESTIES CAN SMOOTH THINGS OUT.
DON'T SAY "BESTIES," DAD.
OH LOOK, THERE SHE IS.
CASSIE?
TURN, TURN, TURN...AND BURN WITH THE FIRE OF LOVE.

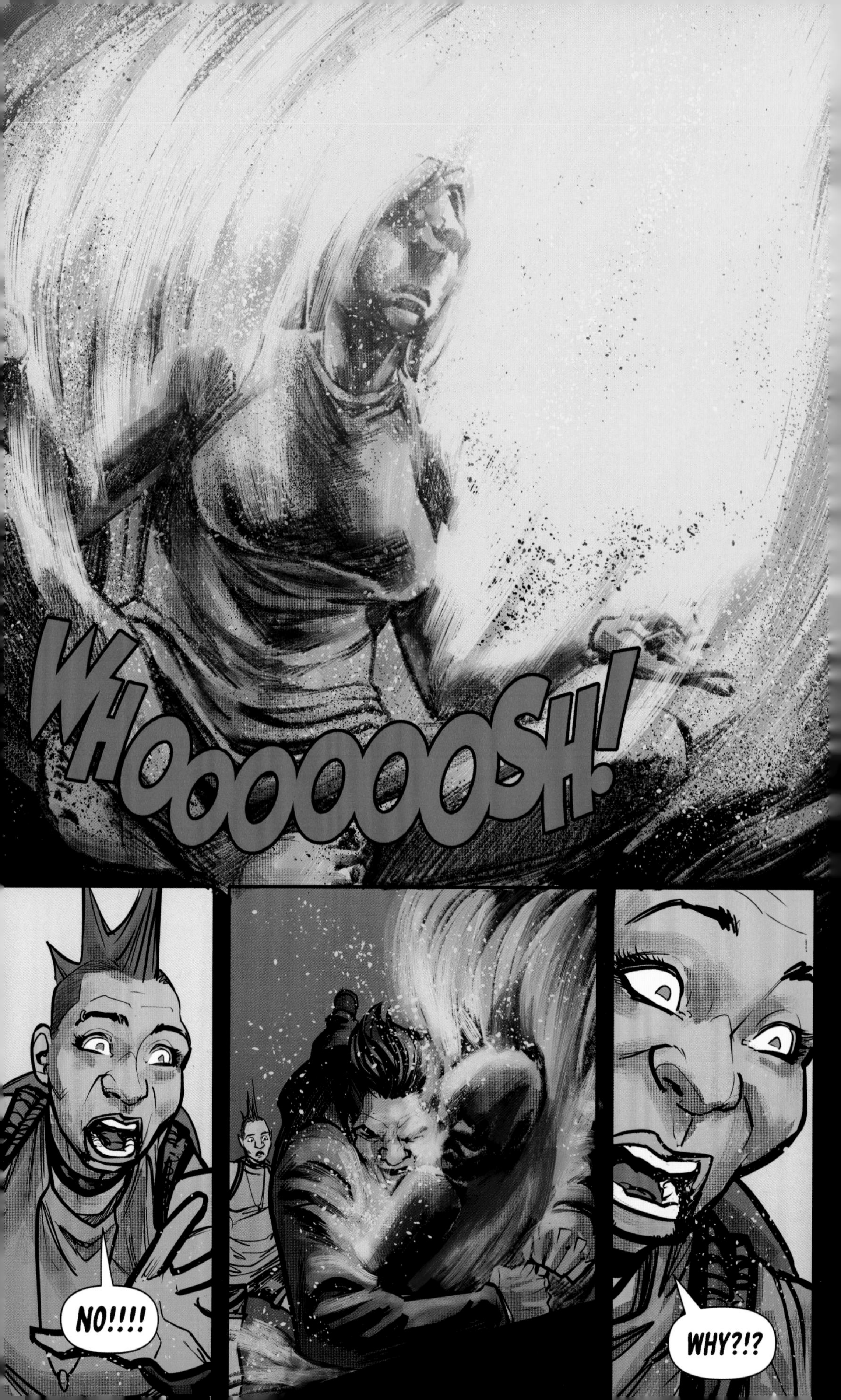
WHOOOOOOSH!
NO!!!!
WHY?!?

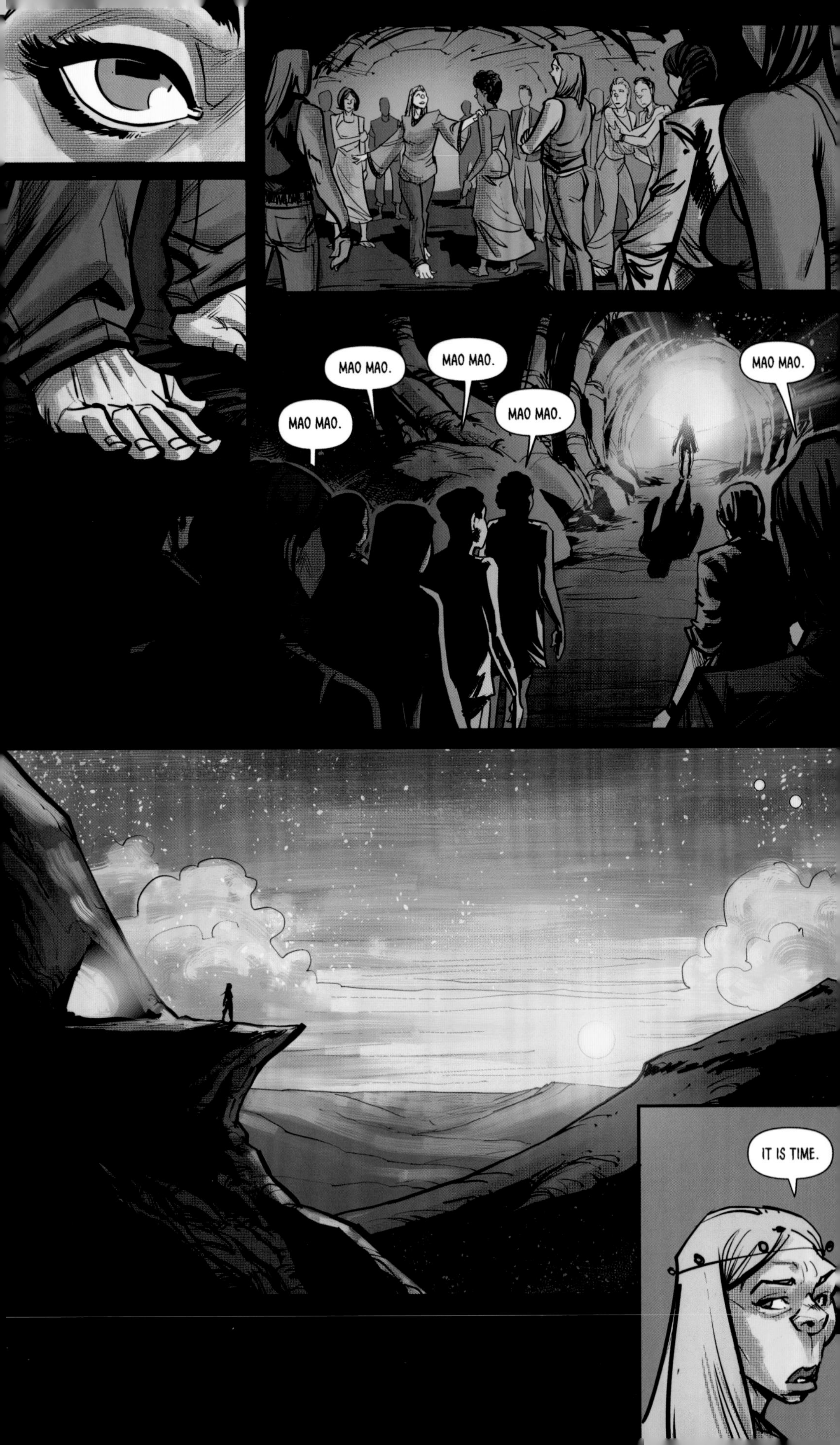
MAO MAO.
MAO MAO.
MAO MAO.
MAO MAO.
MAO MAO.
IT IS TIME.

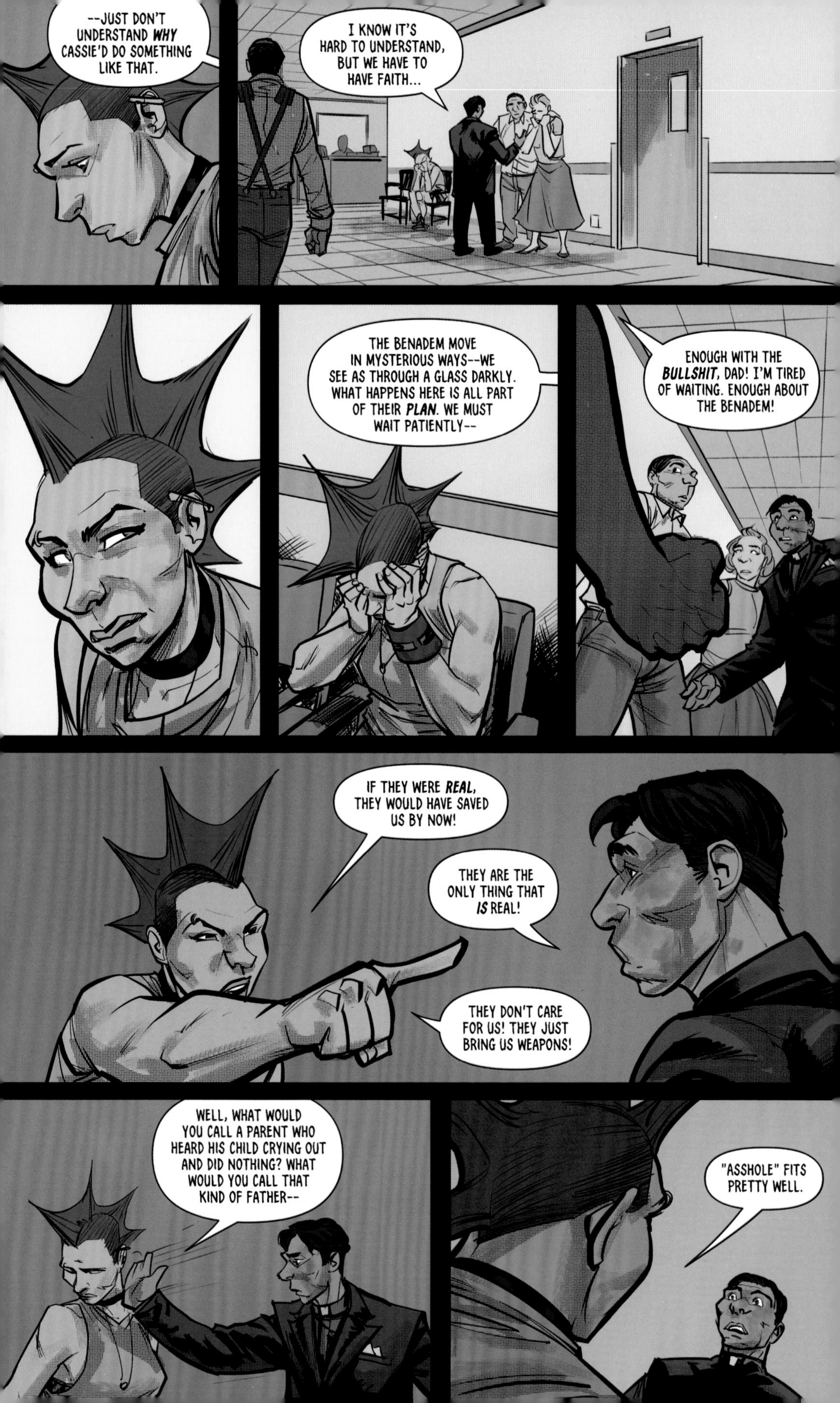
--JUST DON'T UNDERSTAND WHY CASSIE'D DO SOMETHING LIKE THAT.
I KNOW IT'S HARD TO UNDERSTAND, BUT WE HAVE TO HAVE FAITH...
THE BENADEM MOVE IN MYSTERIOUS WAYS--WE SEE AS THROUGH A GLASS DARKLY. WHAT HAPPENS HERE IS ALL PART OF THEIR PLAN. WE MUST WAIT PATIENTLY--
ENOUGH WITH THE BULLSHIT, DAD! I'M TIRED OF WAITING. ENOUGH ABOUT THE BENADEM!
IF THEY WERE REAL, THEY WOULD HAVE SAVED US BY NOW!
THEY ARE THE ONLY THING THAT IS REAL!
THEY DON'T CARE FOR US! THEY JUST BRING US WEAPONS!
WELL, WHAT WOULD YOU CALL A PARENT WHO HEARD HIS CHILD CRYING OUT AND DID NOTHING? WHAT WOULD YOU CALL THAT KIND OF FATHER--
"ASSHOLE" FITS PRETTY WELL.

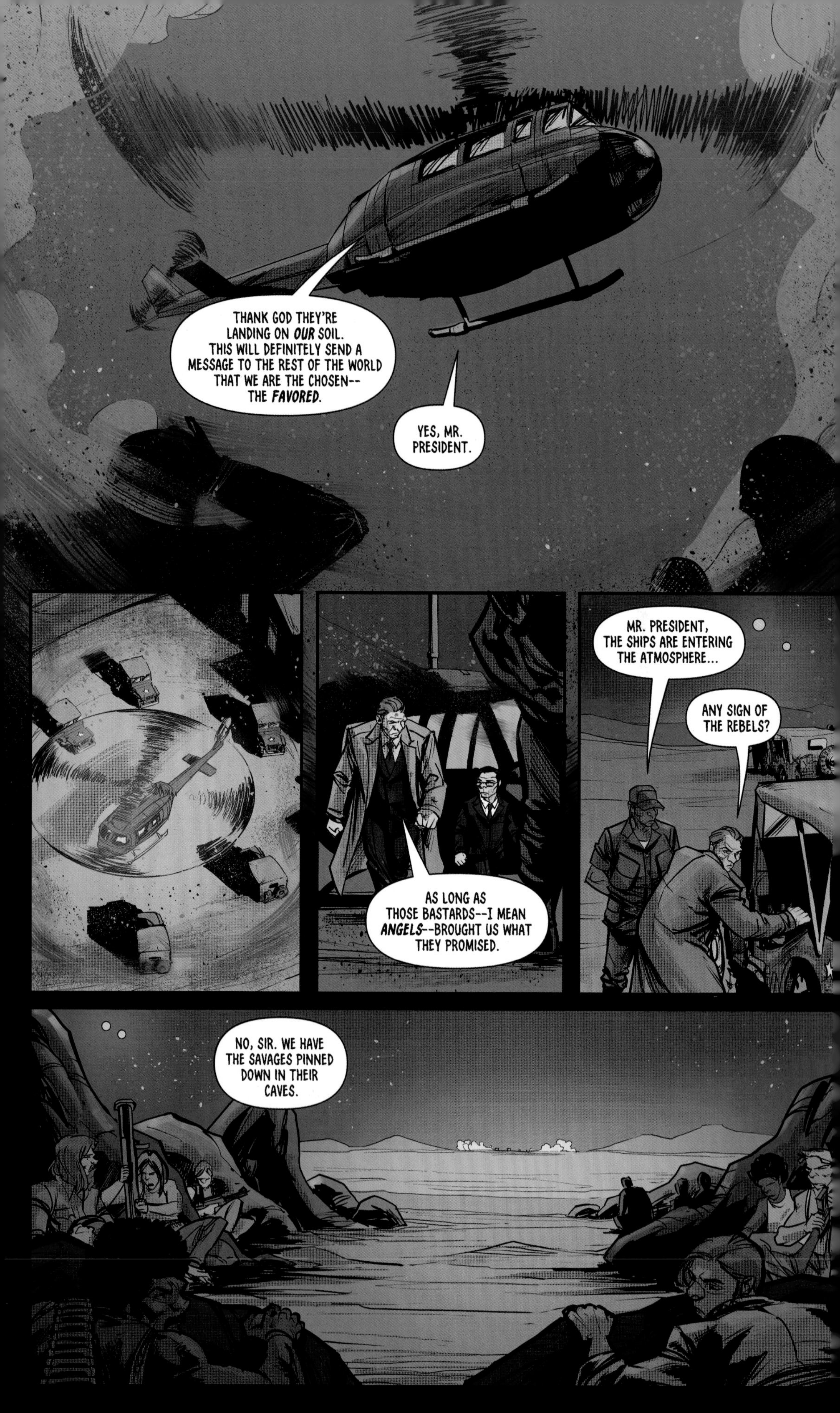
THANK GOD THEY'RE LANDING ON *OUR* SOIL. THIS WILL DEFINITELY SEND A MESSAGE TO THE REST OF THE WORLD THAT WE ARE THE CHOSEN-- THE *FAVORED*.
YES, MR. PRESIDENT.
AS LONG AS THOSE BASTARDS--I MEAN *ANGELS*--BROUGHT US WHAT THEY PROMISED.
MR. PRESIDENT, THE SHIPS ARE ENTERING THE ATMOSPHERE...
ANY SIGN OF THE REBELS?
NO, SIR. WE HAVE THE SAVAGES PINNED DOWN IN THEIR CAVES.

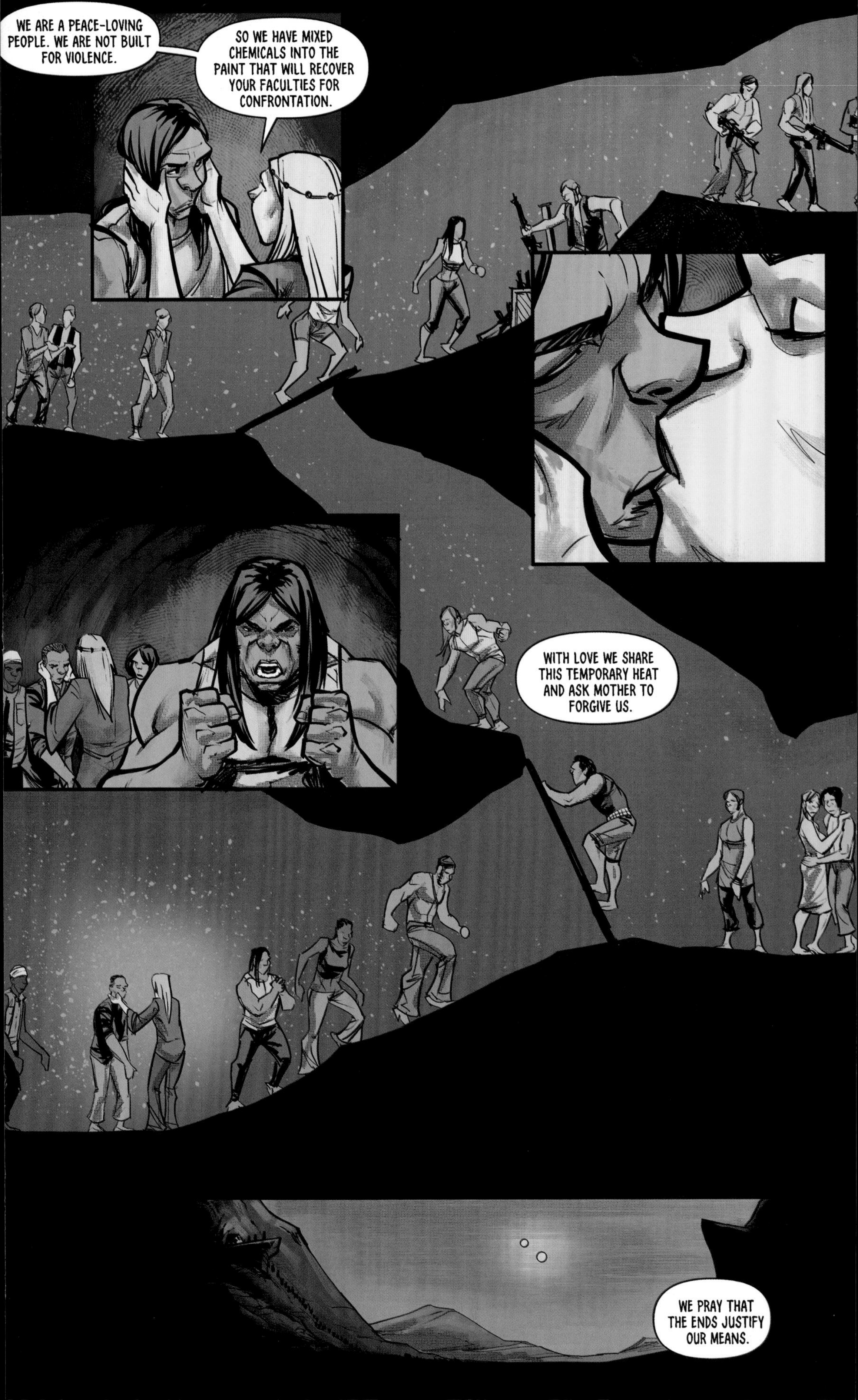
WE ARE A PEACE-LOVING PEOPLE. WE ARE NOT BUILT FOR VIOLENCE.
SO WE HAVE MIXED CHEMICALS INTO THE PAINT THAT WILL RECOVER YOUR FACULTIES FOR CONFRONTATION.
WITH LOVE WE SHARE THIS TEMPORARY HEAT AND ASK MOTHER TO FORGIVE US.
WE PRAY THAT THE ENDS JUSTIFY OUR MEANS.

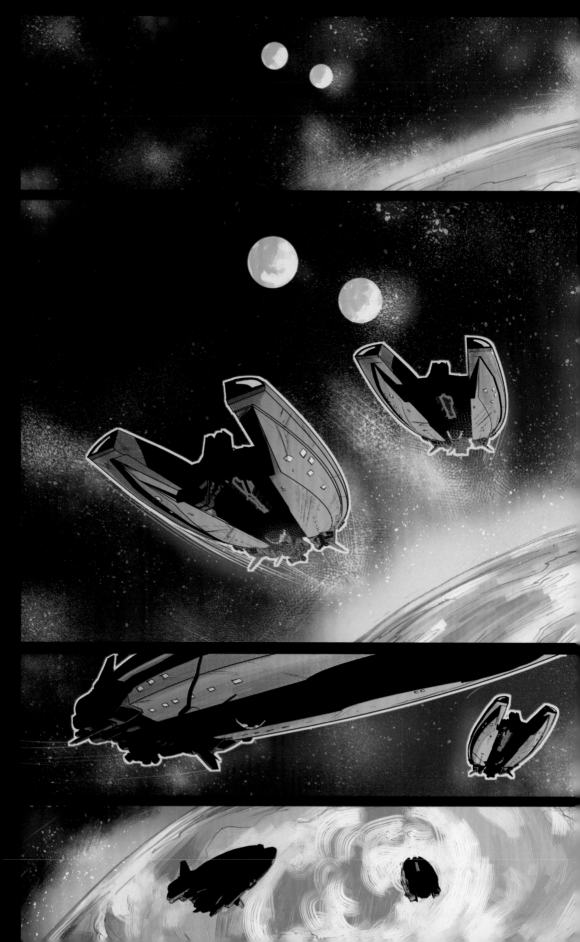

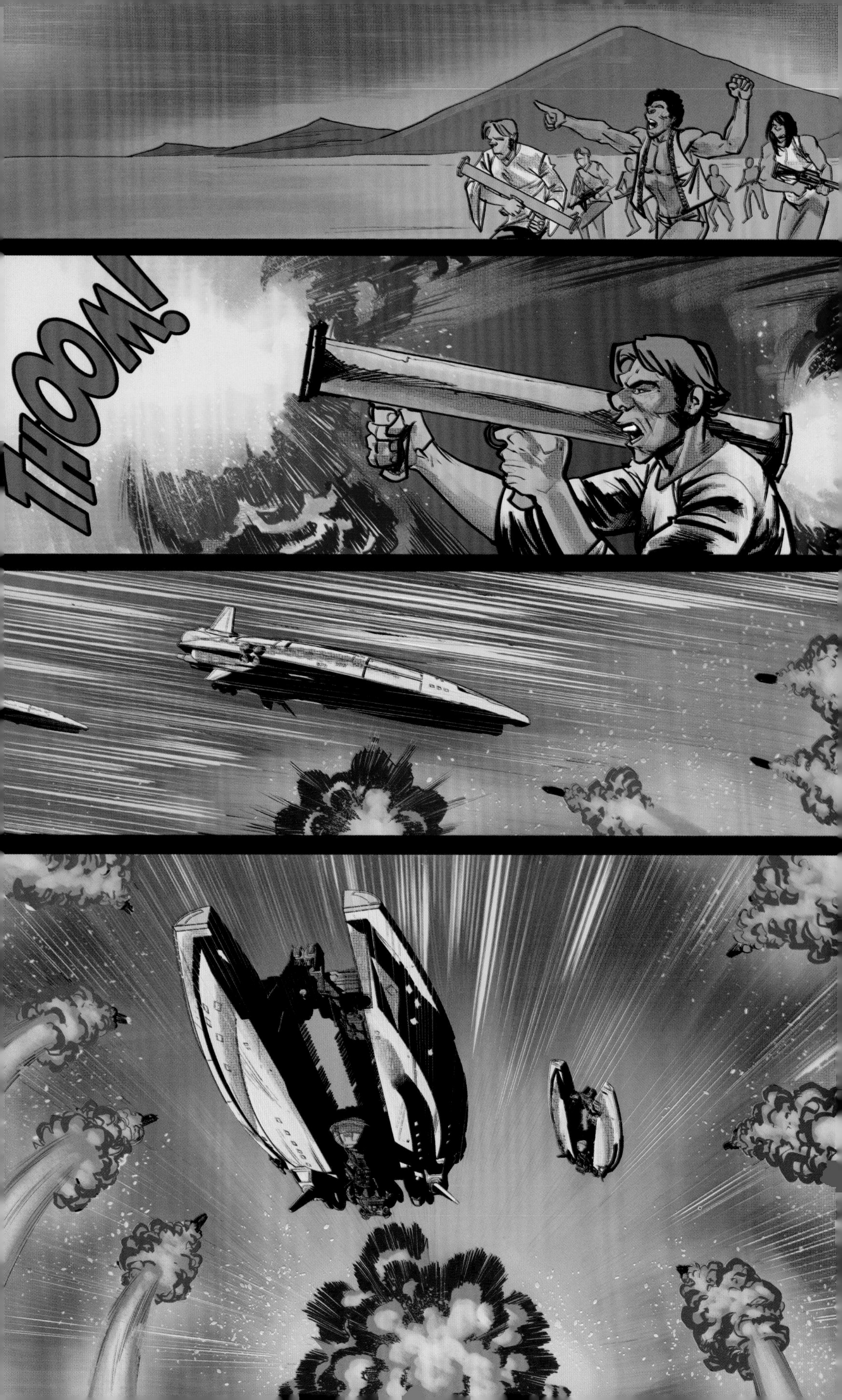
THOOM!

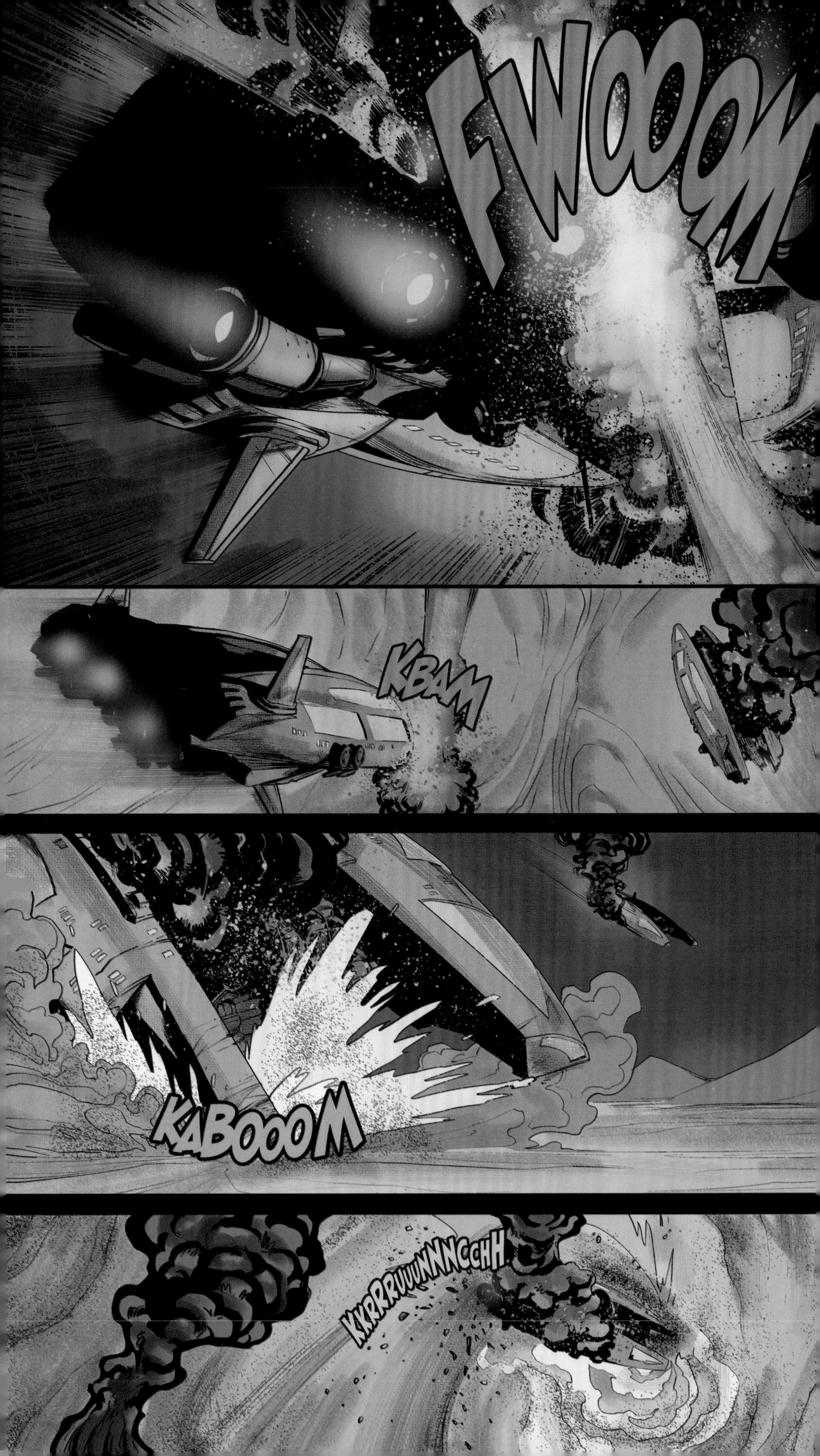
FWOOOM
KBAM
KABOOOM
KKRRUUUNNNCCHH

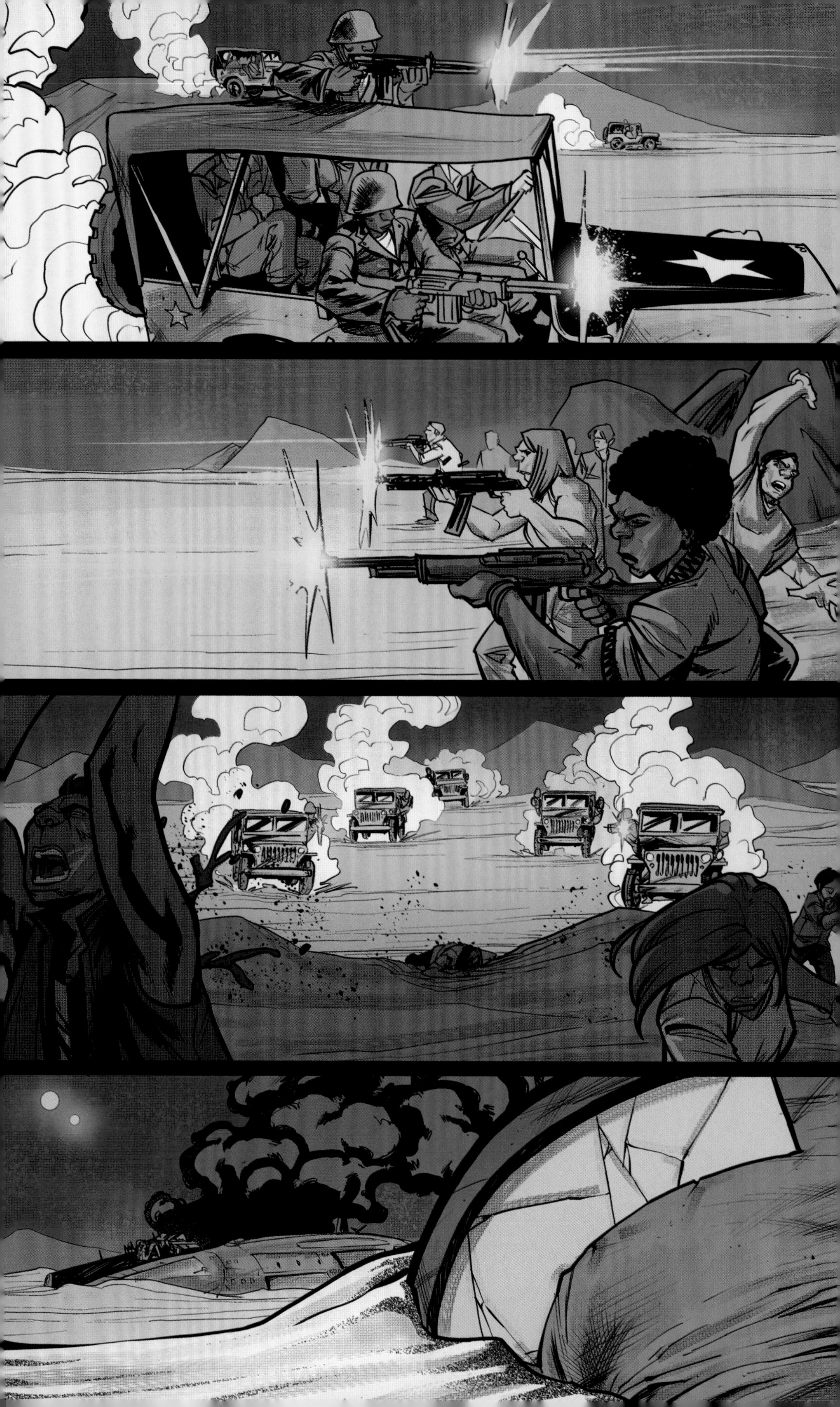

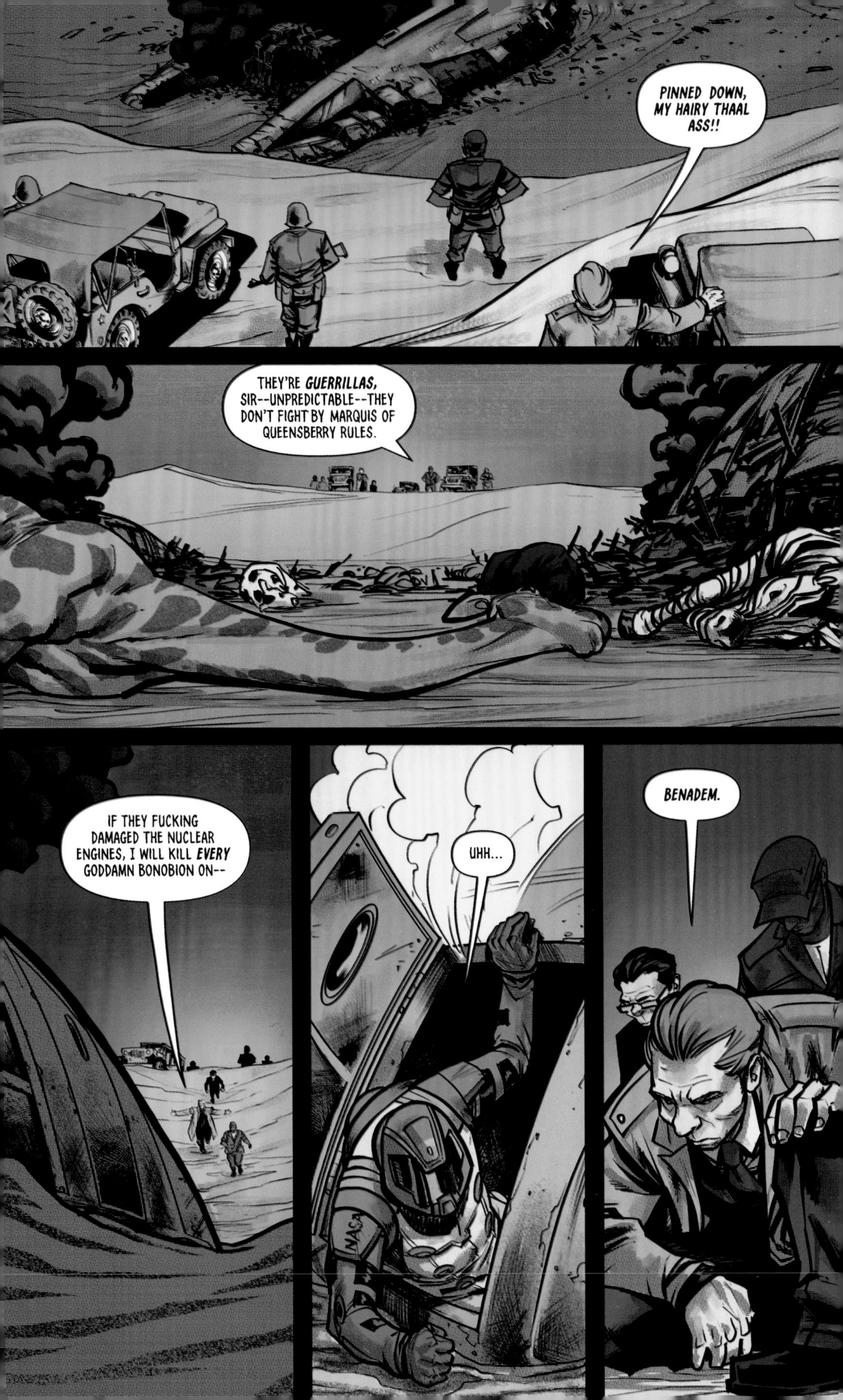
PINNED DOWN, MY HAIRY THAAL ASS!!
THEY'RE GUERRILLAS, SIR--UNPREDICTABLE--THEY DON'T FIGHT BY MARQUIS OF QUEENSBERRY RULES.
IF THEY FUCKING DAMAGED THE NUCLEAR ENGINES, I WILL KILL EVERY GODDAMN BONOBION ON--
UHH...
BENADEM.
NASA

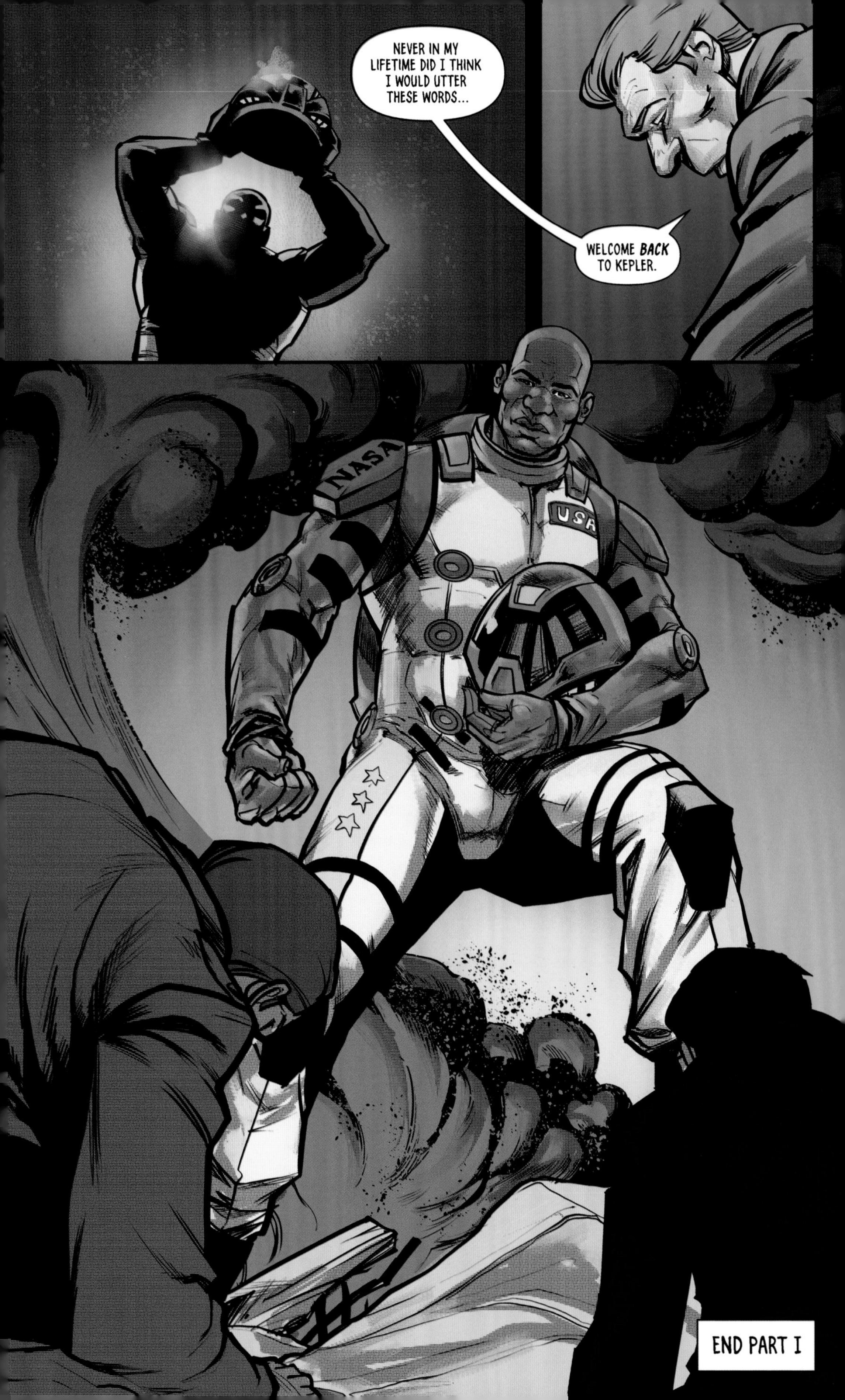
NEVER IN MY LIFETIME DID I THINK I WOULD UTTER THESE WORDS...
WELCOME BACK TO KEPLER.
NASA
USA
END PART I

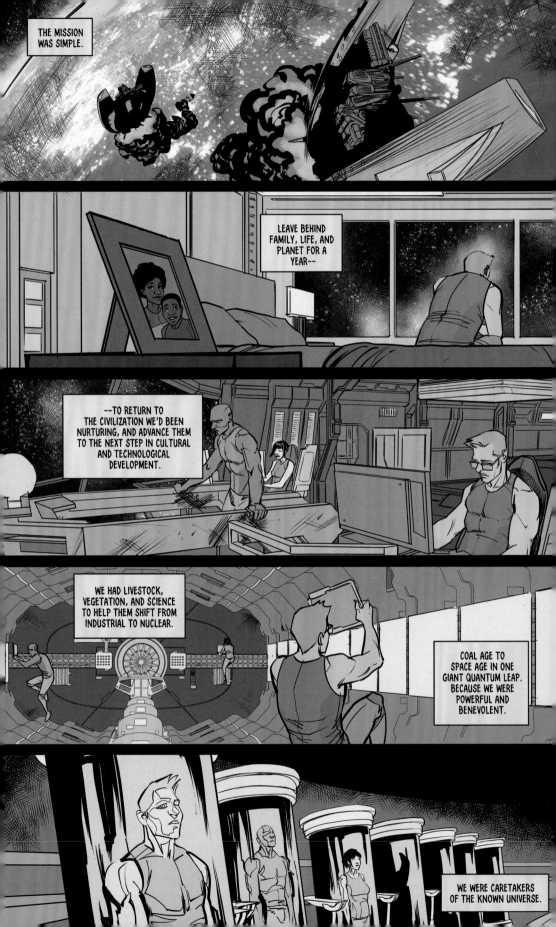

THE MISSION WAS SIMPLE.

LEAVE BEHIND FAMILY, LIFE, AND PLANET FOR A YEAR--

--TO RETURN TO THE CIVILIZATION WE'D BEEN NURTURING, AND ADVANCE THEM TO THE NEXT STEP IN CULTURAL AND TECHNOLOGICAL DEVELOPMENT.

WE HAD LIVESTOCK, VEGETATION, AND SCIENCE TO HELP THEM SHIFT FROM INDUSTRIAL TO NUCLEAR.

COAL AGE TO SPACE AGE IN ONE GIANT QUANTUM LEAP. BECAUSE WE WERE POWERFUL AND BENEVOLENT.

WE WERE CARETAKERS OF THE KNOWN UNIVERSE.

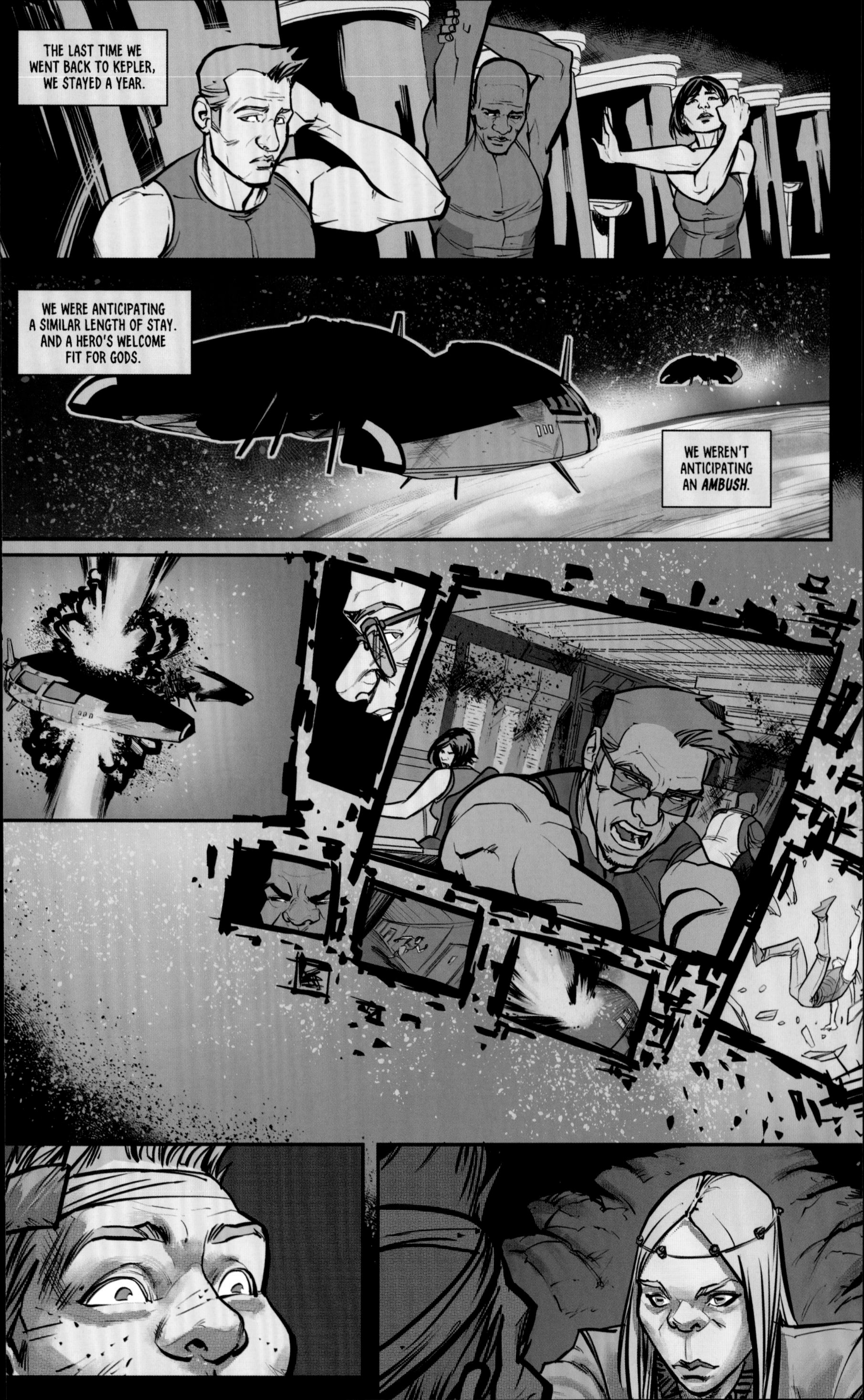
THE LAST TIME WE WENT BACK TO KEPLER, WE STAYED A YEAR.
WE WERE ANTICIPATING A SIMILAR LENGTH OF STAY. AND A HERO'S WELCOME FIT FOR GODS.
WE WEREN'T ANTICIPATING AN *AMBUSH*.

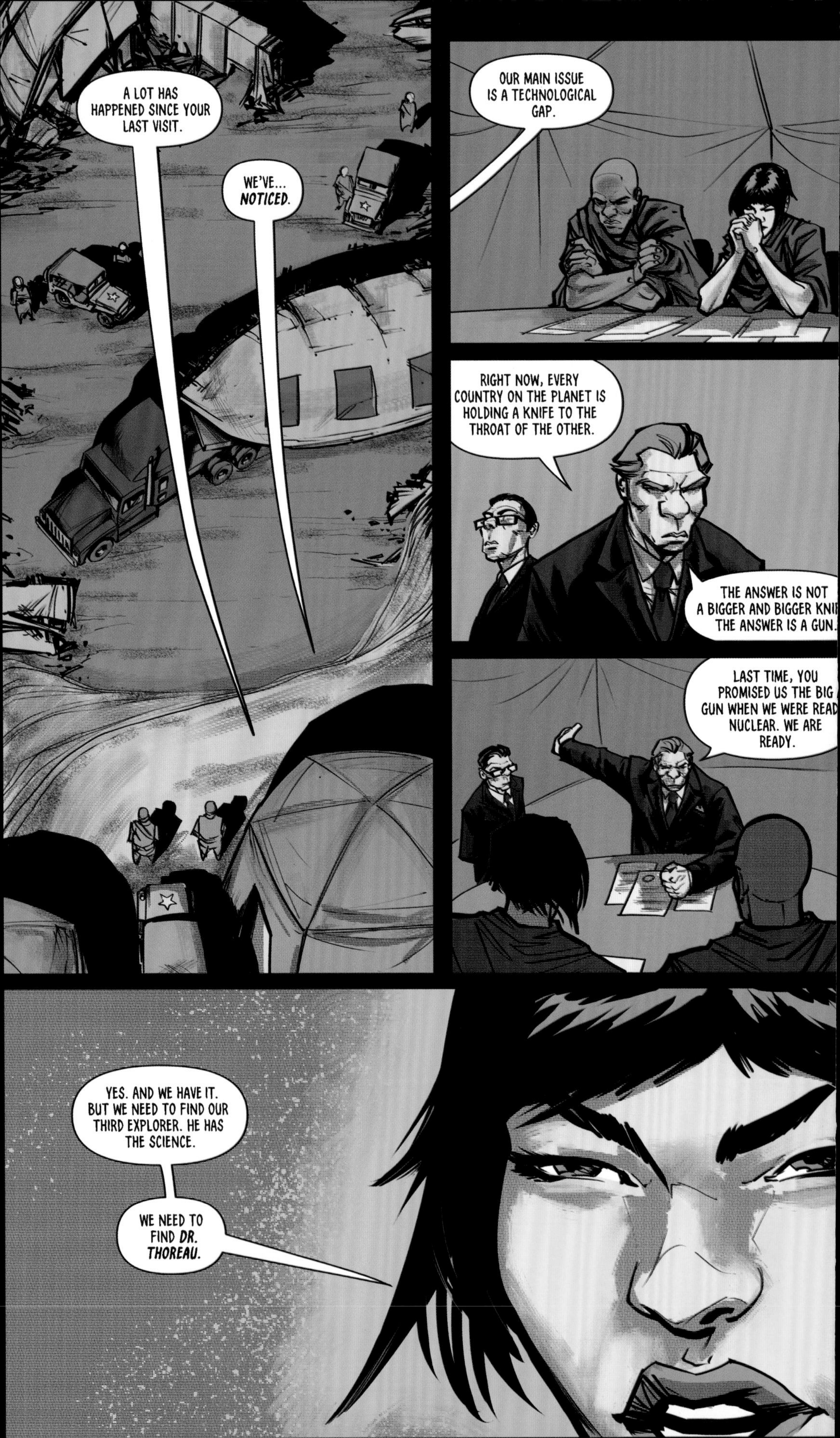

A LOT HAS HAPPENED SINCE YOUR LAST VISIT.
WE'VE... *NOTICED*.
OUR MAIN ISSUE IS A TECHNOLOGICAL GAP.
RIGHT NOW, EVERY COUNTRY ON THE PLANET IS HOLDING A KNIFE TO THE THROAT OF THE OTHER.
THE ANSWER IS NOT A BIGGER AND BIGGER KNIF THE ANSWER IS A GUN.
LAST TIME, YOU PROMISED US THE BIG GUN WHEN WE WERE READ NUCLEAR. WE ARE READY.
YES. AND WE HAVE IT. BUT WE NEED TO FIND OUR THIRD EXPLORER. HE HAS THE SCIENCE.
WE NEED TO FIND *DR. THOREAU*.

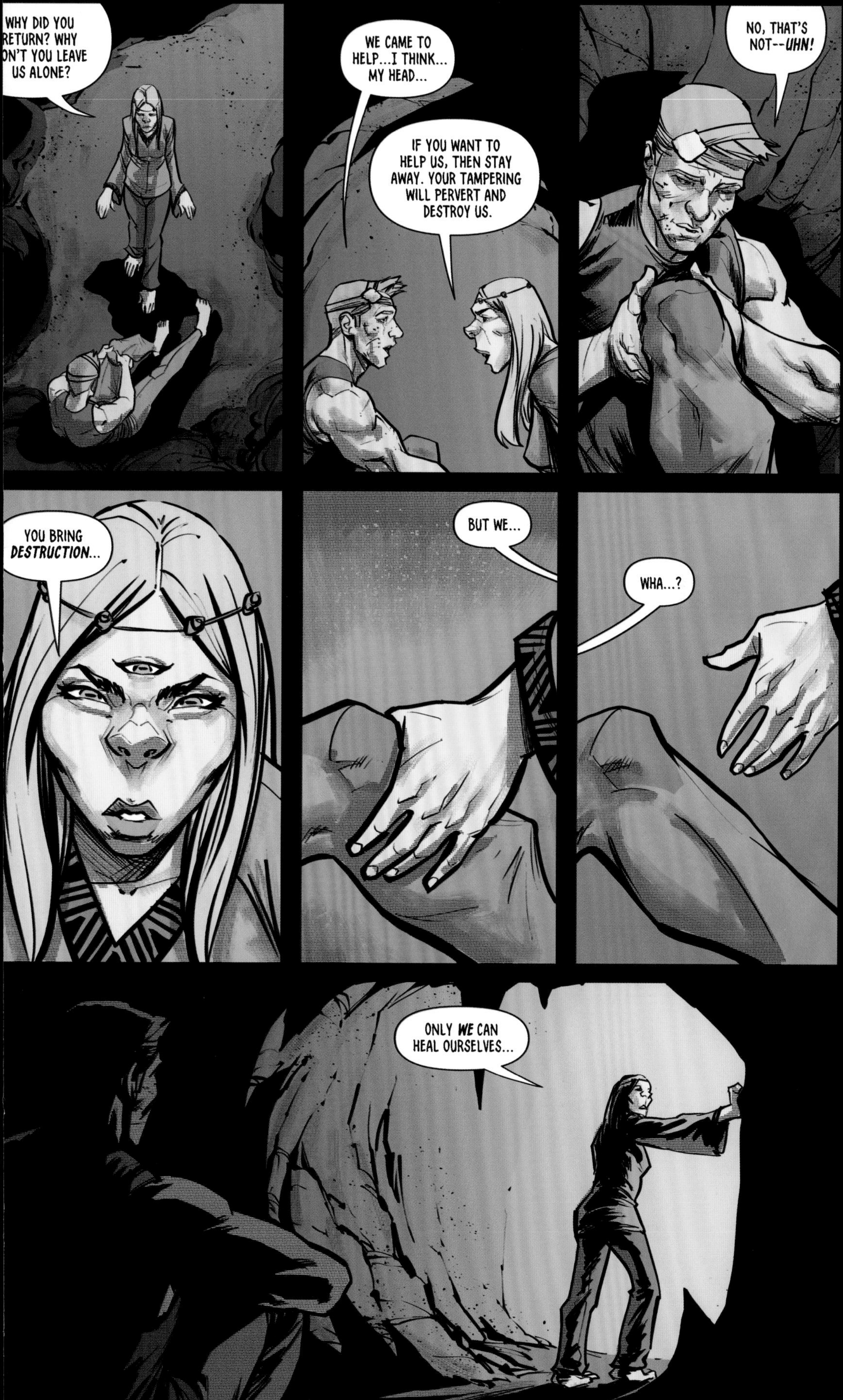

WHY DID YOU RETURN? WHY N'T YOU LEAVE US ALONE?
WE CAME TO HELP...I THINK... MY HEAD...
IF YOU WANT TO HELP US, THEN STAY AWAY. YOUR TAMPERING WILL PERVERT AND DESTROY US.
NO, THAT'S NOT--*UHN!*
YOU BRING *DESTRUCTION*...
BUT WE...
WHA...?
ONLY *WE* CAN HEAL OURSELVES...

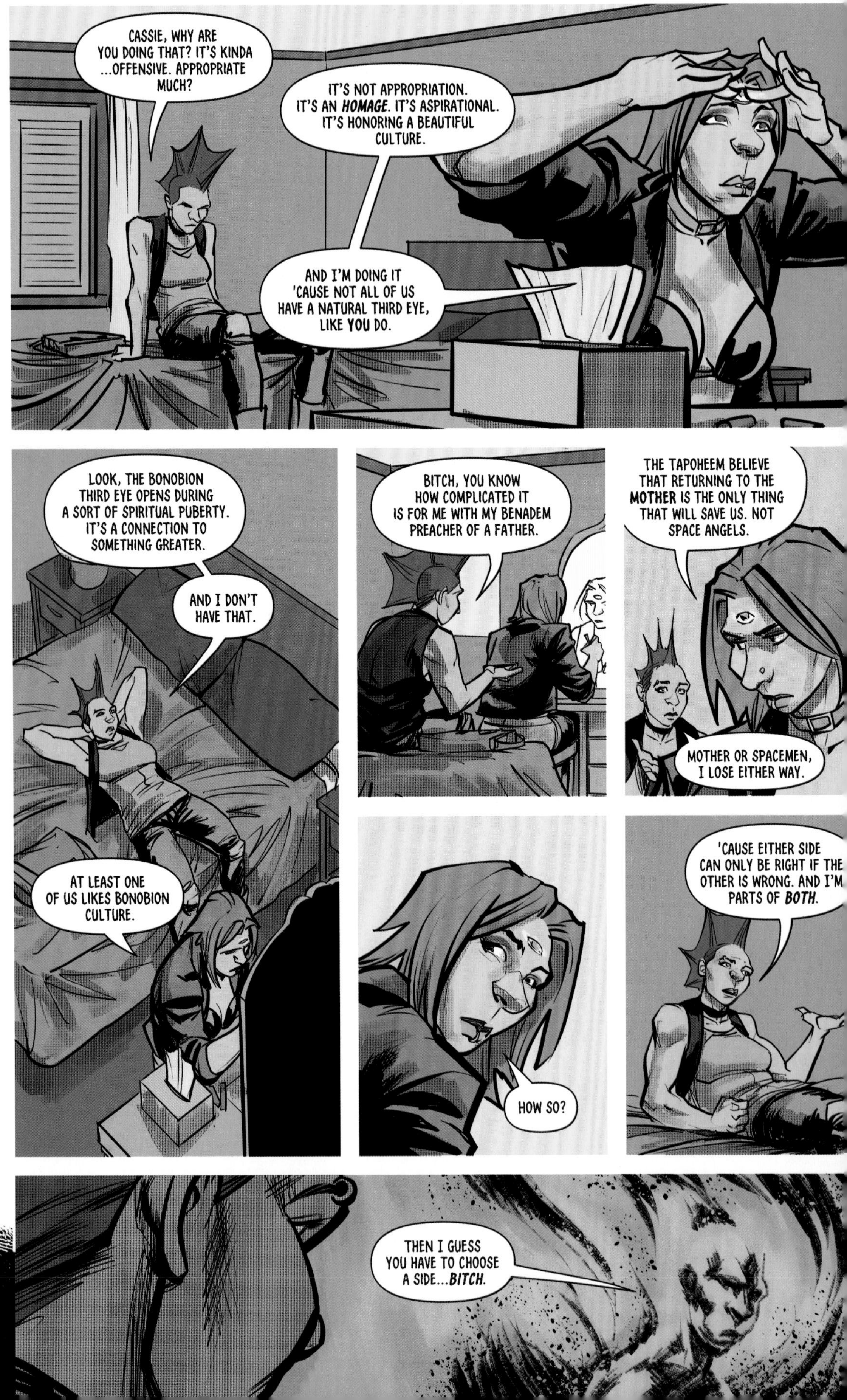
CASSIE, WHY ARE YOU DOING THAT? IT'S KINDA ...OFFENSIVE. APPROPRIATE MUCH?
IT'S NOT APPROPRIATION. IT'S AN *HOMAGE*. IT'S ASPIRATIONAL. IT'S HONORING A BEAUTIFUL CULTURE.
AND I'M DOING IT 'CAUSE NOT ALL OF US HAVE A NATURAL THIRD EYE, LIKE **YOU** DO.
LOOK, THE BONOBION THIRD EYE OPENS DURING A SORT OF SPIRITUAL PUBERTY. IT'S A CONNECTION TO SOMETHING GREATER.
AND I DON'T HAVE THAT.
AT LEAST ONE OF US LIKES BONOBION CULTURE.
BITCH, YOU KNOW HOW COMPLICATED IT IS FOR ME WITH MY BENADEM PREACHER OF A FATHER.
THE TAPOHEEM BELIEVE THAT RETURNING TO THE **MOTHER** IS THE ONLY THING THAT WILL SAVE US. NOT SPACE ANGELS.
MOTHER OR SPACEMEN, I LOSE EITHER WAY.
HOW SO?
'CAUSE EITHER SIDE CAN ONLY BE RIGHT IF THE OTHER IS WRONG. AND I'M PARTS OF *BOTH*.
THEN I GUESS YOU HAVE TO CHOOSE A SIDE...*BITCH*.

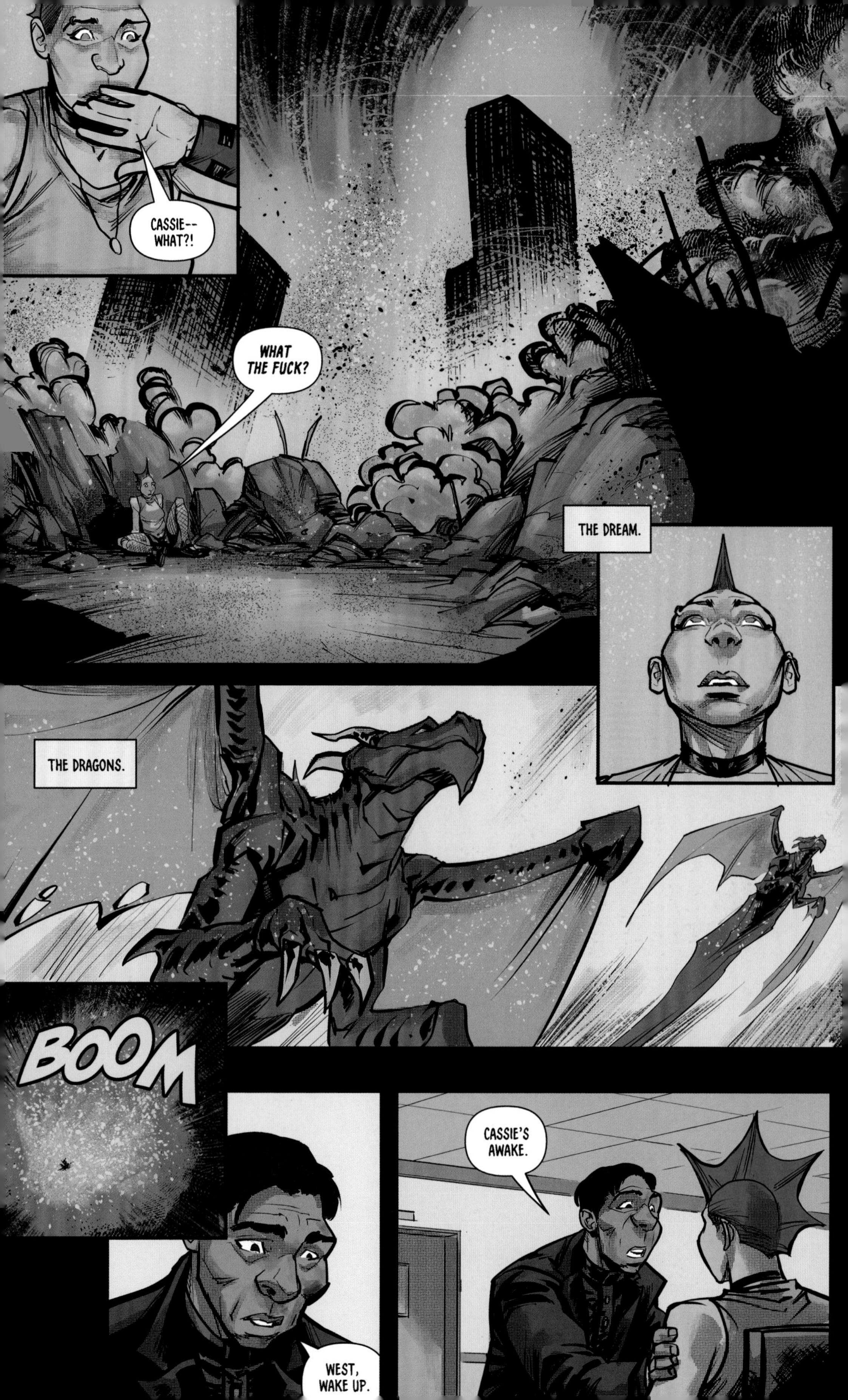
CASSIE--
WHAT?!
WHAT
THE FUCK?
THE DREAM.
THE DRAGONS.
BOOM
WEST,
WAKE UP.
CASSIE'S
AWAKE.

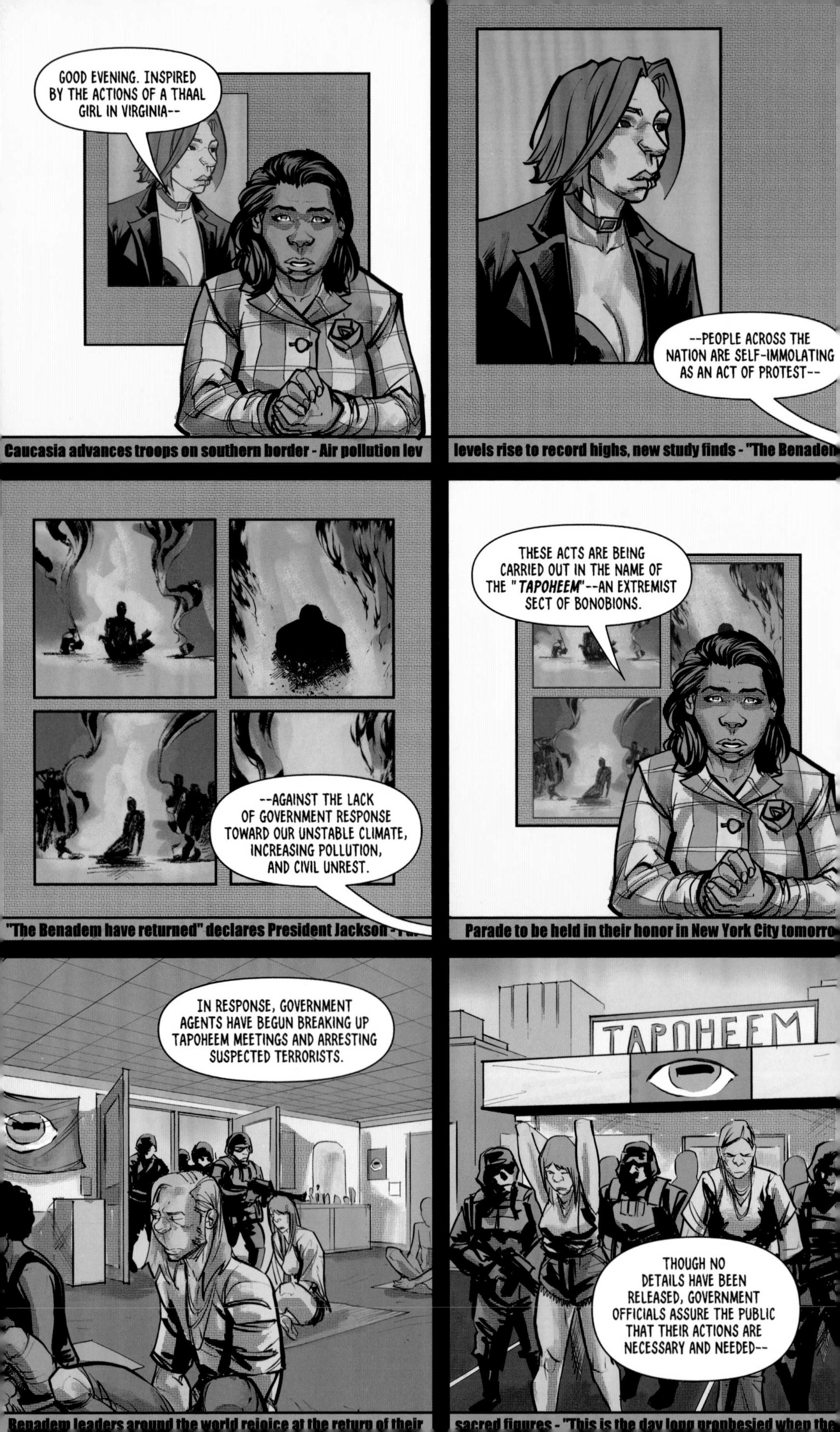
GOOD EVENING. INSPIRED BY THE ACTIONS OF A THAAL GIRL IN VIRGINIA--
Caucasia advances troops on southern border - Air pollution lev
--PEOPLE ACROSS THE NATION ARE SELF-IMMOLATING AS AN ACT OF PROTEST--
levels rise to record highs, new study finds - "The Benadem
--AGAINST THE LACK OF GOVERNMENT RESPONSE TOWARD OUR UNSTABLE CLIMATE, INCREASING POLLUTION, AND CIVIL UNREST.
"The Benadem have returned" declares President Jackson
THESE ACTS ARE BEING CARRIED OUT IN THE NAME OF THE "*TAPOHEEM*"--AN EXTREMIST SECT OF BONOBIONS.
Parade to be held in their honor in New York City tomorro
IN RESPONSE, GOVERNMENT AGENTS HAVE BEGUN BREAKING UP TAPOHEEM MEETINGS AND ARRESTING SUSPECTED TERRORISTS.
Benadem leaders around the world rejoice at the return of their
TAPOHEEM
THOUGH NO DETAILS HAVE BEEN RELEASED, GOVERNMENT OFFICIALS ASSURE THE PUBLIC THAT THEIR ACTIONS ARE NECESSARY AND NEEDED--
sacred figures - "This is the day long prophesied when the

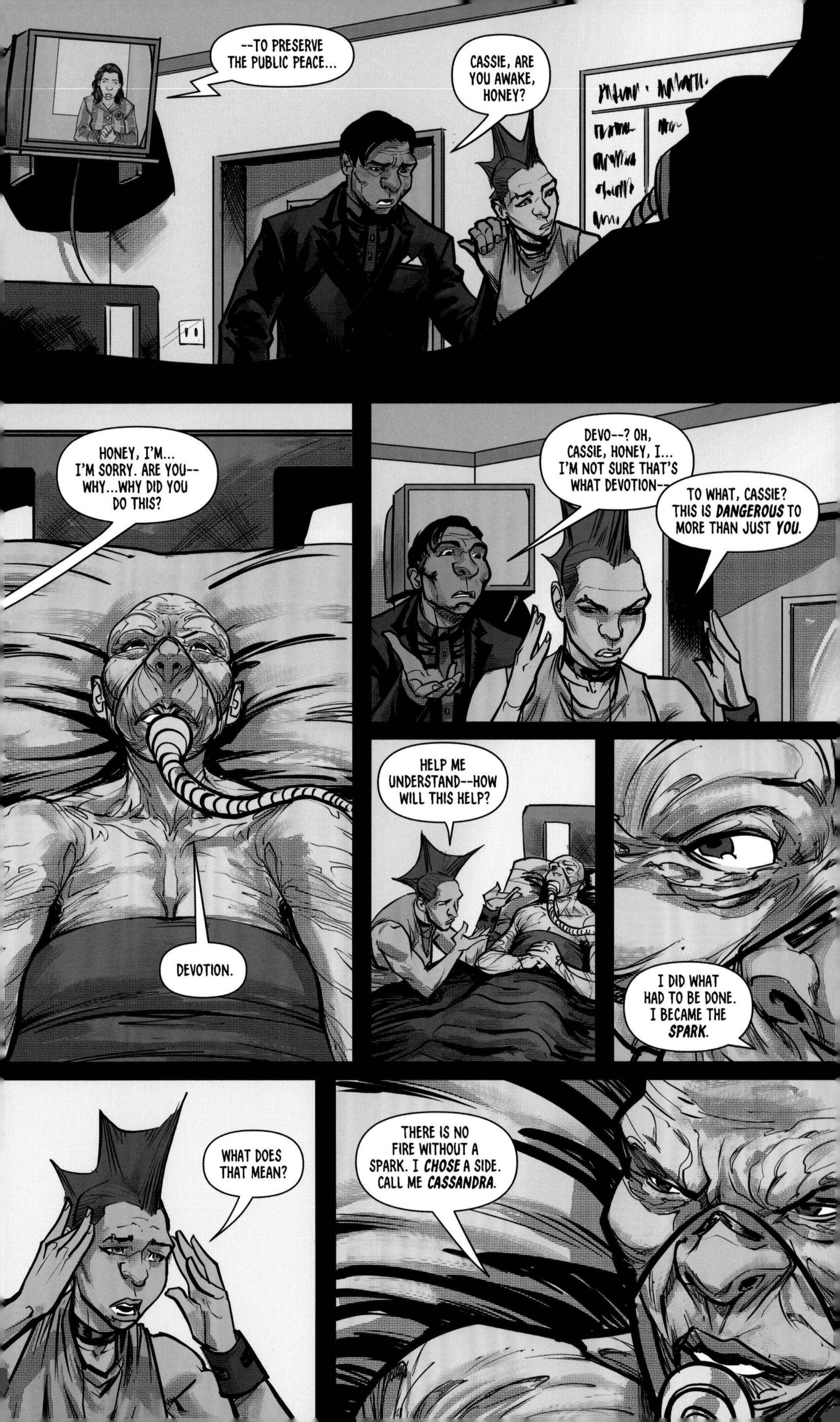
--TO PRESERVE THE PUBLIC PEACE...
CASSIE, ARE YOU AWAKE, HONEY?
HONEY, I'M... I'M SORRY. ARE YOU-- WHY...WHY DID YOU DO THIS?
DEVOTION.
DEVO--? OH, CASSIE, HONEY, I... I'M NOT SURE THAT'S WHAT DEVOTION--
TO WHAT, CASSIE? THIS IS *DANGEROUS* TO MORE THAN JUST *YOU*.
HELP ME UNDERSTAND--HOW WILL THIS HELP?
I DID WHAT HAD TO BE DONE. I BECAME THE *SPARK*.
WHAT DOES THAT MEAN?
THERE IS NO FIRE WITHOUT A SPARK. I *CHOSE* A SIDE. CALL ME *CASSANDRA*.

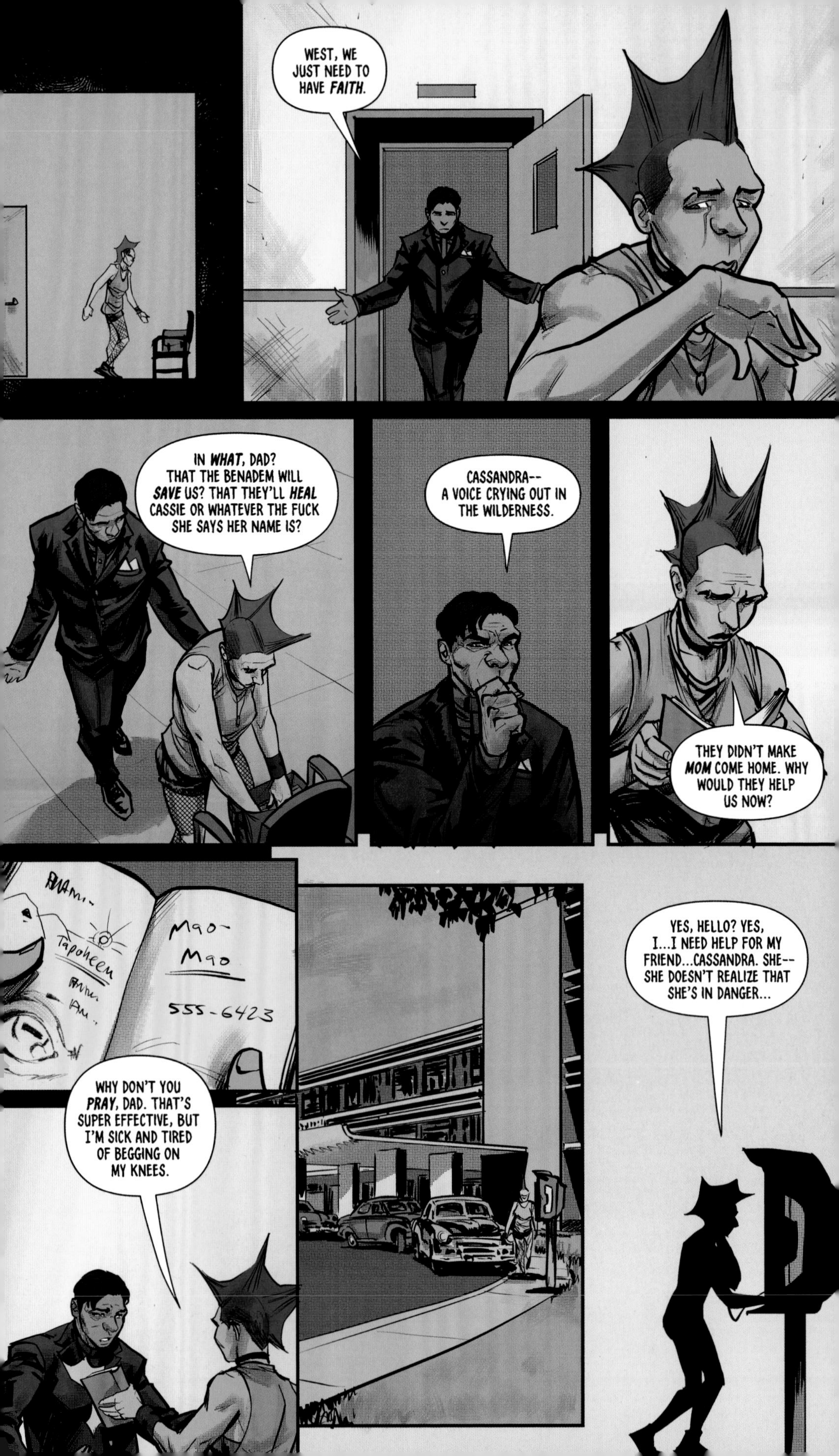
WEST, WE JUST NEED TO HAVE FAITH.
IN WHAT, DAD? THAT THE BENADEM WILL SAVE US? THAT THEY'LL HEAL CASSIE OR WHATEVER THE FUCK SHE SAYS HER NAME IS?
CASSANDRA-- A VOICE CRYING OUT IN THE WILDERNESS.
THEY DIDN'T MAKE MOM COME HOME. WHY WOULD THEY HELP US NOW?
Mao-Mao
555-6423
WHY DON'T YOU PRAY, DAD. THAT'S SUPER EFFECTIVE, BUT I'M SICK AND TIRED OF BEGGING ON MY KNEES.
YES, HELLO? YES, I...I NEED HELP FOR MY FRIEND...CASSANDRA. SHE-- SHE DOESN'T REALIZE THAT SHE'S IN DANGER...

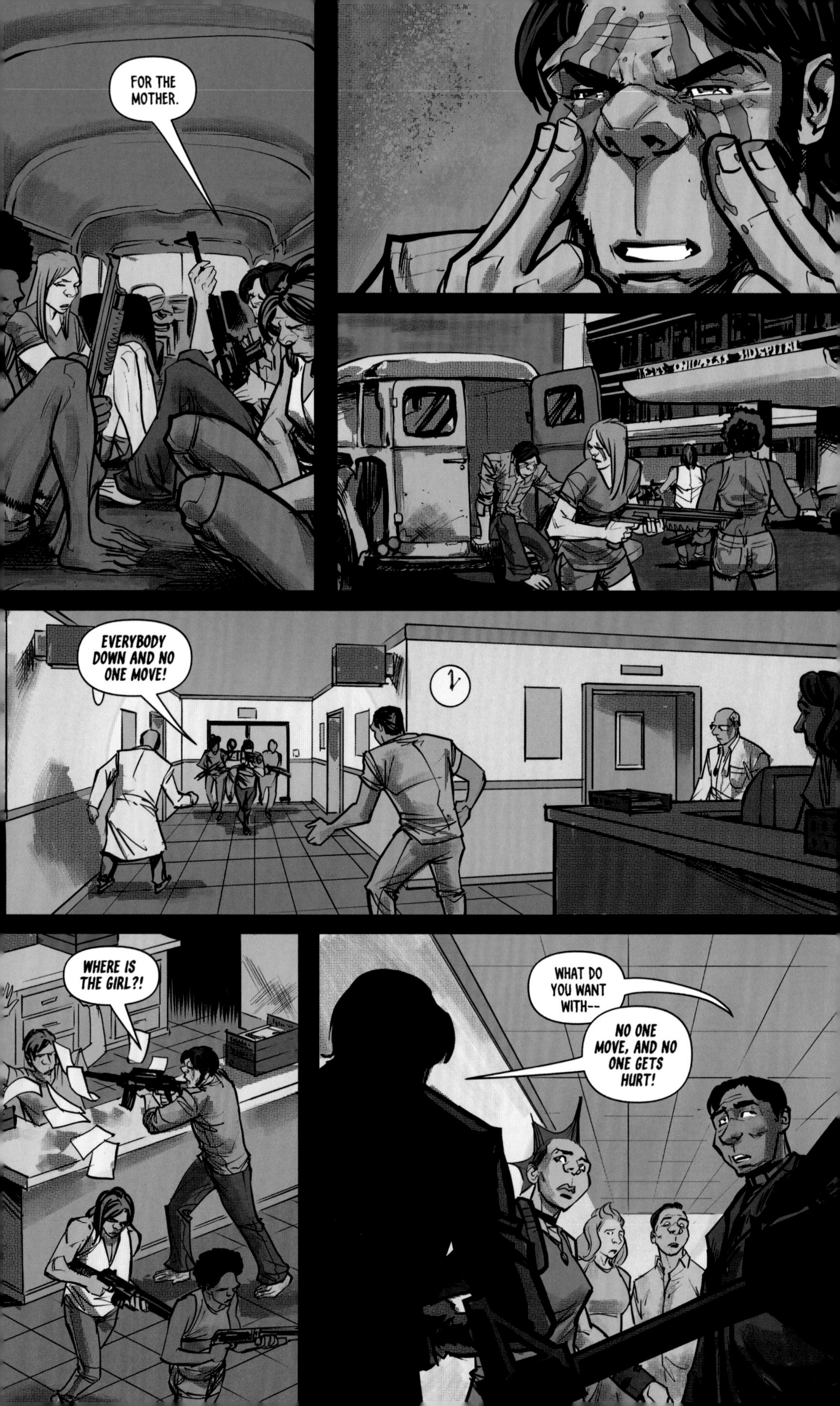
FOR THE MOTHER.
EVERYBODY DOWN AND NO ONE MOVE!
WHERE IS THE GIRL?!
WHAT DO YOU WANT WITH--
NO ONE MOVE, AND NO ONE GETS HURT!

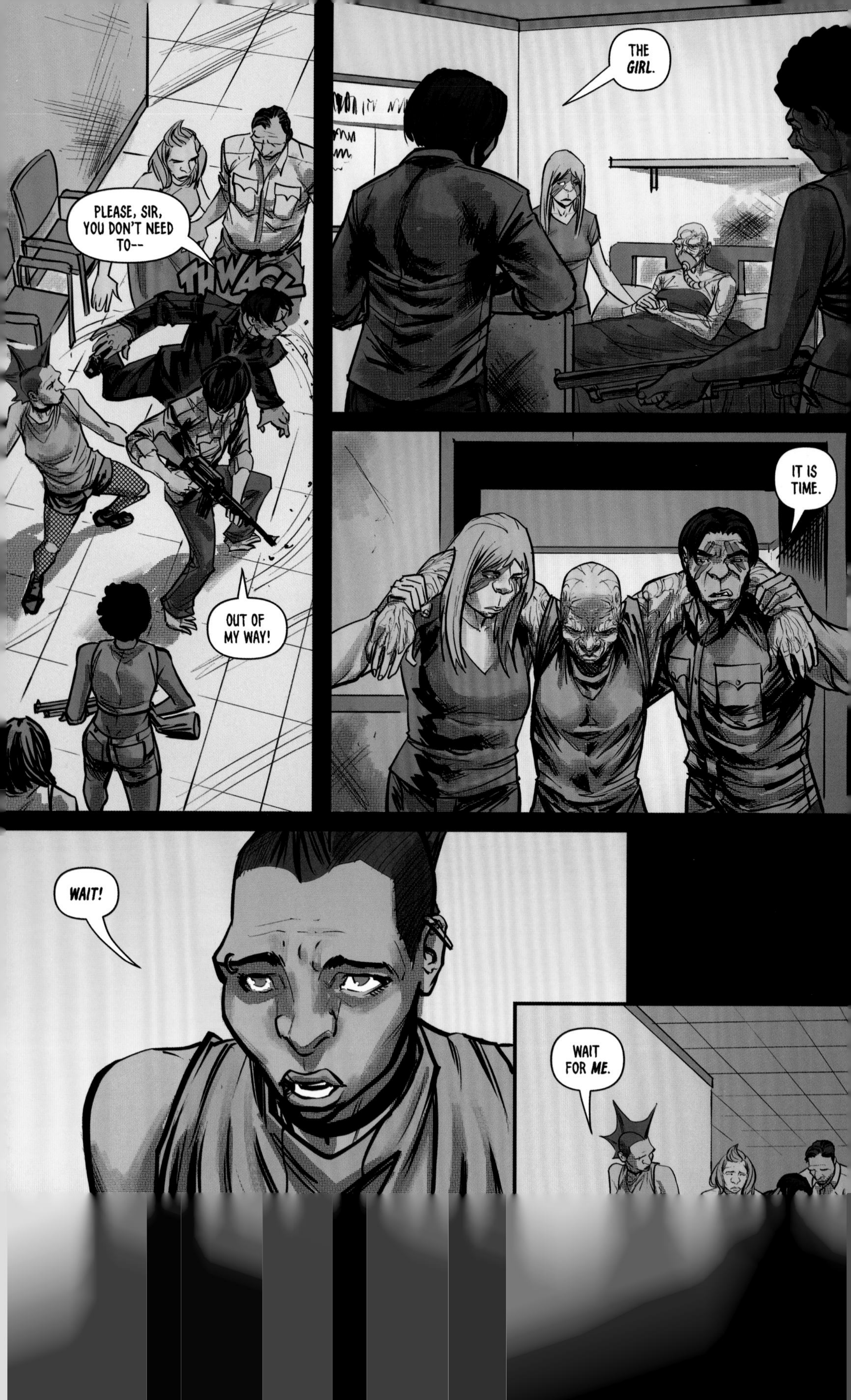
PLEASE, SIR, YOU DON'T NEED TO--
THWACK
OUT OF MY WAY!
THE GIRL.
IT IS TIME.
WAIT!
WAIT FOR ME.

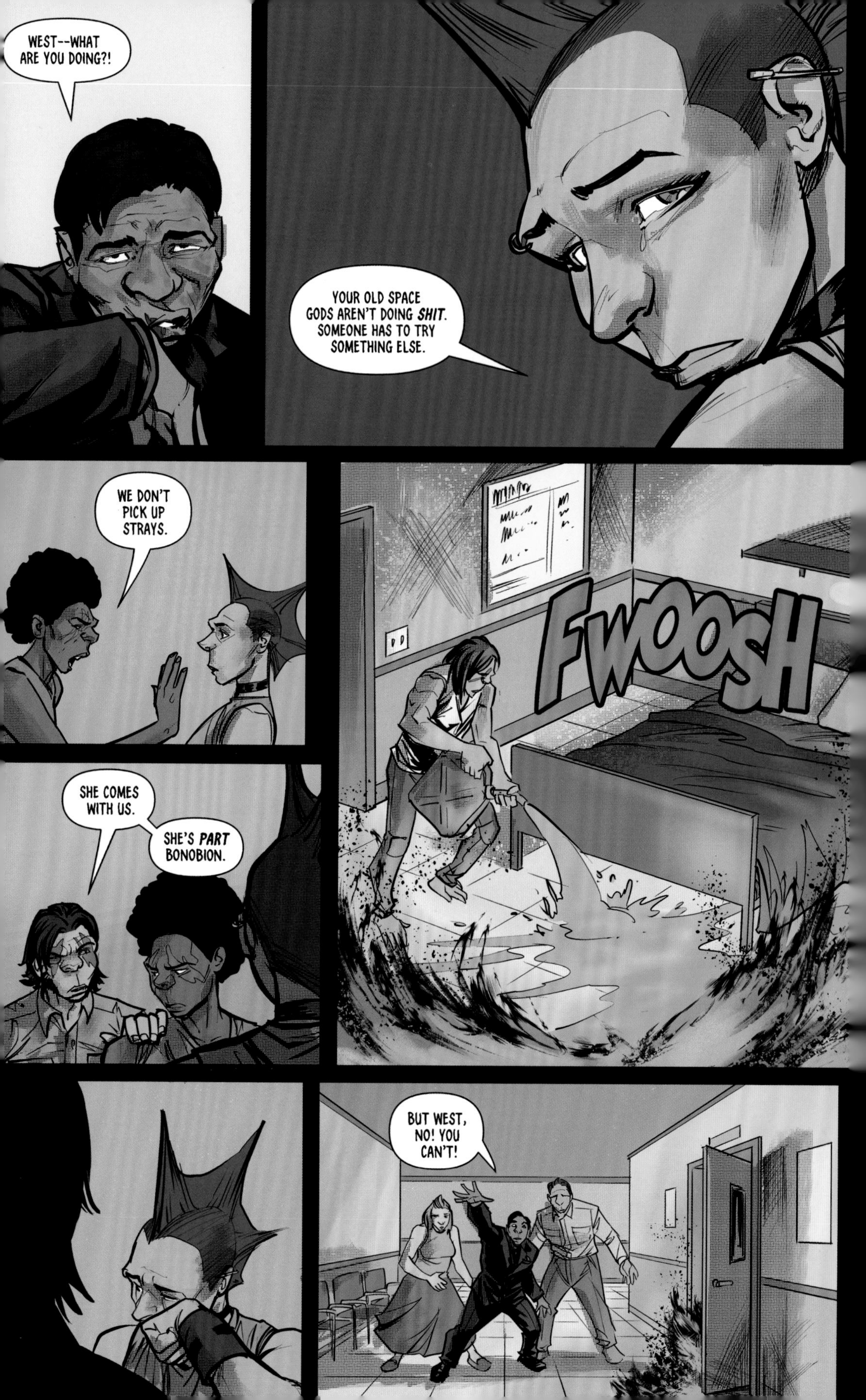
WEST--WHAT ARE YOU DOING?!
YOUR OLD SPACE GODS AREN'T DOING *SHIT*. SOMEONE HAS TO TRY SOMETHING ELSE.
WE DON'T PICK UP STRAYS.
SHE COMES WITH US.
SHE'S *PART* BONOBION.
FWOOSH
BUT WEST, NO! YOU CAN'T!

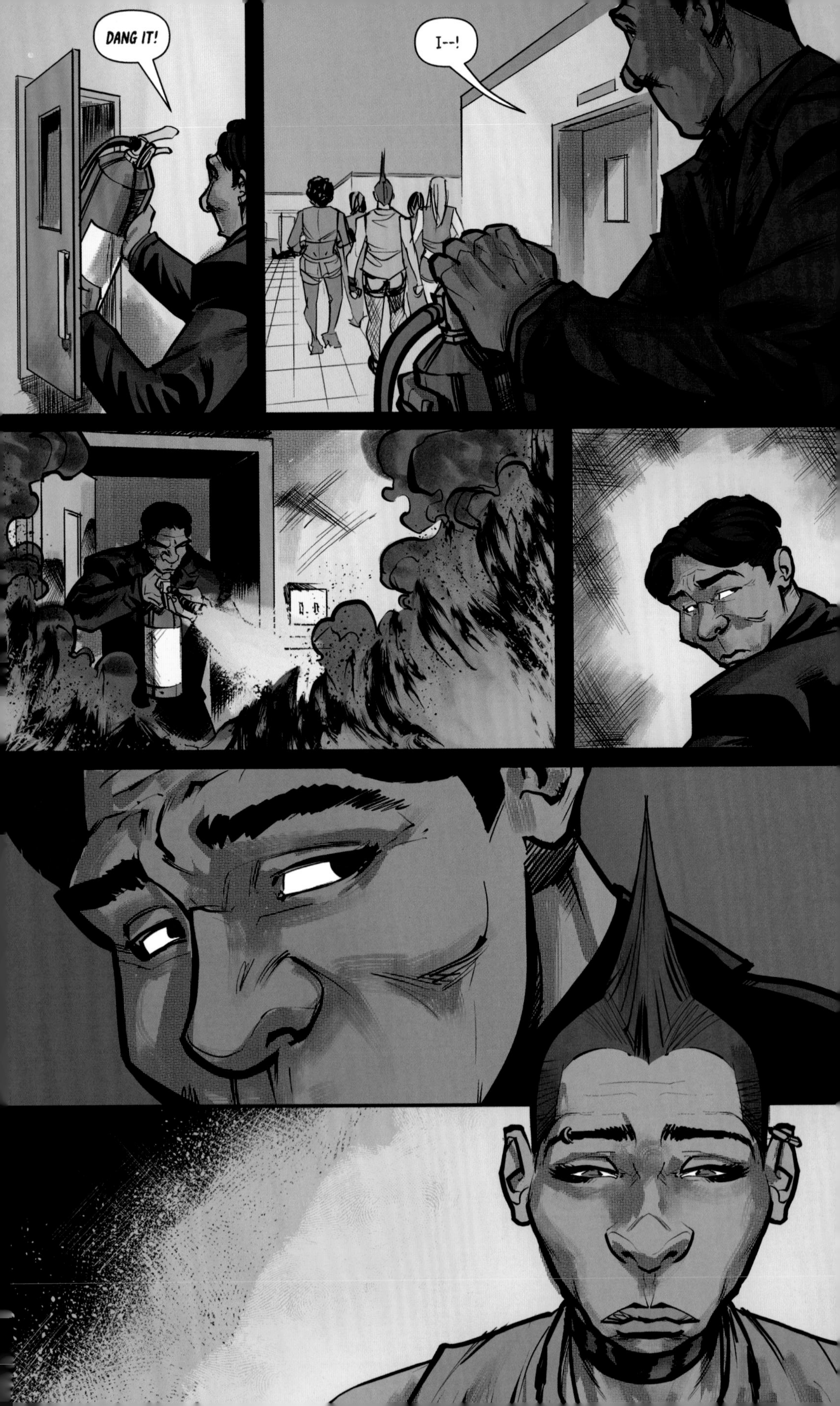
DANG IT!
I--!

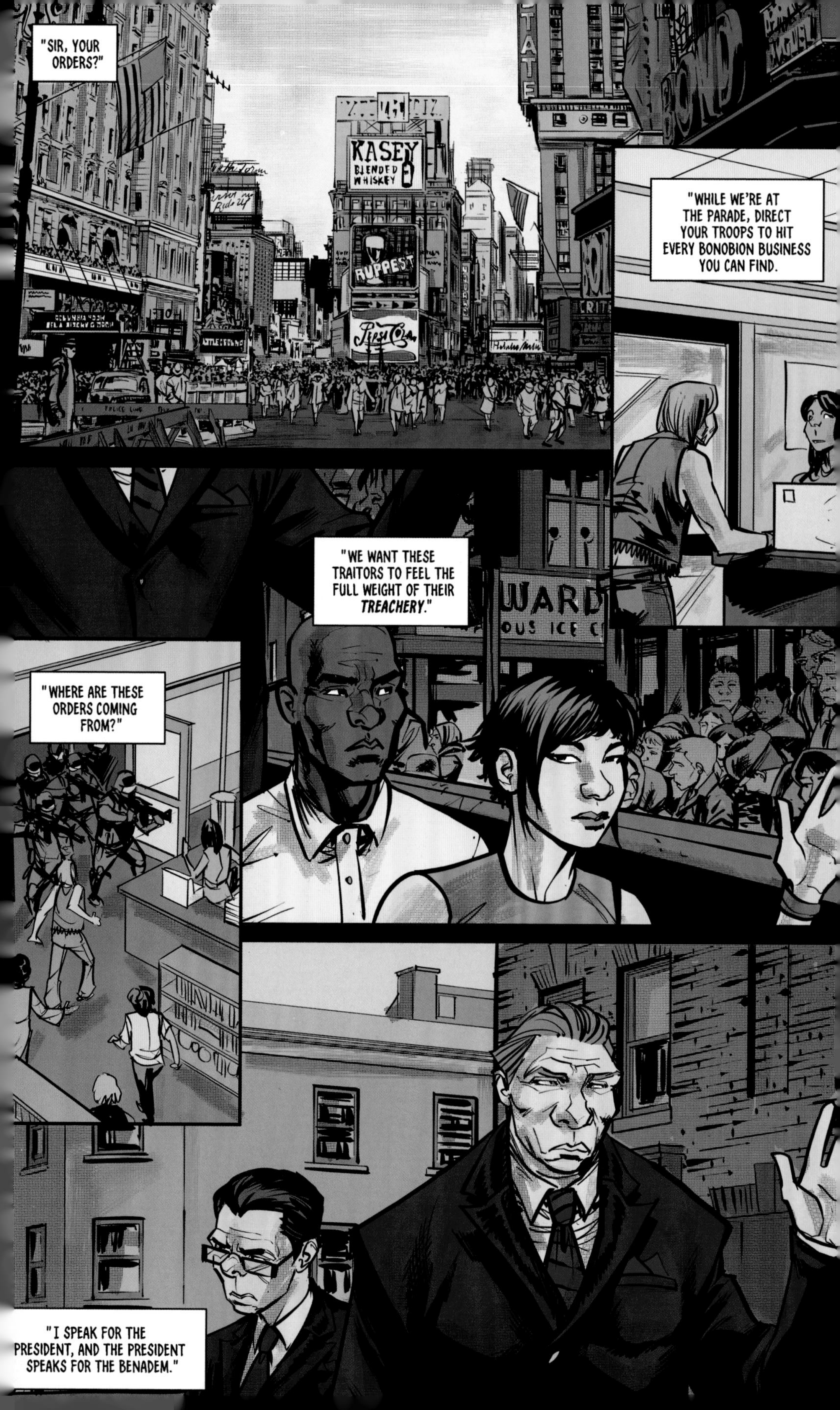
"SIR, YOUR ORDERS?"
KASEY BLENDED WHISKEY
RUPPEST
Pepsi-Cola
"WHILE WE'RE AT THE PARADE, DIRECT YOUR TROOPS TO HIT EVERY BONOBION BUSINESS YOU CAN FIND.
"WE WANT THESE TRAITORS TO FEEL THE FULL WEIGHT OF THEIR *TREACHERY*."
"WHERE ARE THESE ORDERS COMING FROM?"
"I SPEAK FOR THE PRESIDENT, AND THE PRESIDENT SPEAKS FOR THE BENADEM."

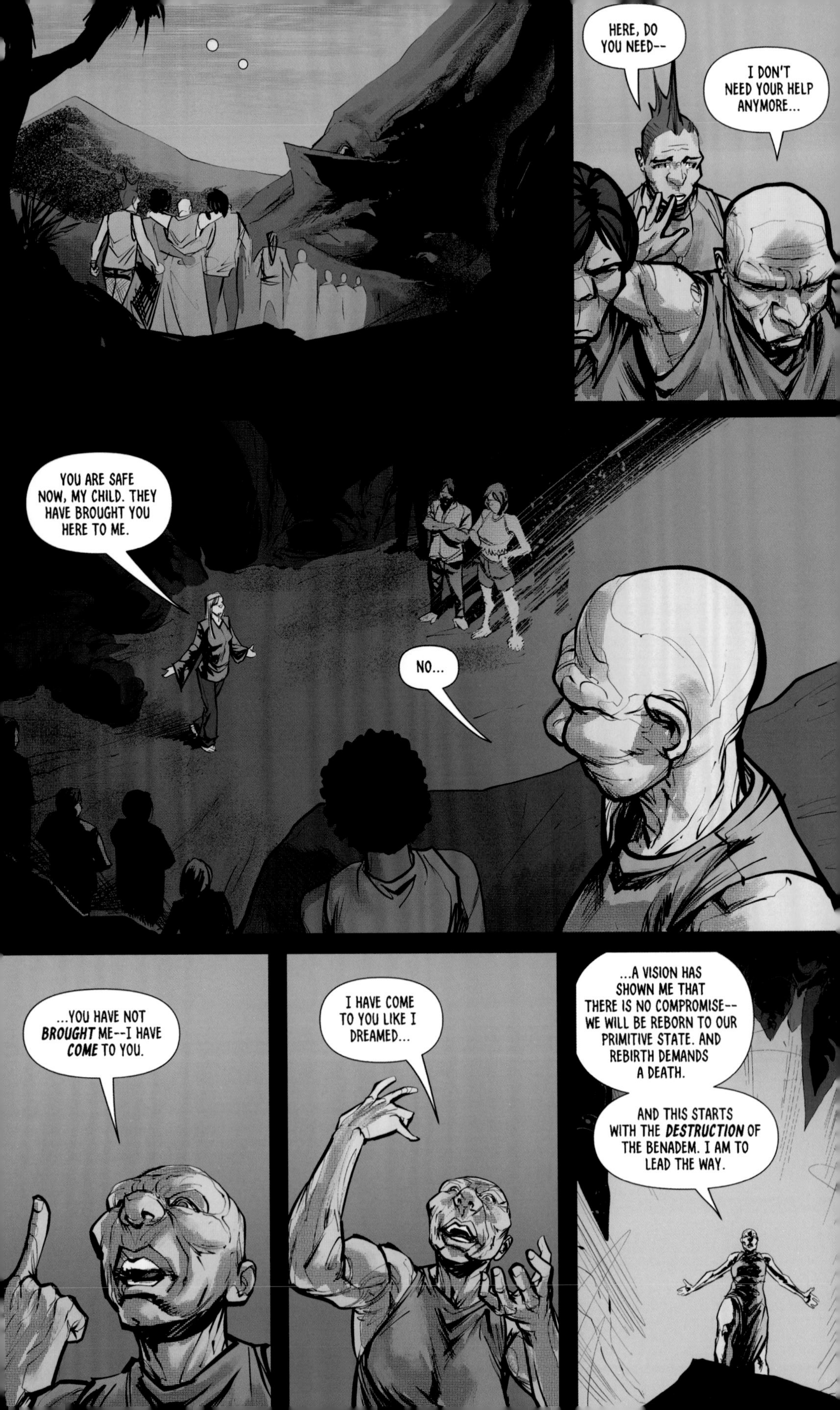
HERE, DO YOU NEED--
I DON'T NEED YOUR HELP ANYMORE...
YOU ARE SAFE NOW, MY CHILD. THEY HAVE BROUGHT YOU HERE TO ME.
NO...
...YOU HAVE NOT *BROUGHT* ME--I HAVE *COME* TO YOU.
I HAVE COME TO YOU LIKE I DREAMED...
...A VISION HAS SHOWN ME THAT THERE IS NO COMPROMISE-- WE WILL BE REBORN TO OUR PRIMITIVE STATE. AND REBIRTH DEMANDS A DEATH.
AND THIS STARTS WITH THE *DESTRUCTION* OF THE BENADEM. I AM TO LEAD THE WAY.

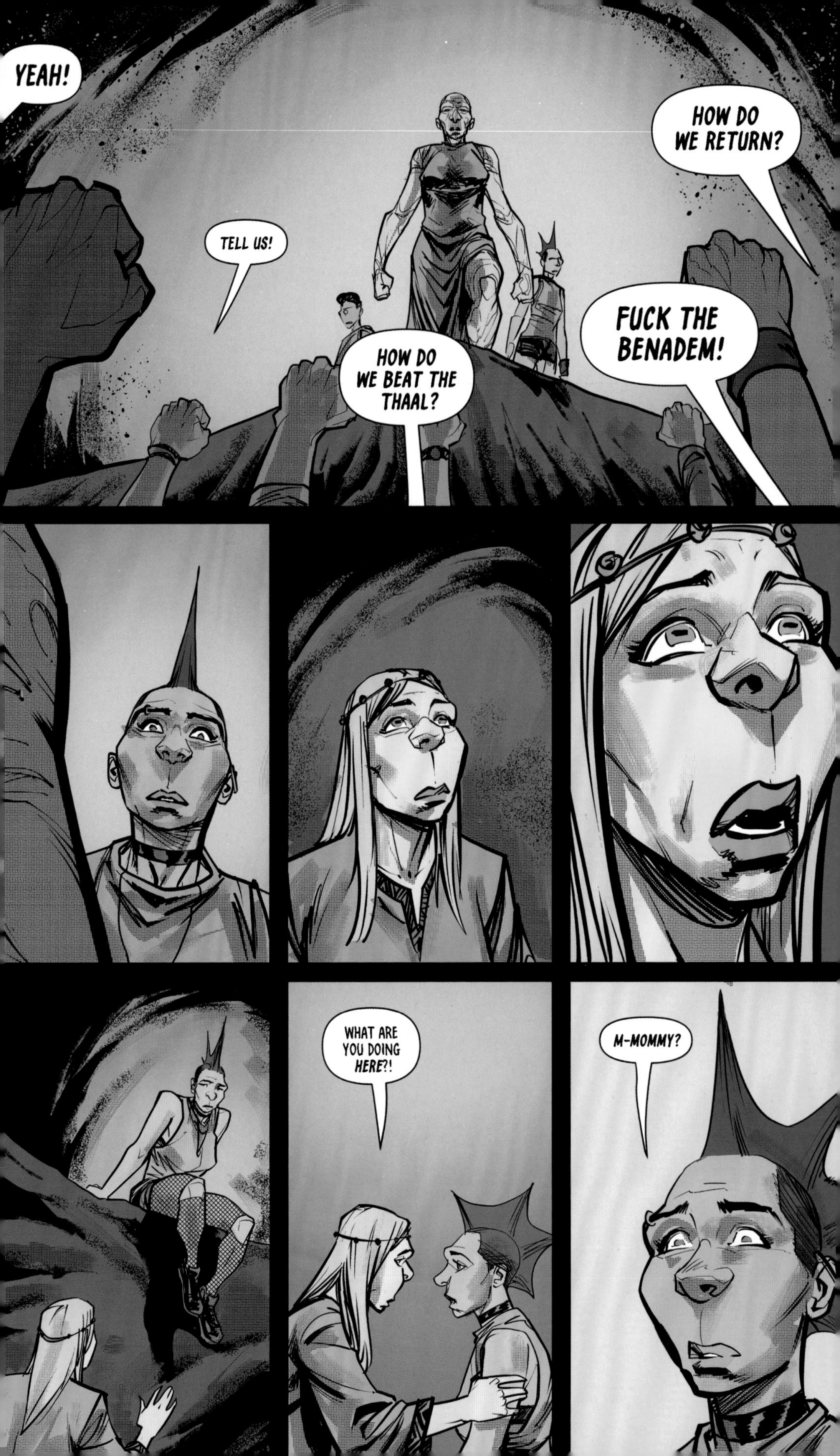
YEAH!
HOW DO WE RETURN?
TELL US!
HOW DO WE BEAT THE THAAL?
FUCK THE BENADEM!
WHAT ARE YOU DOING HERE?!
M-MOMMY?

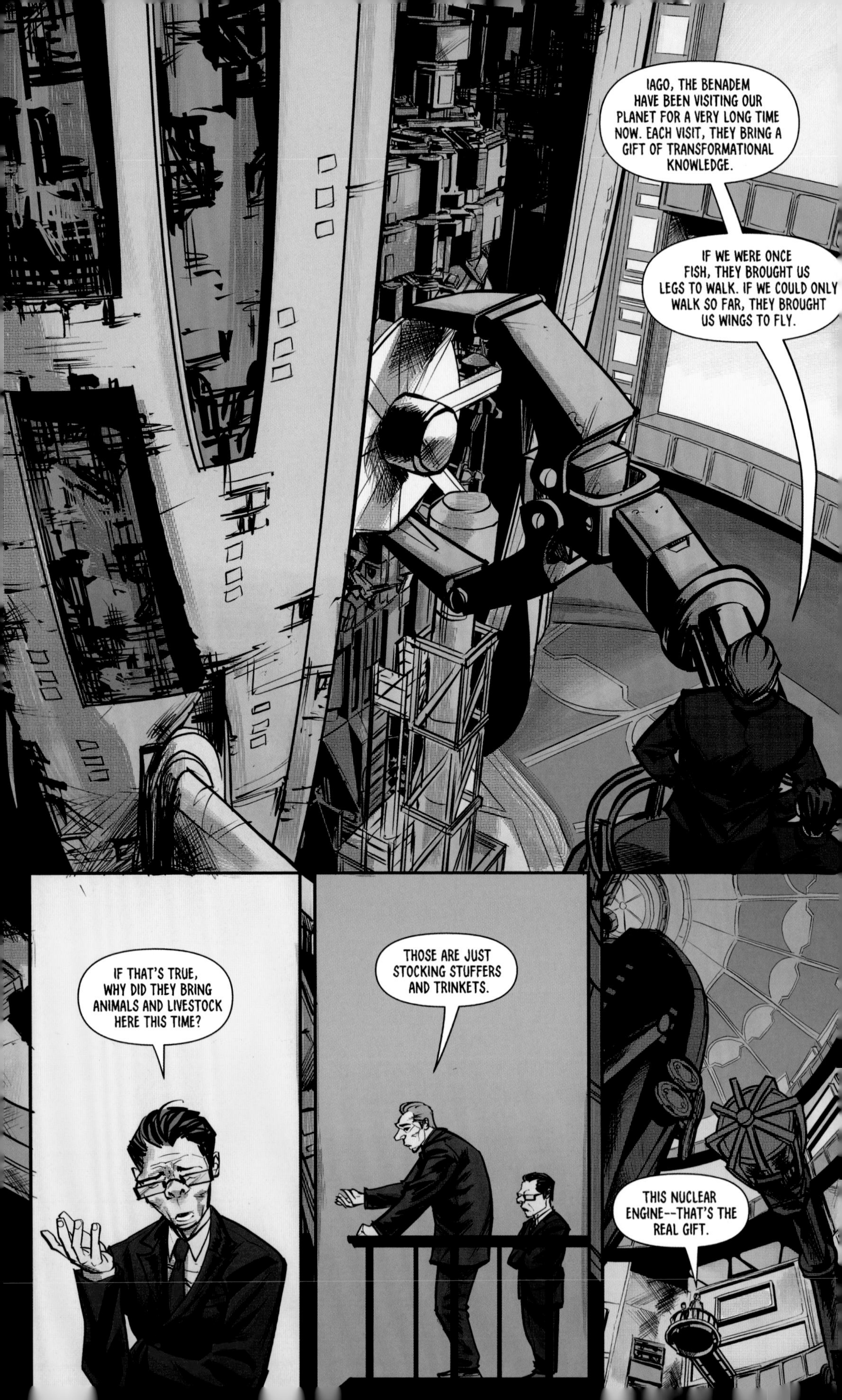
IAGO, THE BENADEM HAVE BEEN VISITING OUR PLANET FOR A VERY LONG TIME NOW. EACH VISIT, THEY BRING A GIFT OF TRANSFORMATIONAL KNOWLEDGE.
IF WE WERE ONCE FISH, THEY BROUGHT US LEGS TO WALK. IF WE COULD ONLY WALK SO FAR, THEY BROUGHT US WINGS TO FLY.
IF THAT'S TRUE, WHY DID THEY BRING ANIMALS AND LIVESTOCK HERE THIS TIME?
THOSE ARE JUST STOCKING STUFFERS AND TRINKETS.
THIS NUCLEAR ENGINE--THAT'S THE REAL GIFT.

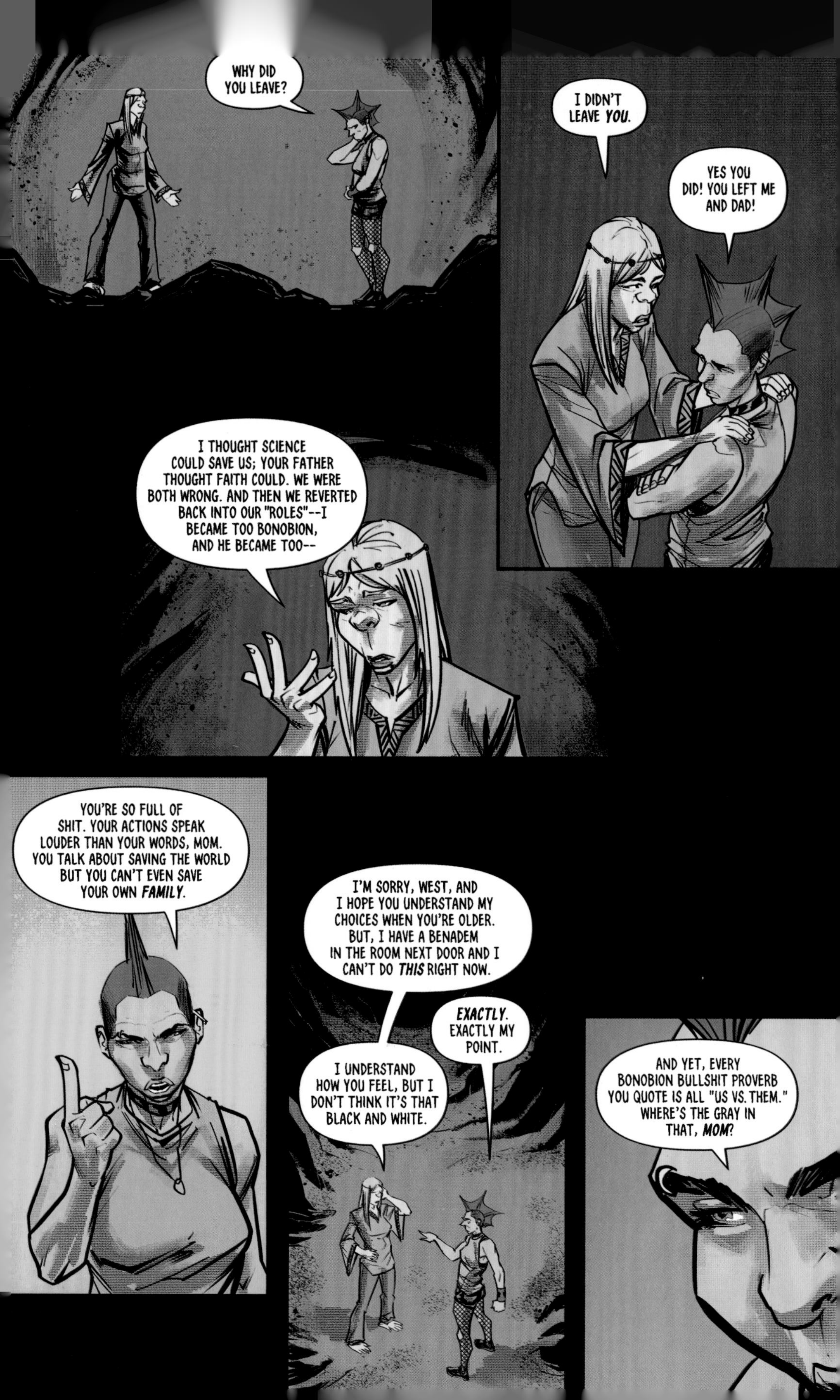
WHY DID YOU LEAVE?
I DIDN'T LEAVE *YOU*.
YES YOU DID! YOU LEFT ME AND DAD!
I THOUGHT SCIENCE COULD SAVE US; YOUR FATHER THOUGHT FAITH COULD. WE WERE BOTH WRONG. AND THEN WE REVERTED BACK INTO OUR "ROLES"--I BECAME TOO BONOBION, AND HE BECAME TOO--
YOU'RE SO FULL OF SHIT. YOUR ACTIONS SPEAK LOUDER THAN YOUR WORDS, MOM. YOU TALK ABOUT SAVING THE WORLD BUT YOU CAN'T EVEN SAVE YOUR OWN *FAMILY*.
I'M SORRY, WEST, AND I HOPE YOU UNDERSTAND MY CHOICES WHEN YOU'RE OLDER. BUT, I HAVE A BENADEM IN THE ROOM NEXT DOOR AND I CAN'T DO *THIS* RIGHT NOW.
I UNDERSTAND HOW YOU FEEL, BUT I DON'T THINK IT'S THAT BLACK AND WHITE.
EXACTLY. EXACTLY MY POINT.
AND YET, EVERY BONOBION BULLSHIT PROVERB YOU QUOTE IS ALL "US VS. THEM." WHERE'S THE GRAY IN THAT, *MOM*?

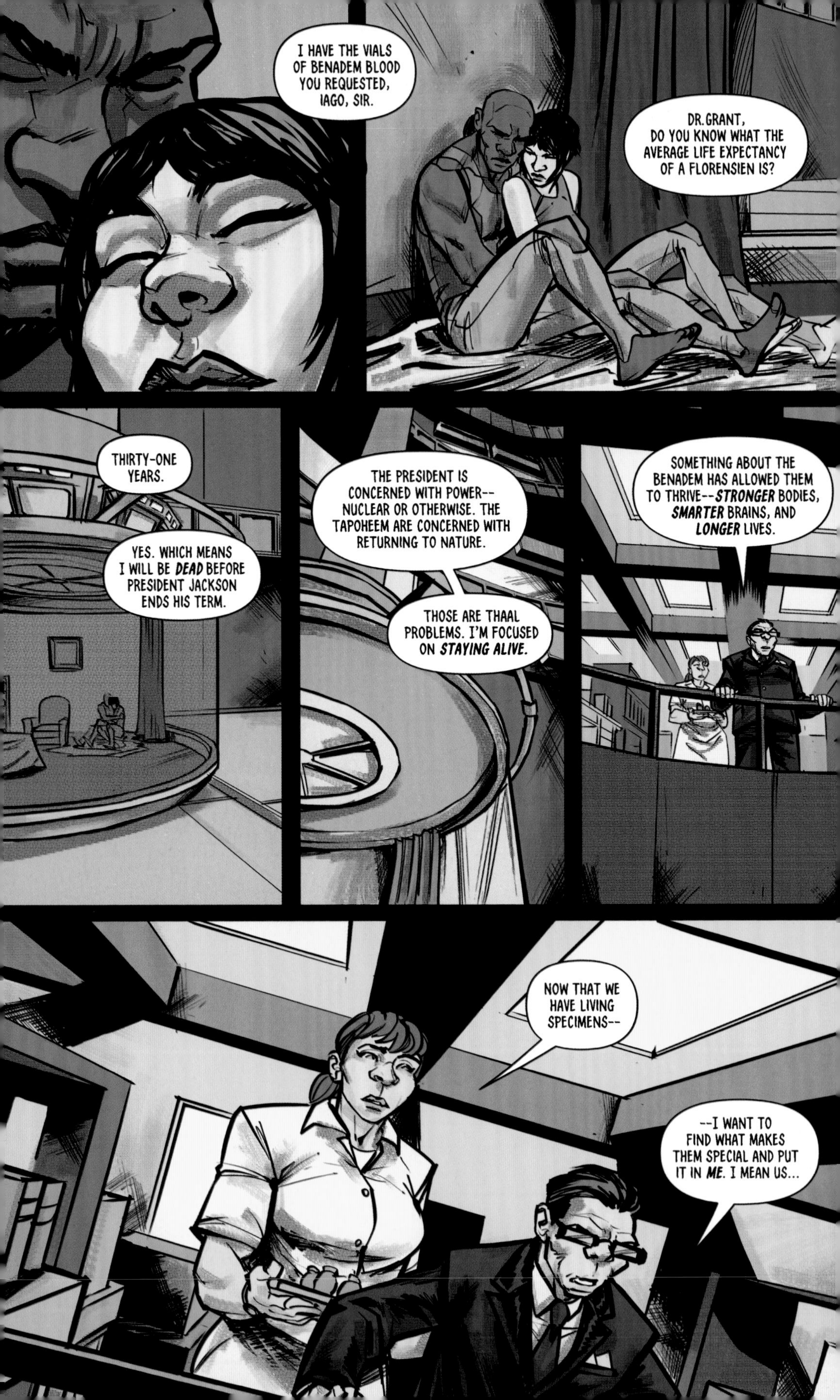
I HAVE THE VIALS OF BENADEM BLOOD YOU REQUESTED, IAGO, SIR.
DR. GRANT, DO YOU KNOW WHAT THE AVERAGE LIFE EXPECTANCY OF A FLORENSIEN IS?
THIRTY-ONE YEARS.
YES. WHICH MEANS I WILL BE *DEAD* BEFORE PRESIDENT JACKSON ENDS HIS TERM.
THE PRESIDENT IS CONCERNED WITH POWER-- NUCLEAR OR OTHERWISE. THE TAPOHEEM ARE CONCERNED WITH RETURNING TO NATURE.
THOSE ARE THAAL PROBLEMS. I'M FOCUSED ON *STAYING ALIVE.*
SOMETHING ABOUT THE BENADEM HAS ALLOWED THEM TO THRIVE--*STRONGER* BODIES, *SMARTER* BRAINS, AND *LONGER* LIVES.
NOW THAT WE HAVE LIVING SPECIMENS--
--I WANT TO FIND WHAT MAKES THEM SPECIAL AND PUT IT IN *ME*. I MEAN US...

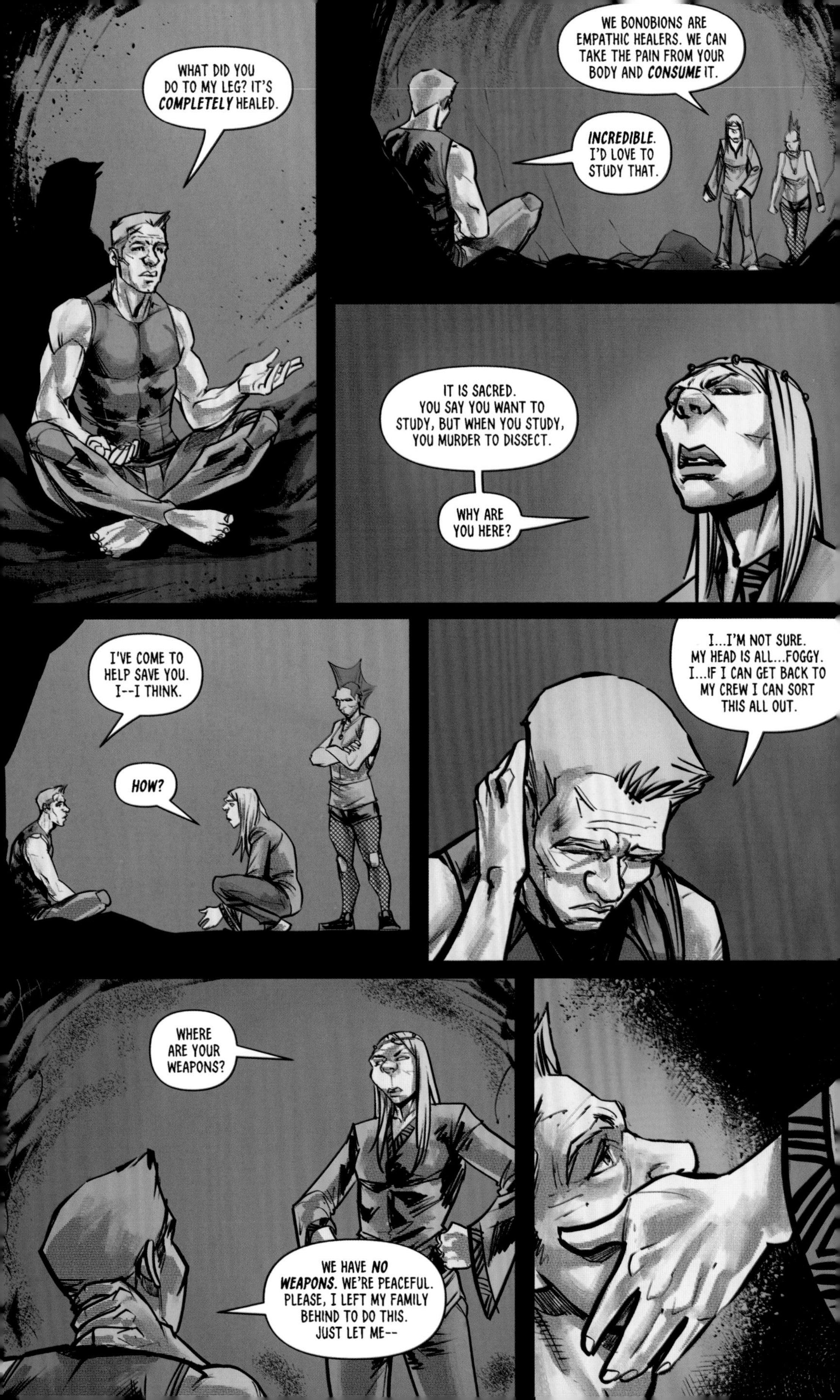
WHAT DID YOU DO TO MY LEG? IT'S *COMPLETELY* HEALED.
WE BONOBIONS ARE EMPATHIC HEALERS. WE CAN TAKE THE PAIN FROM YOUR BODY AND *CONSUME* IT.
INCREDIBLE. I'D LOVE TO STUDY THAT.
IT IS SACRED. YOU SAY YOU WANT TO STUDY, BUT WHEN YOU STUDY, YOU MURDER TO DISSECT.
WHY ARE YOU HERE?
I'VE COME TO HELP SAVE YOU. I--I THINK.
HOW?
I...I'M NOT SURE. MY HEAD IS ALL...FOGGY. I...IF I CAN GET BACK TO MY CREW I CAN SORT THIS ALL OUT.
WHERE ARE YOUR WEAPONS?
WE HAVE *NO WEAPONS.* WE'RE PEACEFUL. PLEASE, I LEFT MY FAMILY BEHIND TO DO THIS. JUST LET ME--

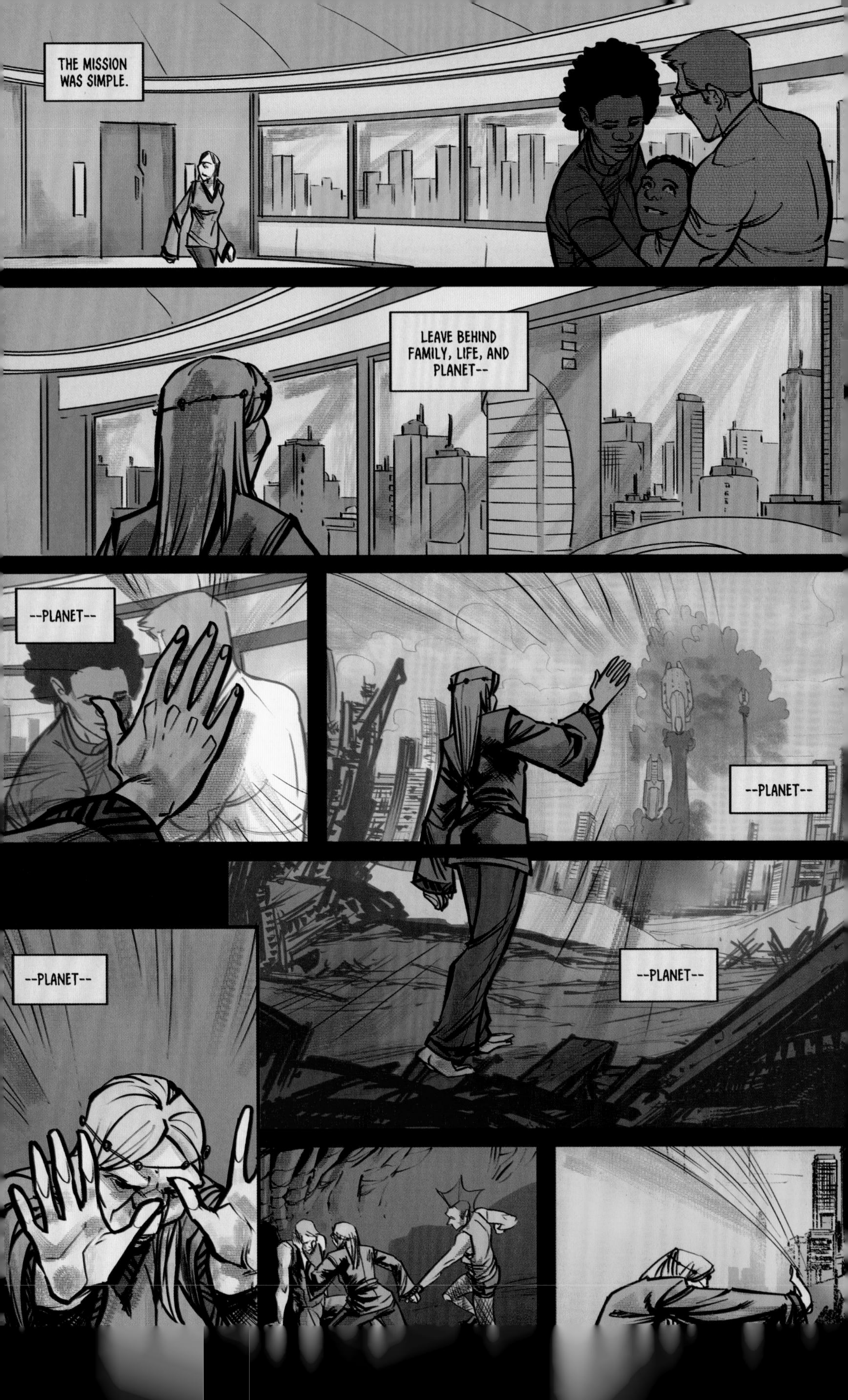
THE MISSION WAS SIMPLE.
LEAVE BEHIND FAMILY, LIFE, AND PLANET--
--PLANET--
--PLANET--
--PLANET--
--PLANET--

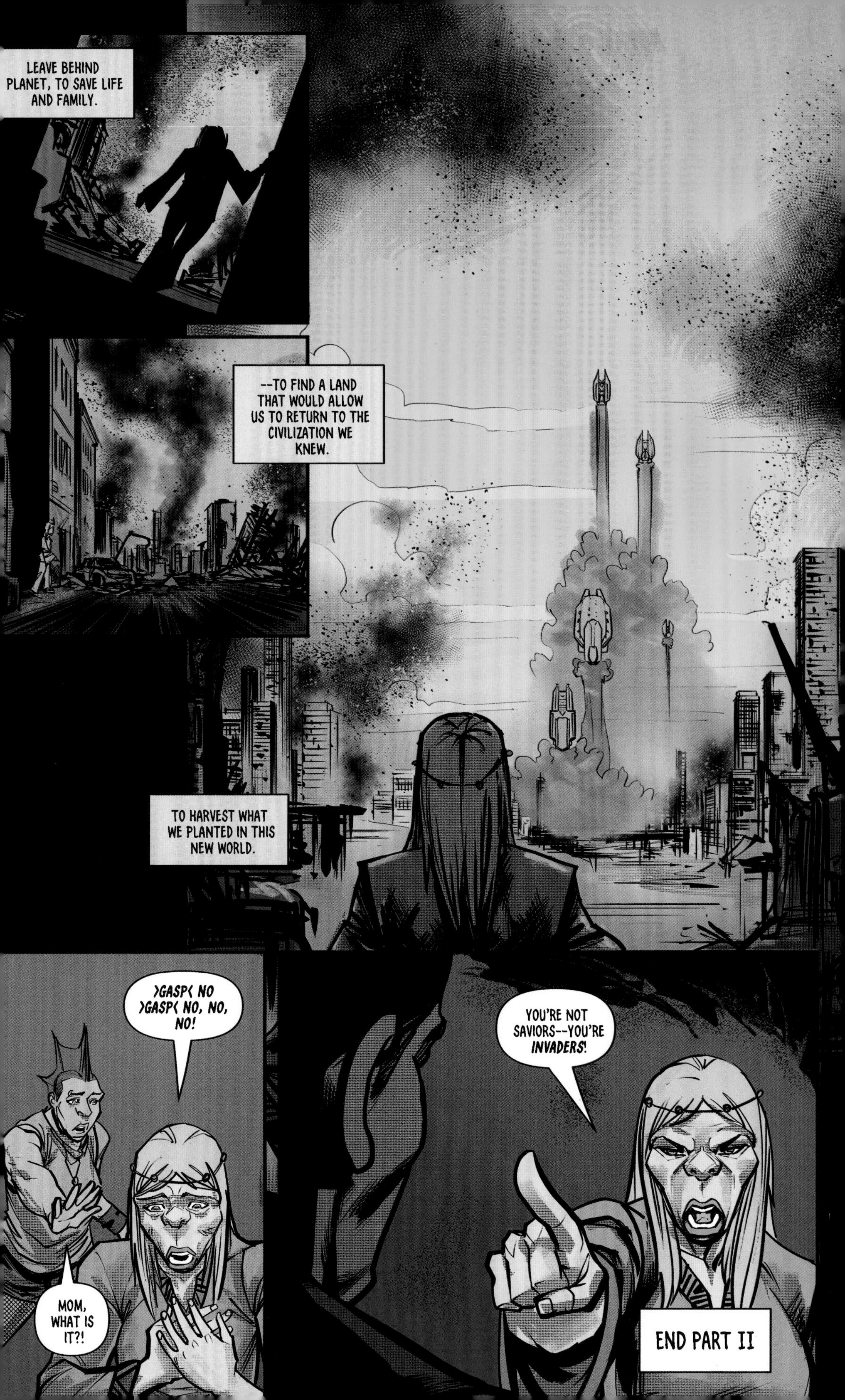
LEAVE BEHIND PLANET, TO SAVE LIFE AND FAMILY.
--TO FIND A LAND THAT WOULD ALLOW US TO RETURN TO THE CIVILIZATION WE KNEW.
TO HARVEST WHAT WE PLANTED IN THIS NEW WORLD.
>GASP< NO >GASP< NO, NO, NO!
MOM, WHAT IS IT?!
YOU'RE NOT SAVIORS--YOU'RE INVADERS!
END PART II

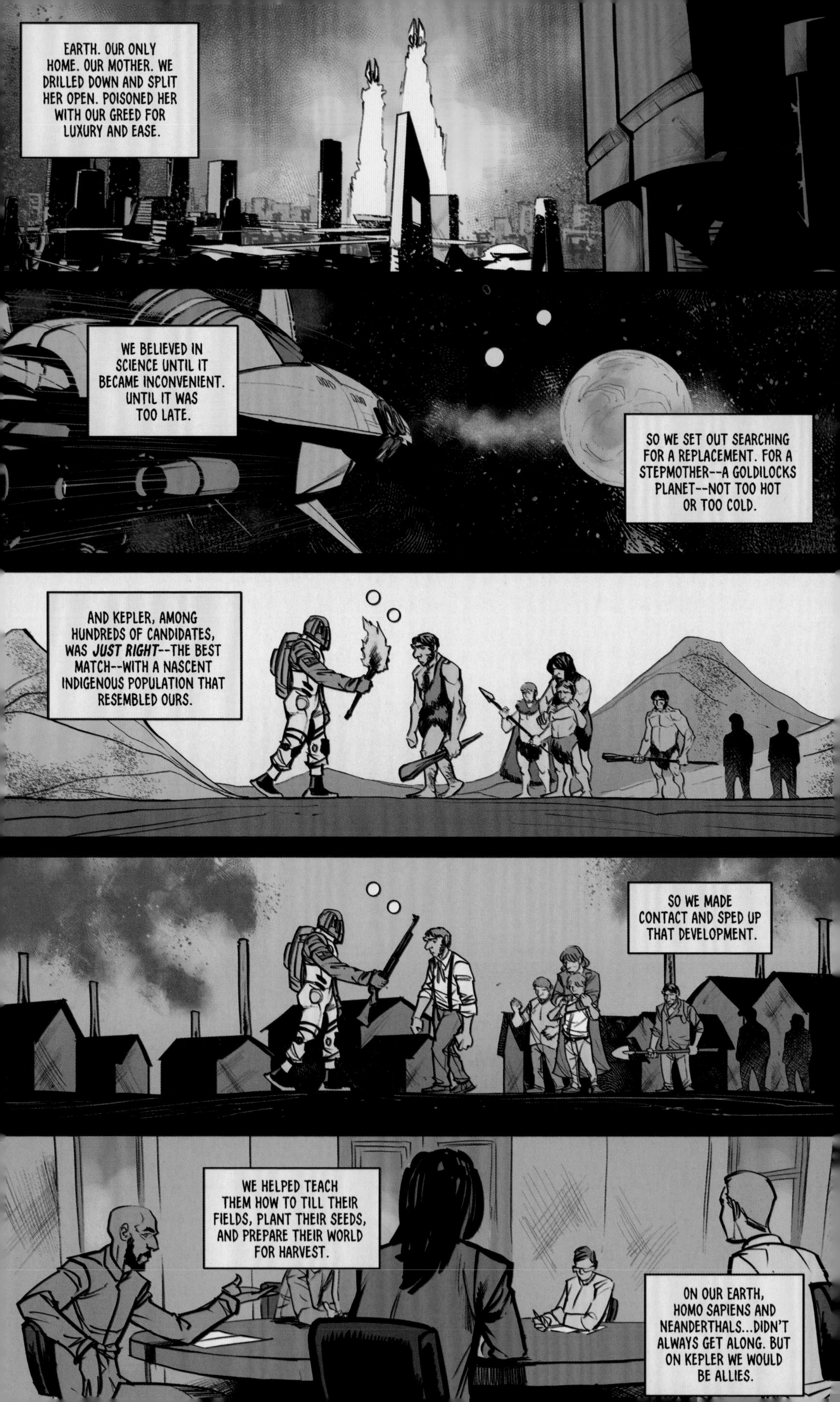
EARTH. OUR ONLY HOME. OUR MOTHER. WE DRILLED DOWN AND SPLIT HER OPEN. POISONED HER WITH OUR GREED FOR LUXURY AND EASE.
WE BELIEVED IN SCIENCE UNTIL IT BECAME INCONVENIENT. UNTIL IT WAS TOO LATE.
SO WE SET OUT SEARCHING FOR A REPLACEMENT. FOR A STEPMOTHER--A GOLDILOCKS PLANET--NOT TOO HOT OR TOO COLD.
AND KEPLER, AMONG HUNDREDS OF CANDIDATES, WAS *JUST RIGHT*--THE BEST MATCH--WITH A NASCENT INDIGENOUS POPULATION THAT RESEMBLED OURS.
SO WE MADE CONTACT AND SPED UP THAT DEVELOPMENT.
WE HELPED TEACH THEM HOW TO TILL THEIR FIELDS, PLANT THEIR SEEDS, AND PREPARE THEIR WORLD FOR HARVEST.
ON OUR EARTH, HOMO SAPIENS AND NEANDERTHALS...DIDN'T ALWAYS GET ALONG. BUT ON KEPLER WE WOULD BE ALLIES.

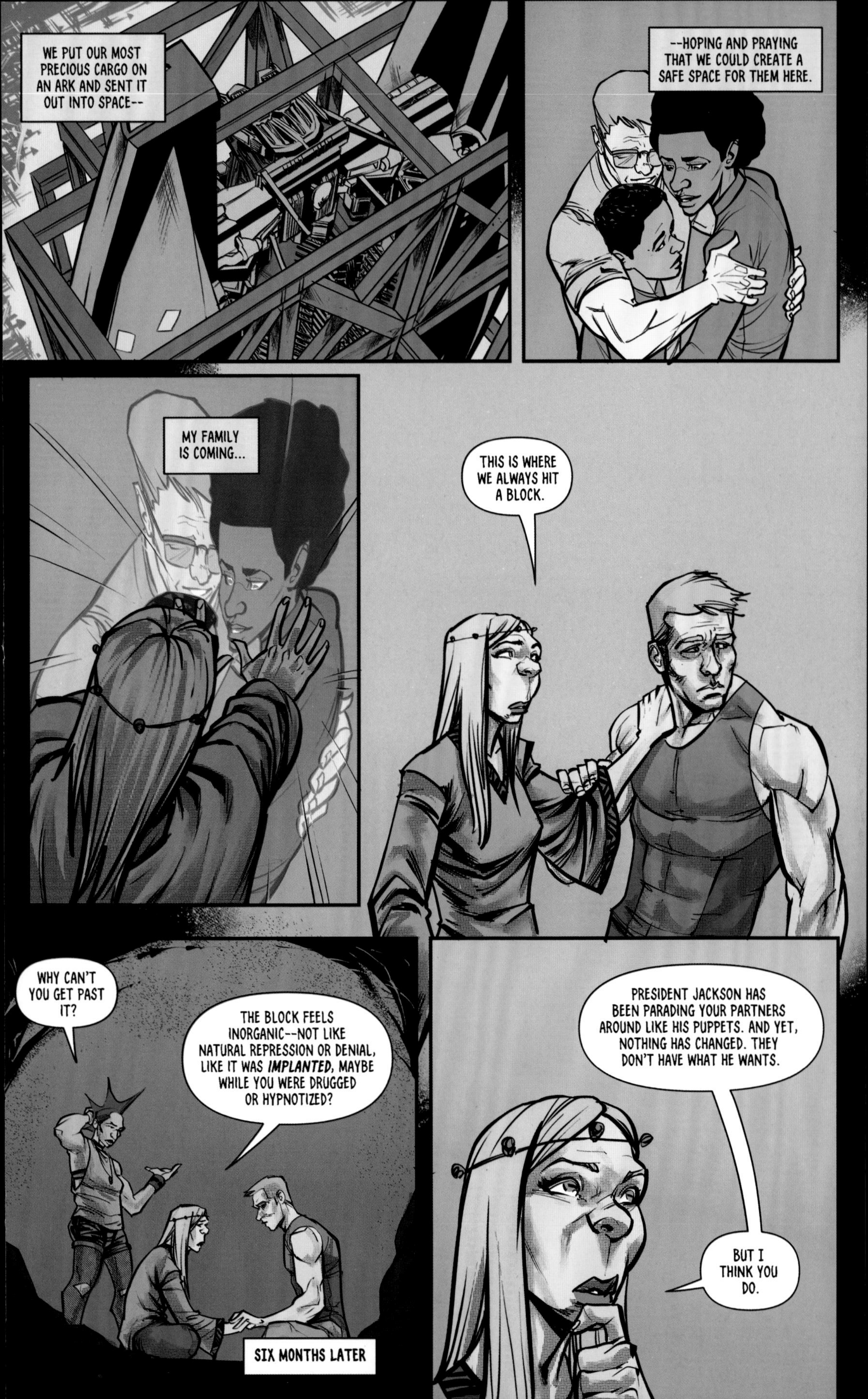
WE PUT OUR MOST PRECIOUS CARGO ON AN ARK AND SENT IT OUT INTO SPACE--
--HOPING AND PRAYING THAT WE COULD CREATE A SAFE SPACE FOR THEM HERE.
MY FAMILY IS COMING...
THIS IS WHERE WE ALWAYS HIT A BLOCK.
WHY CAN'T YOU GET PAST IT?
THE BLOCK FEELS INORGANIC--NOT LIKE NATURAL REPRESSION OR DENIAL, LIKE IT WAS *IMPLANTED*, MAYBE WHILE YOU WERE DRUGGED OR HYPNOTIZED?
SIX MONTHS LATER
PRESIDENT JACKSON HAS BEEN PARADING YOUR PARTNERS AROUND LIKE HIS PUPPETS. AND YET, NOTHING HAS CHANGED. THEY DON'T HAVE WHAT HE WANTS.
BUT I THINK YOU DO.

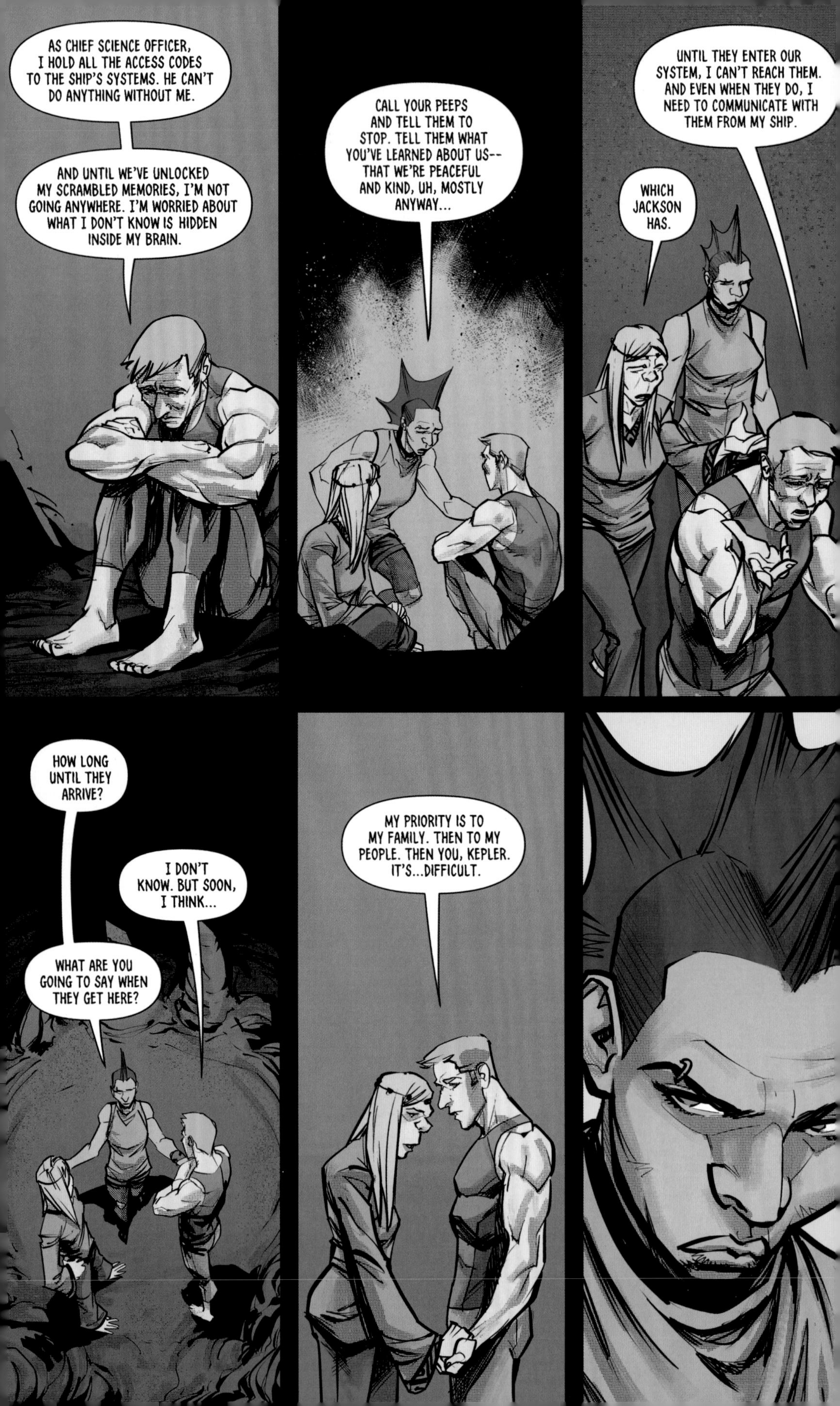
AS CHIEF SCIENCE OFFICER, I HOLD ALL THE ACCESS CODES TO THE SHIP'S SYSTEMS. HE CAN'T DO ANYTHING WITHOUT ME.
AND UNTIL WE'VE UNLOCKED MY SCRAMBLED MEMORIES, I'M NOT GOING ANYWHERE. I'M WORRIED ABOUT WHAT I DON'T KNOW IS HIDDEN INSIDE MY BRAIN.
CALL YOUR PEEPS AND TELL THEM TO STOP. TELL THEM WHAT YOU'VE LEARNED ABOUT US-- THAT WE'RE PEACEFUL AND KIND, UH, MOSTLY ANYWAY...
UNTIL THEY ENTER OUR SYSTEM, I CAN'T REACH THEM. AND EVEN WHEN THEY DO, I NEED TO COMMUNICATE WITH THEM FROM MY SHIP.
WHICH JACKSON HAS.
HOW LONG UNTIL THEY ARRIVE?
I DON'T KNOW. BUT SOON, I THINK...
WHAT ARE YOU GOING TO SAY WHEN THEY GET HERE?
MY PRIORITY IS TO MY FAMILY. THEN TO MY PEOPLE. THEN YOU, KEPLER. IT'S...DIFFICULT.

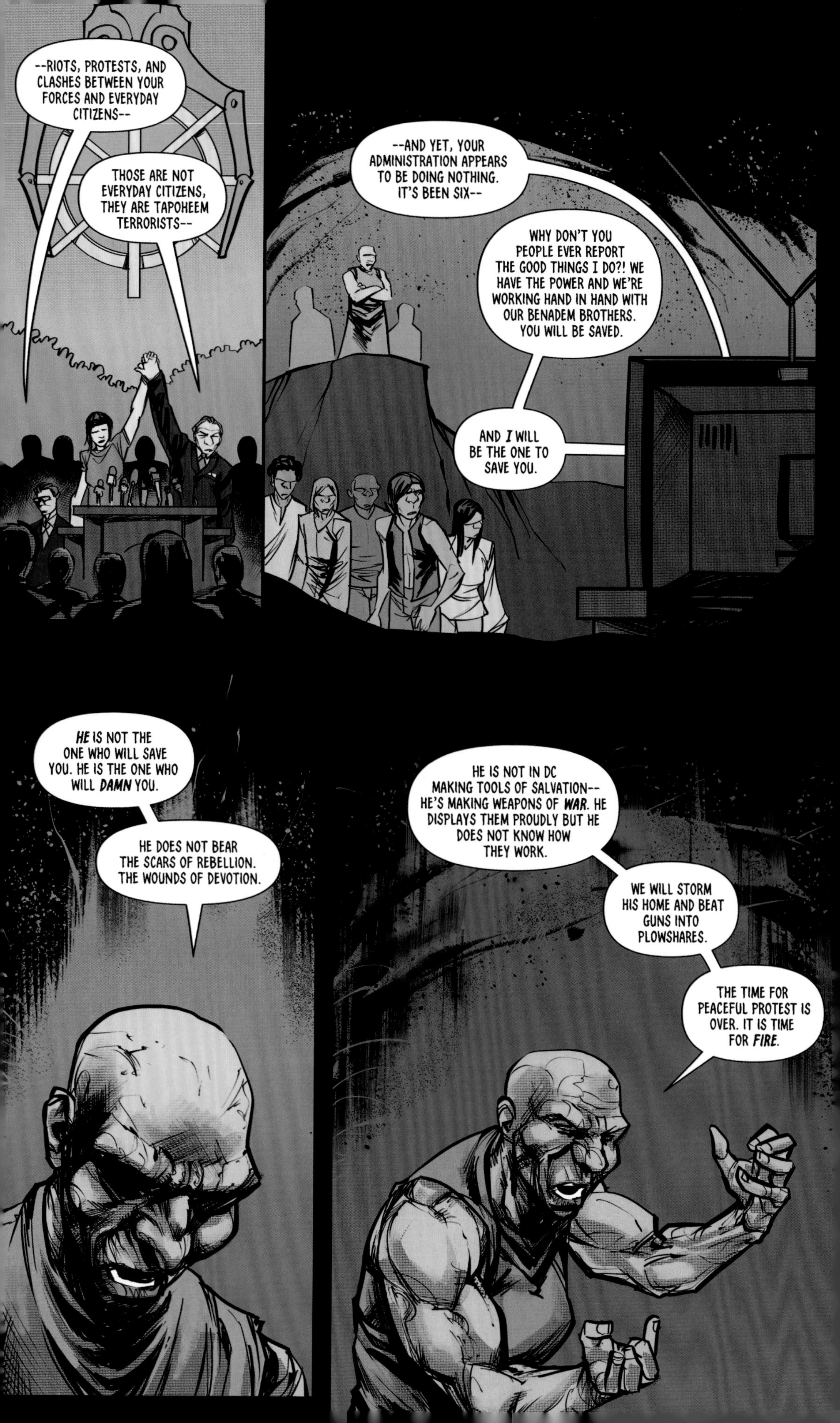
--RIOTS, PROTESTS, AND CLASHES BETWEEN YOUR FORCES AND EVERYDAY CITIZENS--
THOSE ARE NOT EVERYDAY CITIZENS, THEY ARE TAPOHEEM TERRORISTS--
--AND YET, YOUR ADMINISTRATION APPEARS TO BE DOING NOTHING. IT'S BEEN SIX--
WHY DON'T YOU PEOPLE EVER REPORT THE GOOD THINGS I DO?! WE HAVE THE POWER AND WE'RE WORKING HAND IN HAND WITH OUR BENADEM BROTHERS. YOU WILL BE SAVED.
AND *I* WILL BE THE ONE TO SAVE YOU.
HE IS NOT THE ONE WHO WILL SAVE YOU. HE IS THE ONE WHO WILL *DAMN* YOU.
HE DOES NOT BEAR THE SCARS OF REBELLION. THE WOUNDS OF DEVOTION.
HE IS NOT IN DC MAKING TOOLS OF SALVATION-- HE'S MAKING WEAPONS OF *WAR*. HE DISPLAYS THEM PROUDLY BUT HE DOES NOT KNOW HOW THEY WORK.
WE WILL STORM HIS HOME AND BEAT GUNS INTO PLOWSHARES.
THE TIME FOR PEACEFUL PROTEST IS OVER. IT IS TIME FOR *FIRE*.

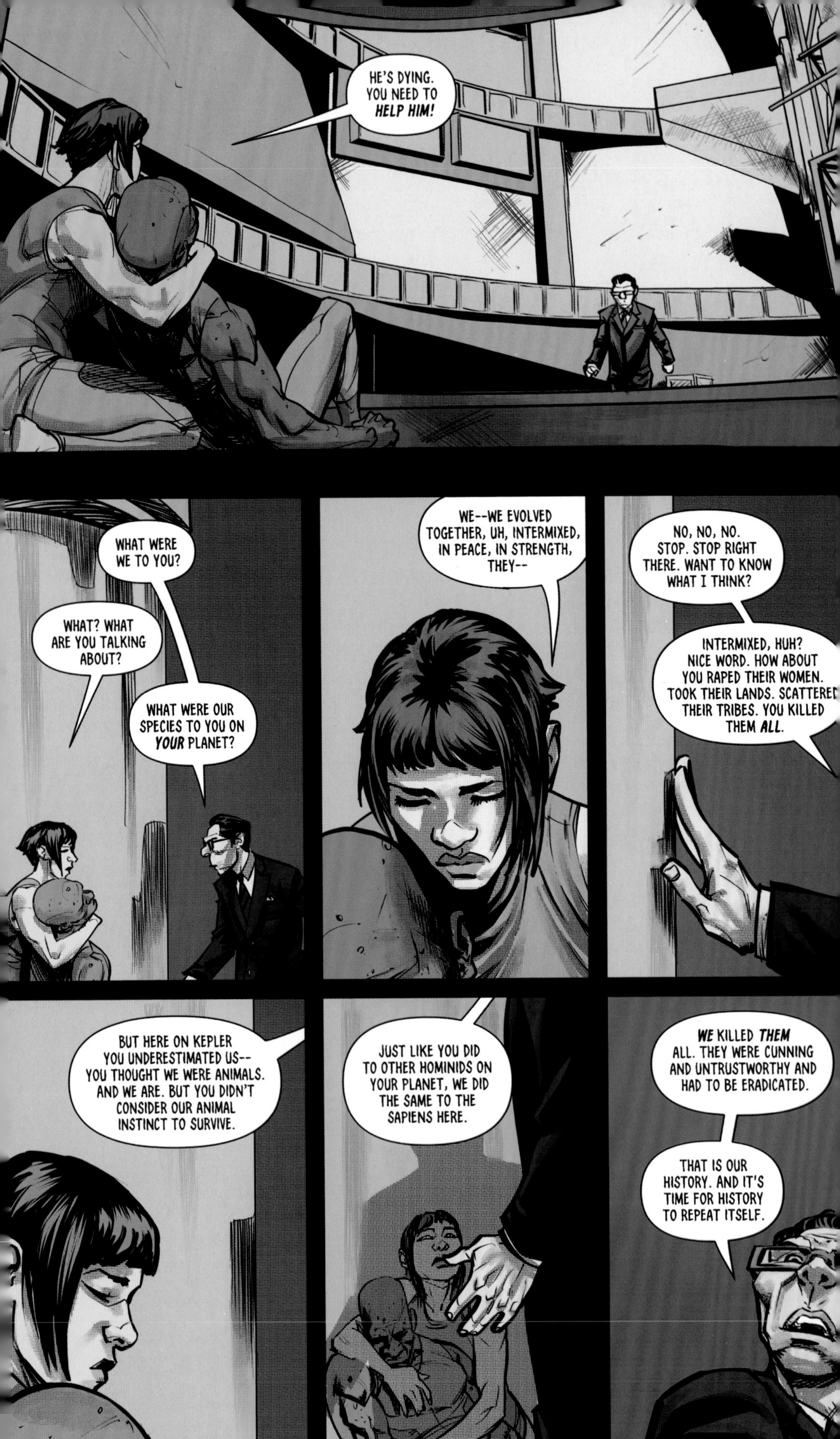
HE'S DYING. YOU NEED TO HELP HIM!
WHAT WERE WE TO YOU?
WHAT? WHAT ARE YOU TALKING ABOUT?
WHAT WERE OUR SPECIES TO YOU ON YOUR PLANET?
WE--WE EVOLVED TOGETHER, UH, INTERMIXED, IN PEACE, IN STRENGTH, THEY--
NO, NO, NO. STOP. STOP RIGHT THERE. WANT TO KNOW WHAT I THINK?
INTERMIXED, HUH? NICE WORD. HOW ABOUT YOU RAPED THEIR WOMEN. TOOK THEIR LANDS. SCATTERED THEIR TRIBES. YOU KILLED THEM ALL.
BUT HERE ON KEPLER YOU UNDERESTIMATED US-- YOU THOUGHT WE WERE ANIMALS. AND WE ARE. BUT YOU DIDN'T CONSIDER OUR ANIMAL INSTINCT TO SURVIVE.
JUST LIKE YOU DID TO OTHER HOMINIDS ON YOUR PLANET, WE DID THE SAME TO THE SAPIENS HERE.
WE KILLED THEM ALL. THEY WERE CUNNING AND UNTRUSTWORTHY AND HAD TO BE ERADICATED.
THAT IS OUR HISTORY. AND IT'S TIME FOR HISTORY TO REPEAT ITSELF.

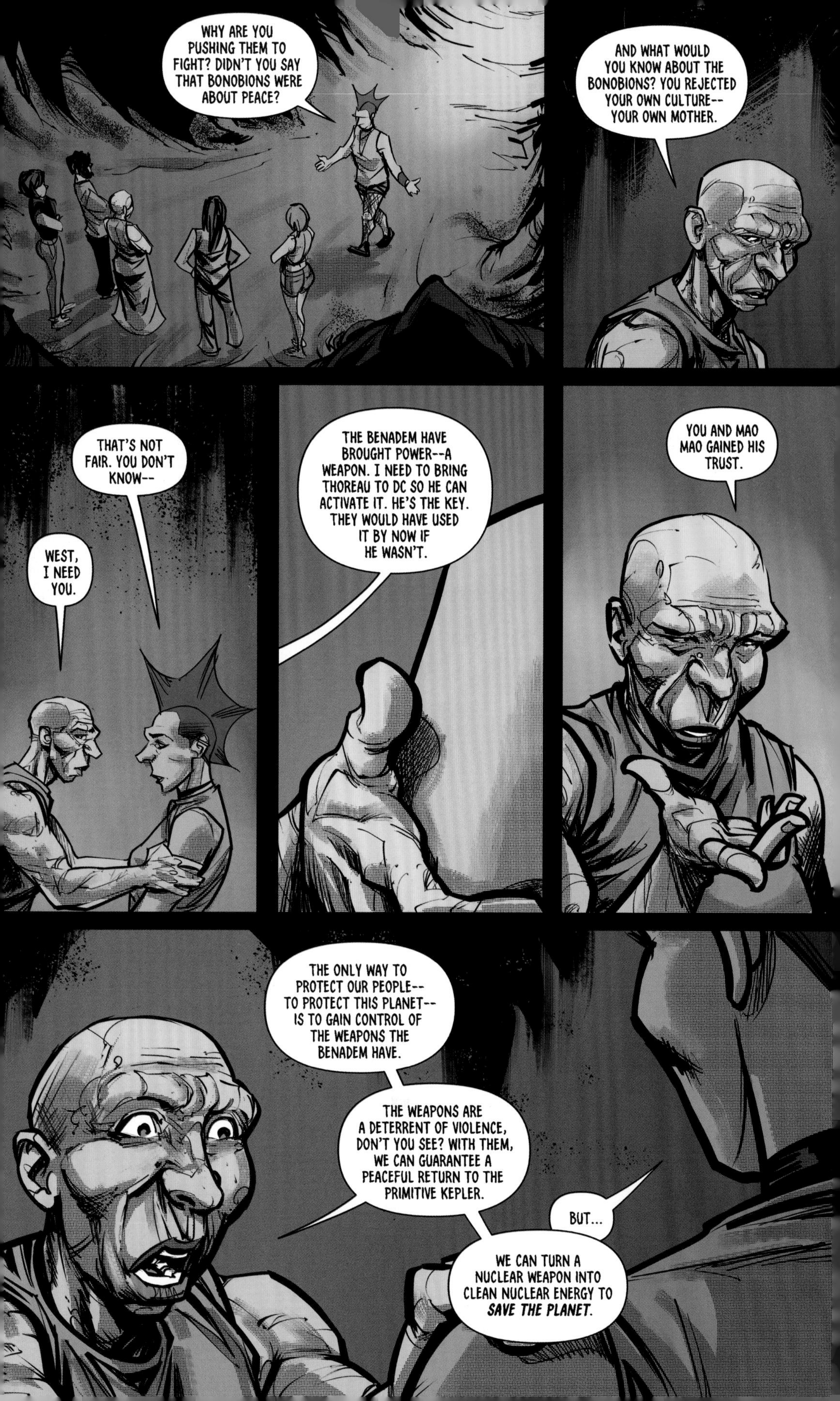
WHY ARE YOU PUSHING THEM TO FIGHT? DIDN'T YOU SAY THAT BONOBIONS WERE ABOUT PEACE?
AND WHAT WOULD YOU KNOW ABOUT THE BONOBIONS? YOU REJECTED YOUR OWN CULTURE-- YOUR OWN MOTHER.
THAT'S NOT FAIR. YOU DON'T KNOW--
WEST, I NEED YOU.
THE BENADEM HAVE BROUGHT POWER--A WEAPON. I NEED TO BRING THOREAU TO DC SO HE CAN ACTIVATE IT. HE'S THE KEY. THEY WOULD HAVE USED IT BY NOW IF HE WASN'T.
YOU AND MAO MAO GAINED HIS TRUST.
THE ONLY WAY TO PROTECT OUR PEOPLE-- TO PROTECT THIS PLANET-- IS TO GAIN CONTROL OF THE WEAPONS THE BENADEM HAVE.
THE WEAPONS ARE A DETERRENT OF VIOLENCE, DON'T YOU SEE? WITH THEM, WE CAN GUARANTEE A PEACEFUL RETURN TO THE PRIMITIVE KEPLER.
BUT...
WE CAN TURN A NUCLEAR WEAPON INTO CLEAN NUCLEAR ENERGY TO *SAVE THE PLANET*.

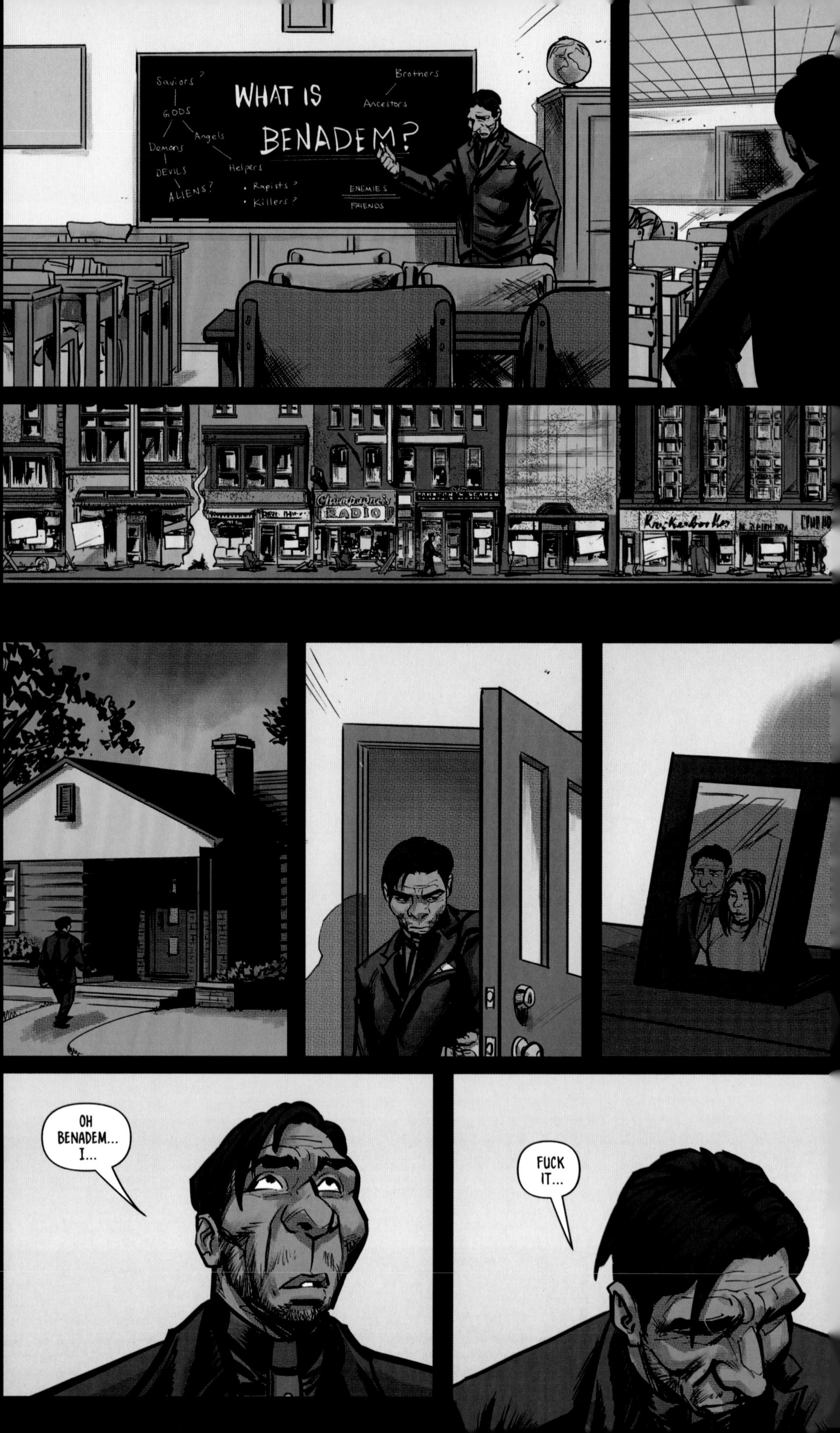
Saviors?
GODS
Angels
Demons
DEVILS
ALIENS?
Helpers
WHAT IS
BENADEM?
• Rapists?
• Killers?
Brothers
Ancestors
ENEMIES
FRIENDS
OH BENADEM... I...
FUCK IT...

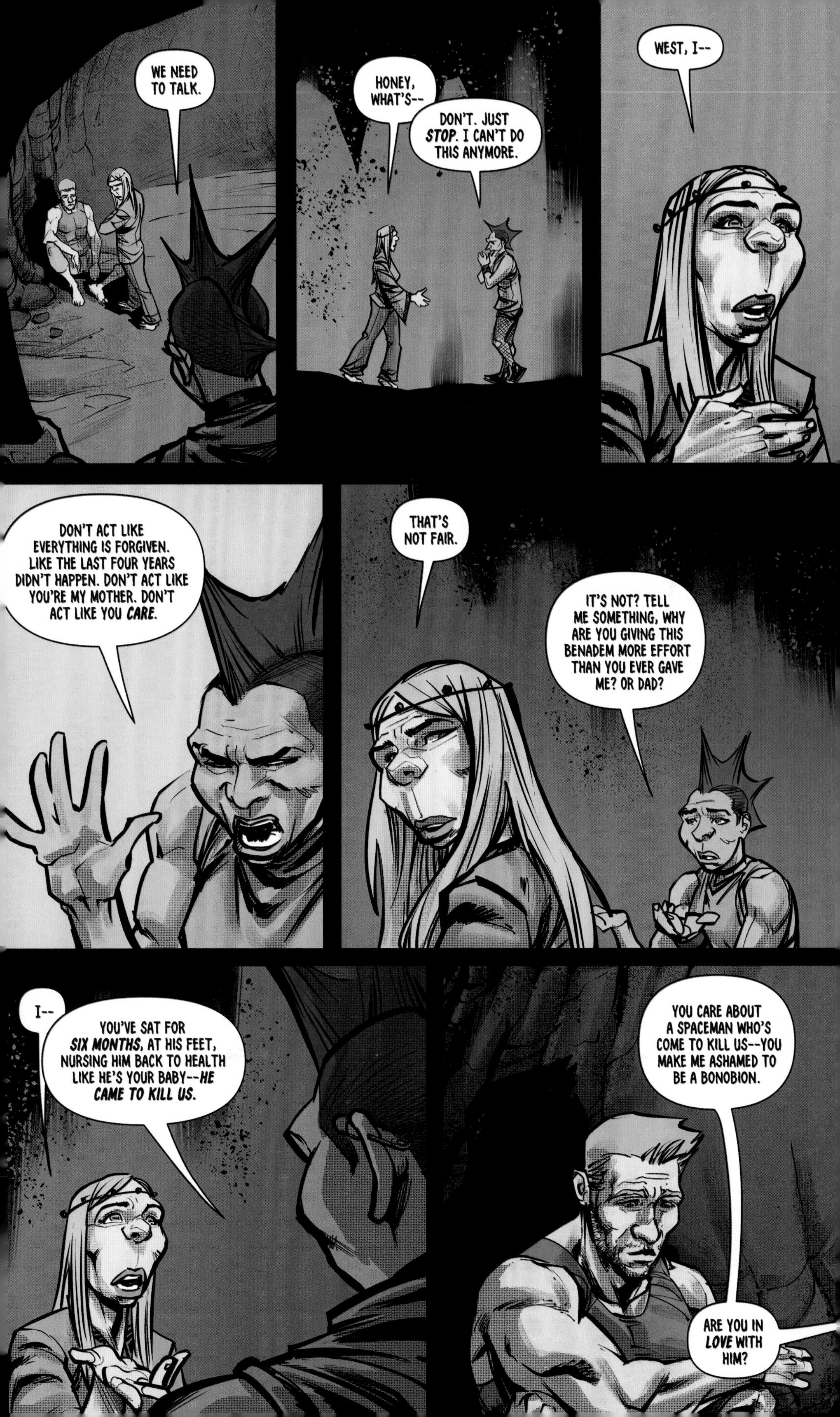
WE NEED TO TALK.
HONEY, WHAT'S--
DON'T. JUST *STOP*. I CAN'T DO THIS ANYMORE.
WEST, I--
DON'T ACT LIKE EVERYTHING IS FORGIVEN. LIKE THE LAST FOUR YEARS DIDN'T HAPPEN. DON'T ACT LIKE YOU'RE MY MOTHER. DON'T ACT LIKE YOU *CARE*.
THAT'S NOT FAIR.
IT'S NOT? TELL ME SOMETHING, WHY ARE YOU GIVING THIS BENADEM MORE EFFORT THAN YOU EVER GAVE ME? OR DAD?
I--
YOU'VE SAT FOR *SIX MONTHS*, AT HIS FEET, NURSING HIM BACK TO HEALTH LIKE HE'S YOUR BABY--*HE CAME TO KILL US*.
YOU CARE ABOUT A SPACEMAN WHO'S COME TO KILL US--YOU MAKE ME ASHAMED TO BE A BONOBION.
ARE YOU IN *LOVE* WITH HIM?

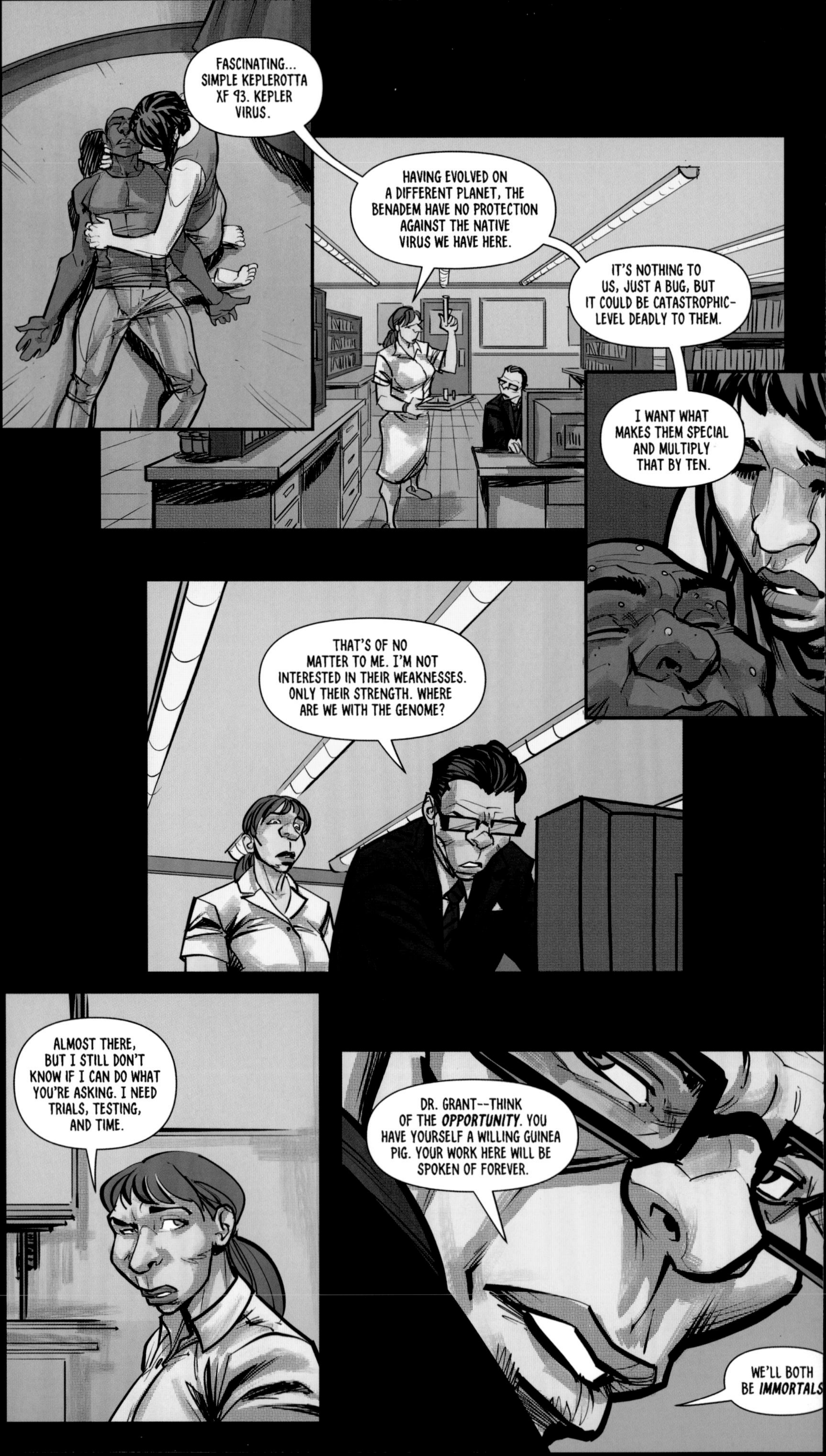
FASCINATING... SIMPLE KEPLEROTTA XF 93. KEPLER VIRUS.
HAVING EVOLVED ON A DIFFERENT PLANET, THE BENADEM HAVE NO PROTECTION AGAINST THE NATIVE VIRUS WE HAVE HERE.
IT'S NOTHING TO US, JUST A BUG, BUT IT COULD BE CATASTROPHIC-LEVEL DEADLY TO THEM.
I WANT WHAT MAKES THEM SPECIAL AND MULTIPLY THAT BY TEN.
THAT'S OF NO MATTER TO ME. I'M NOT INTERESTED IN THEIR WEAKNESSES. ONLY THEIR STRENGTH. WHERE ARE WE WITH THE GENOME?
ALMOST THERE, BUT I STILL DON'T KNOW IF I CAN DO WHAT YOU'RE ASKING. I NEED TRIALS, TESTING, AND TIME.
DR. GRANT--THINK OF THE *OPPORTUNITY*. YOU HAVE YOURSELF A WILLING GUINEA PIG. YOUR WORK HERE WILL BE SPOKEN OF FOREVER.
WE'LL BOTH BE *IMMORTALS*

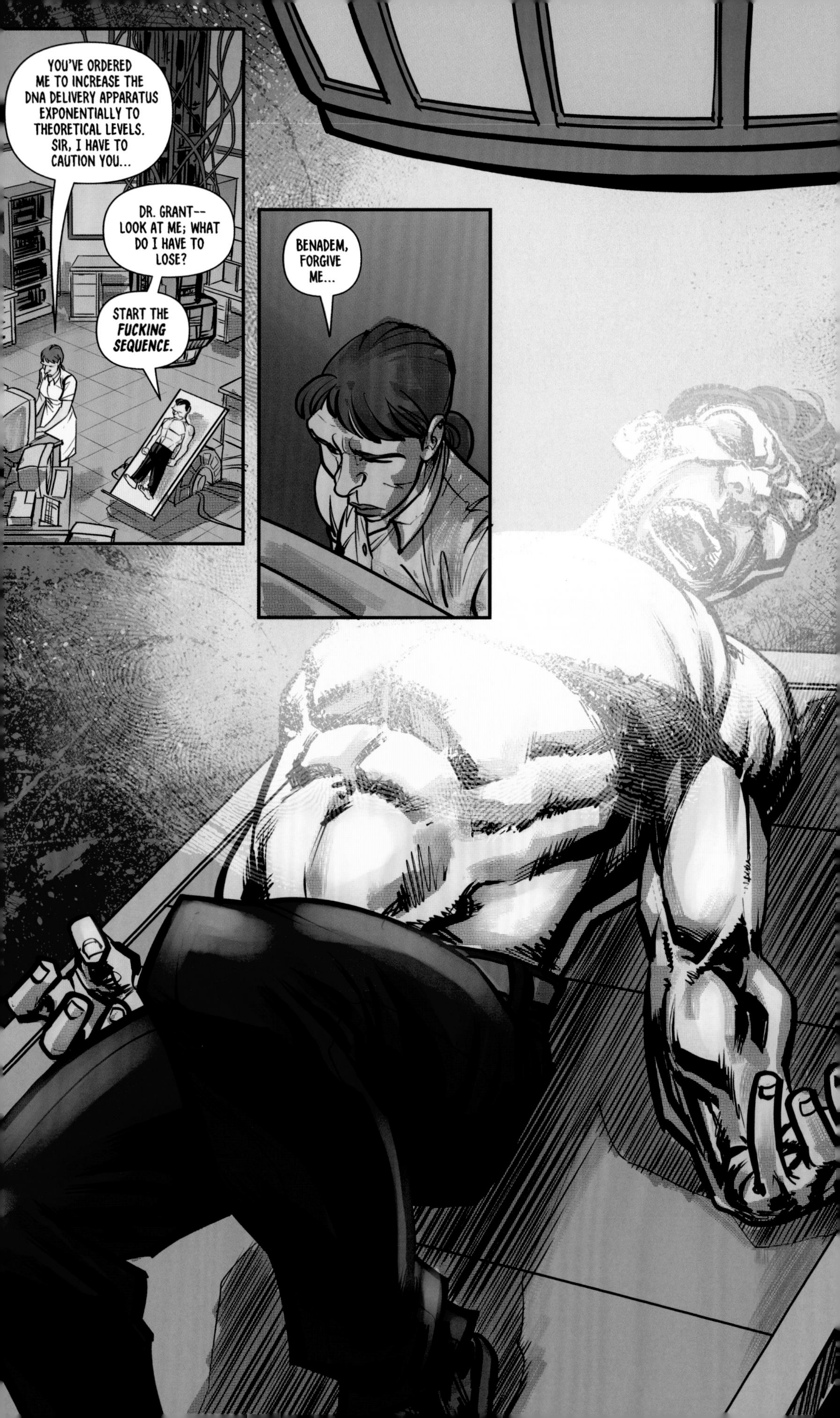

YOU'VE ORDERED ME TO INCREASE THE DNA DELIVERY APPARATUS EXPONENTIALLY TO THEORETICAL LEVELS. SIR, I HAVE TO CAUTION YOU...
DR. GRANT-- LOOK AT ME; WHAT DO I HAVE TO LOSE?
START THE *FUCKING SEQUENCE*.
BENADEM, FORGIVE ME...

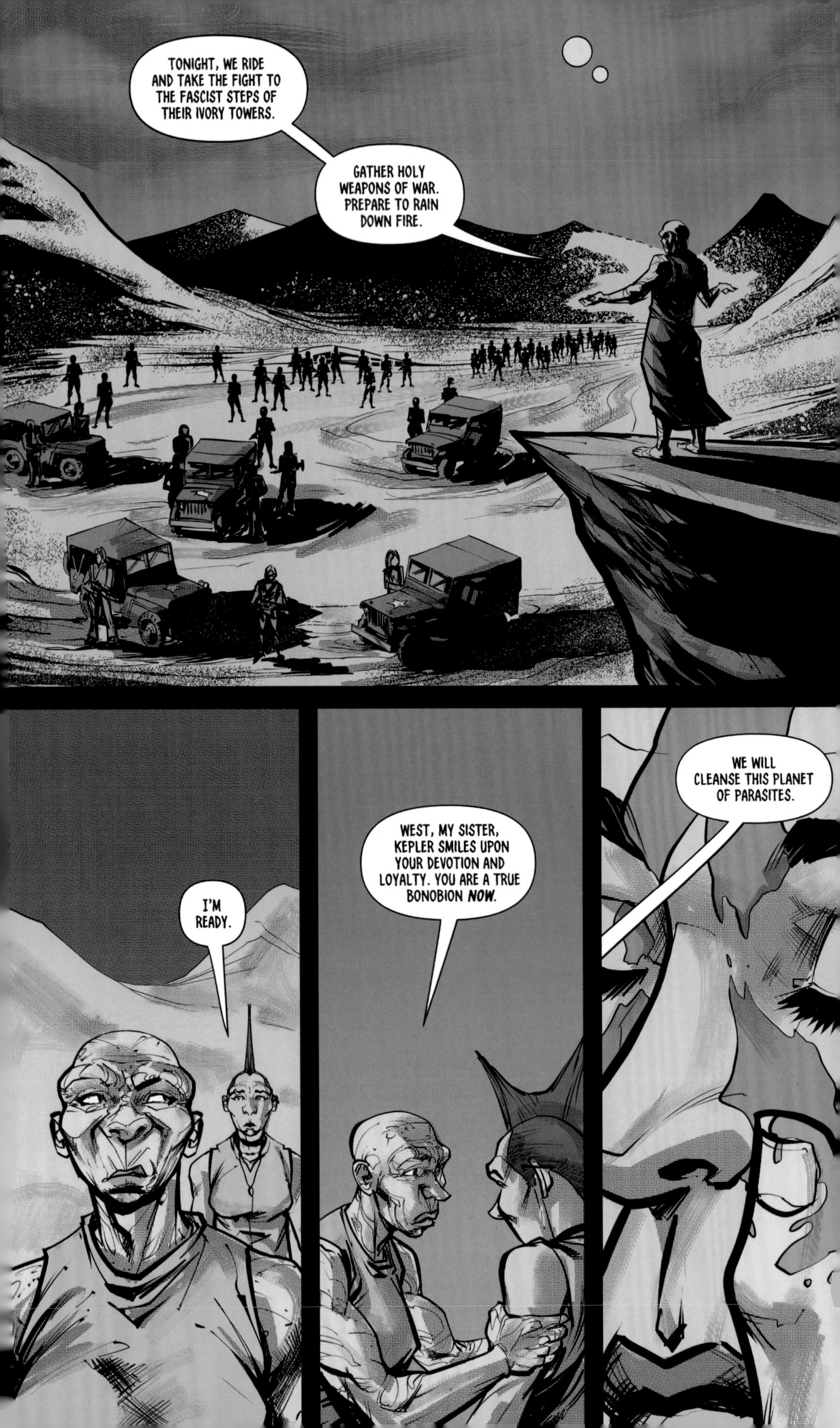
TONIGHT, WE RIDE AND TAKE THE FIGHT TO THE FASCIST STEPS OF THEIR IVORY TOWERS.
GATHER HOLY WEAPONS OF WAR. PREPARE TO RAIN DOWN FIRE.
I'M READY.
WEST, MY SISTER, KEPLER SMILES UPON YOUR DEVOTION AND LOYALTY. YOU ARE A TRUE BONOBION *NOW*.
WE WILL CLEANSE THIS PLANET OF PARASITES.

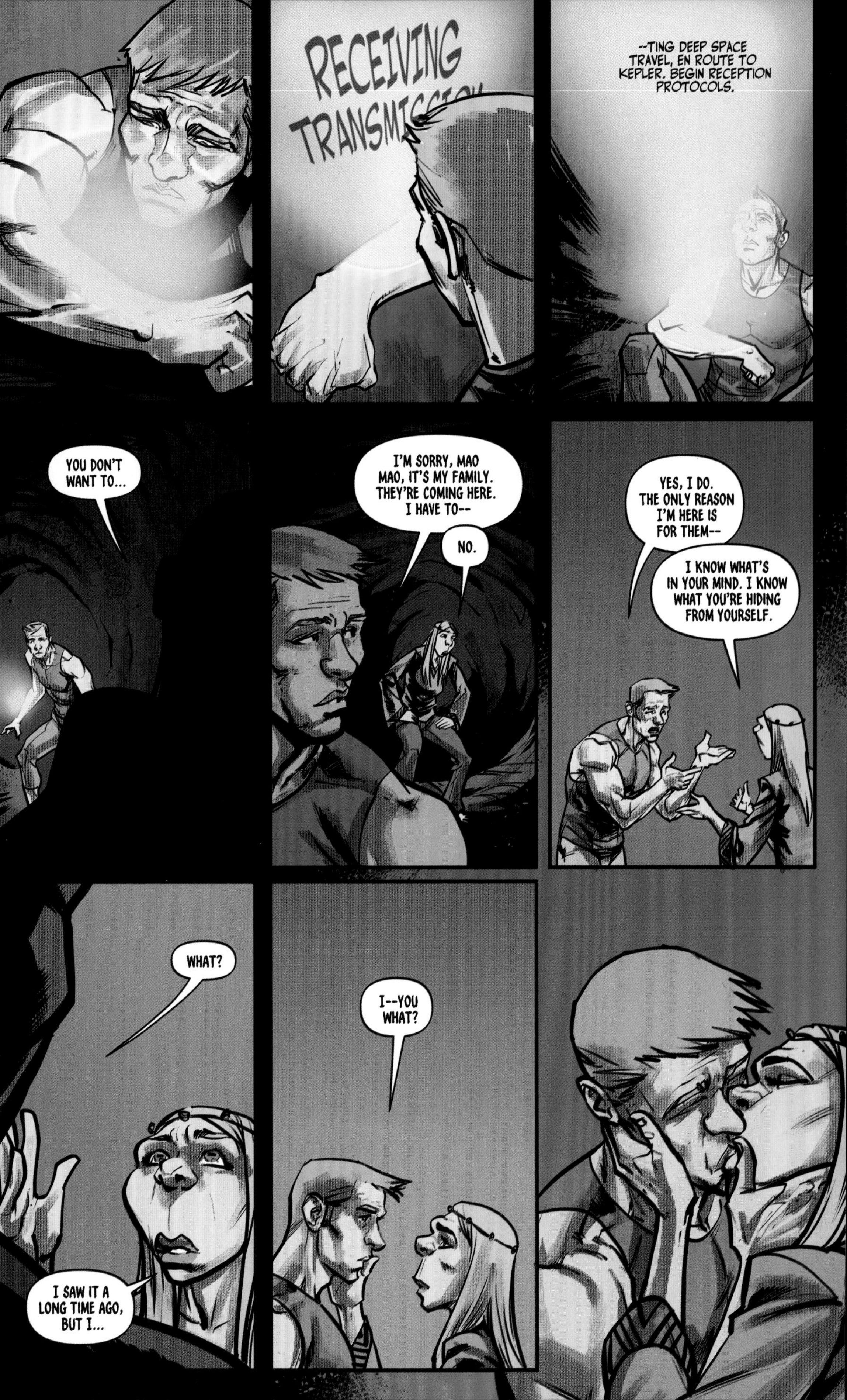
RECEIVING TRANSMISSION
--TING DEEP SPACE TRAVEL, EN ROUTE TO KEPLER. BEGIN RECEPTION PROTOCOLS.
YOU DON'T WANT TO...
I'M SORRY, MAO MAO, IT'S MY FAMILY. THEY'RE COMING HERE. I HAVE TO--
NO.
YES, I DO. THE ONLY REASON I'M HERE IS FOR THEM--
I KNOW WHAT'S IN YOUR MIND. I KNOW WHAT YOU'RE HIDING FROM YOURSELF.
WHAT?
I SAW IT A LONG TIME AGO, BUT I...
I--YOU WHAT?

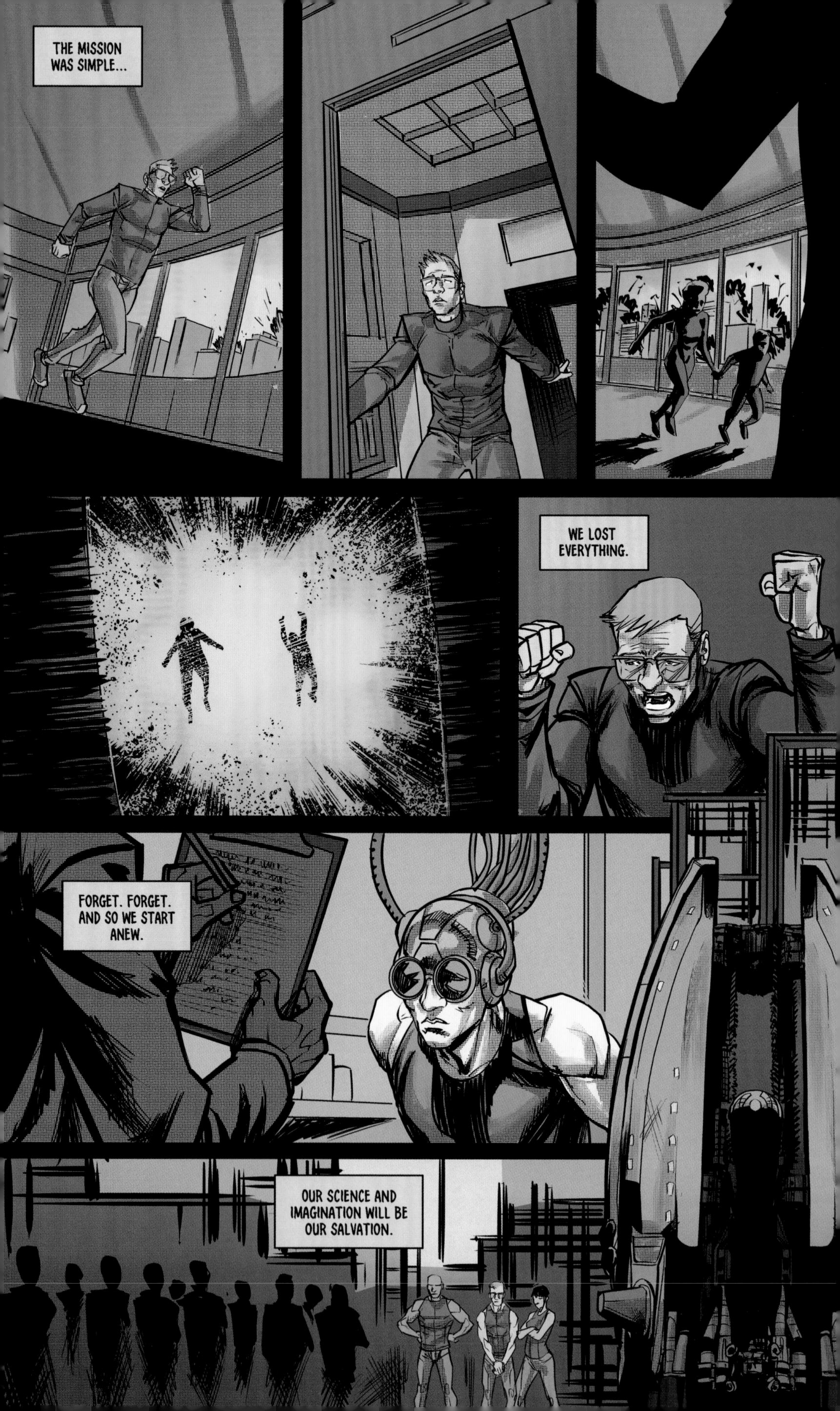
THE MISSION WAS SIMPLE...
WE LOST EVERYTHING.
FORGET. FORGET. AND SO WE START ANEW.
OUR SCIENCE AND IMAGINATION WILL BE OUR SALVATION.

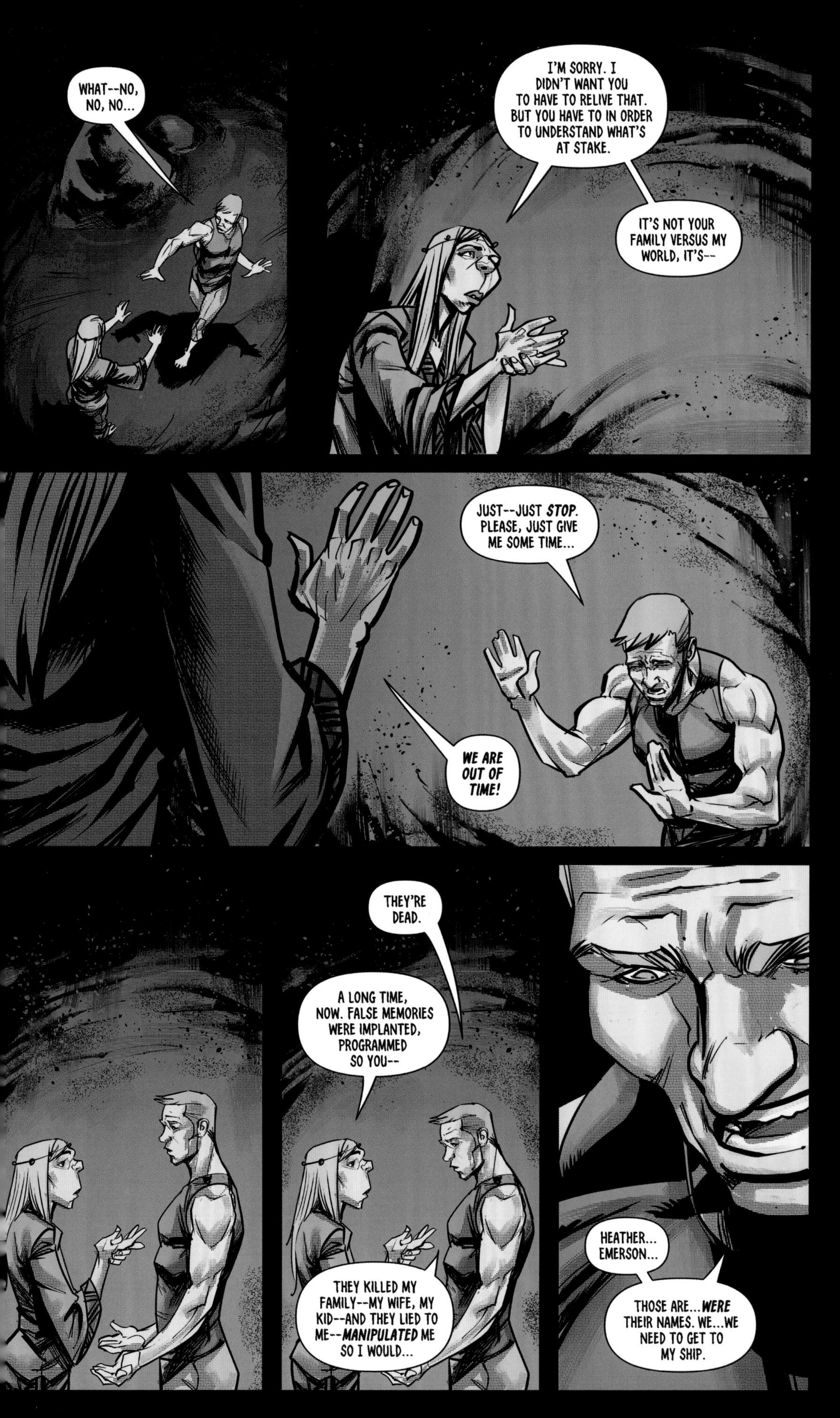
WHAT--NO, NO, NO...
I'M SORRY. I DIDN'T WANT YOU TO HAVE TO RELIVE THAT. BUT YOU HAVE TO IN ORDER TO UNDERSTAND WHAT'S AT STAKE.
IT'S NOT YOUR FAMILY VERSUS MY WORLD, IT'S--
JUST--JUST STOP. PLEASE, JUST GIVE ME SOME TIME...
WE ARE OUT OF TIME!
THEY'RE DEAD.
A LONG TIME, NOW. FALSE MEMORIES WERE IMPLANTED, PROGRAMMED SO YOU--
THEY KILLED MY FAMILY--MY WIFE, MY KID--AND THEY LIED TO ME--MANIPULATED ME SO I WOULD...
HEATHER... EMERSON...
THOSE ARE...WERE THEIR NAMES. WE...WE NEED TO GET TO MY SHIP.

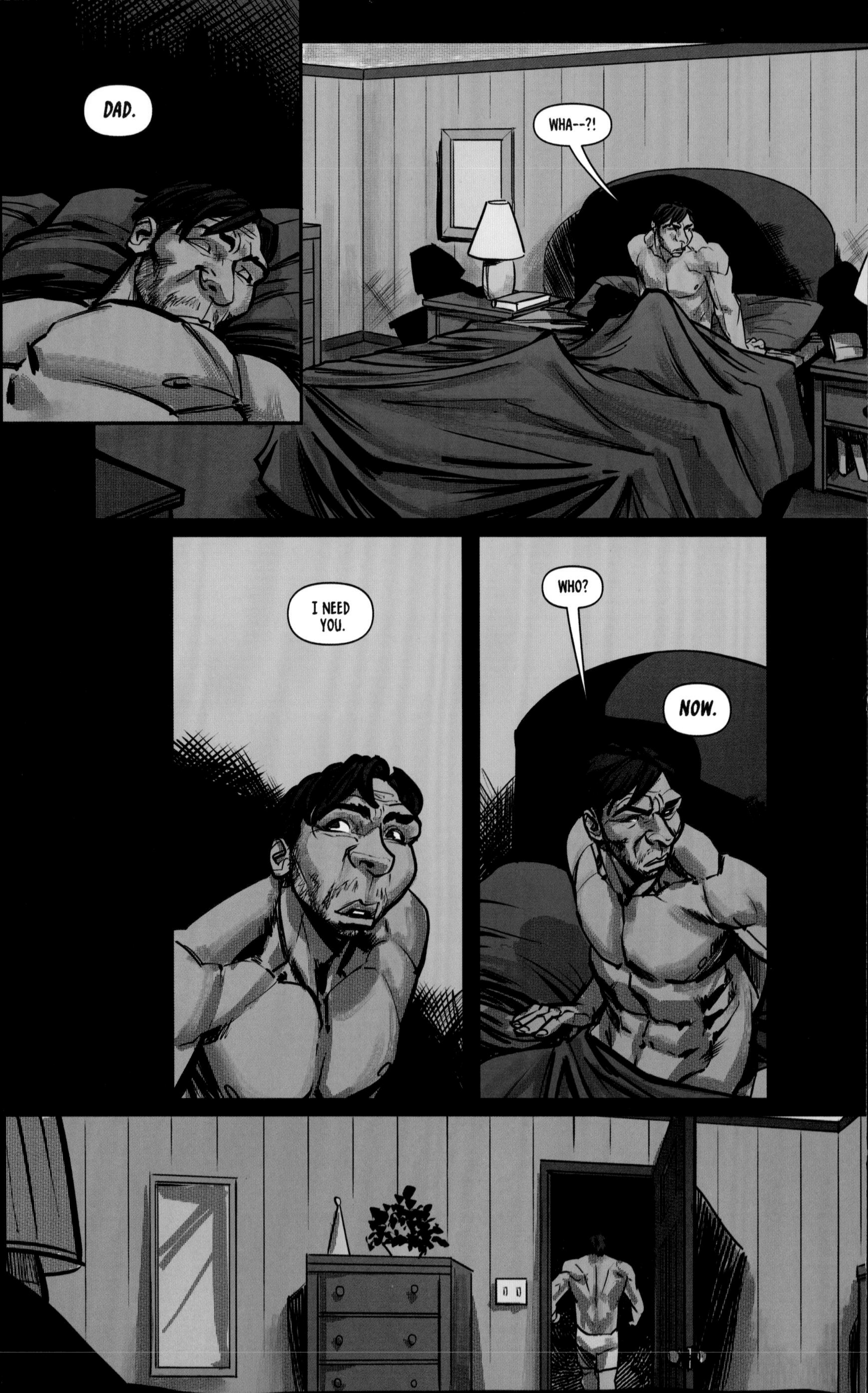
DAD.
WHA--?!
I NEED YOU.
WHO?
NOW.

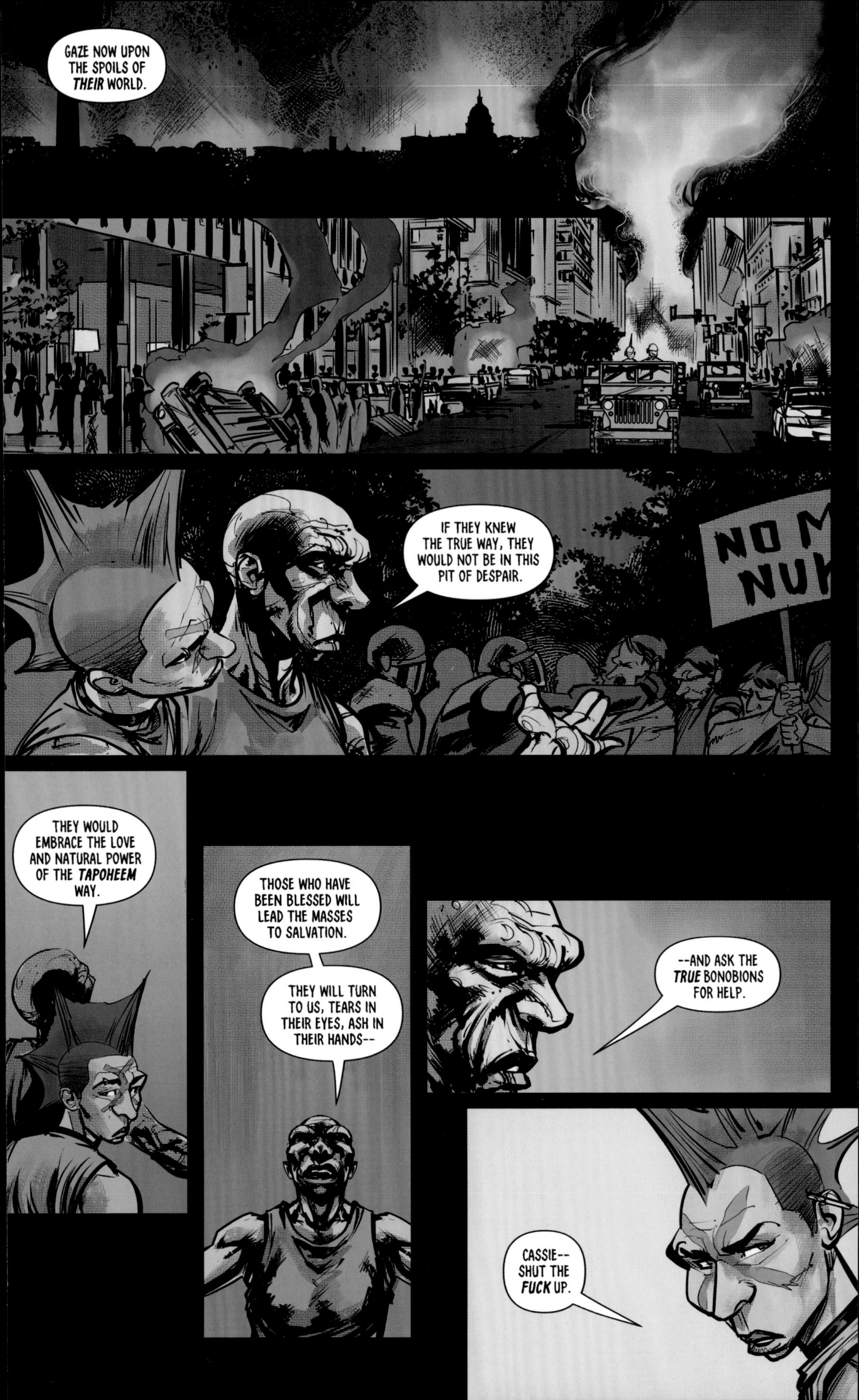
GAZE NOW UPON THE SPOILS OF *THEIR* WORLD.
IF THEY KNEW THE TRUE WAY, THEY WOULD NOT BE IN THIS PIT OF DESPAIR.
NO M
NUK
THEY WOULD EMBRACE THE LOVE AND NATURAL POWER OF THE *TAPOHEEM* WAY.
THOSE WHO HAVE BEEN BLESSED WILL LEAD THE MASSES TO SALVATION.
THEY WILL TURN TO US, TEARS IN THEIR EYES, ASH IN THEIR HANDS--
--AND ASK THE *TRUE* BONOBIONS FOR HELP.
CASSIE-- SHUT THE *FUCK* UP.

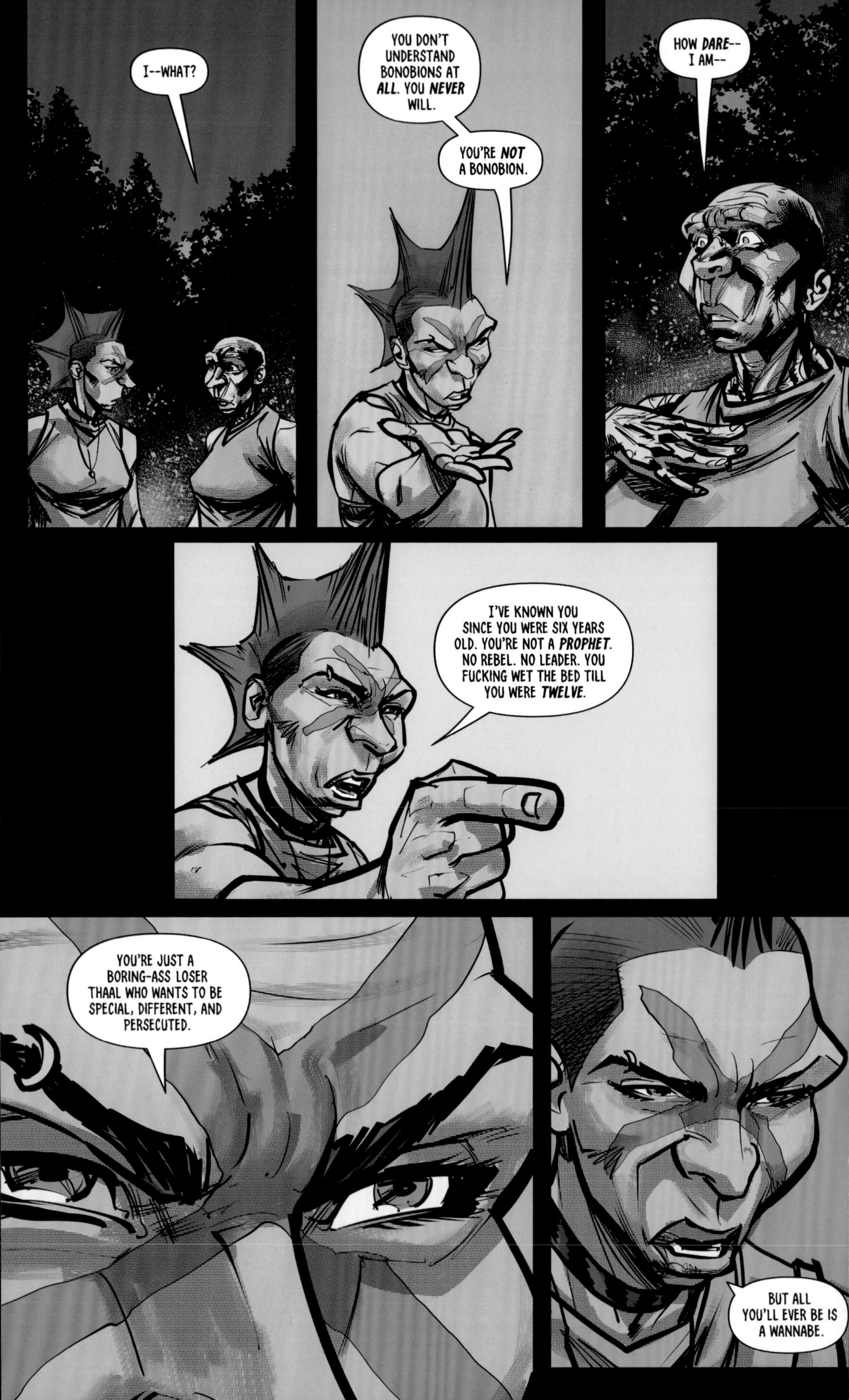
I--WHAT?
YOU DON'T UNDERSTAND BONOBIONS AT ALL. YOU NEVER WILL.
YOU'RE NOT A BONOBION.
HOW DARE-- I AM--
I'VE KNOWN YOU SINCE YOU WERE SIX YEARS OLD. YOU'RE NOT A PROPHET. NO REBEL. NO LEADER. YOU FUCKING WET THE BED TILL YOU WERE TWELVE.
YOU'RE JUST A BORING-ASS LOSER THAAL WHO WANTS TO BE SPECIAL, DIFFERENT, AND PERSECUTED.
BUT ALL YOU'LL EVER BE IS A WANNABE.

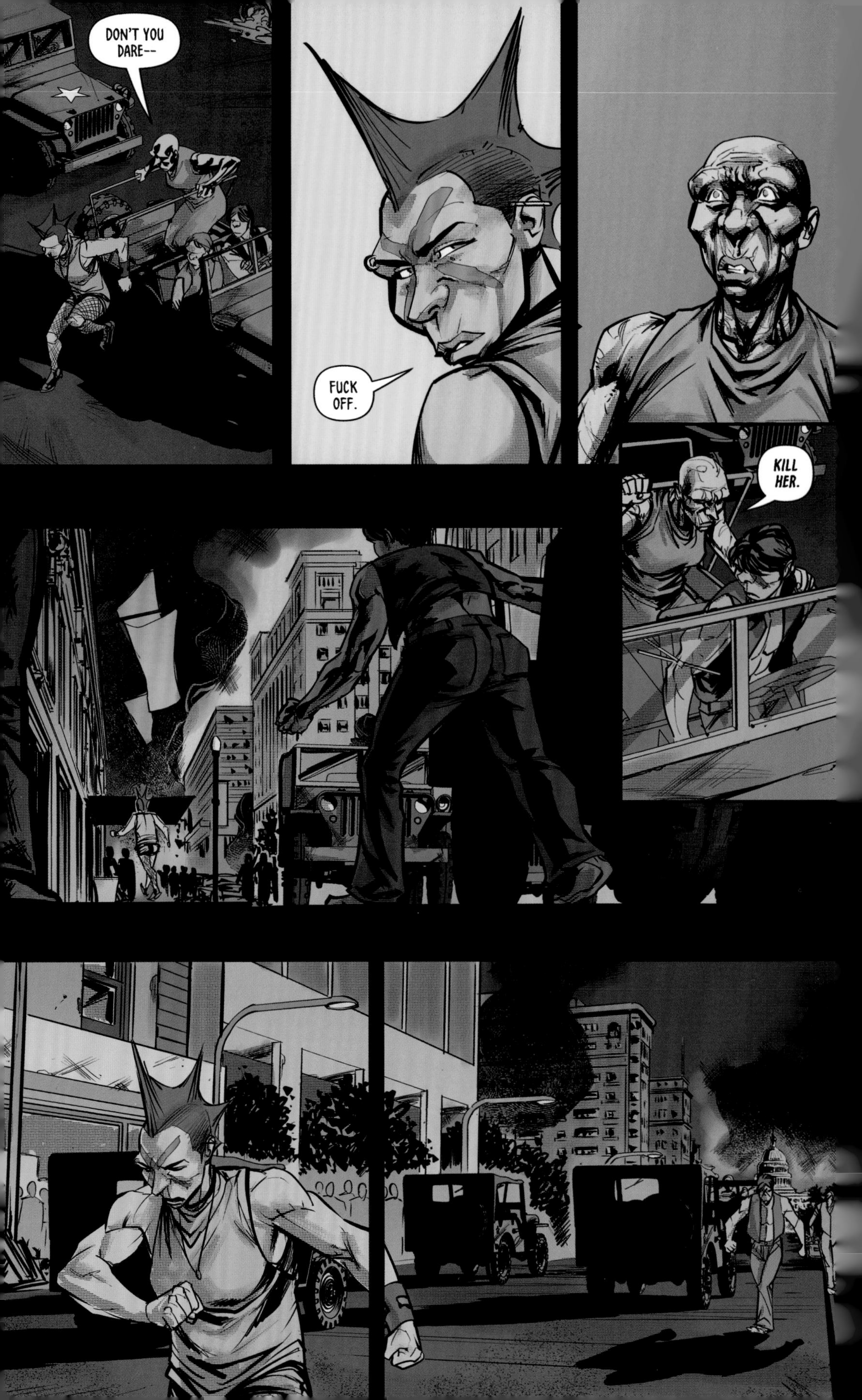
DON'T YOU DARE--
FUCK OFF.
KILL HER.

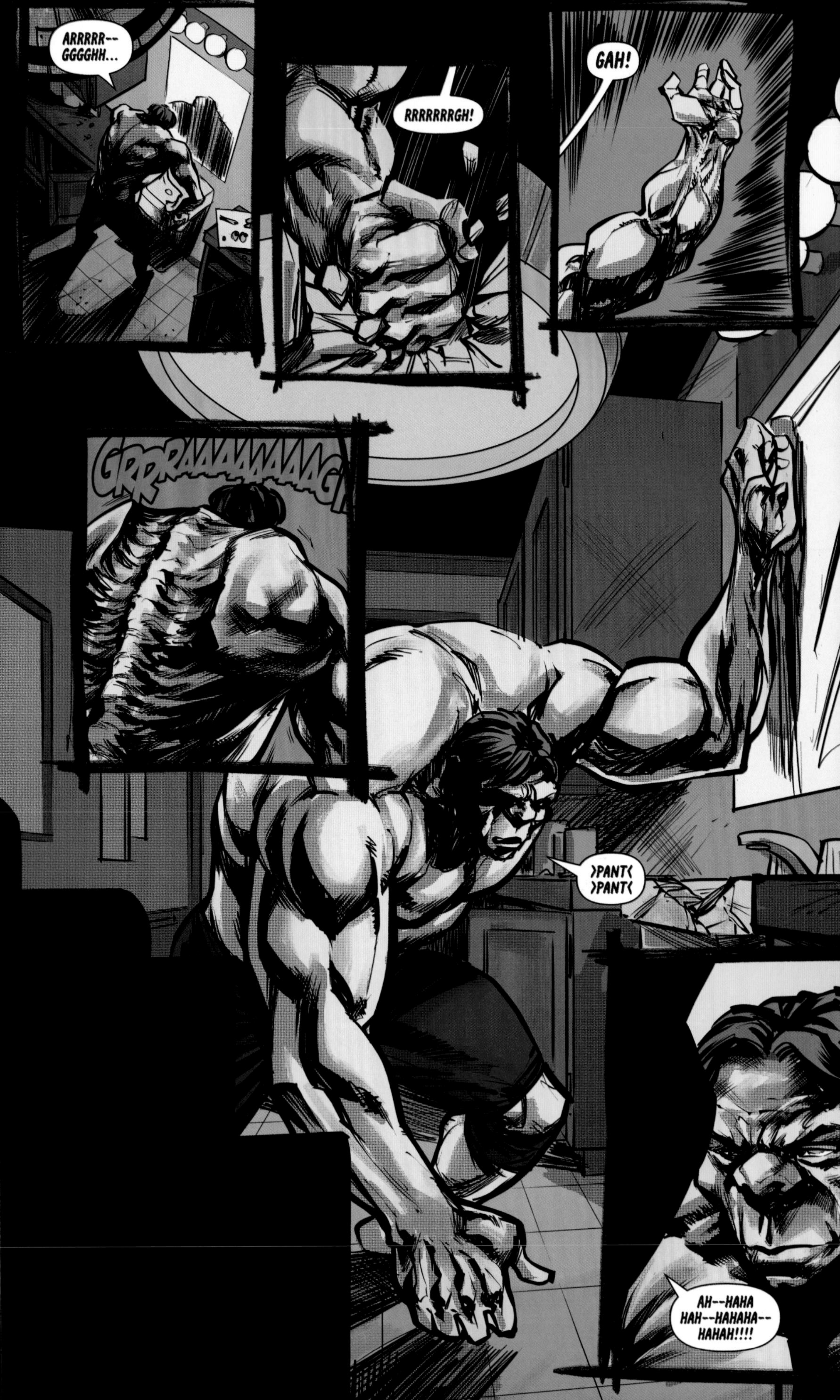
ARRRRR--
GGGGHH...
RRRRRRRGH!
GAH!
GRRRAAAAAAAAG!
›PANT‹
›PANT‹
AH--HAHA
HAH--HAHAHA--
HAHAH!!!!

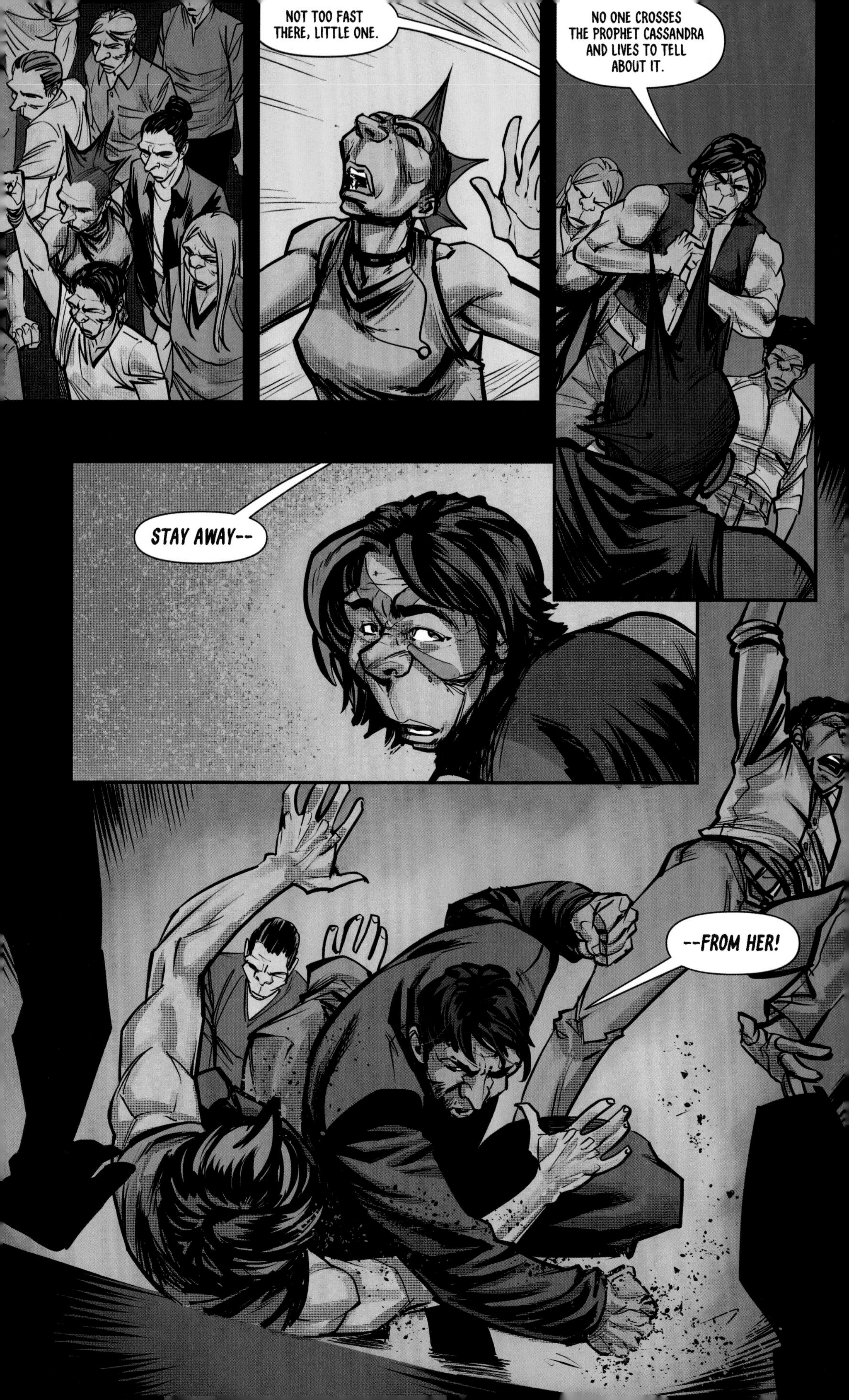
NOT TOO FAST THERE, LITTLE ONE.
NO ONE CROSSES THE PROPHET CASSANDRA AND LIVES TO TELL ABOUT IT.
STAY AWAY--
--FROM HER!

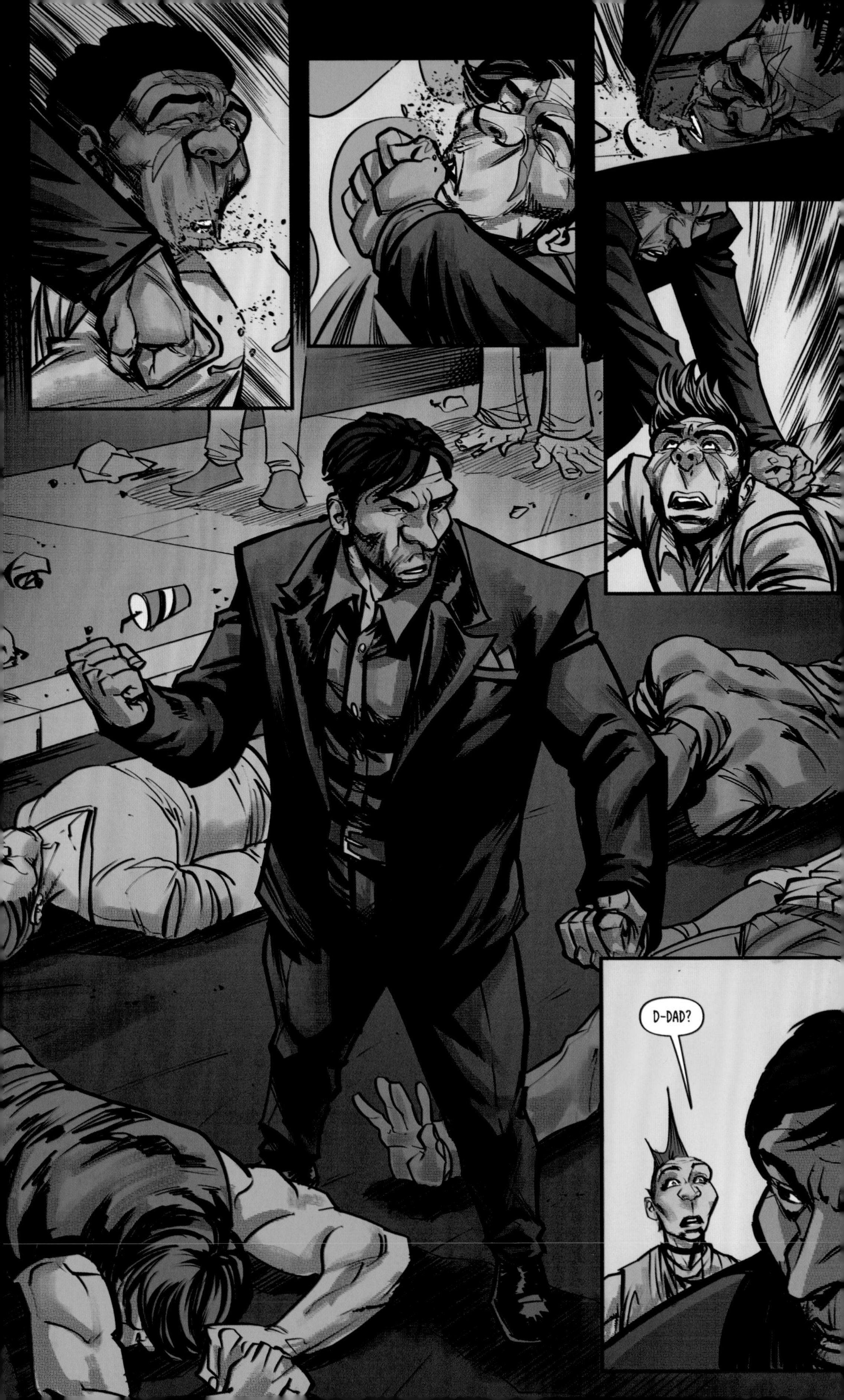
D-DAD?

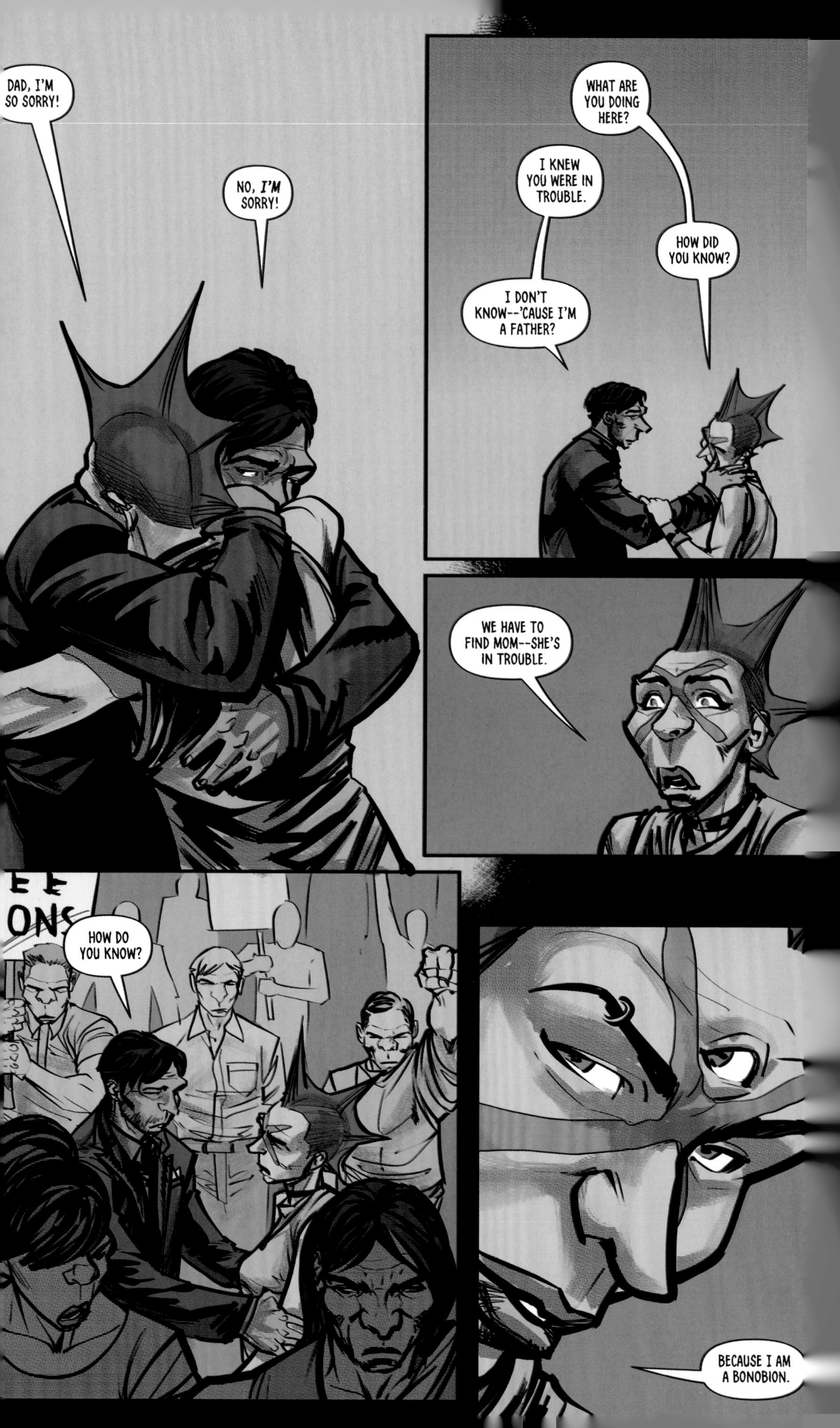
DAD, I'M SO SORRY!
NO, *I'M* SORRY!
WHAT ARE YOU DOING HERE?
I KNEW YOU WERE IN TROUBLE.
HOW DID YOU KNOW?
I DON'T KNOW--'CAUSE I'M A FATHER?
WE HAVE TO FIND MOM--SHE'S IN TROUBLE.
HOW DO YOU KNOW?
BECAUSE I AM A BONOBION.

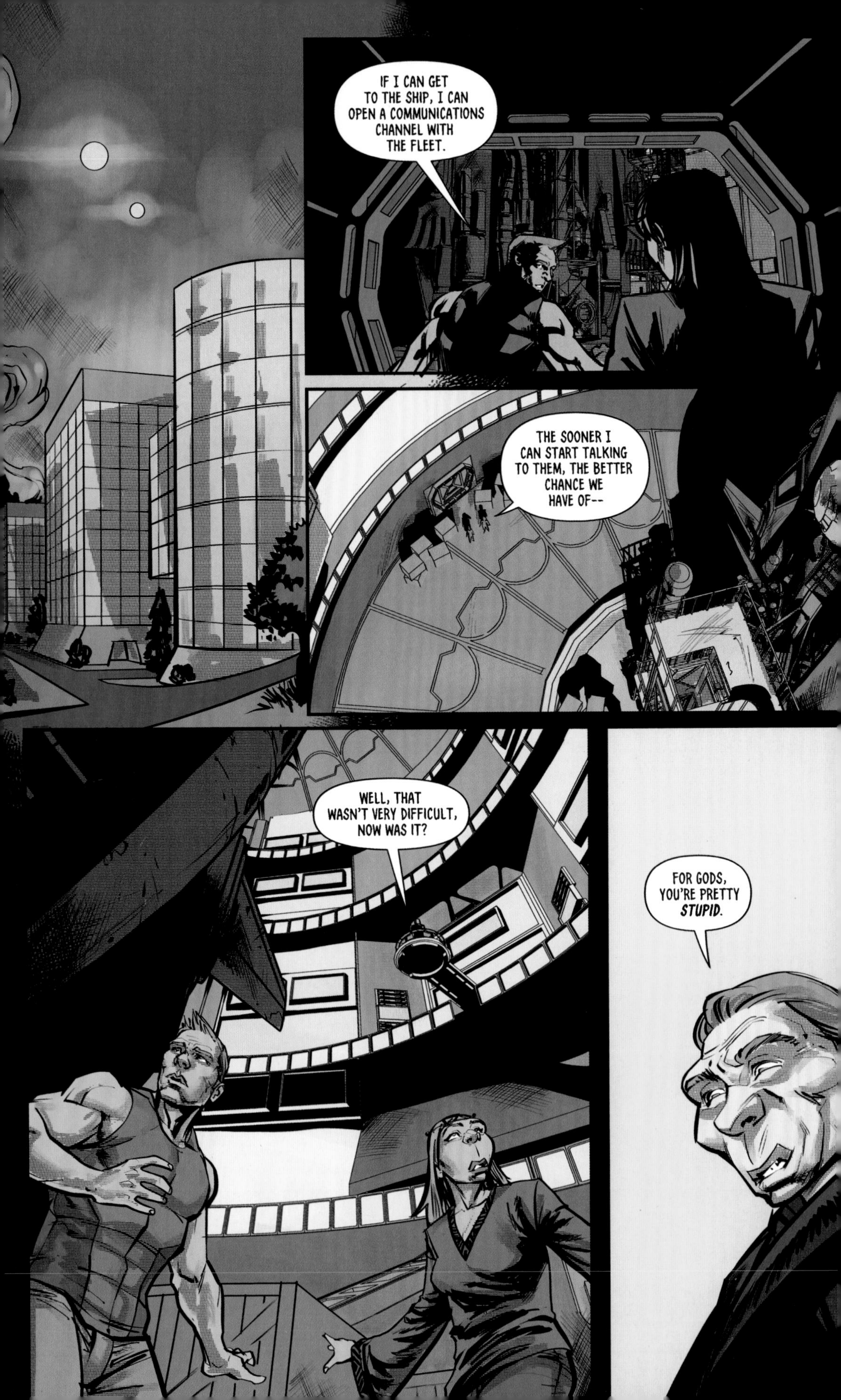
IF I CAN GET TO THE SHIP, I CAN OPEN A COMMUNICATIONS CHANNEL WITH THE FLEET.
THE SOONER I CAN START TALKING TO THEM, THE BETTER CHANCE WE HAVE OF--
WELL, THAT WASN'T VERY DIFFICULT, NOW WAS IT?
FOR GODS, YOU'RE PRETTY *STUPID*.

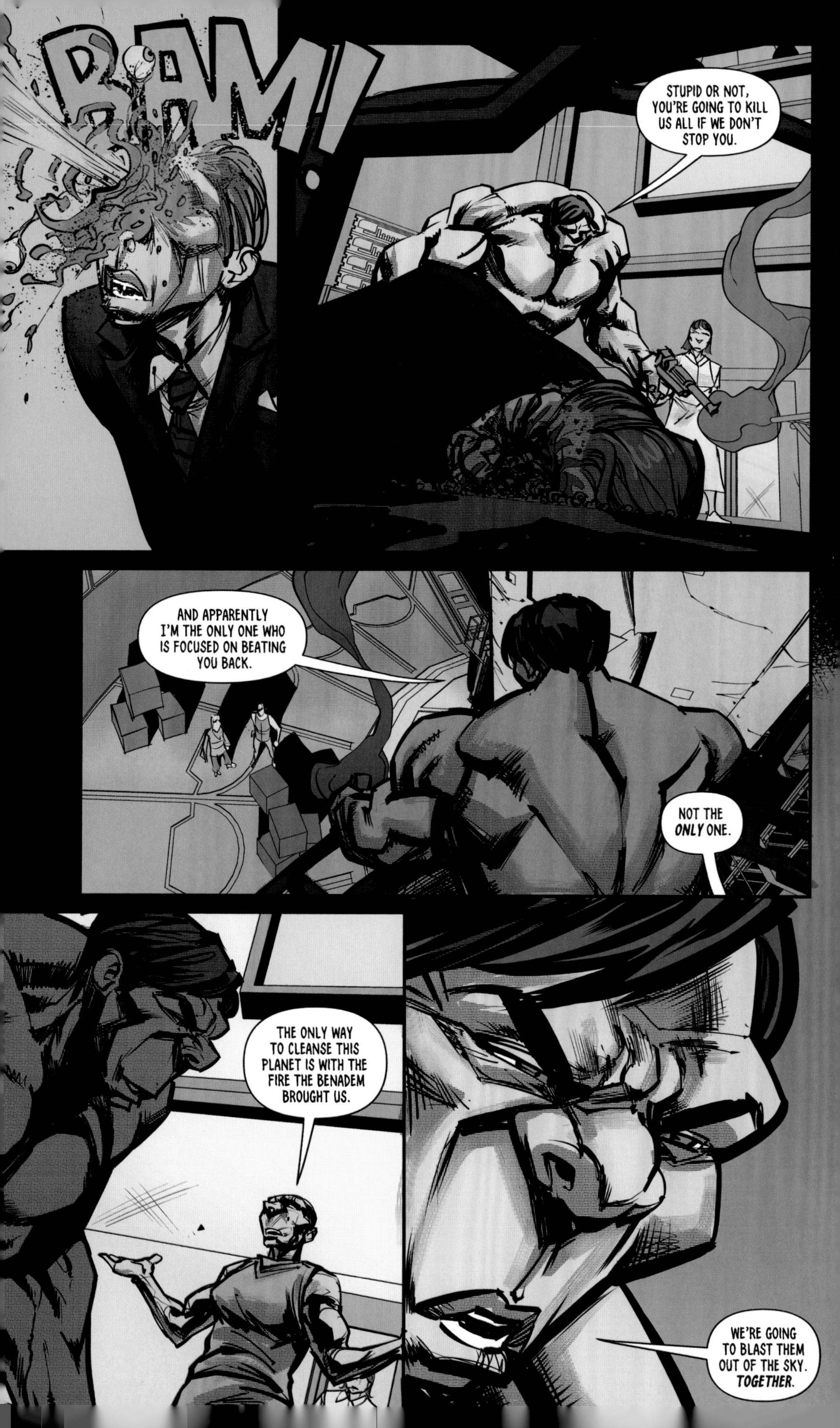
BAM!
STUPID OR NOT, YOU'RE GOING TO KILL US ALL IF WE DON'T STOP YOU.
AND APPARENTLY I'M THE ONLY ONE WHO IS FOCUSED ON BEATING YOU BACK.
NOT THE *ONLY* ONE.
THE ONLY WAY TO CLEANSE THIS PLANET IS WITH THE FIRE THE BENADEM BROUGHT US.
WE'RE GOING TO BLAST THEM OUT OF THE SKY. ***TOGETHER***.

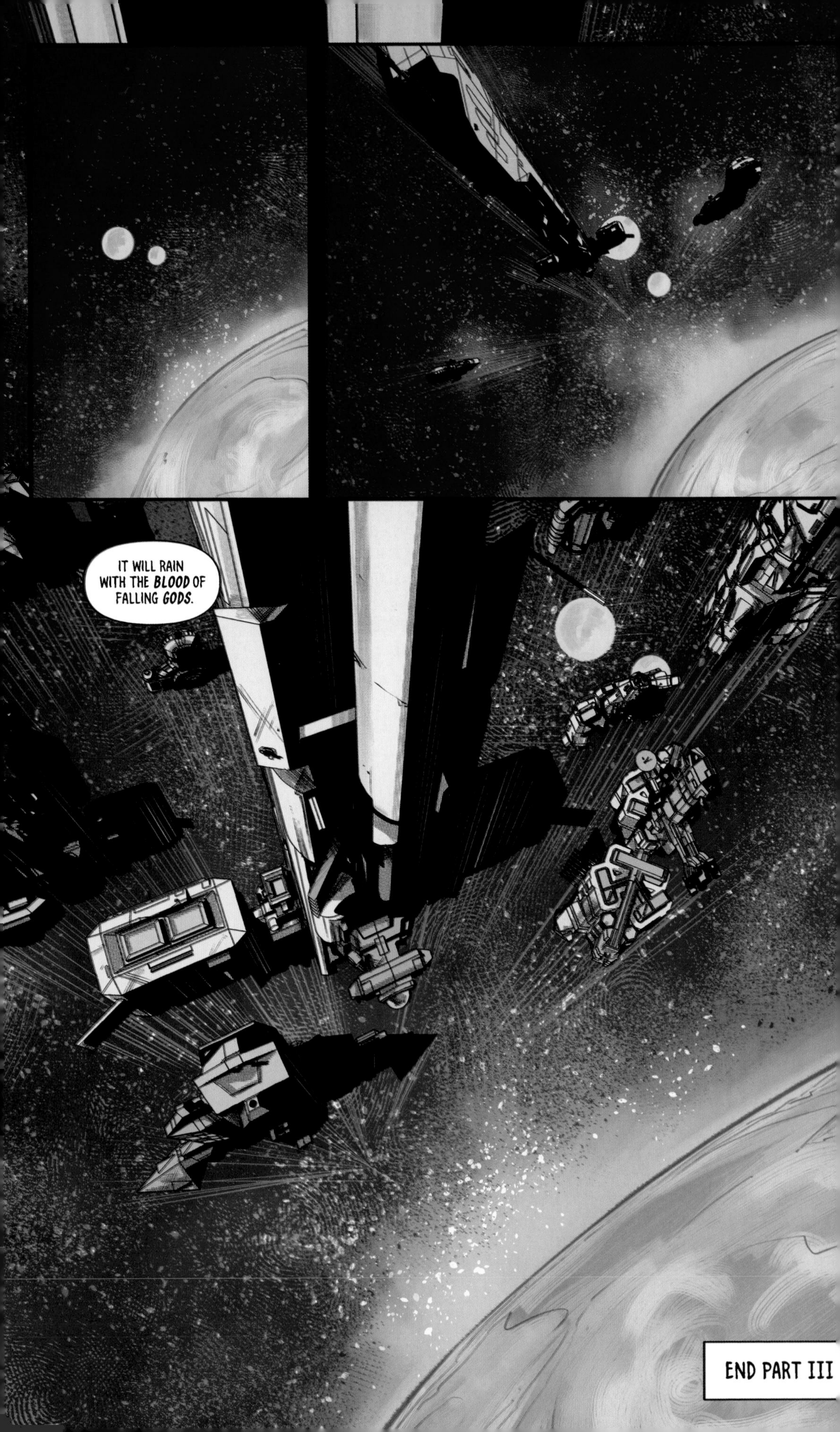
IT WILL RAIN WITH THE BLOOD OF FALLING GODS.
END PART III

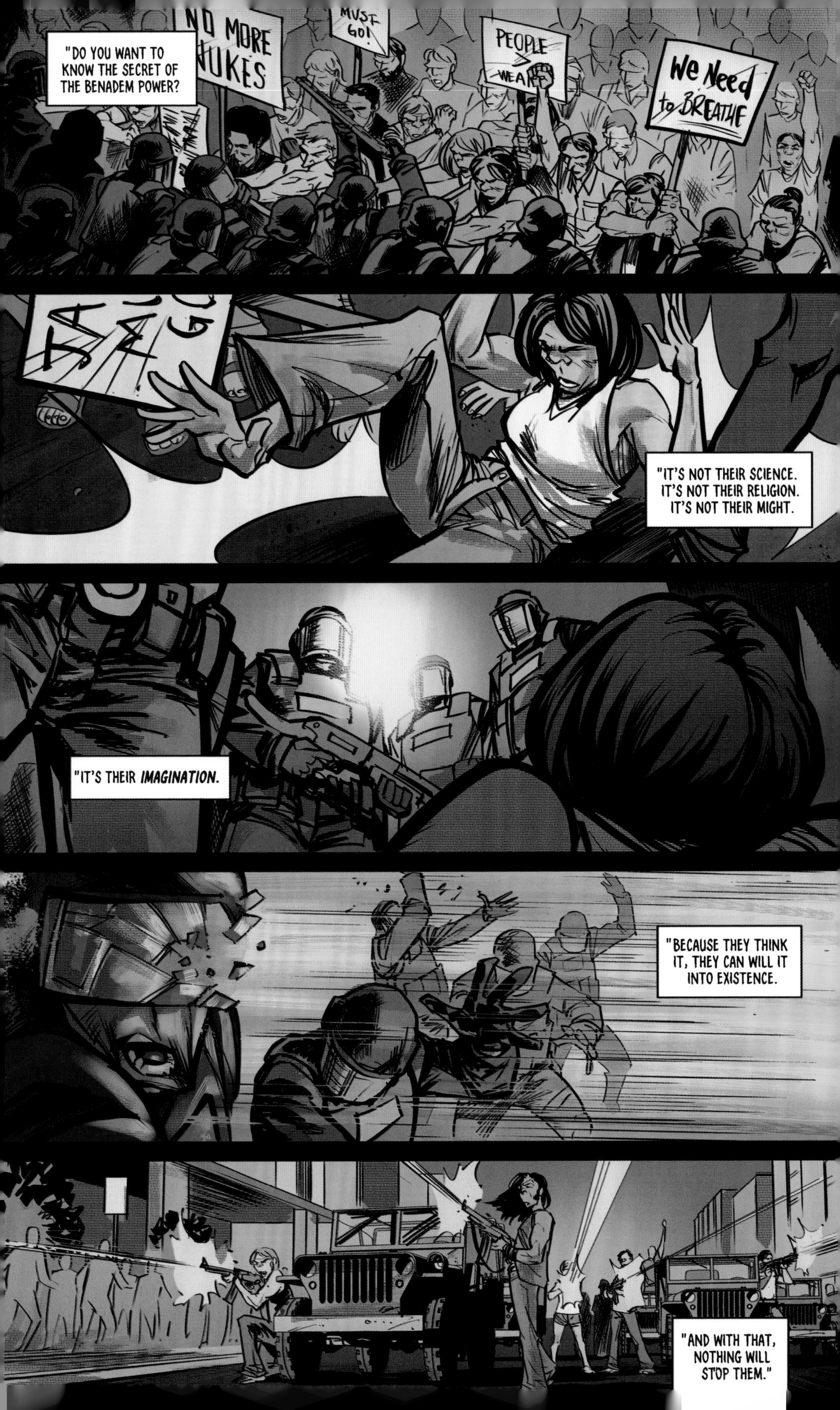
"DO YOU WANT TO KNOW THE SECRET OF THE BENADEM POWER?
NO MORE NUKES
MUST GO!
PEOPLE > WEA
We Need to BREATHE
"IT'S NOT THEIR SCIENCE. IT'S NOT THEIR RELIGION. IT'S NOT THEIR MIGHT.
"IT'S THEIR *IMAGINATION*.
"BECAUSE THEY THINK IT, THEY CAN WILL IT INTO EXISTENCE.
"AND WITH THAT, NOTHING WILL STOP THEM."

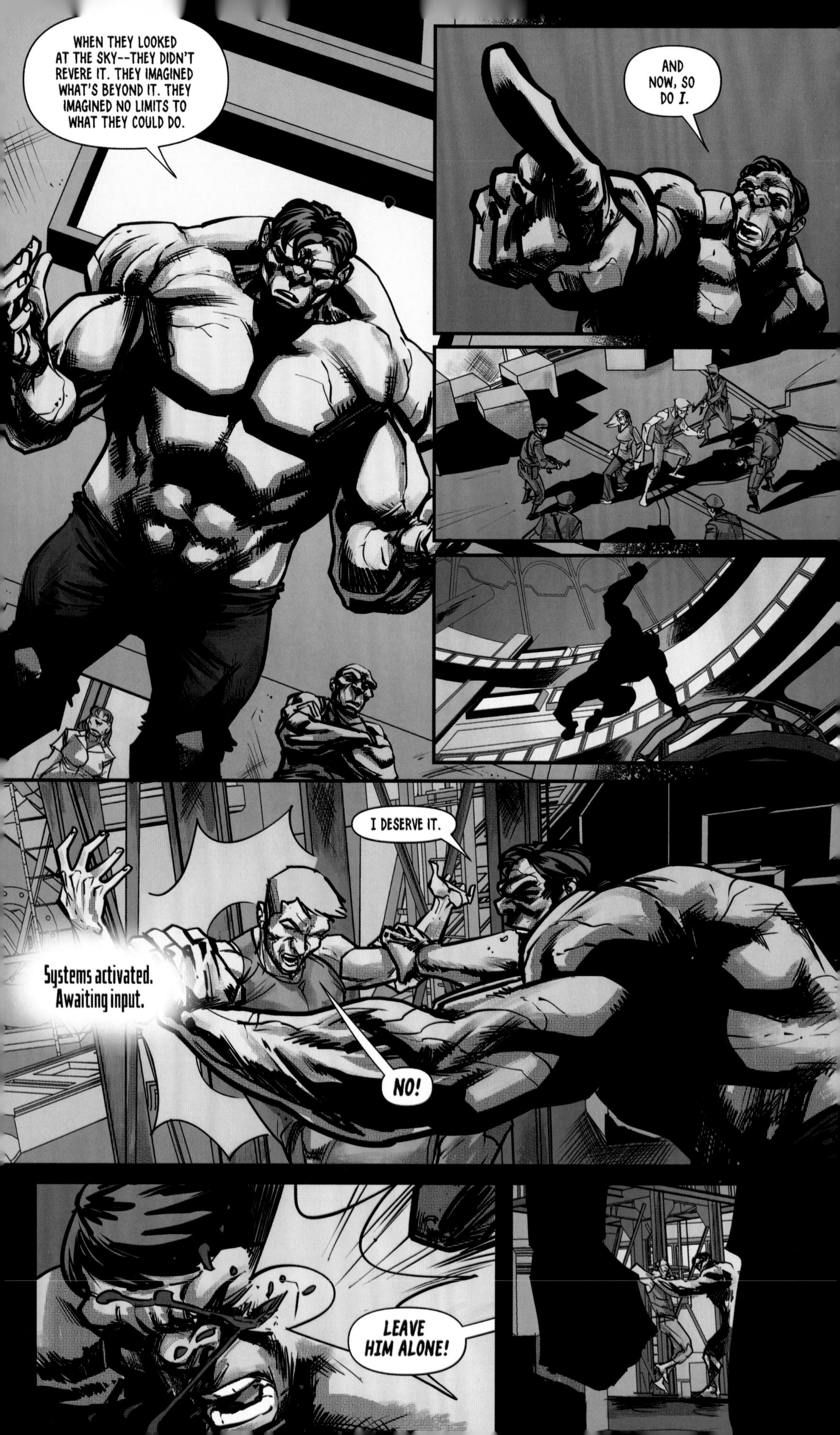
WHEN THEY LOOKED AT THE SKY--THEY DIDN'T REVERE IT. THEY IMAGINED WHAT'S BEYOND IT. THEY IMAGINED NO LIMITS TO WHAT THEY COULD DO.
AND NOW, SO DO *I*.
I DESERVE IT.
Systems activated. Awaiting input.
NO!
LEAVE HIM ALONE!

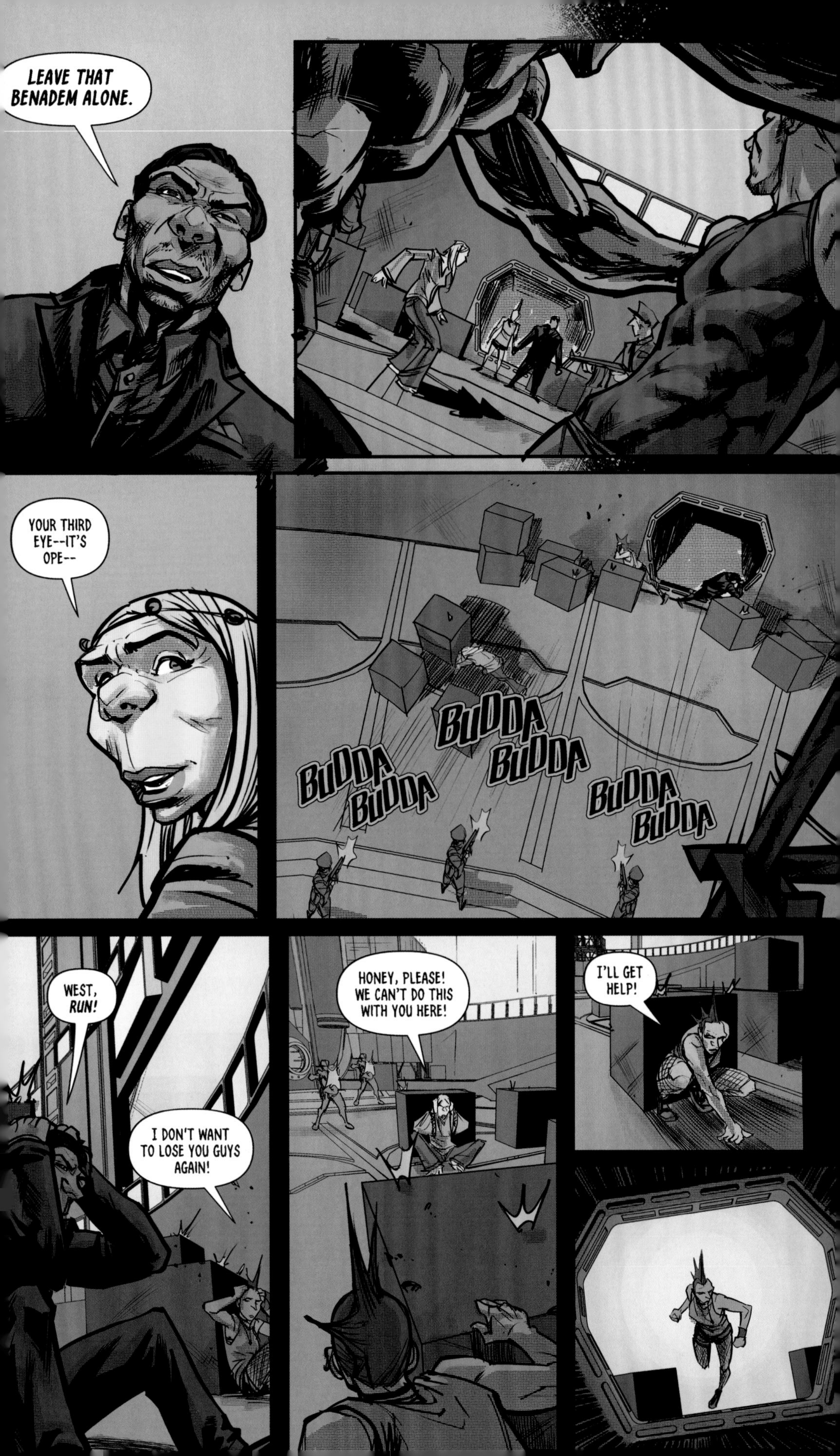
LEAVE THAT BENADEM ALONE.
YOUR THIRD EYE--IT'S OPE--
BUDDA BUDDA
BUDDA BUDDA
BUDDA BUDDA
WEST, RUN!
I DON'T WANT TO LOSE YOU GUYS AGAIN!
HONEY, PLEASE! WE CAN'T DO THIS WITH YOU HERE!
I'LL GET HELP!

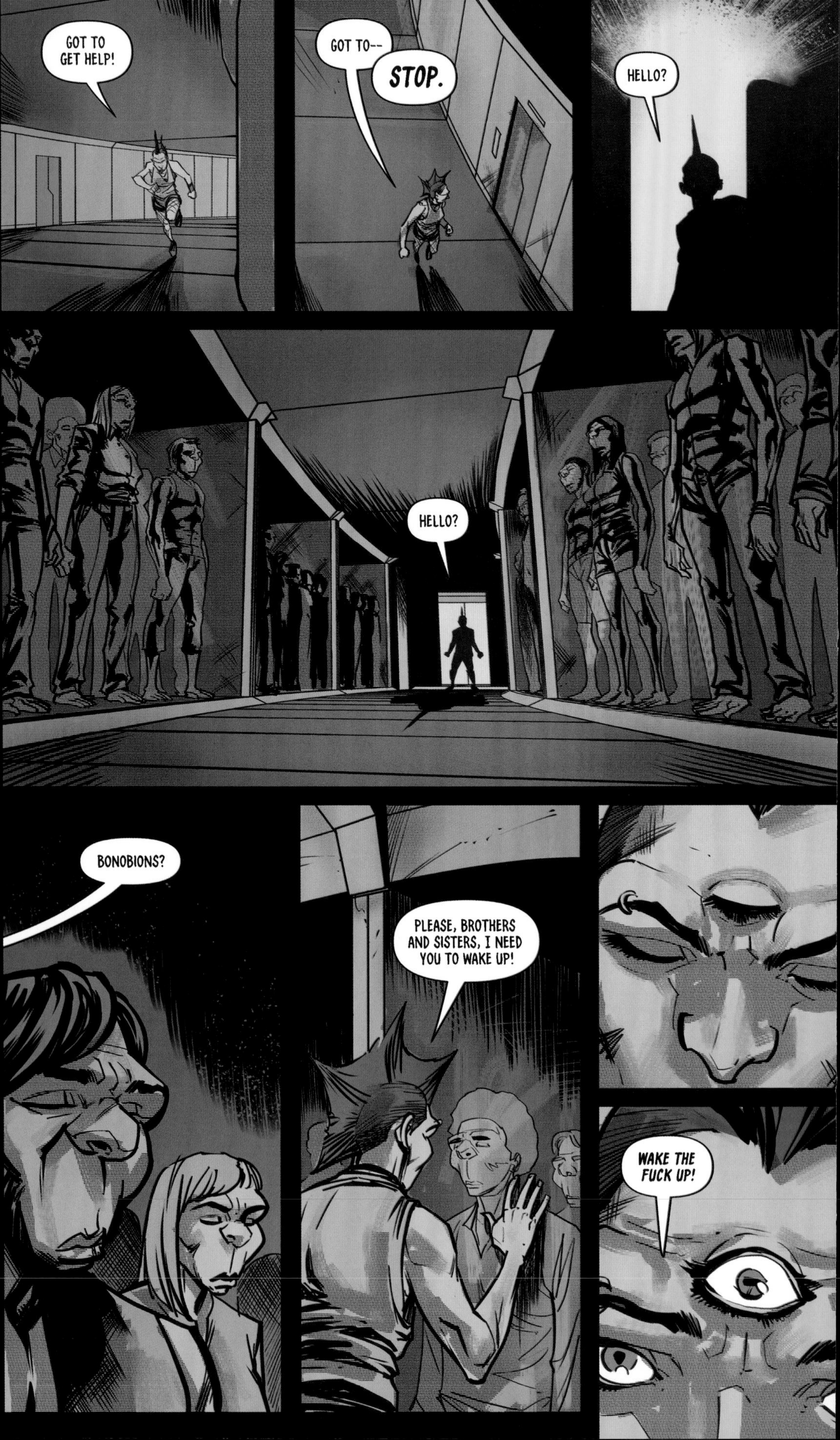

GOT TO GET HELP!
GOT TO--
STOP.
HELLO?
HELLO?
BONOBIONS?
PLEASE, BROTHERS AND SISTERS, I NEED YOU TO WAKE UP!
WAKE THE FUCK UP!

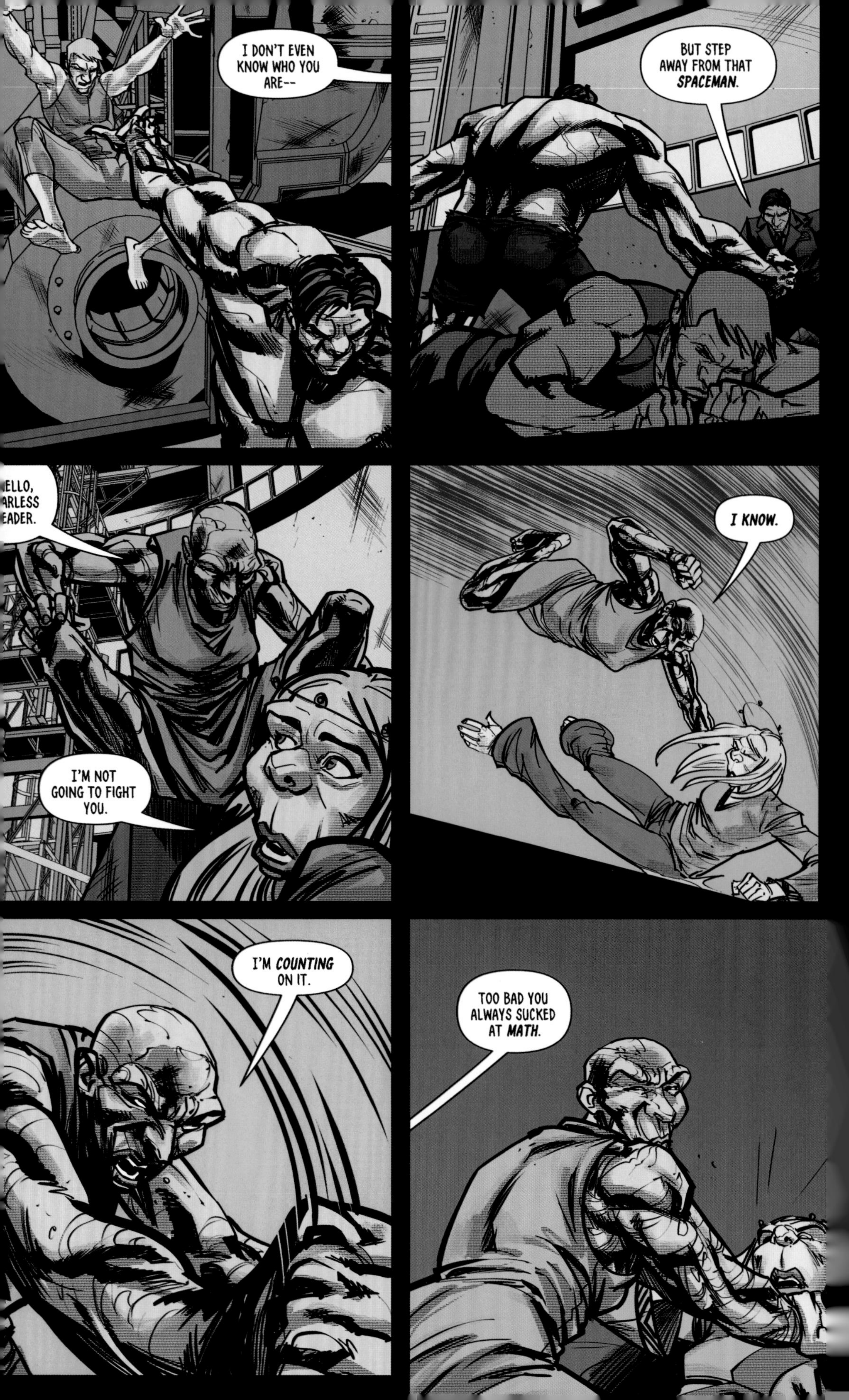
I DON'T EVEN KNOW WHO YOU ARE--
BUT STEP AWAY FROM THAT SPACEMAN.
ELLO, ARLESS EADER.
I'M NOT GOING TO FIGHT YOU.
I KNOW.
I'M COUNTING ON IT.
TOO BAD YOU ALWAYS SUCKED AT MATH.

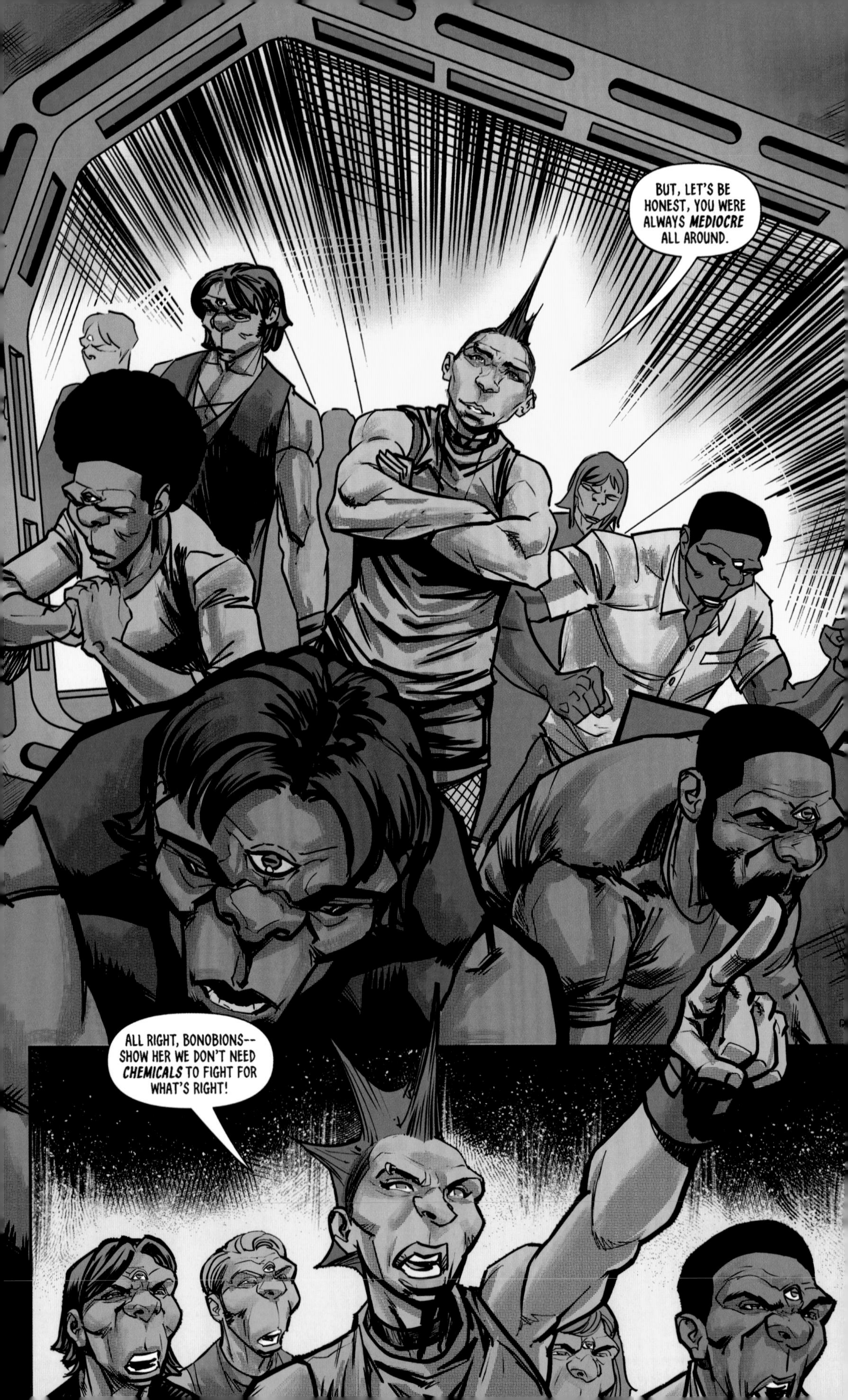
BUT, LET'S BE HONEST, YOU WERE ALWAYS MEDIOCRE ALL AROUND.
ALL RIGHT, BONOBIONS-- SHOW HER WE DON'T NEED CHEMICALS TO FIGHT FOR WHAT'S RIGHT!

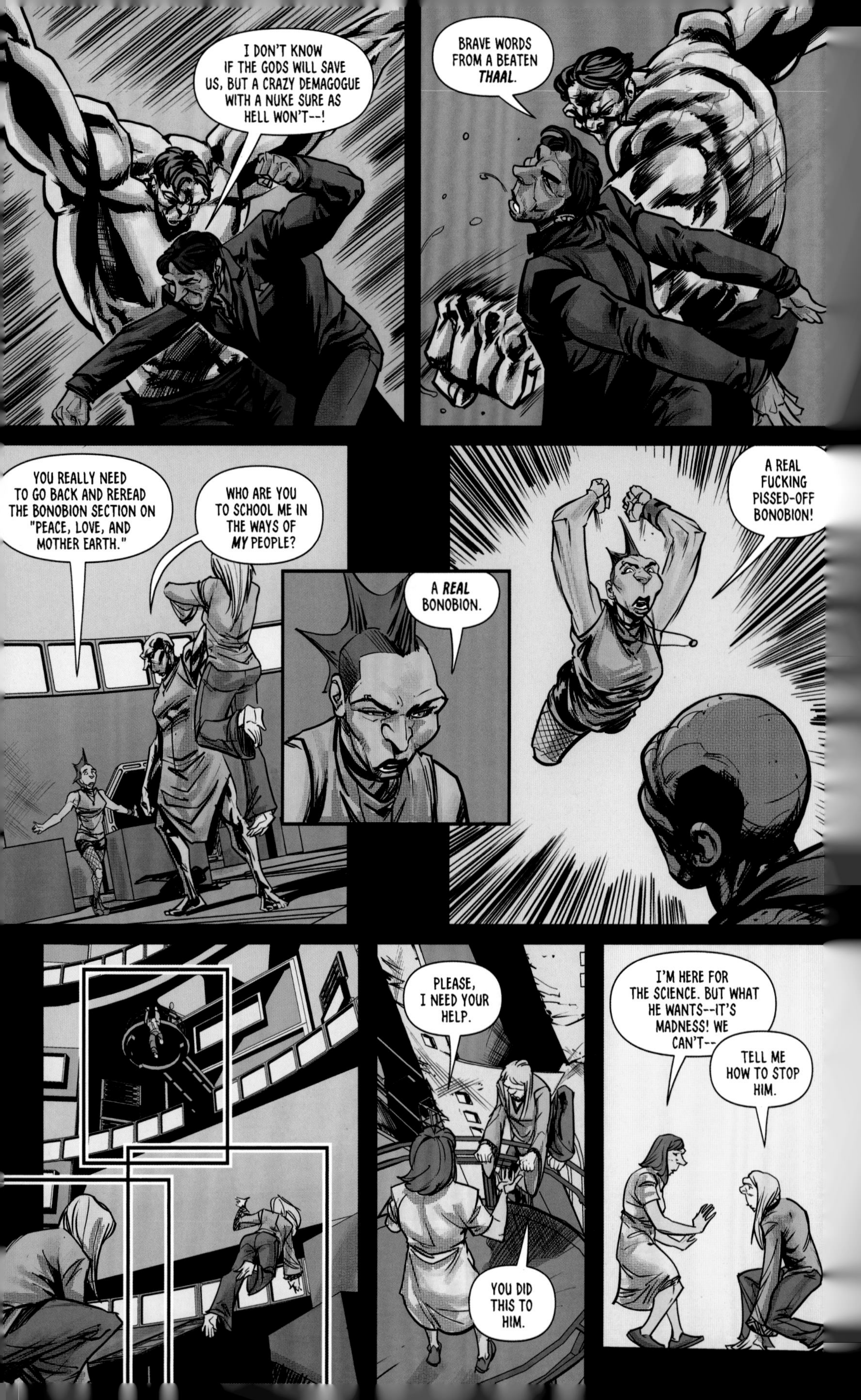
I DON'T KNOW IF THE GODS WILL SAVE US, BUT A CRAZY DEMAGOGUE WITH A NUKE SURE AS HELL WON'T--!
BRAVE WORDS FROM A BEATEN *THAAL*.
YOU REALLY NEED TO GO BACK AND REREAD THE BONOBION SECTION ON "PEACE, LOVE, AND MOTHER EARTH."
WHO ARE YOU TO SCHOOL ME IN THE WAYS OF *MY* PEOPLE?
A *REAL* BONOBION.
A REAL FUCKING PISSED-OFF BONOBION!
PLEASE, I NEED YOUR HELP.
YOU DID THIS TO HIM.
I'M HERE FOR THE SCIENCE. BUT WHAT HE WANTS--IT'S MADNESS! WE CAN'T--
TELL ME HOW TO STOP HIM.

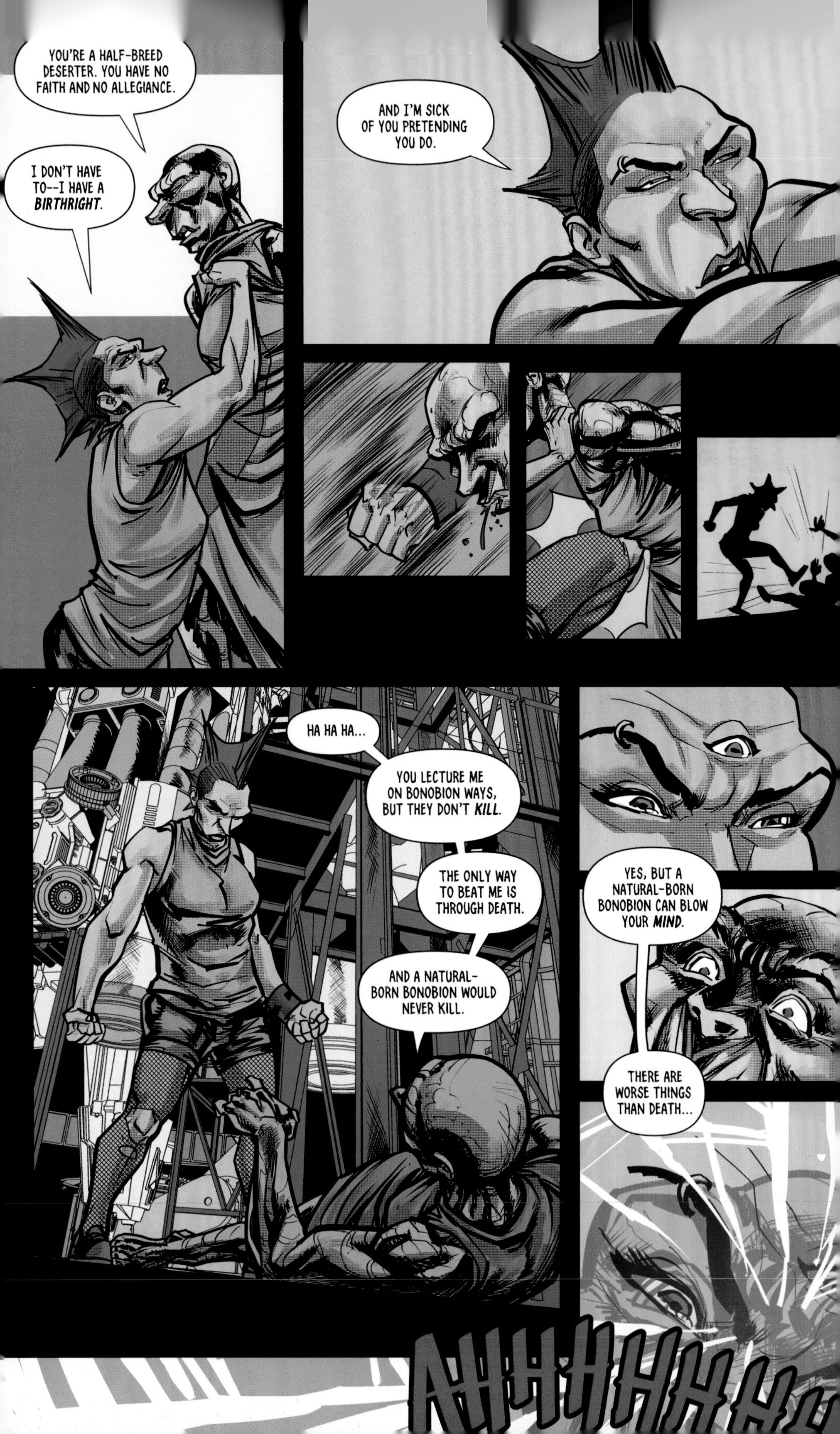

YOU'RE A HALF-BREED DESERTER. YOU HAVE NO FAITH AND NO ALLEGIANCE.
I DON'T HAVE TO--I HAVE A *BIRTHRIGHT*.
AND I'M SICK OF YOU PRETENDING YOU DO.
HA HA HA...
YOU LECTURE ME ON BONOBION WAYS, BUT THEY DON'T *KILL*.
THE ONLY WAY TO BEAT ME IS THROUGH DEATH.
AND A NATURAL-BORN BONOBION WOULD NEVER KILL.
YES, BUT A NATURAL-BORN BONOBION CAN BLOW YOUR *MIND*.
THERE ARE WORSE THINGS THAN DEATH...
AHHHHHHH

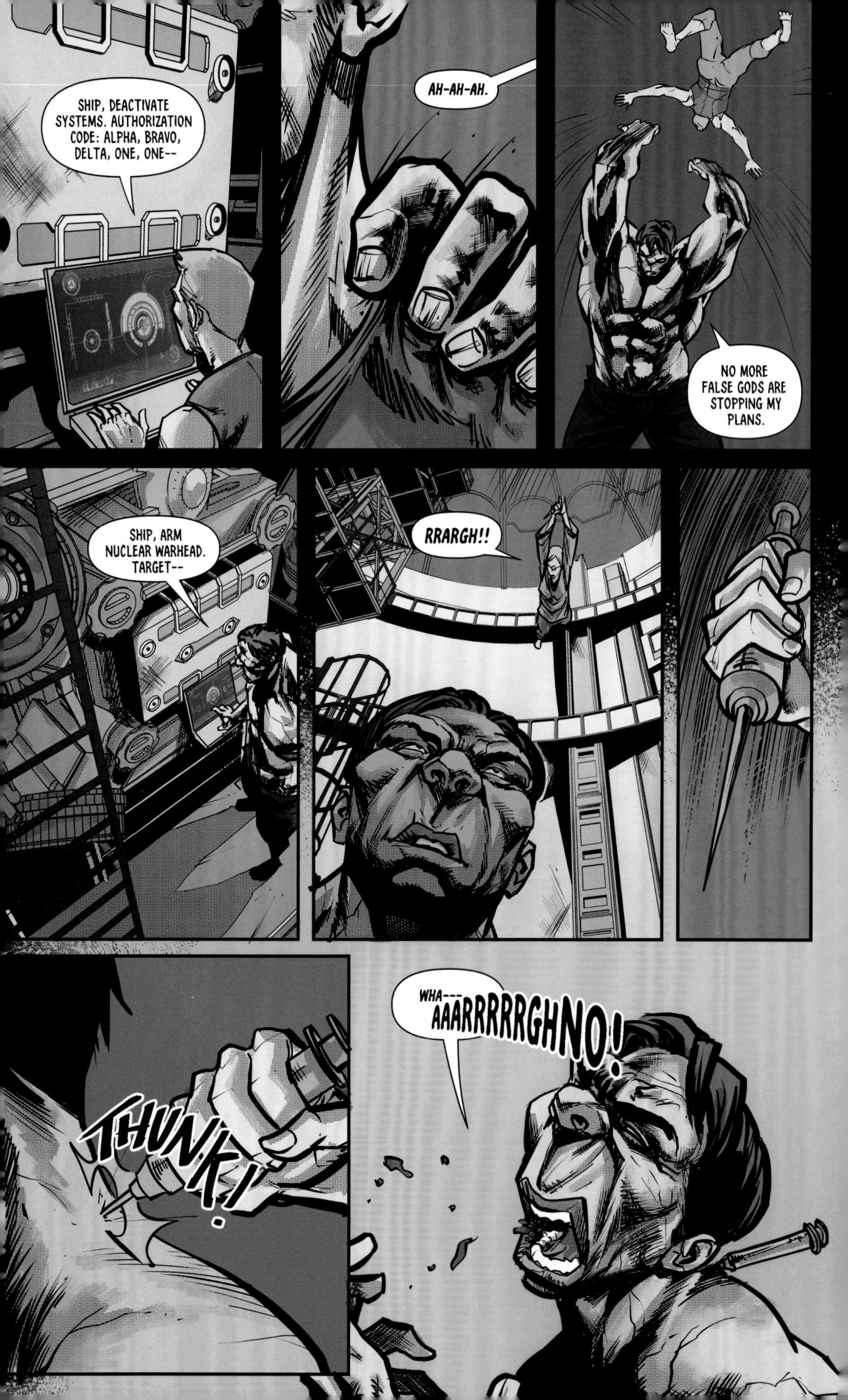
SHIP, DEACTIVATE SYSTEMS. AUTHORIZATION CODE: ALPHA, BRAVO, DELTA, ONE, ONE--
AH-AH-AH.
NO MORE FALSE GODS ARE STOPPING MY PLANS.
SHIP, ARM NUCLEAR WARHEAD. TARGET--
RRARGH!!
THUNK!
WHA---
AAARRRRRGHNO!

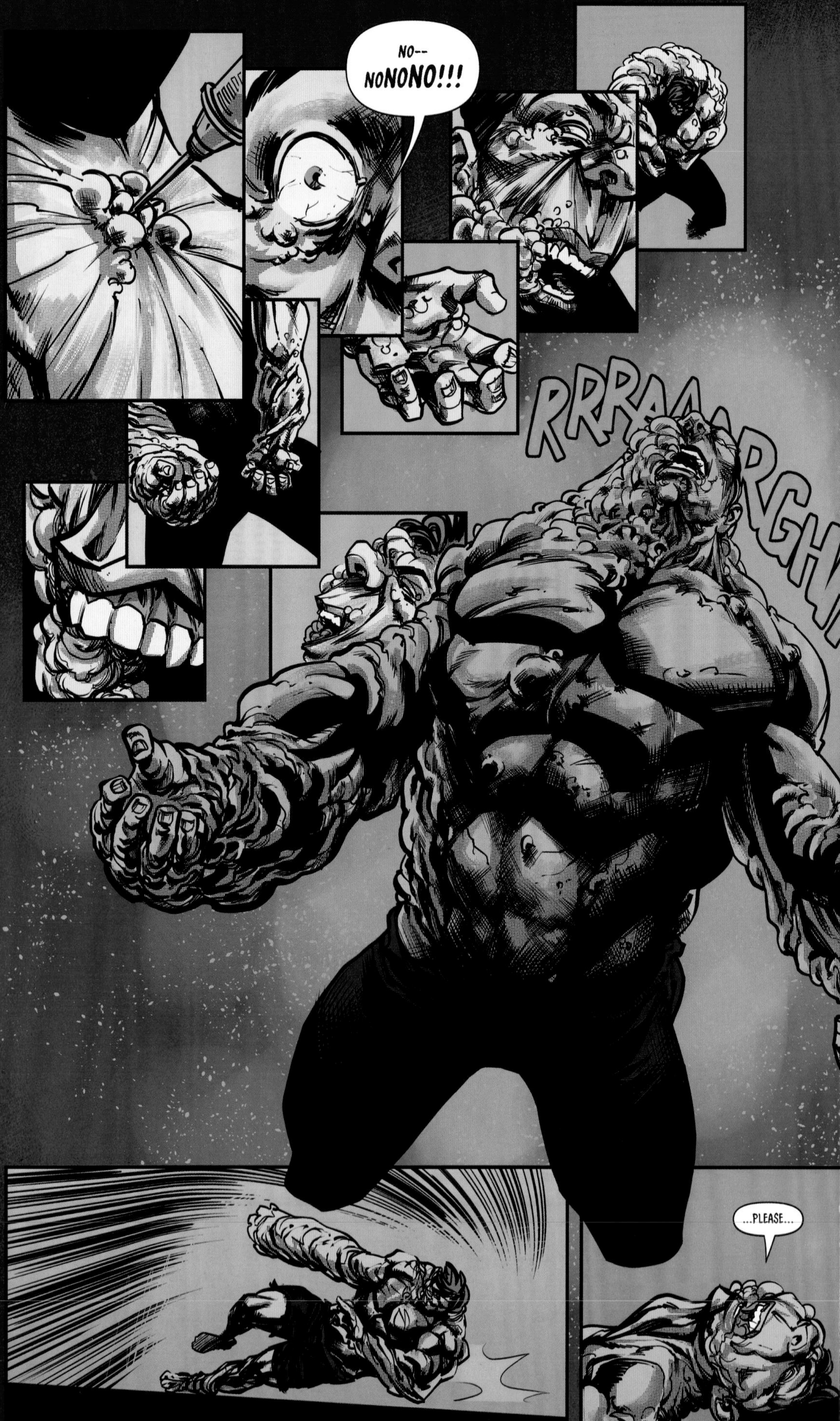
NO--
NONONO!!!
RRRAAAARGH
...PLEASE...

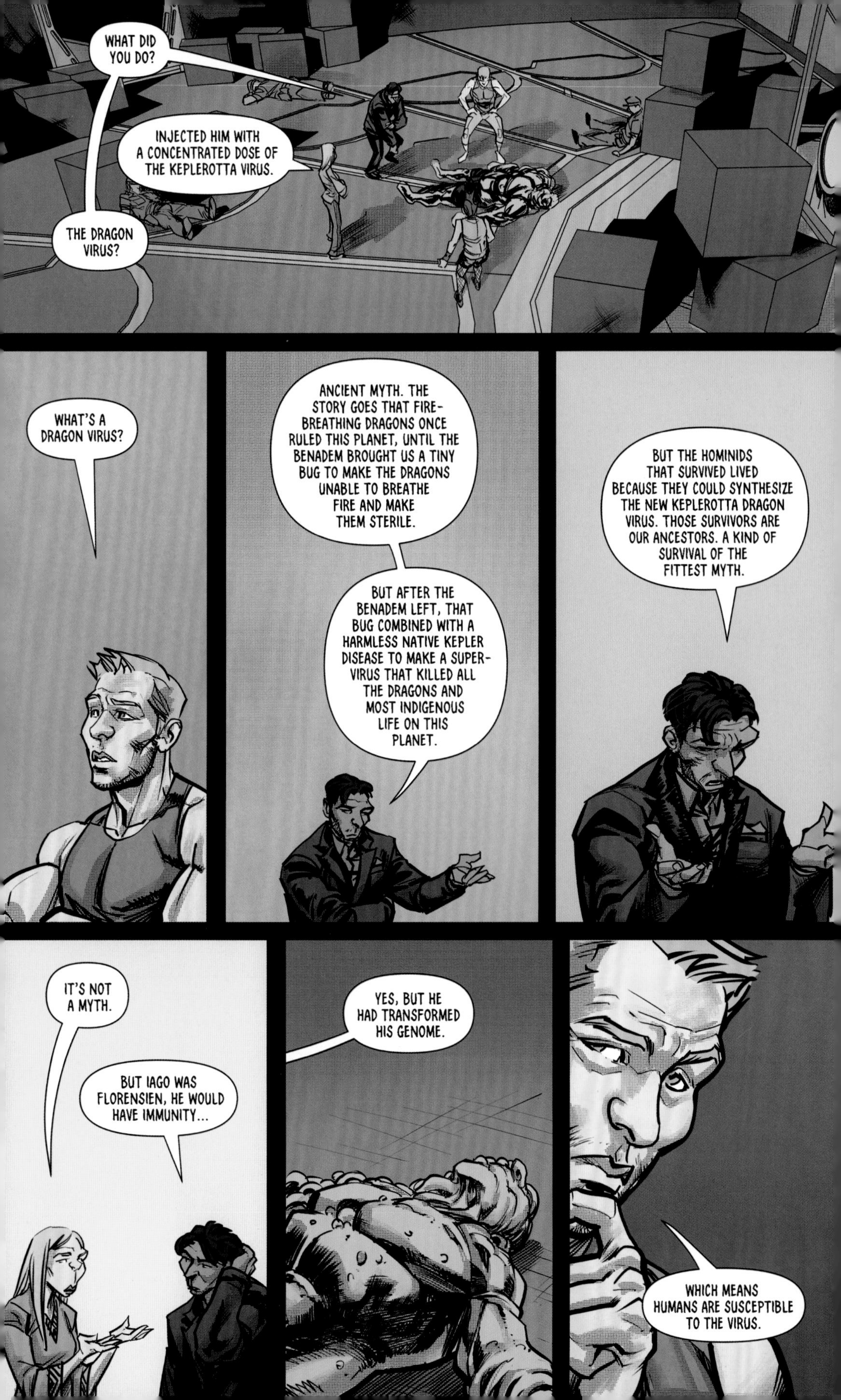

WHAT DID YOU DO?
INJECTED HIM WITH A CONCENTRATED DOSE OF THE KEPLEROTTA VIRUS.
THE DRAGON VIRUS?
WHAT'S A DRAGON VIRUS?
ANCIENT MYTH. THE STORY GOES THAT FIRE-BREATHING DRAGONS ONCE RULED THIS PLANET, UNTIL THE BENADEM BROUGHT US A TINY BUG TO MAKE THE DRAGONS UNABLE TO BREATHE FIRE AND MAKE THEM STERILE.
BUT AFTER THE BENADEM LEFT, THAT BUG COMBINED WITH A HARMLESS NATIVE KEPLER DISEASE TO MAKE A SUPER-VIRUS THAT KILLED ALL THE DRAGONS AND MOST INDIGENOUS LIFE ON THIS PLANET.
BUT THE HOMINIDS THAT SURVIVED LIVED BECAUSE THEY COULD SYNTHESIZE THE NEW KEPLEROTTA DRAGON VIRUS. THOSE SURVIVORS ARE OUR ANCESTORS. A KIND OF SURVIVAL OF THE FITTEST MYTH.
IT'S NOT A MYTH.
BUT IAGO WAS FLORENSIEN, HE WOULD HAVE IMMUNITY...
YES, BUT HE HAD TRANSFORMED HIS GENOME.
WHICH MEANS HUMANS ARE SUSCEPTIBLE TO THE VIRUS.

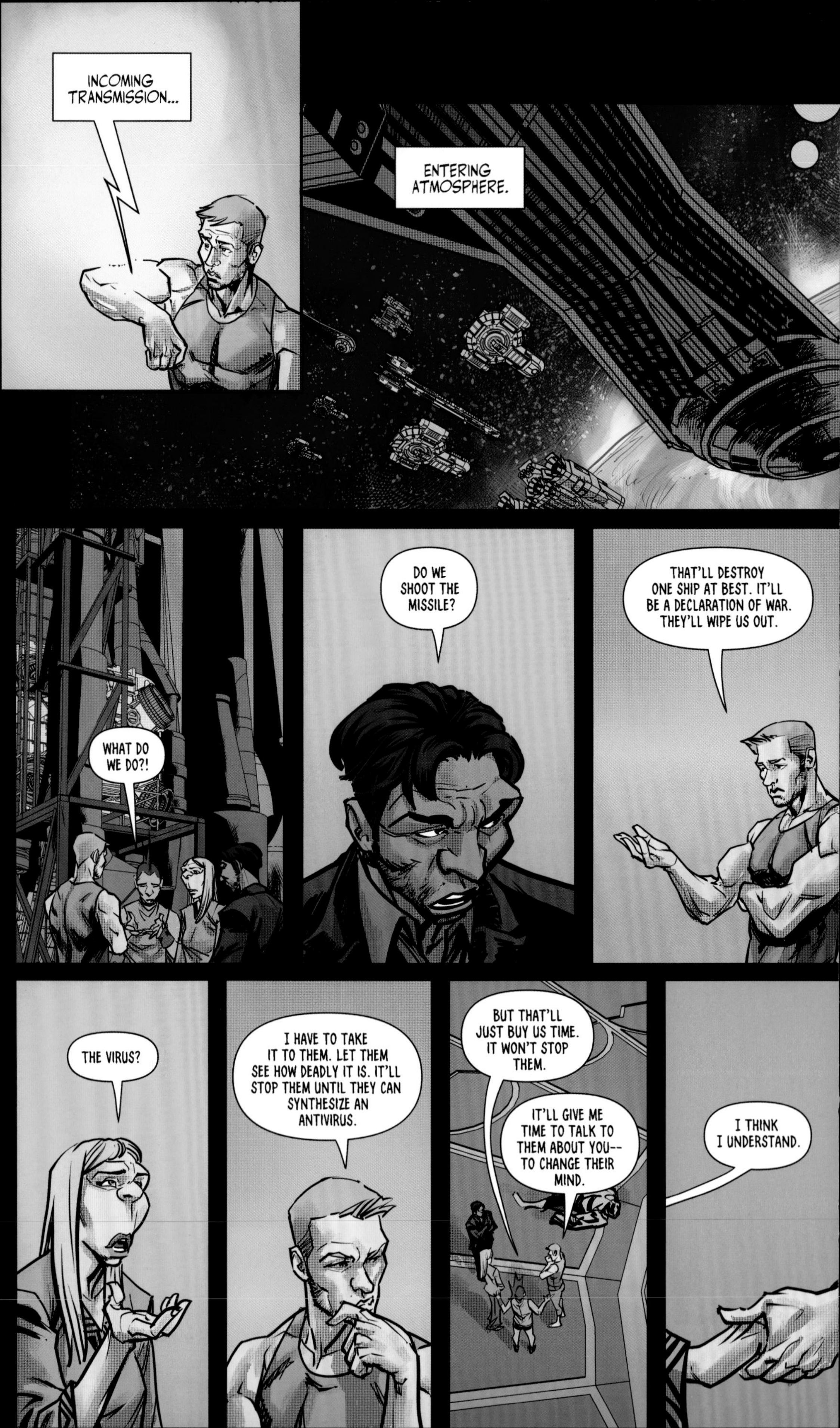
INCOMING TRANSMISSION...
ENTERING ATMOSPHERE.
WHAT DO WE DO?!
DO WE SHOOT THE MISSILE?
THAT'LL DESTROY ONE SHIP AT BEST. IT'LL BE A DECLARATION OF WAR. THEY'LL WIPE US OUT.
THE VIRUS?
I HAVE TO TAKE IT TO THEM. LET THEM SEE HOW DEADLY IT IS. IT'LL STOP THEM UNTIL THEY CAN SYNTHESIZE AN ANTIVIRUS.
BUT THAT'LL JUST BUY US TIME. IT WON'T STOP THEM.
IT'LL GIVE ME TIME TO TALK TO THEM ABOUT YOU-- TO CHANGE THEIR MIND.
I THINK I UNDERSTAND.

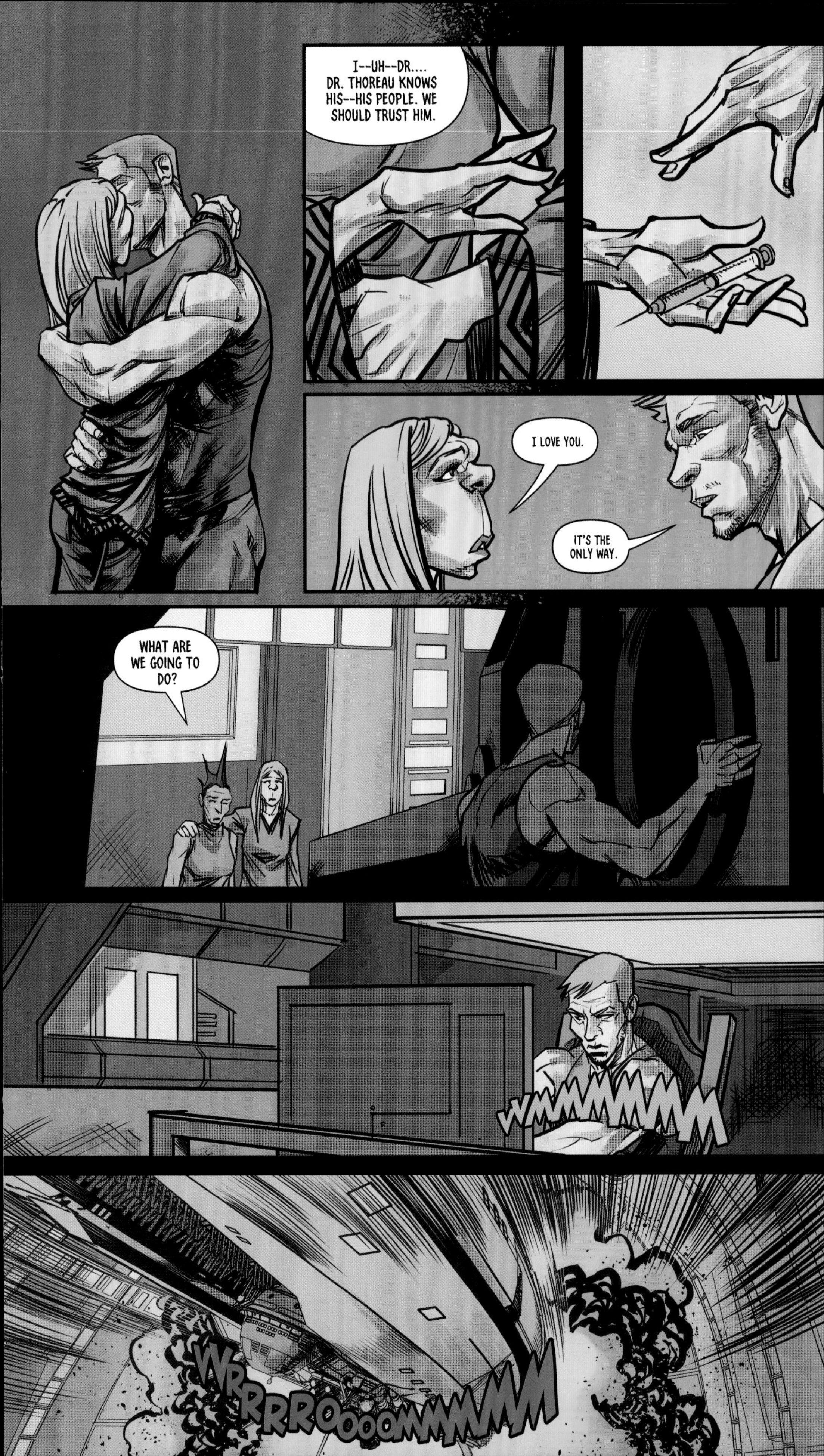
I--UH--DR....
DR. THOREAU KNOWS
HIS--HIS PEOPLE. WE
SHOULD TRUST HIM.
I LOVE YOU.
IT'S THE
ONLY WAY.
WHAT ARE
WE GOING TO
DO?
VMMMMMMMM
VVRRRROOOOMMMMMM

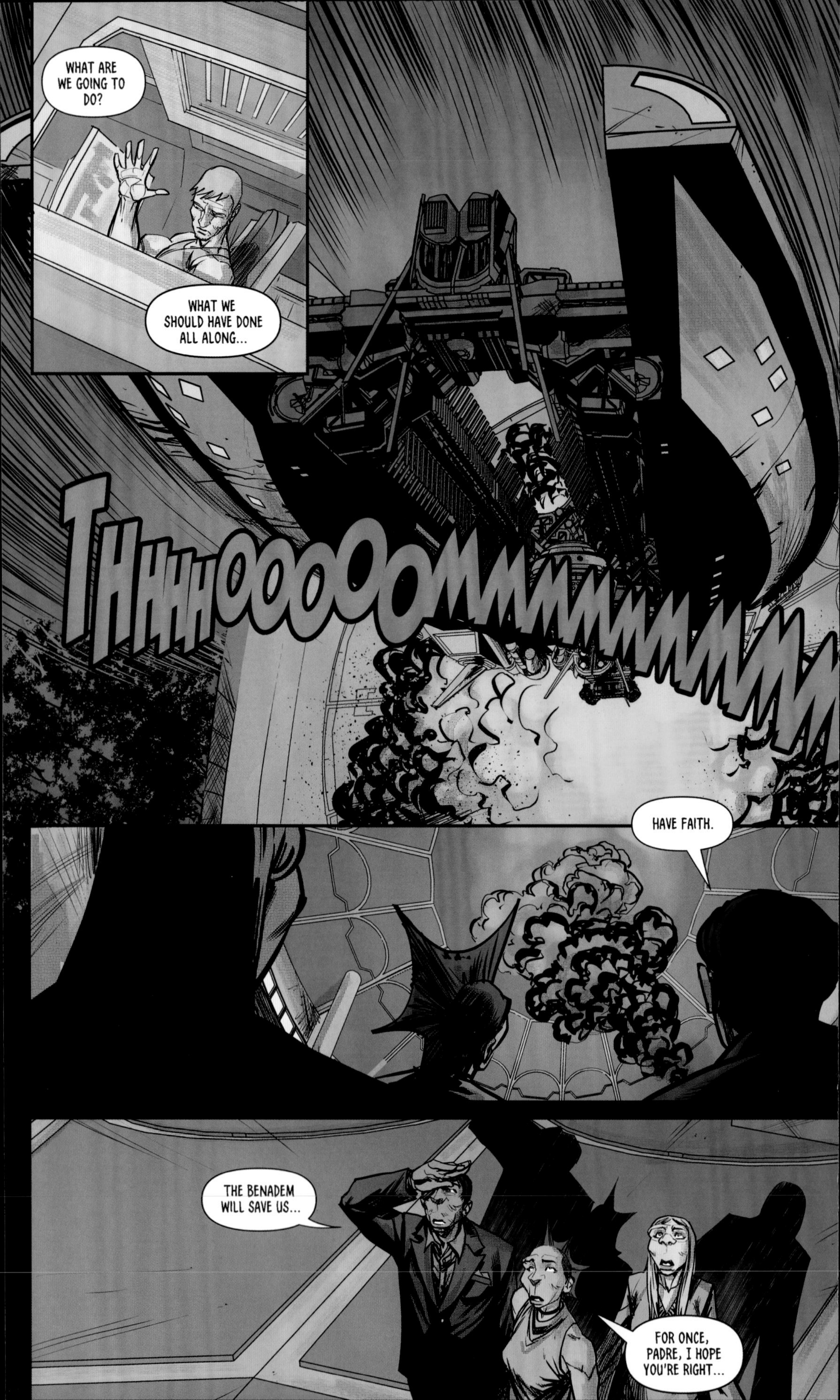
WHAT ARE WE GOING TO DO?
WHAT WE SHOULD HAVE DONE ALL ALONG...
THHHOOOOOMMMMMMMMMMMM
HAVE FAITH.
THE BENADEM WILL SAVE US...
FOR ONCE, PADRE, I HOPE YOU'RE RIGHT...

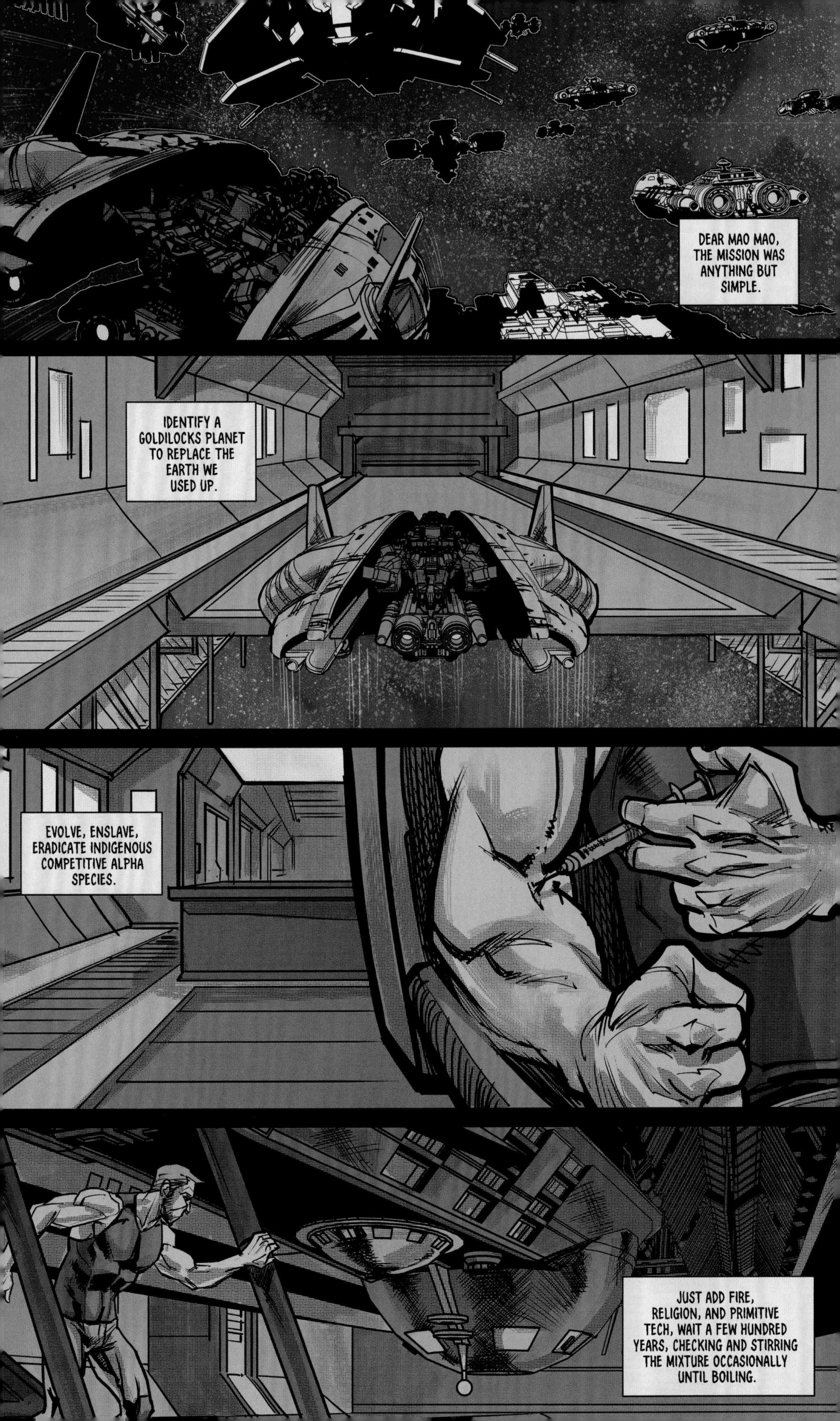
DEAR MAO MAO, THE MISSION WAS ANYTHING BUT SIMPLE.
IDENTIFY A GOLDILOCKS PLANET TO REPLACE THE EARTH WE USED UP.
EVOLVE, ENSLAVE, ERADICATE INDIGENOUS COMPETITIVE ALPHA SPECIES.
JUST ADD FIRE, RELIGION, AND PRIMITIVE TECH, WAIT A FEW HUNDRED YEARS, CHECKING AND STIRRING THE MIXTURE OCCASIONALLY UNTIL BOILING.

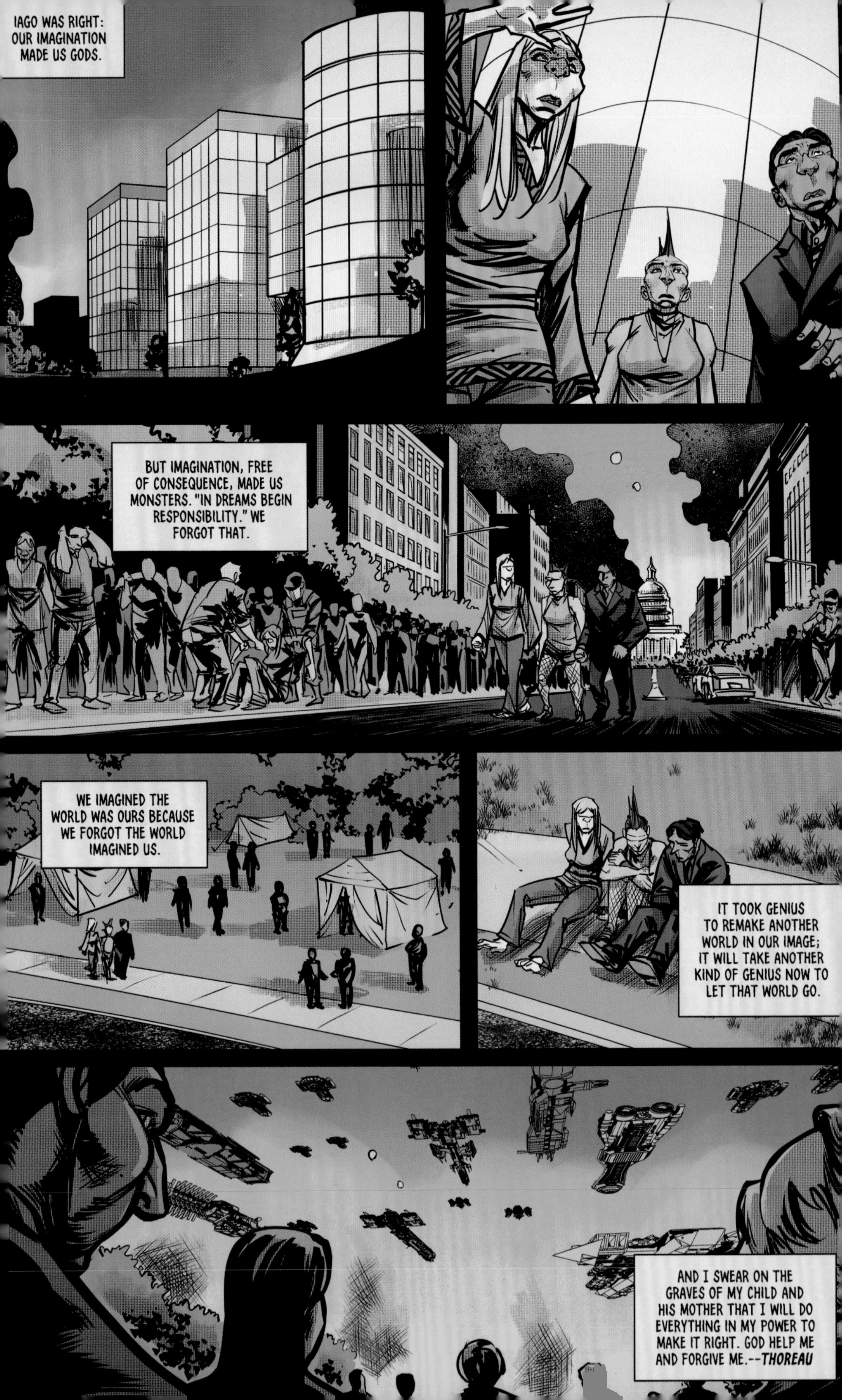
IAGO WAS RIGHT: OUR IMAGINATION MADE US GODS.
BUT IMAGINATION, FREE OF CONSEQUENCE, MADE US MONSTERS. "IN DREAMS BEGIN RESPONSIBILITY." WE FORGOT THAT.
WE IMAGINED THE WORLD WAS OURS BECAUSE WE FORGOT THE WORLD IMAGINED US.
IT TOOK GENIUS TO REMAKE ANOTHER WORLD IN OUR IMAGE; IT WILL TAKE ANOTHER KIND OF GENIUS NOW TO LET THAT WORLD GO.
AND I SWEAR ON THE GRAVES OF MY CHILD AND HIS MOTHER THAT I WILL DO EVERYTHING IN MY POWER TO MAKE IT RIGHT. GOD HELP ME AND FORGIVE ME.--THOREAU

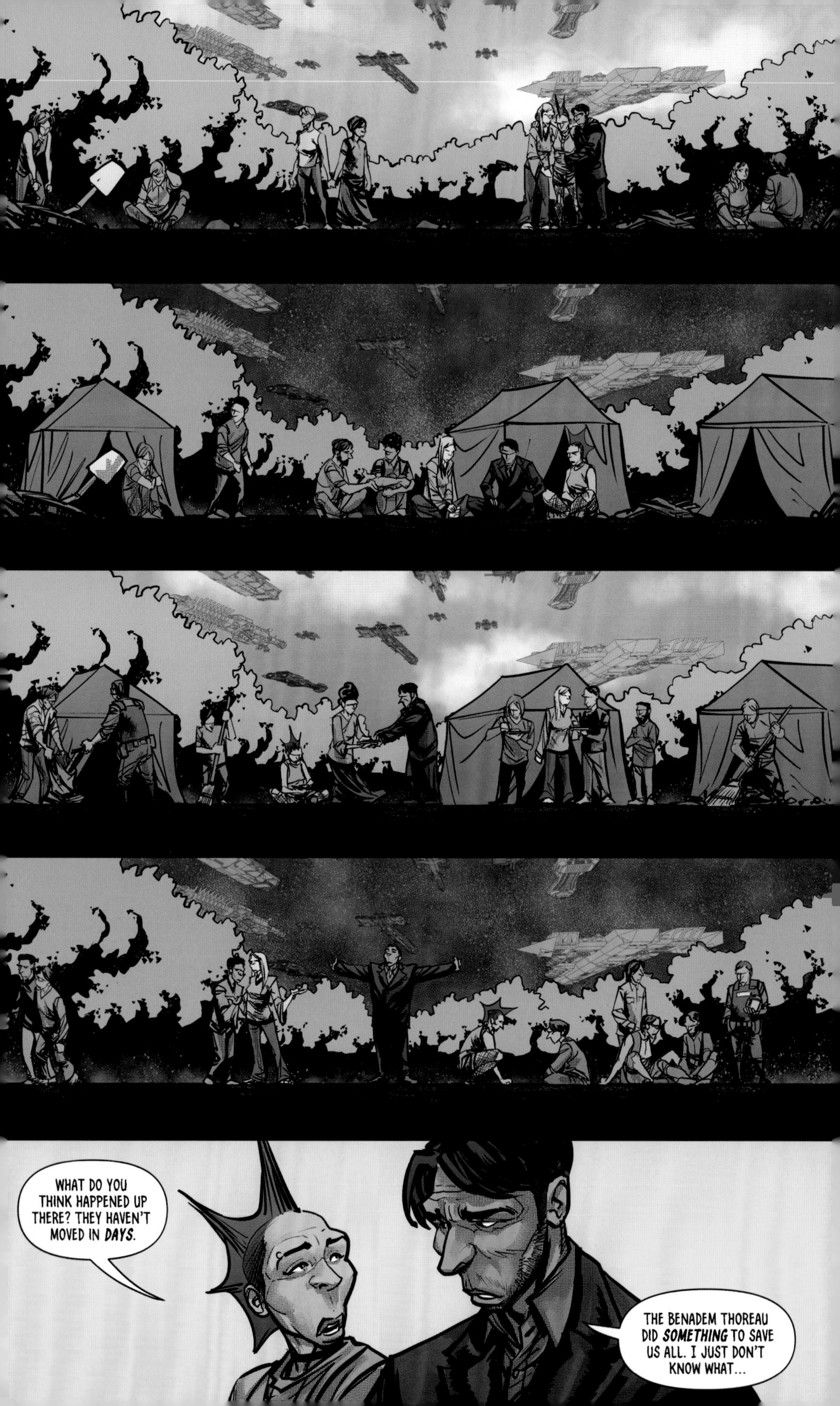
WHAT DO YOU THINK HAPPENED UP THERE? THEY HAVEN'T MOVED IN *DAYS*.
THE BENADEM THOREAU DID *SOMETHING* TO SAVE US ALL. I JUST DON'T KNOW WHAT...

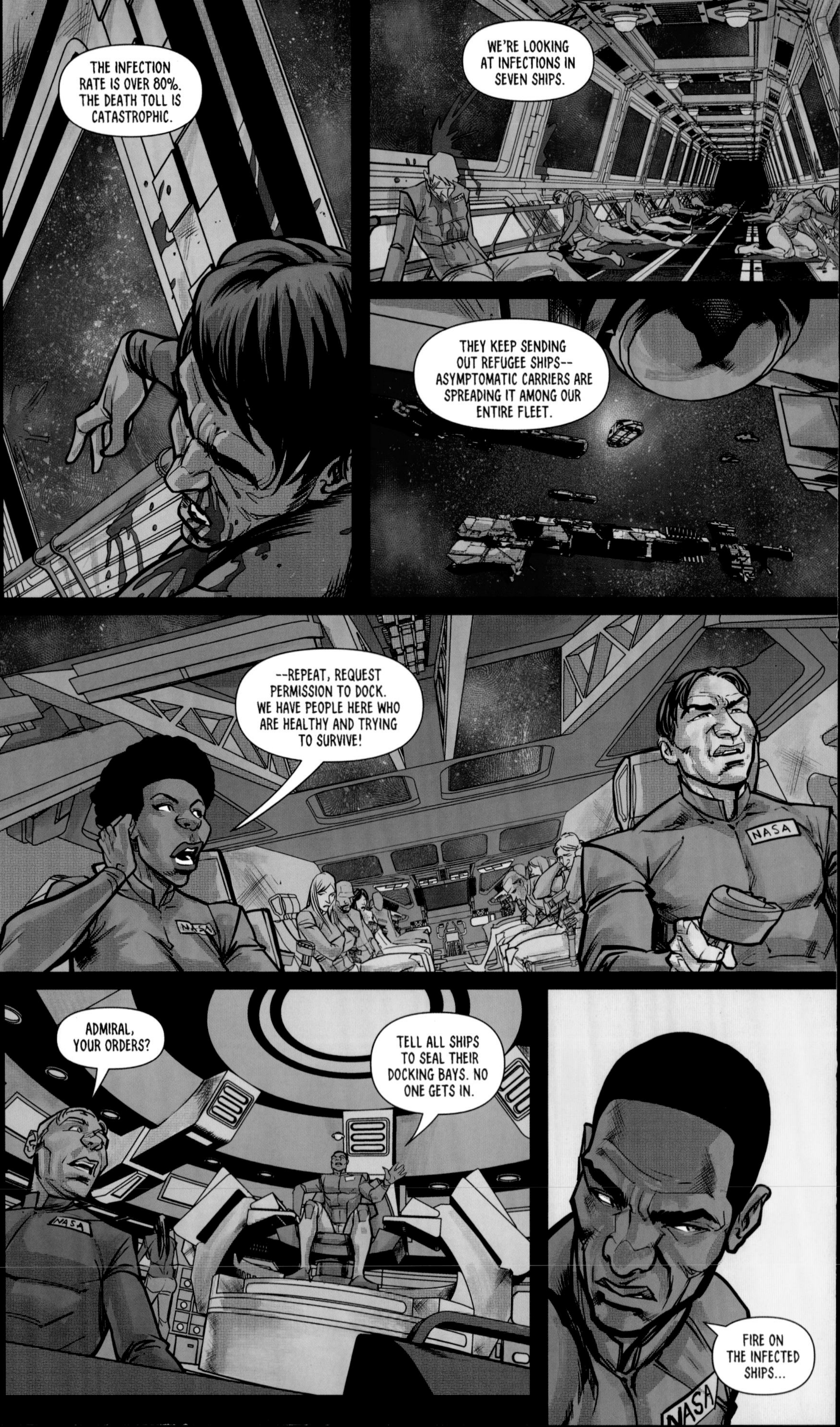
THE INFECTION RATE IS OVER 80%. THE DEATH TOLL IS CATASTROPHIC.
WE'RE LOOKING AT INFECTIONS IN SEVEN SHIPS.
THEY KEEP SENDING OUT REFUGEE SHIPS-- ASYMPTOMATIC CARRIERS ARE SPREADING IT AMONG OUR ENTIRE FLEET.
--REPEAT, REQUEST PERMISSION TO DOCK. WE HAVE PEOPLE HERE WHO ARE HEALTHY AND TRYING TO SURVIVE!
NASA
NASA
ADMIRAL, YOUR ORDERS?
TELL ALL SHIPS TO SEAL THEIR DOCKING BAYS. NO ONE GETS IN.
NASA
FIRE ON THE INFECTED SHIPS...
NASA

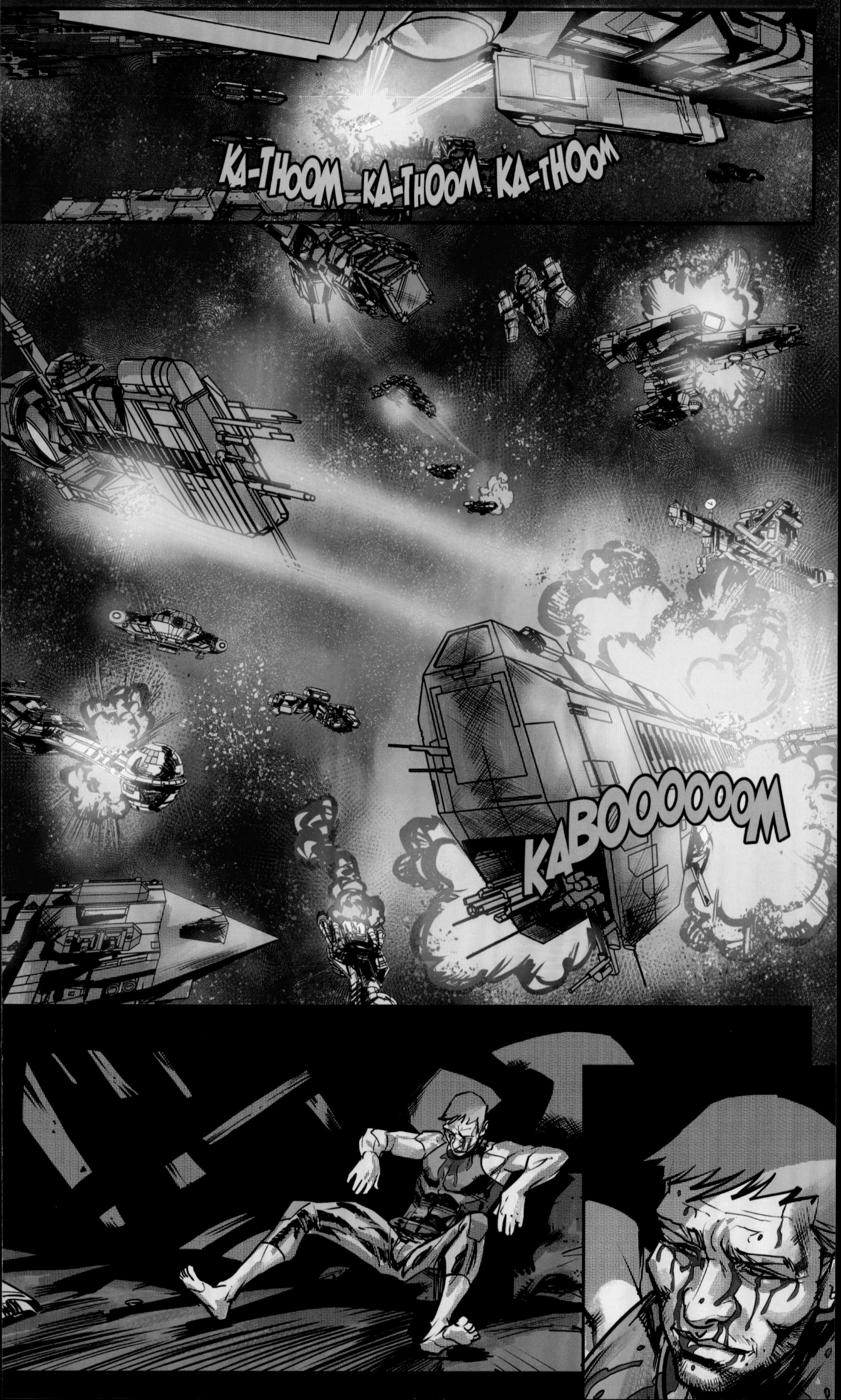
KA-THOOM KA-THOOM KA-THOOM
KABOOOOOOM

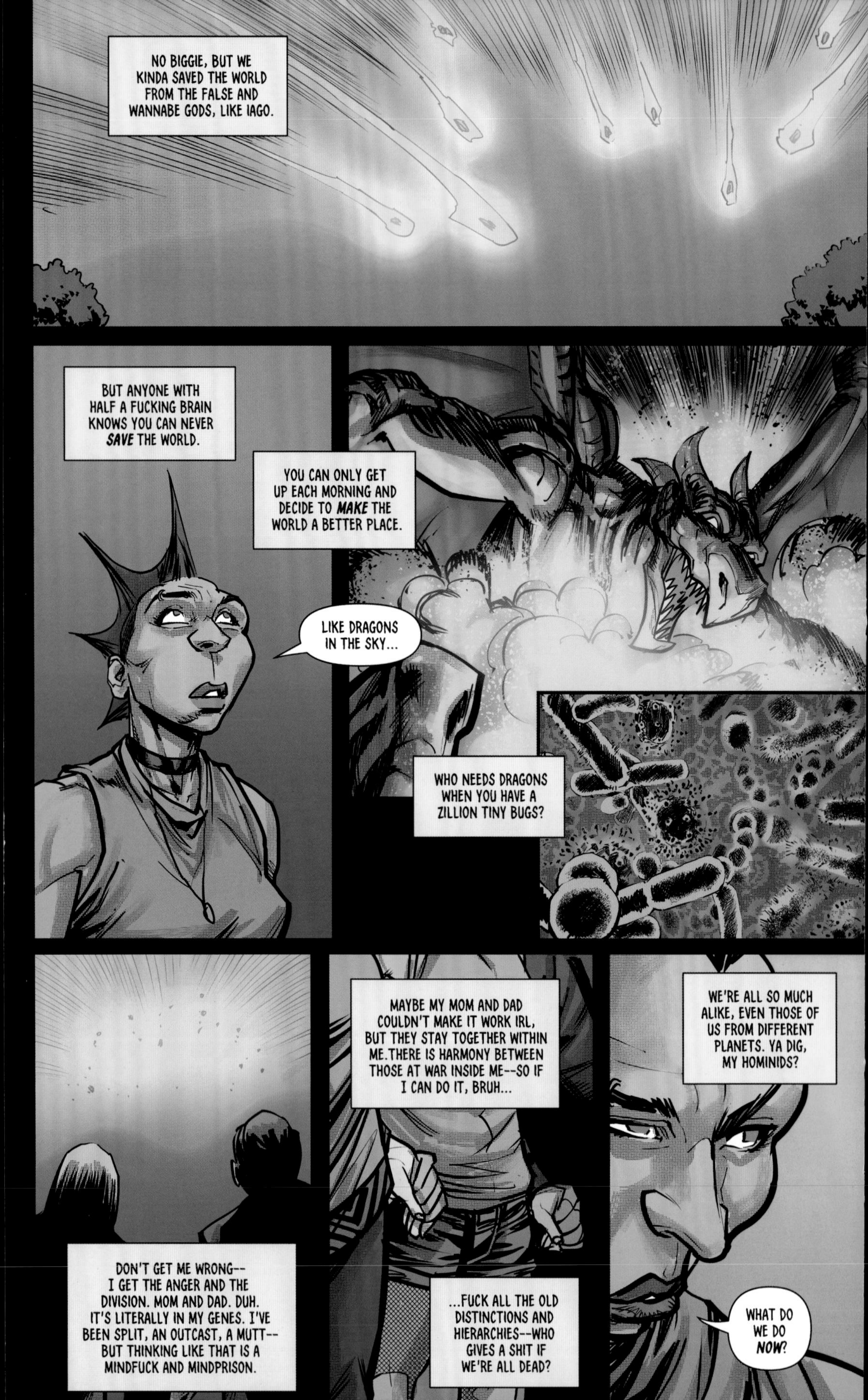
NO BIGGIE, BUT WE KINDA SAVED THE WORLD FROM THE FALSE AND WANNABE GODS, LIKE IAGO.
BUT ANYONE WITH HALF A FUCKING BRAIN KNOWS YOU CAN NEVER *SAVE* THE WORLD.
YOU CAN ONLY GET UP EACH MORNING AND DECIDE TO *MAKE* THE WORLD A BETTER PLACE.
LIKE DRAGONS IN THE SKY...
WHO NEEDS DRAGONS WHEN YOU HAVE A ZILLION TINY BUGS?
DON'T GET ME WRONG-- I GET THE ANGER AND THE DIVISION. MOM AND DAD. DUH. IT'S LITERALLY IN MY GENES. I'VE BEEN SPLIT, AN OUTCAST, A MUTT-- BUT THINKING LIKE THAT IS A MINDFUCK AND MINDPRISON.
MAYBE MY MOM AND DAD COULDN'T MAKE IT WORK IRL, BUT THEY STAY TOGETHER WITHIN ME. THERE IS HARMONY BETWEEN THOSE AT WAR INSIDE ME--SO IF I CAN DO IT, BRUH...
...FUCK ALL THE OLD DISTINCTIONS AND HIERARCHIES--WHO GIVES A SHIT IF WE'RE ALL DEAD?
WE'RE ALL SO MUCH ALIKE, EVEN THOSE OF US FROM DIFFERENT PLANETS. YA DIG, MY HOMINIDS?
WHAT DO WE DO *NOW*?

WE CAN'T START OVER, BUT WE CAN MOVE FORWARD.

TOGETHER.

WHAT DOES THAT MEAN, THOUGH?

WE DON'T KNOW, WEST.

IT DOESN'T MEAN THINGS ARE BACK TO THE WAY THEY WERE.

OR EVER CAN BE. WOULD YOU BE OKAY WITH THAT?

YEP.

IF WE ARE TO SURVIVE AND THRIVE WE GOTTA WAKE UP TO WHAT JOINS US--ALL SUFFERING, HOPEFUL DUDES OF THE UNIVERSE WITH SIMPLE-ASS DREAMS FOR LOVE AND JOY AND A TOMORROW AND SHIT...'CAUSE...

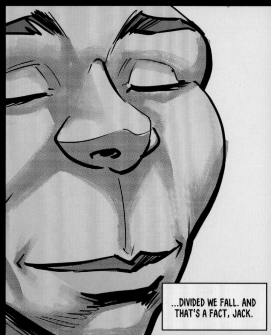

...DIVIDED WE FALL. AND THAT'S A FACT, JACK.

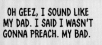

OH GEEZ, I SOUND LIKE MY DAD. I SAID I WASN'T GONNA PREACH. MY BAD.

BUT SOMETIMES YOU GOTTA SPEAK THE FUCK UP.

LATER, SPACE INVADERS.

THE END

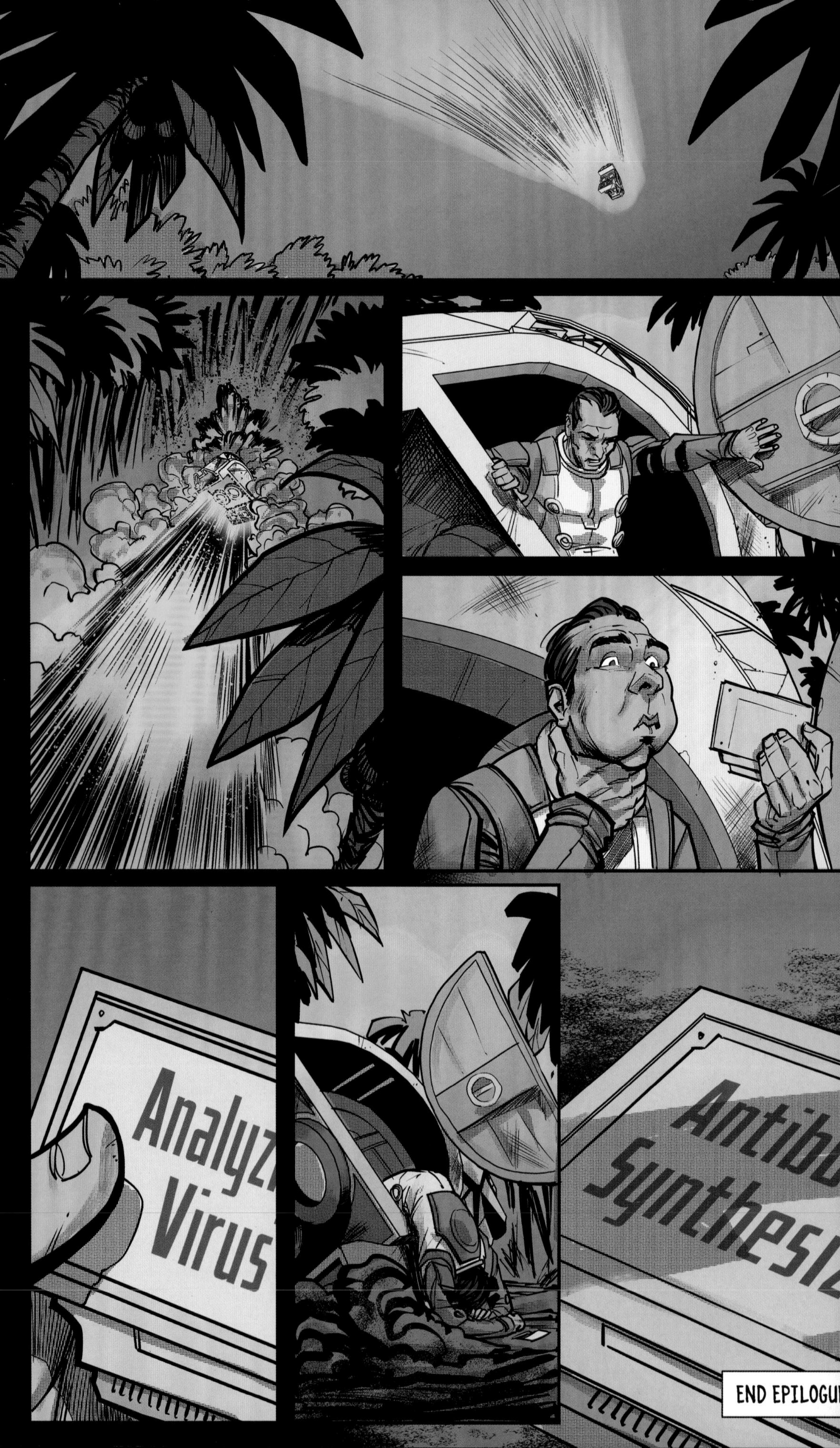
Analyz
Virus
Antib
Synthesi
END EPILOGU

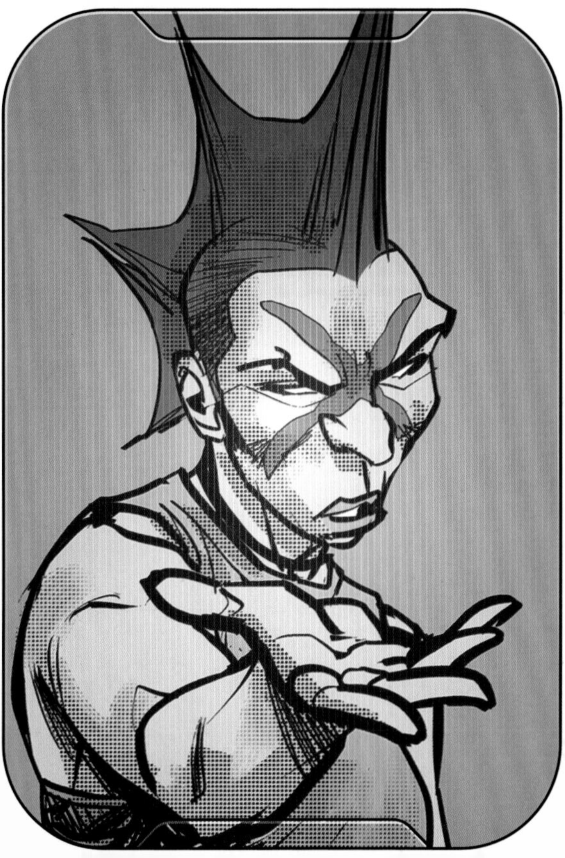

AFTERWORD

n August 2020, my champion editor Megan Walker reached out to check my availability for a project she'd been working on. She explained it was adapting a television pilot that David Duchovny had written. They wanted to turn it into a comic, and she'd been working with David, but they had gotten to a point where they wanted to bring in a comics professional to begin shaping it. She sent me the pilot and the outline for a first-season graphic novel they had put together and I set about seeing if there was a way I could adapt it for the comics medium.

See, what I've managed to not say to David or Megan up until this very point is how much of a fan of David's I was and am. When working in any form of entertainment, it does no one any good to just fanboy all over someone. I started watching X-Files as a youth—the first episode I caught was "Squeeze," the first Eugene Tooms episode—I was nine and at a birthday party. And it scared the shit out of me. And I was hooked. From the intricate conspiracy plots that folded in on themselves to the horrific and addicting monster of the week to the goofy, hilarious, and inventive one-offs—everything about that show shaped how I love and tell stories. 'd followed David's career outside of the FBI as well the Ronnie Hunt-directed Return to Me is one of

my all-time favorite rom-coms) and was impressed to discover how much of a writing career he'd been creating over the last decade or so. The opportunit to work with him got me really excited.

But I kept that part of me in check and set about seeing if I could do my job on this project. Thankfully it was a really cool script with a lot of fun visual potential. I was also able to see how the story could be compressed and shaped down to a graphic nove So I replied that I was interested, and we started talking about how we would adapt this.

Whenever you work with someone you've admired for years, especially when they're coming from outside of comics (which is its own unique interesting, and somewhat mystifying medium) there's always a little apprehension as to how the collaboration will go. Not every day do you get to work with an icon of generations (the number o bisexual friends I have who told me watching X-Files was the first time they realized they were bi is 100 percent). Thankfully, and almost immediately, any concerns I had disappeared. David was warm genuine, humble, excited, and very generous abou collaborating. From the beginning, he wa comfortable saying, "The television thing is th television thing. We can make this its own version

The process of adapting an entire season of TV to an 88-page story (which ended up at 92) was the hardest thing I've ever done. I spent hours parked in the backyard of the house I was in at the time, thinking, scribbling notes, talking out loud, and listening to the *Interstellar* soundtrack (my unofficial soundtrack of the book). Once I had the outline together and received notes from David and Megan, I set about breaking it down into a page-by-page outline (vital for comics). And that was when I realized I had outlined a 124-page graphic novel. Back to the cutting room! After losing roughly 30 pages, we arrived at the outline that more or less resembles the story you have here.

I spent the next few months scripting the story into a comics format, getting notes from David along the way. One of the most amazing things that David did was read a million drafts of the same script with a fresh pair of eyes. Every. Time. And his ability to look at things fresh, over and over, was vital. He'd come back with notes like "On page 24, this character says this one thing. And then on page 67, another character says this other thing. And those two ideas are in conflict with each other. What about this . . . ?" There were so many little things that he noticed and then refined. He did pass after pass on the dialogue—every line was important (which makes sense coming from an actor—who also writes, produces, directs, sings, etc.).

All while writing the scripts, I was drawing hominid designs. Originally, we had all the hominid species in the book—but the design process was starting to get overwhelming, and our main cast were only from the three main species that exist in the book. So we decided to pare them down. The biggest challenge was to not draw all the Thaals like the GEICO Caveman. That's our visual shorthand for Neanderthals. Whether it's accurate or not, that's a common image that quickly communicates an idea. And comics live or die by easily recognizable and understood visual shorthand. Stylistically, I wanted to go in a direction that was more cartoony, bold, and expressive. My mind wanted to see this book as Mike Mignola and Gabriel Bá's love child with my approach. So, create characters that don't look like cavemen, but are obviously not humans. But they also have to be attractive in their own way. We knew we had at least one moment when a human kissed a Bonobion and we wanted the viewers to be focused on what the characters are feeling, not "Ew, that dude's kissing a monkey." My friend coined the look I was searching for as "Fuckable Monkeys." That was my goal.

Once we narrowed the species down to just the main three, it was lots of refinement to get the right look, shapes, and physicality. At the same time, I was looking at how I wanted to approach the visuals of the world. We had established that the world looks firmly set in the late '50s to mid-'60s aesthetic. Looking at lots of reference photos of locations, vehicles, and clothing helped shape the look of the book. I decided to use toning as a way to add volume and form to my figures, and it also matched the look of that era. We went through a lot of variations—for Spenser especially—but we landed on a really fun look for the characters and the world.

David and I both took a break on the book for a few months as he was off shooting *The Bubble* and I hopped over to draw half a graphic novel for another publisher. We both got back and dove into the art in mid-2021. Life changes and events slowed me down on the book, but after about six months, the line art and lettering were complete and I dove into colors. Another month or two, and the book was done. There was constant polishing and tweaking up until the end, and I think it's the best version of the story we could tell.

Wrapping up my little nine-year-old fanboy self, as I was drawing the book, I was talking to David one day and he said he'd sent the script to his friend Chris—he paused to clarify it was Chris Carter, creator of *The X-Files*, and asked if I knew who that was—and Chris really liked it. David said other things, but I was just spinning on "Chris Carter, shaper of my narrative tastes and style, likes a script I wrote with David Duchovny. What is life?" It was a surreal moment, as many moments working on this book were.

We, essentially, worked in silence for a year and a half. The book was done and nearly locked before it was even announced. David had shot multiple movies, written several books, and recorded at least one music album, I believe. I had done quite a few things as well. We both fought through COVID diagnoses, worried over our families and friends, and tried to live life in this very weird and scary time.

You've read the result of all of that work and time. It's something we're very proud of. Something we hope we can do more with if time and attention warrant. It's a story about accepting and embracing what makes us different. Of working together to preserve life, the fight for love and survival. It's a cautionary but hopeful tale.

—PHILLIP SEVY

KEPLER™

SKETCHBOOK

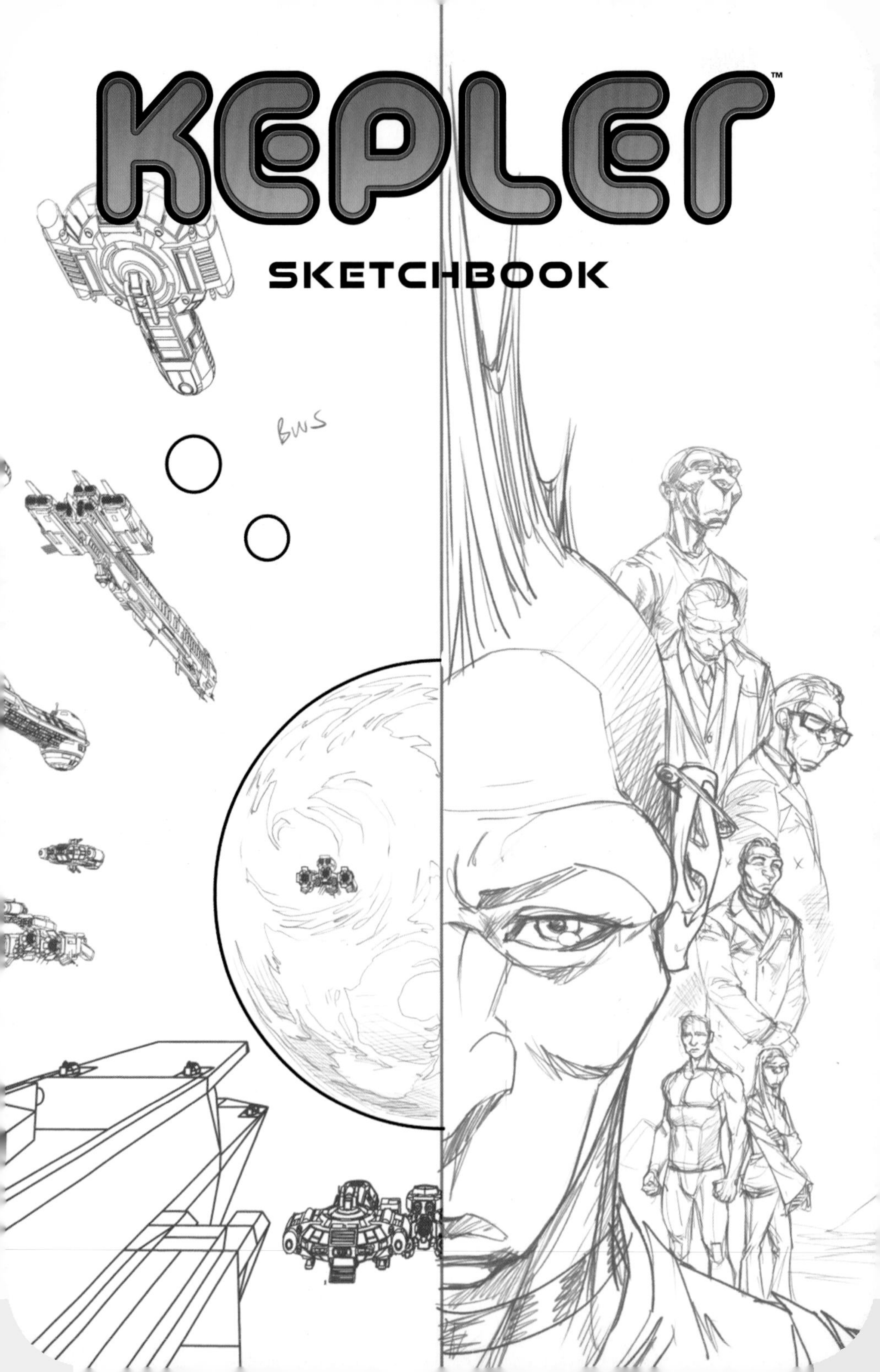

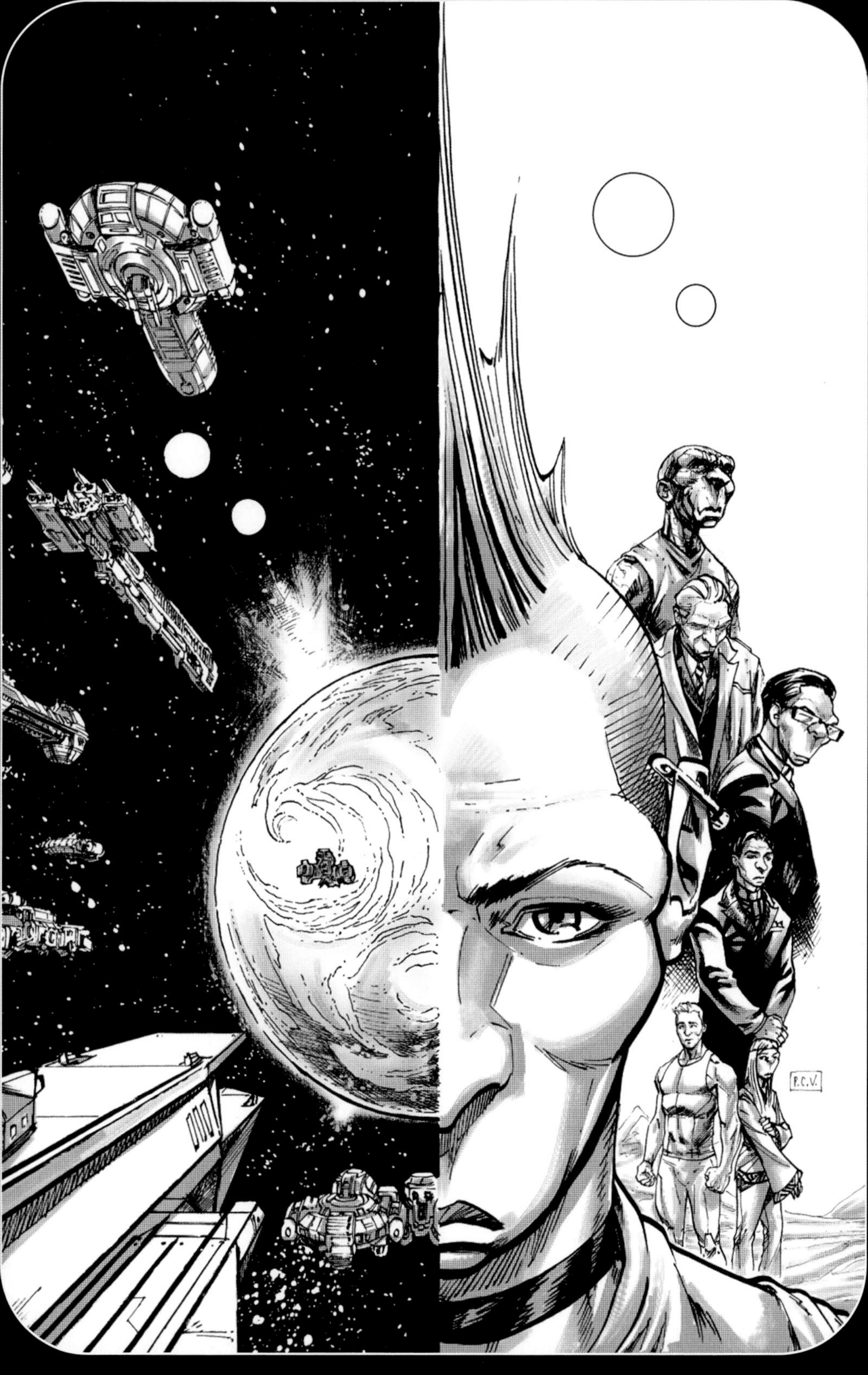
P.C.V.

Artist Phillip Sevy's inks for the front cover of *Kepler*.

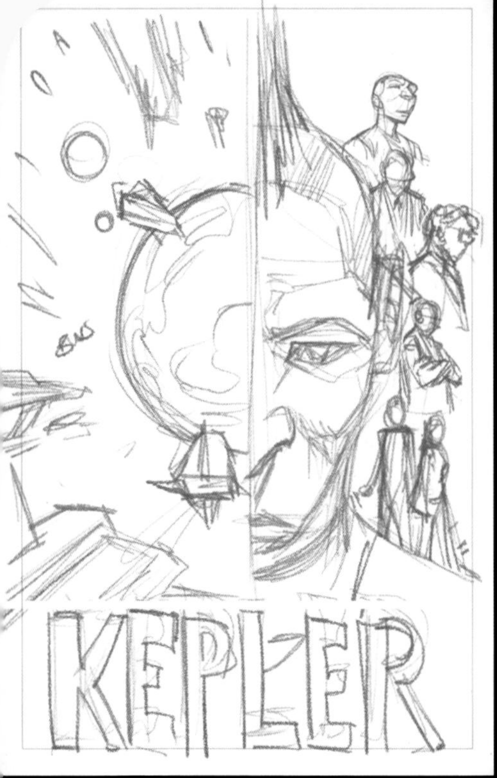
KEPLER

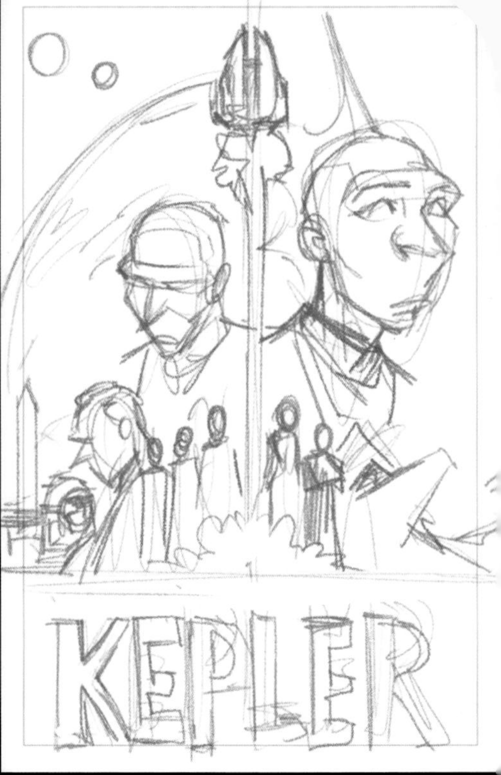
KEPLER

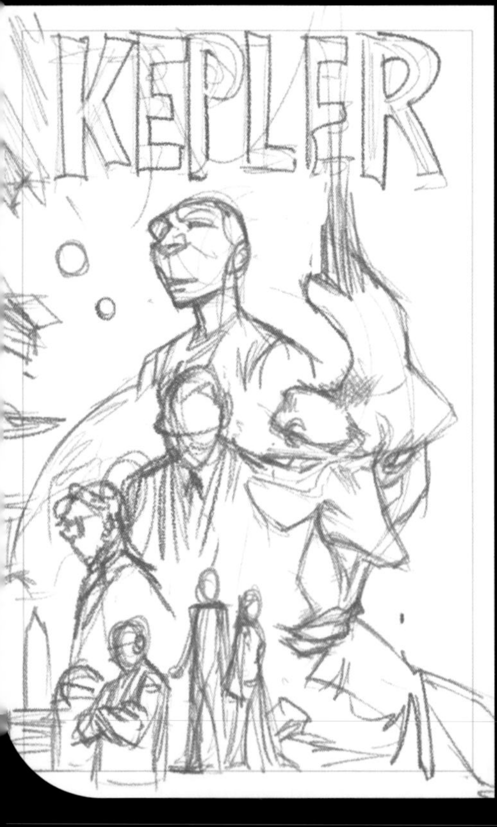
KEPLER

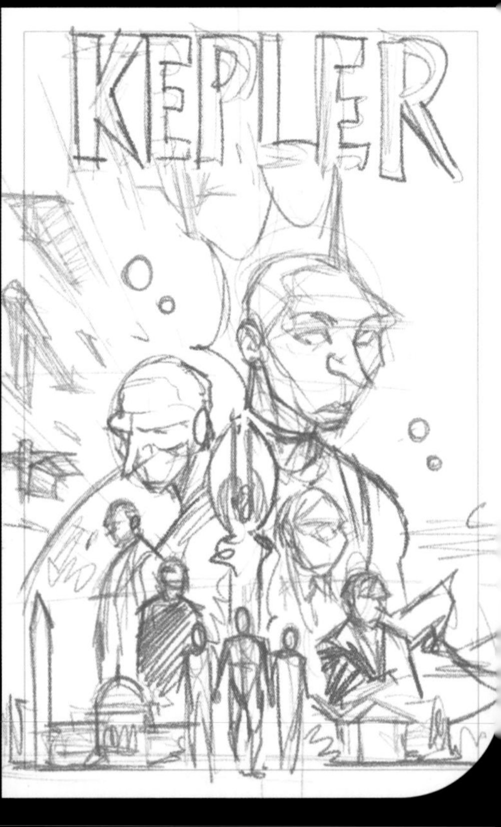
KEPLER

For the cover, I wanted to present images that felt like a movie poster. David ended up liking the one that was the least like a traditional poster—one that was bolder. And it was totally the right choice. I had to play with the elements to make them work, but I really like it.

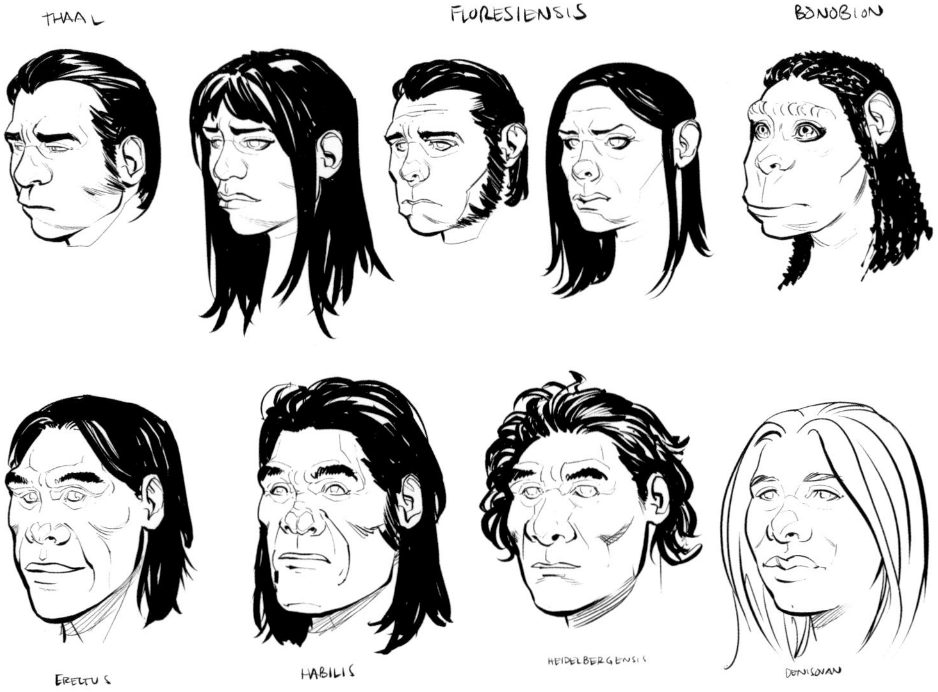
THAAL
FLORESIENSIS
BONOBION
ERECTUS
HABILIS
HEIDELBERGENSIS
DENISOVAN

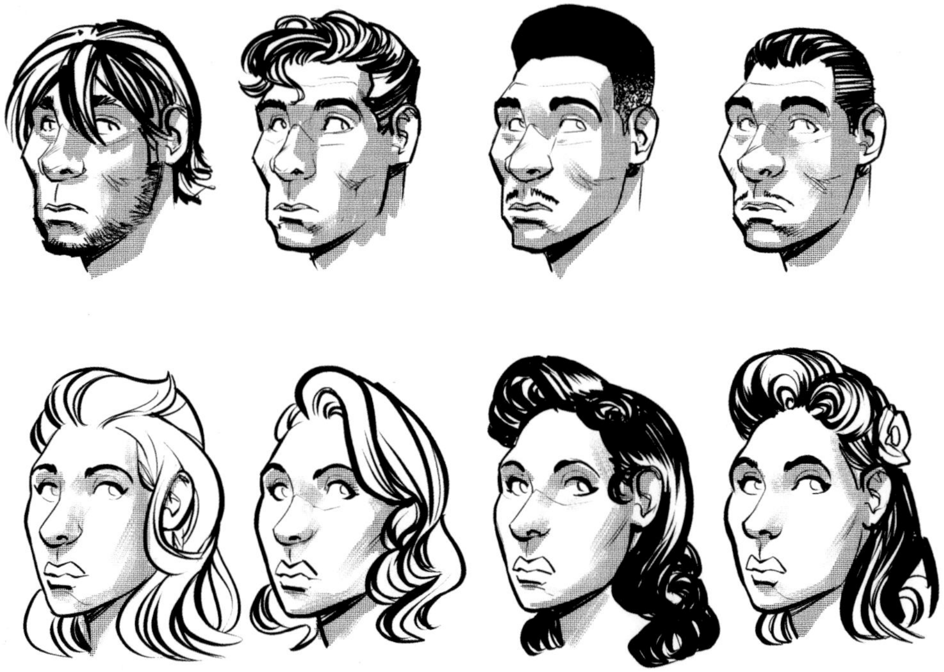

Early on, we were going to have many different hominid species, and it was a challenge to make them distinct and different. We eventually pared them down (to my relief) to the main three. The lower image is an exploration of Thaal looks and styles fitting the time period.

Getting the proportions and physicality of the species took so much work (there are SO many drawings to find the right look). The top two images were early style explorations. The bottom image was a body guide for female and male Thaals and a quick costume guide (there were many others). The opposite page shows explorations of Bonobion forms, proportions, and styles. Bonobions were closer aligned to hippie culture, whereas Thaals were more *Mad Men*-esque.

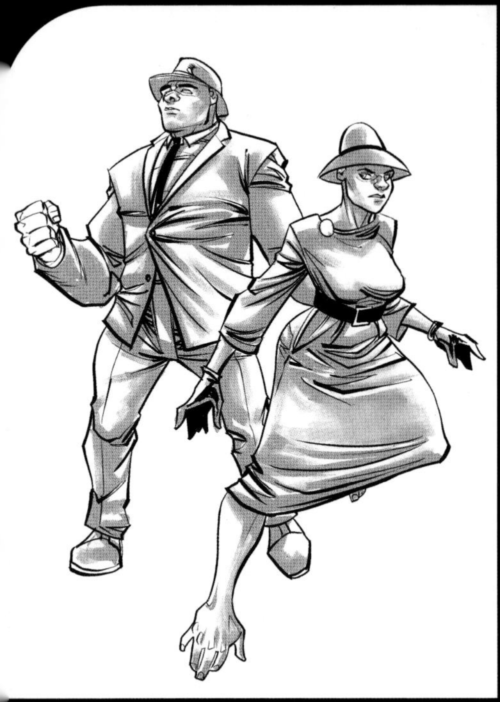

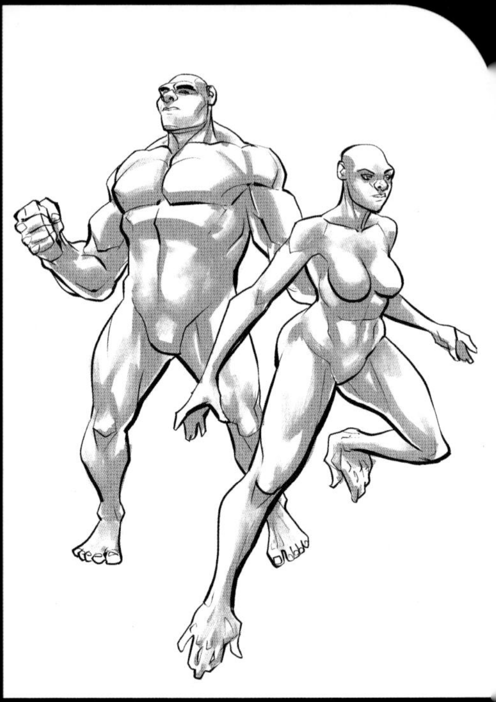

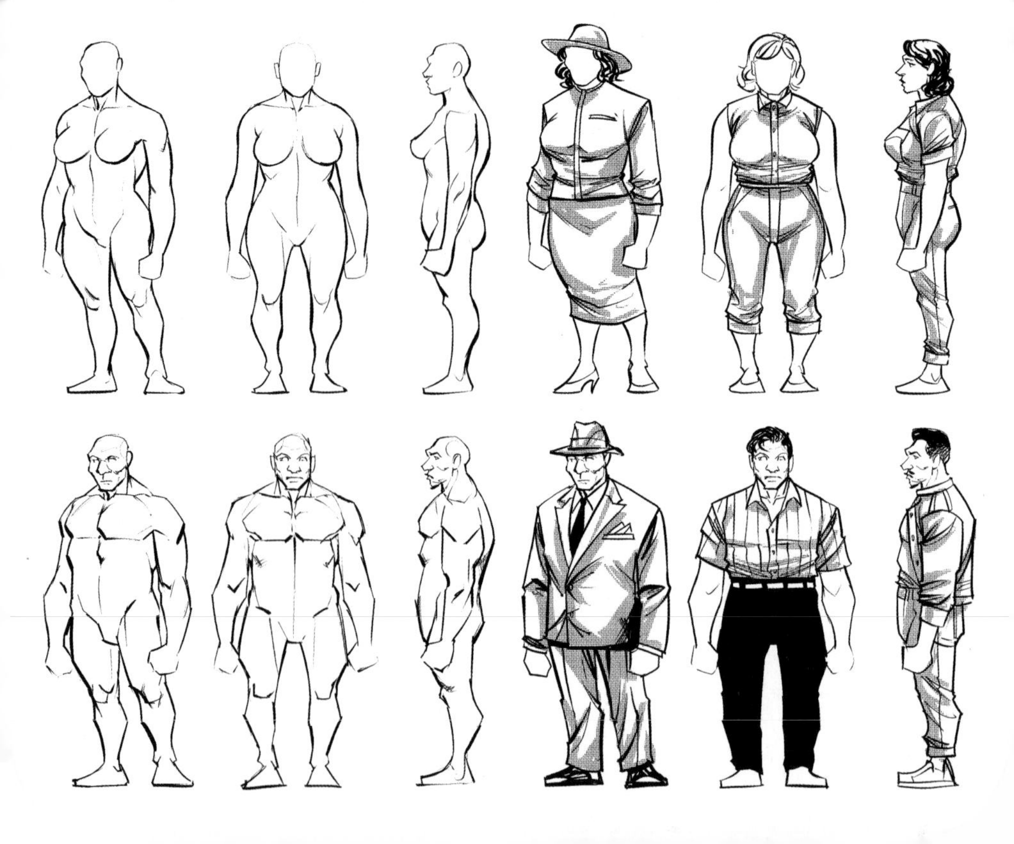

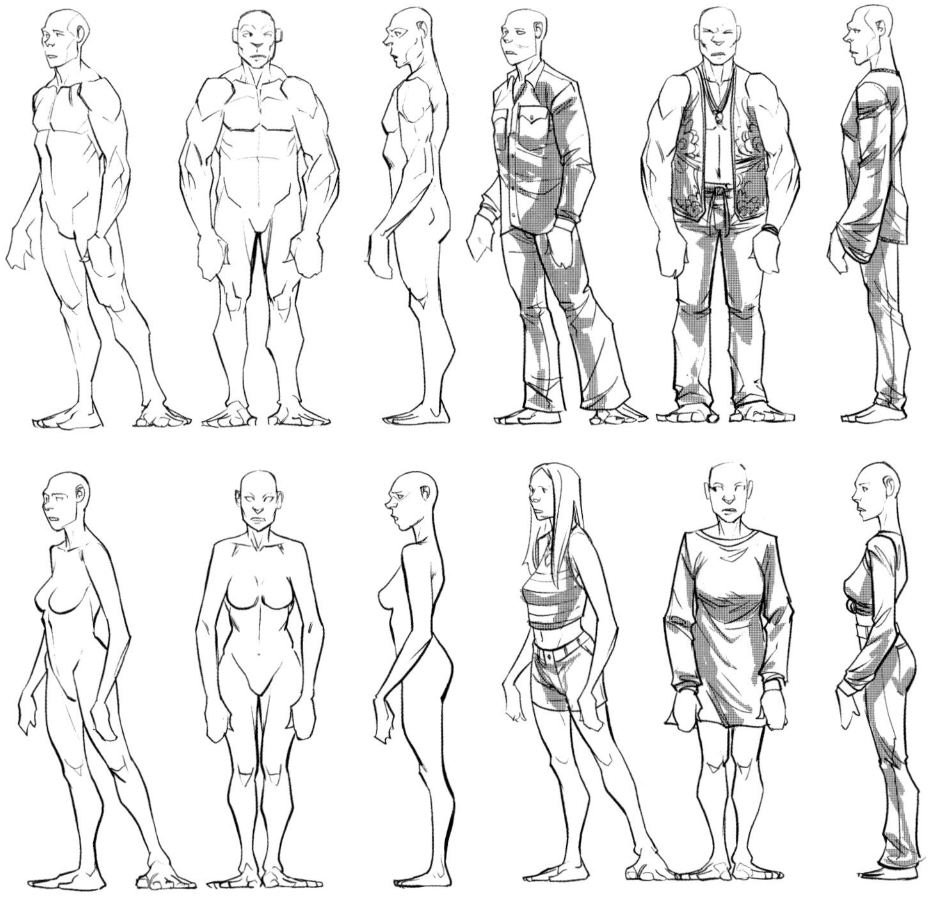

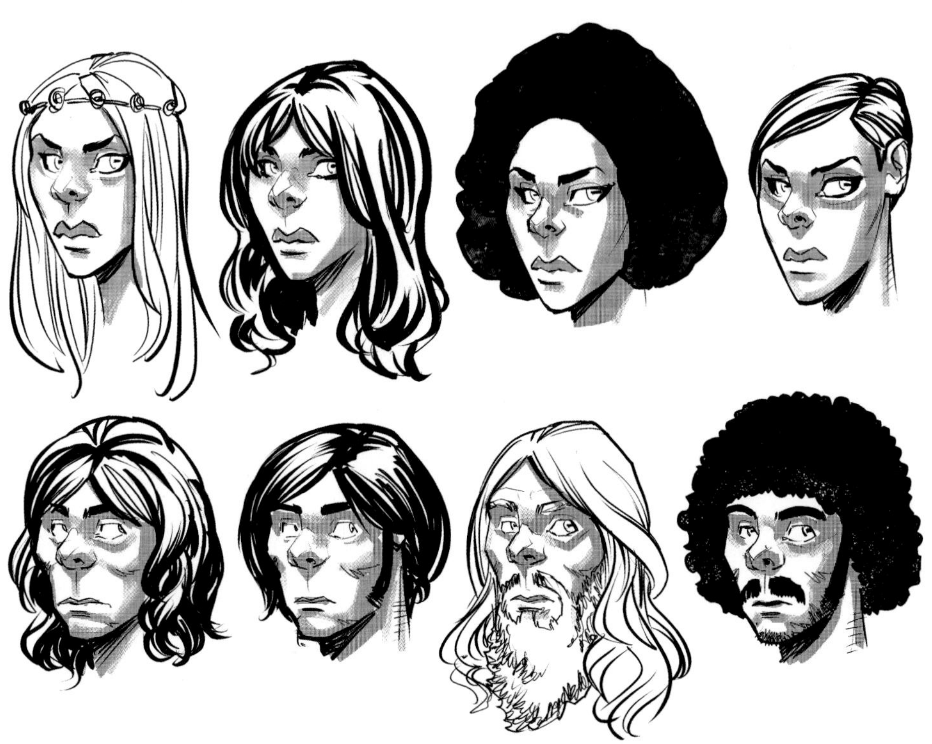

These were explorations of the world, the environment, and the style I was going to use to draw the book.

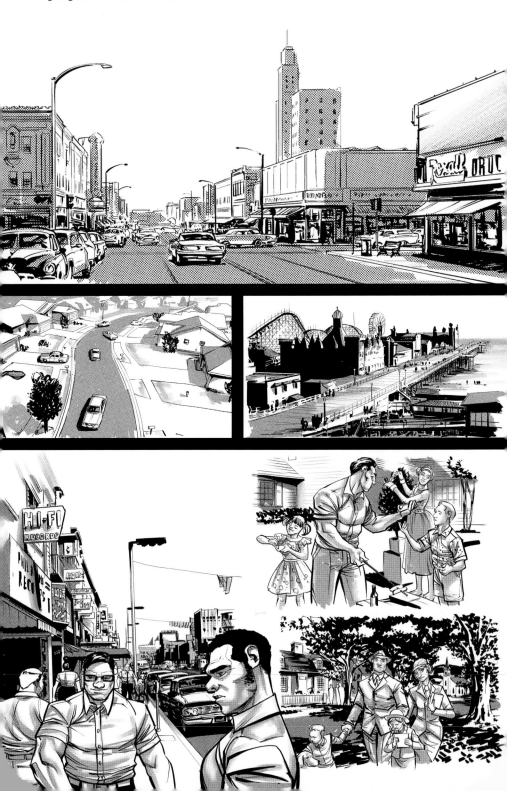

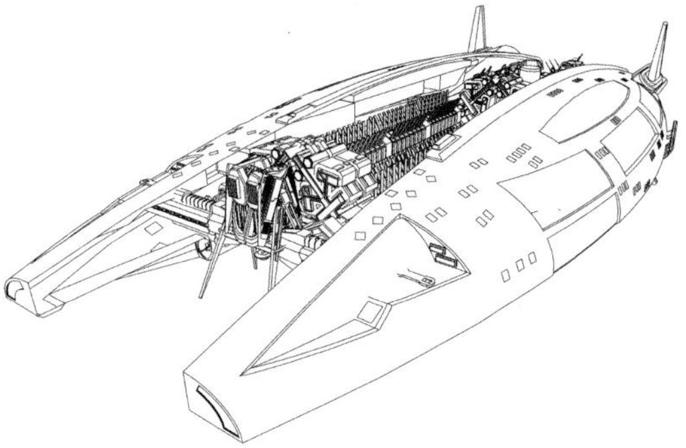

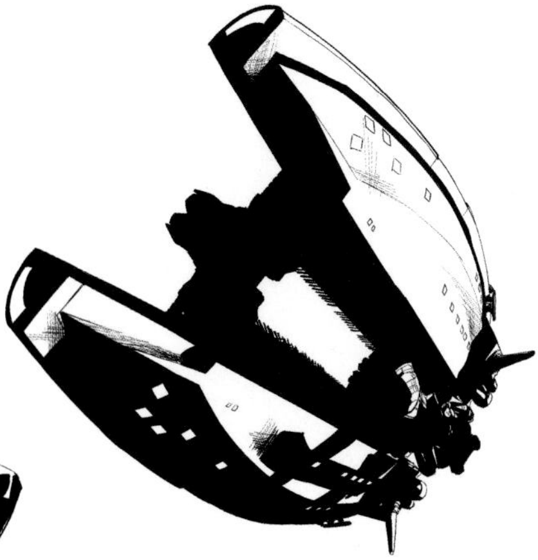

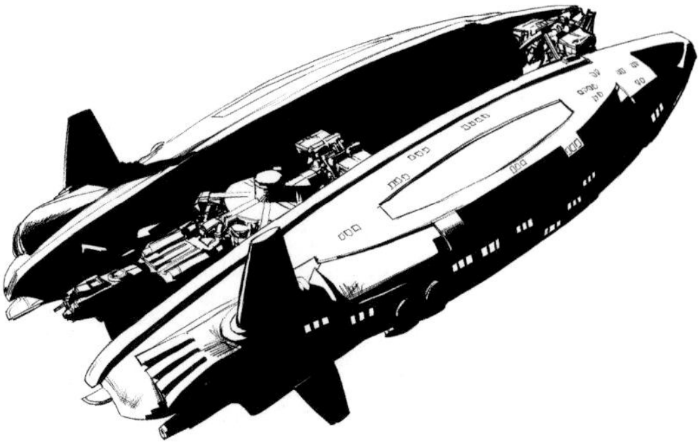

I had built this ship for another book that never came to fruition, but the look fit this world perfectly! Ship exploration with the Benadem astronauts in various stylings.

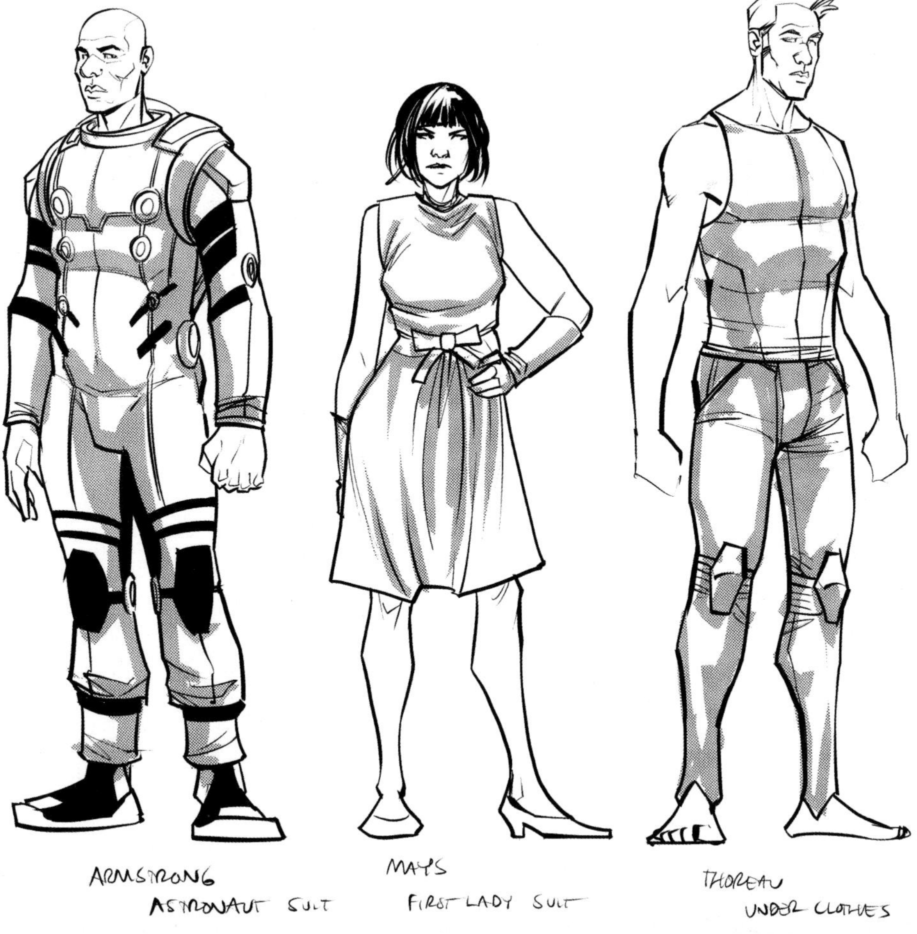
ARMSTRONG
ASTRONAUT SUIT
MAYS
FIRST LADY SUIT
THOREAU
UNDER CLOTHES